Green Fields #9

EXODUS

Adrienne Lecter

Exodus

Green Fields #9

ISBN: 9781718010475

Editing by Marti Lynch
Interior design & cover by Adrienne Lecter

www.adriennelecter.com

Give feedback on the book at:
adrienne@adriennelecter.com

Twitter: @AdrienneLecter

First Edition August 2018
Second Print Edition November 2021
Produced and published by Barbara Klein, Vienna, Austria

To M

Because I'd go back for you, too. Maybe.

(he laughed when he read it)

Chapter 1

"I am Elle Moreau. We have been expecting you."

I couldn't help but crack a smile, which the tall, dark-skinned woman returned. Bucky Hamilton, next to me? Not so much, but, if anything, that was a bonus. This was going to be good, I just knew it!

Ignoring me, he focused on the French woman. "You're welcome," he huffed out, making a show of crossing his arms over his chest, making himself appear more at ease than I knew he was. It helped that he was the only one of us who'd put away his weapons, not that he needed them at close range to be deadly. "For saving your people's asses."

Elle's mouth twisted as she compressed her lips, but she didn't comment.

I should probably have let Hamilton handle this, but I was still too hyper to just stand there and gloat. Slaughtering what had felt like a million zombies—and feeling like myself for the first time in fucking forever—would do that to you. "It's great to finally meet some people," I offered. "Haven't encountered a single living soul all the way from the coast until this afternoon." It seemed like a good idea not to stress that it was true that we were the only reason why the group we'd encountered—presumably a part of the French Resistance here near Ajou—was still alive. I was sure that they would sing our praises in time if they were so inclined.

The woman's eyes skipped from Bucky to me, and her features evened out into a more pleasant expression. Apparently, we had something in common already in our dislike for the asshole in charge.

"No wonder. Now that it's winter, we have withdrawn most of our lookouts," she professed. "You would have had to know where the remaining posts are to encounter anyone." Her gaze skipped to Bucky once more for a second but returned to me as she went on. "Thank you for helping Noah and his group. They got delayed yesterday because of bad weather and had to find a different route back. We will have trouble with the influx of corpse eaters so close to our base, but we appreciate your effort in trying to cull the hunting ones."

And she was great at delivering backhanded compliments. I could see us getting along splendidly already. She didn't react to my grin, but I was sure that she noticed it.

Bucky finally remembered his manners, or figured introducing himself was a good way to draw her attention away from me. "I'm Capt. Hamilton, United States Army, and these are my men." No mention of rejects this time, for once. That was a pleasant surprise. "I would like to talk to whoever is in charge here."

Elle held his challenging gaze evenly. "You are talking to her," she stated rather coolly—and turned to me. Booyah! "It is a pleasure welcoming you, Dr. Lewis. We have been hoping to have the honor of meeting you in person for a long time, but dared not expect that it would come to this encounter." My smile grew exponentially, and not just because she was blowing Bucky off. My name she could have gotten from talking to the survivors, but my background? Not so much. I had a certain idea where she'd gotten that information from, going along with her statement that they'd been expecting us.

Question was whether that was a good thing or not. I was sure it was only a matter of time until we found out. For now, I was ready to take whatever positive fate slammed in my way.

"The pleasure is all mine," I replied jovially, taking a step forward so I was standing closer to her than Bucky was. Let the grown-ups talk.

Hamilton had other ideas. "Listen—"

He shut up when Elle gave him a scathing glare, and yet again she addressed me instead. "I was under the impression that these were your guards? Is this man speaking for you?"

I quickly responded before Bucky could. "No, he is definitely not."

Elle cocked her head to the side, a light frown of confusion making her brows draw together. "Are you in any kind of duress, Dr. Lewis? I only brought a fraction of the fighters that are stationed in the base up with me as I didn't want to turn our welcome into a hostile gesture, but I can have two hundred more ready within five minutes."

Oh, and there it was, the second opportunity of the day to figuratively bend Bucky over the next hard surface. Yet as tempted as I was, like with fighting the undead, I already knew I had to pass it up. It was still highly amusing to see a wave of tension run through his guys as if the better part of them was afraid I'd sic my newfound French friends on them. Part of me was a little offended. Nobody had actually expected me to wade into a sea of zombies, and I hadn't hesitated to join them for a moment. The least I deserved was a modicum of trust. The smart thing would have been to disband their unease immediately before any accidents could happen, but I just couldn't help myself. Turning to Bucky, I gave him a calculating look. "What do you think? Do I have any reason whatsoever to ask for assistance?"

Bucky's stoic glare was surprisingly satisfying; that he, for once, didn't offer up a slur-ridden opinion, too. Behind him, I saw Hill trying to give me a look of warning, while Cole's reaction was more of a, "Seriously? I thought you were better than this," heavily mixed with exasperation. Well, that wouldn't do. In this, they definitely acted differently from my guys as, even in the gloom, I could make out Burns's bright grin that was so ready to cheer on any shit I was about to stir up. Ah, well. Baby steps, I reminded myself. As much as taunting Bucky could have become my new purpose in life—and a very fulfilling one at that—I still had to deal with the others, and I wasn't going to sacrifice all the hard-earned respect I'd gained by being a petty bitch.

Addressing Elle, I did my best to appear jovial as I responded. "Of course not. As I already told your friends, for me there are only two sides in this conflict—the living and the dead. Survival always has to supersede personal issues we may or may not have with one another. If you could spare some shelter for the night for us and maybe an opportunity to exchange information, we would be much obliged."

The previous tension drained from Elle, making me wonder if she chalked my antics up to inside jokes she wasn't privy to, or misguided American grandstanding that cultured Europeans didn't feel the need to concern themselves with. Probably the latter. I really didn't give a shit either way, as her next words were warm—and inviting to everyone present.

"Of course. And we can provide much better than simple bare necessities." She gestured toward where her guards were posted. "Please follow me to our main entrance. There is room aplenty where you can store your dirty gear"—which meant pretty much everything we were carrying—"underground. It will be safe there but of course you are free to post guards as you see fit. Please." She waited for me to join her, then led the way herself, the guards already dispersing.

I knew something was off with me when I didn't feel the slightest thread of trepidation come up inside of me considering the setup waiting for us. So far, most settlements hadn't exactly been welcoming to us, and my experience with the few military bases was far from pleasant, for different reasons. Sure, Elle had—so far—done nothing to provoke any suspicion from me, but trusting wasn't exactly an attribute I would have assigned to myself any longer. As much as Hamilton's obvious ire amused me, exacerbating it wasn't enough of a motive to head blindly into danger. But I also seemed to lack concern about my lack of threat-assessment paranoia, so I figured, what the hell. Someone else would likely have spoken up if they'd thought we were headed into actual danger.

About halfway to what appeared to be a heavy iron or steel door leading underground, Elle paused for a second, hesitating. "I'm afraid we will have to insist on a safety check before letting you into the base proper. You have proven that you can handle yourselves in a fight, but there is always the risk of infection."

I'd been waiting for something like this. Glancing at Bucky, who was following close enough that he could have tripped over my heels had I slowed down just a little, I found him giving me a blank stare. Apparently this was my circus now, and my monkeys.

"Most of us can't actually get infected," I professed, closely watching Elle's reaction. She gave none—including surprise—which made me guess she was at least somewhat aware of this. That made me wonder if she also knew the potential consequences. "But I presume that's only part of your concern?"

She gave a curt nod. "You are allowed to bring weapons into our base but only in reasonable quantities. For safety reasons, any explosives will have to remain with your gear. We have showers ready that you can use." Showers we were in dire need of, which she omitted to note. "While you are cleaning up, we will quickly inspect what items you want to bring inside, and after you pass inspection that none of you have any open wounds that could be infected, you are free to enter the base. Should you object, you can still access the showers and we will provide food and water, but I'm afraid that you will need to remain in the outer storerooms."

Probably the most elaborate way of telling someone you wanted to see them naked, but it wasn't like I'd expected anything else. It was funny to see both Bucky and Red look a little squeamish. Apparently, we filthy scavengers had been treated very differently than the brave soldiers were used to. I felt tempted to tell Elle that I could kiss her for that, and considering that she was French, she might just let me. Maybe not.

"Our security measures amuse you?" she inquired, her tone gently chiding.

Grinning, I shook my head. "Not that different from how we handle things at home. Although, in most places, we didn't get showers and hot food until after negotiating, so this is actually a step up."

She looked downright appalled at that but moved on when I didn't elaborate. I was dying to know more about how she knew who I was, but clearly, showers first.

The heavy steel doors opened up onto concrete stairs, leading into a large room lined with empty shelves. Already, it was warm inside, almost balmy compared to the outside environs. The air inside wasn't stale so I figured they had good ventilation, but the scent of burning wood from the torches—actual, Medieval-style torches—tickled my nostrils. There were two other doors leading from the concrete oval room farther into the base. Seeing as the guards barred the entrance to the left, I presumed the showers would be behind the right one.

"Please take all the time you need with stowing your gear away. Once you have passed the check, you are free to return here anytime to get something or clean your things," Elle instructed. "When you are ready, please hand everything you want to bring inside the base to the guards. Your things will be waiting for you on the other side. We have racks for cleaning your clothes by the shower room. You can undress there for easy convenience." Her eyes briefly skipped over the lot of us—counting heads, I figured. "You are free to decide on how you want to split up your group. The showers have room for around ten people. You can do the ladies first—"

I didn't miss exactly how miserable both Gita and Rodriguez looked at that idea, so I spoke up quickly.

"The five of us will go first." I indicated me and my people. "The rest can draw straws for all I care. I'm sure they have their own preferences."

Elle didn't ask about the distinction, but I was sure that she'd noticed that, for the most part, the five of us had differently colored gear and lacked any form of rank or group insignia. Well, I had a feeling that she'd soon get to see mine.

"Perfect. I will leave you to coordinate now, and tell the cook to get dinner started." The guards let her through the left door but immediately closed it after her, the sound of several deadbolts engaging from the other side somewhat ominous.

I wondered if we should coordinate with the others, but seeing as Bucky was still silent, I left it at dropping my things on a shelf, peeling myself out of the worst of the outer layers that were dirty as hell, and grabbed some clean clothes from my pack before handing them—and my knife, handguns, and quickly cleaned boots—to the guards. The others followed suit while the soldiers were more or less waiting for someone to tell them what to do. I was sure that Red would start the briefing once it was obvious that we couldn't listen in anymore. Again it occurred to me that, just maybe, I should have been a little more paranoid, but so far, nothing had set me off. The truth was, I was tired, exhausted, in dire need of that shower, and longing to spend some downtime without having to watch my back, preferably somewhere cozy and warm. If the French wanted to kill us, they could have easily gunned us all down outside their neat little bunker, rather than letting us inside where there was blood to be washed off later.

And speaking of washing off blood—not only was there electric lighting in the room lined with shower stalls, but they had hot, running water. The level of care I had in me for who was about to see my naked, scarred, scrawny ass was quickly dropping toward zero.

It took me a few minutes to ditch the rest of my clothes. Most of it went straight into the trash bags provided for that very cause. Not being able to do proper cleaning beyond what hastily stuffed-in baby wipes would accomplish, I'd expected to have developed some lovely rashes in the meantime, but except for dirty skin ready to be scraped off, there was only the bandage from Parker's hack job of a surgery that needed any attention. The scar was already fading, no longer angry red, but the general area was still tender. Maybe if I could go another day or two without anyone poking me there, it would heal for good. The bruises I'd accumulated from today's fight were much more visible all over my body.

As usual under these circumstances, I did my best not to get a faceful of anyone's body parts that I didn't need to see too closely before I hopped into a stall, only moderately surprised that Nate followed. The stalls were large enough to accommodate two people, and seeing as I had a week of sweat and grime, with some undefinable fluids from earlier today, plastered on my back, I didn't mind having someone handy who could wash it all off. I certainly wouldn't have minded a lot more physical contact of a different nature, but I didn't want to subject the others to having to listen to that. Nate appeared indifferent himself so I took that as a sign that he was thinking along the same lines.

They had real shampoo, conditioner, and body wash in an overflowing rack inside the stall, not just something that was closer to dish soap than personal hygiene products. Ah, the luxury. I was liking the French more and more by the second.

I perfectly hated having to admit that I was as clean as I was going to get—and, more importantly, having to leave the hot stream of water—but as I stepped out to grab a towel to dry off, I did my best not to let much of that show. Having to fight with keeping my balance—again—was bad enough, but I didn't want to go all frowny-face at anyone for our inspection. If Elle's dislike for Bucky had been any indication, I could win a lot more favor by being as easygoing and relaxed as possible, so that's what I was going for. The others were mostly ready by then—untangling and washing my hair had taken a small eternity—with only Gita looking positively miserable where she remained cocooned in her towel. I wondered if I should say something to her, but was honestly too tired and worked up at the same time to get my diplomatic side working. Tanner noticed as well, clapping her amicably on the back—after discarding his own towel in a corner. Modesty had not survived the apocalypse. That, or I was surrounded by out-of-the-closet exhibitionists.

"Don't worry, girl. I'm sure those yahoos over there are going to steal the show, anyway." He pointedly looked in my direction where I was waiting next to the exit.

I gave him the most innocent expression I could manage, but that held up for exactly the three seconds it took me to drop my own towel and check my scar in the partly foggy full-length mirror next to the door. Most recent scar, I amended to myself, because damnit, parts of my body closely resembled expressionistic art. I did my humanly best to ignore that—my ego really didn't need that reminder. It was so much easier to focus on the rest. Turning to Nate, I asked, "Did you see my ass? That's some serious booty developing there." I got the deadpan stare I deserved for that, which made it easy to crack a smile. Checking again, I made sure that the light peach fuzz on my face hadn't started to turn into black bristles. "My eyebrows could do with some plucking," I observed critically, more interested in the scabbed-over cuts on my forehead and cheek—also from this afternoon. "But you still like hairy little women, right?"

Rather than verbally reply, Nate gave my left shoulder a hard push that made me stagger away from the mirror and toward the exit. Gita's snicker kept my previous smile firmly planted on my face. Mission accomplished. Then again, her eyebrows were perfectly plucked, so what did she have to lose?

The room beyond the showers was a rectangular box, floor, ceiling, and walls tiled white except for the huge viewing window opposite the entrance. There was a very sturdy-looking steel door next to the window. The interior was so brightly lit that my eyes immediately started to tear up; there was barely a shadow left directly below my body between my feet, and even that was only a light one. Beyond the glass, Elle, a handful of guards, a woman who I presumed was a doctor, judging from the scrubs and white lab coat she was wearing, and a few less distinctive people were waiting for us, doing a rather good job of not appearing particularly interested or impressed by us as we filed into the room. I ended up between Nate and Burns, which certainly detracted from some of the visible changes my body had gone through over the past weeks, but might also distract from the marked additions—and losses. I tried my very best to appear confident and like I didn't give a shit, keeping my hands on my hips and my fingers slightly splayed. Because the room beyond the glass window was much darker, I could see my own reflection all too well, not something I cared for particularly. But I certainly was something to look at now, that much was true.

I was by far not a stranger to my husband's unclothed form, but we didn't actually spend a lot of time around each other fully naked. I might win the contest of who got the most scars since the shit hit the fan, but he wasn't as far behind as might have been preferable. And while I felt like the Frankensteinesque appearance of my left thigh in particular and my toes and fingers in general were impossible not to stare at, there was plenty to ogle between the five of us, also including a lot more ink than I'd have guessed.

The voice of the doctor—heavily accented but very melodic in a smokey contralto—tore me out of my reverie. "Please turn around. When the light changes, please face forward again."

We all shuffled our feet as we followed her directions. Burns snickered, and when I looked at him over my shoulder, I caught him staring at my ass. Very likely it was about Nate's name and the anatomical heart tattooed there, but I couldn't just let that fly—particularly as the somewhat cooler air in the room seemed to do nothing whatsoever to decrease his obvious sense of comfort, so to speak.

"If you even think about whacking off to this, I'll castrate you," I threatened.

The snicker turned into a full-blown laugh. "Well, aren't we glad you're not a mind reader," Burns shot back, feeling not the least bit intimidated. "Besides, I'm counting on someone else's attention so that I won't have to spank the monkey."

We grinned at each other, making me miss the face Nate was making—but his response did a great job filling me in on that. "I'm so damn glad you're trying to be professional," he grumbled.

My reaction got postponed when the lights suddenly turned off, leaving me seeing weird shapes and blotches as my vision slowly cleared of the afterimages. It took me a few seconds to realize that the blue hue the room was cast into wasn't due to visual randomness but different sets of lights. Glancing down my body, I found slight fluorescent flickers dancing along the fresh scar, same as across my left middle finger's new tip.

"Turn around, please," the doctor instructed. As I did, I saw that weird greenish flicker in the glass reflection as well, same as across a partly scabbed-over cut on my forehead—but I quickly forgot all about that when I saw that it was my eyes that shone in vivid bright green. And not just mine—the same was true for Nate, Burns, and Tanner. Not that hard to guess what that was all about, but that told me nothing about the why.

Maybe it should have freaked me the fuck out, but I was far too fascinated and curious. Fucking serum.

There was some nervous shifting going on at the right end of our line as the others noticed, but a few seconds later, the bright lights were switched on once more, and no one seemed ready to gun us down any moment now. The invisible locks on the exit disengaged, the door swinging open as someone pushed on it from the other side. Behind the window, Elle motioned us to walk through. There was a small room beyond, open to the other side of the viewing window, our possessions that we'd handed to the guards earlier waiting for us. Nate exchanged cautious glances with me, making me guess that, so far, he'd never experienced that demon-glow eyes test before, but he looked less disturbed by it than I felt. We dressed quickly, the warmth of the shower and observation room quickly dissipating. Just because they had electricity down here didn't mean it was wasted on heating when a few layers of clothes could do the job more effectively and cheaper.

Elle was waiting for us as we filed out of the changing room, the doctor preoccupied with chatting in hushed tones with one of the guards. Still no one seemed disconcerted, or the slightest bit alarmed.

"You passed," Elle offered in a disinterested tone, as if she hadn't expected anything else. That made me wonder if this really was about them inspecting us for bite marks, or simply to see whether we would follow directions well. That blue-light check they could have done with us fully clothed.

"I take it you know what I was talking about when I told you that some of us are immune to the virus," I surmised. Rather than reply, she gave me a tight smile. I took that with a nod, wondering if I should ask her if I could watch on the next two rounds of checks, seeing as I still didn't know exactly who of our illustrious compatriots had been inoculated with the serum, or who hadn't. Parker hadn't been, that much was easy to deduce. Bucky was, of course, and I was sure Nate could have verified most of them, at least from back when he'd still been part of their ranks. With Red, Hill, and Cole I was overwhelmingly positive, but except for Cole's little reveal yesterday about his and Hill's Delta career, they were surprisingly closed-mouthed about their pasts.

But I had more important items on my agenda, at least for the next minutes.

"You are free to head into the base proper, if you'd like," Elle explained, pointing at the corridor behind her. "Or you can wait here."

"Actually, I have a favor to ask," I offered. "Two, but they're connected." She looked surprised, but nodded at me to go on. I couldn't help but grin. The first really wouldn't be hard on them, I was sure. "Uhm, the thing is, I would be much obliged if you could, perhaps, come up with ideas to postpone the progress of the other two thirds of our party? Nothing that might get you shot, but I think just a few minutes around Hamilton have been enough to let you see just what an asshole he is, and if you have ways to legitimately annoy him…"

Elle's laughter was short but came from the heart. "Say no more. We let you through easily because you were very cooperative, and we already knew what to expect. The same is not true for the rest." Her gaze dropped to my midriff. "That scar, it's recent. If you would like to get our doctor's opinion on it, I'm sure she would check on you right away." Rather than wait for my response, Elle called over her shoulder. "Inaya?"

The doctor finished her conversation quickly before joining us, faster than I could turn down Elle's offer. Elle said something to her in French, her vague gesture toward my stomach making it obvious what this was about. Rather than having me strip, the doctor regarded me with an even, somewhat bored, gaze. "You feel healthy?"

"A lot more since I got that," I explained.

"Then there's nothing that needs my attention," she responded, already turning away. Something told me the good doctor had some experience dealing with people who healed unnaturally fast.

Elle pursed her lips. "If she can't set bones, she gets bored easily," she explained. "What else do you need?"

"Well, you see, the situation is this. The past weeks, way longer than I care to count, we've practically spent sitting on top of each other, with Hamilton delighting in making a nuisance of himself. I can't even remember clearly when my husband and I last had a moment to ourselves." One of the guards behind Elle cracked a smile, and I could practically feel Nate roll his eyes where he was standing behind me. Traitor. "You're French," I went on explaining. "I don't think I'll have to spell out the details for you. If you have some kind of maintenance room somewhere with a door that closes where we won't be in the way…"

Elle's snort was rather amused. "Ah, I see. That's why you want me to delay the dear captain's progress?"

I shrugged, not exactly denying it. "Ten minutes. That's all I need." And my, did I have to put my foot in my mouth like that every damn time?

"You have twenty easily, maybe thirty if I can manage," Elle promised, hard-pressed now to keep from smirking. "Head down the corridor, third door on the right, just where the main corridor takes a turn to the left. It's an old storeroom where we keep spare parts. If you don't mind the smell of engine grease, it's all yours. Bolts from the inside."

I thanked her, grabbed Nate's arm before he could come up with anything that would have made me change my mind, and was off in the direction she'd indicated, Burns's laughter following us down the concrete corridor.

Chapter 2

There was a hint of resistance from Nate but no outright protest, so I chose to ignore it. Screw finding out about the immunological status of Bucky's men. I needed this, and right fucking now. Our steps echoed on the concrete floor, two lightbulbs doing a shit job illuminating the over a hundred feet of distance between the entrance and the turn Elle had indicated before. The cracked walls were stained with water and covered with moss in places, making me guess that the tunnel—and likely the entire installation—was older than me, probably by a few decades.

Cold War era, probably some kind of bunker should the Soviets decide Europe was the perfect stomping ground to turn the conflict into a hot one. Part of my mind idly wondered exactly how many thousands of people all over the world had survived simply because of past paranoia.

The much larger part of my mind was hell-bent on getting out of my clothes and into Nate's, so I didn't exactly dwell on those musings.

I found the door unlocked if somewhat hard to open, rusty hinges squeaking loudly as I forced it to swing into the room. There were no working light fixtures but right next to the door was one of those LED stick flashlights perfect for illuminating the underside of cars and the likes. I let go of Nate in favor of switching it on, having to slit my eyes as the sudden glare blinded me. I heard the heavy door close behind me. The next moment, I found my back pressed against the inside of it as Nate grabbed me and whirled me around, his body colliding with mine a second later. I didn't waste another thought, reaching up to twine my fingers through his hair, eagerly opening my mouth to his tongue. His hands pushed between my back and the door, then went lower to grab my ass, pulling the lower half of my body toward him. I moaned, hitching one leg up so I could get closer to the friction I so absolutely needed.

My, but I clearly wasn't the only one needy for attention.

If the apocalypse had taught me one thing, it was to be stealthy but quick about getting things going, but if I had twenty to thirty minutes, I wasn't going to try to be done in five. Nate seemed to be thinking along the same lines, actually taking his time to remove some of my non-essential clothes, and letting me do the same to him. I tensed a few times when he inadvertently put pressure on parts of me that hurt more than I could ignore, but it only took a disgruntled growl for him to continue when he paused. He certainly seemed over that notion by the time his hand found its way inside my underwear. A hint of a satisfied smirk crossed his face as he found me quite ready for more, and he didn't hesitate to follow up on that. I took a moment to sag against the door and close my eyes, enjoying myself. What could I say? There was so much shit going on with my body—of late and still present—that it felt damn good to get an endorphin kick from something pleasurable for once.

But as fun as that was, and as much as he knew what to do to get me going, it wasn't enough, and it wasn't what I was hungering for. So before long, I aimed for his partly undone pants and reached inside with my right hand—only to find him a long shot from where I needed him to be physically able to slake my lust. And as if that wasn't bad enough, he tensed and stepped away, our height difference making my hand fall away while his managed to stay in place.

That was not what my ego needed right now—or ever.

For a few seconds, it was impossible for me to quench the twin wave of rejection and doubt that cut right through the haze of need, my mind still slow because it was too far in one-track territory to react. Spending weeks with a healthy dose of pep talks, exercise, and step-by-step successes in relearning everything my body had forgotten or needed to compensate for was one thing; feeling my latent insecurity roar to life and do a complete mental reset was quite another. It made me want to cringe, curl up, and above all else, cry, and bless Nate for not being an imbecile and not being aware of that. All I could do to keep myself from doing any of that was to stand there, still as a statue, while my ragged breath hitched. I hadn't even realized I'd closed my eyes until I felt his hand—the other one, not the one he'd withdrawn from between my legs—gently cup the side of my face, his nose briefly brushing mine as he leaned in for a feather-light kiss.

"It's not you," he more exhaled than whispered against my lips. "I swear, it's not you."

Maybe it was just the seconds ticking by that finally allowed my intellect to jump-start. Or maybe it was the fact that gentle and soft wasn't anything either of us usually fell back to where sex was concerned—including before the shit hit the fan. Whatever it was,

I was happy to let it tear me out of the deepest levels of misery my ego was still sinking into, allowing me to offer a wry, hard laugh. I opened my eyes and stared into his, too close to really focus on them.

"Yeah, because the idea of a three-fingered hand job wouldn't send anyone running for the hills."

Nate pulled back, just far enough so he could read my expression, and I, in turn, his. He looked conflicted as hell, and not in the "how do I break this to her" way that I'd expected. So not a lie on his part. With a sinking feeling in my stomach I watched him bite his lip, casting around for words. If not for his hand still cradling my face, lending warm and stoic comfort, I might have started to freak out all over again.

The breath he finally let out was full of dejection, and I could see in his gaze that he'd decided to cut the crap, including trying to cushion the blow.

"It's not you," he repeated—stalling. Or not. Anger flared up inside of me, hot and instantaneous, as if it had never receded into the back of my mind. Deep down, warning bells went off again but this once I chose to ignore them. Stabbing Nate in the chest with my right index finger—had to be the right since I wasn't equipped with a left anymore—I opened my mouth to let him have it, yet stopped when he caught my hand in his free one and pressed it to his lips, kissing my knuckles and what little remained of my ring finger, before—

"Did you just gnaw on my stump?!"

The grin taking over his face for a second was answer enough, and it weirdly mollified the rage boiling inside of me. I realized he was distracting me and was a little surprised that it worked. He was also still stalling, and when he saw the twist coming to my lips, he dropped it for real, while keeping his fingers wrapped around my hand, his gaze boring into mine.

"Every time I close my eyes, whether I even try to wank or just want to go to sleep, I still feel my fingers contracting around your throat. I see the panic in your eyes when you realize that I am going to choke you to death and there's nothing you can do to stop me. I still feel my body slamming down on yours as I force you across that table and immobilize you, leaving you just enough air to breathe so you won't clock out because you need to be fully aware of what's going to happen to you next. And I still feel the conviction that what I'm doing is right; that I will keep holding you down while Hamilton does whatever the fuck he wants to do to you, and a simple order is enough and I will do it, too. So, no, I'm not going soft because the sensation of your hand is familiar yet glaringly different at the same time. Happy now?"

It would have been easiest to snap the "Hell, no!" at him that wanted to wrench itself from my very soul—and I didn't miss the fact that his previously tender gestures had transformed into vise grips, if controlled enough not to hurt me—but for once in my life I took the one second that was enough to let my thoughts catch up with my impulse control. I forced myself to relax, even though memory-recruited resentment made me want to tense up and push away from him. Yeah, that would have been a brilliant reaction considering Nate's confession. I held his gaze evenly, doing my very best to keep both judgment that I didn't really feel and anger that he might mistake for resentment off my face.

"I take it that whatever was in that mind-control shit they shot you up with didn't just turn you into a passive passenger in your own meat-suit body?" I ventured a guess. So much for trusting anything Hamilton said.

Nate shook his head. "Nope. I was in control, and I knew exactly what I was doing. I was convinced that I was doing the right thing. A very focused, single-minded conviction, but conviction nevertheless. I was following orders and I had no reason whatsoever to doubt them."

Part of me wanted to scream. Part of me definitely wanted to recoil—thankfully only a very small part of me. I felt like I should give him a hug, but the intensity burning in his eyes told me quite plainly that he wasn't exactly receptive for gestures like that— probably because it would have made him fold in on himself, and right now we simply didn't have the time for a good cry. I almost started laughing when I realized that, in many ways, we'd become so damn similar to each other over the past months. Maybe always had been, only that I'd needed to play catch-up with all the shit he'd been through in his life while for me it had been mostly boring sunshine and happiness. Extrapolating from that, it wasn't that hard to guess what I should—or at least could—do next.

"How about I stalk back down that corridor and finally do what I should have done weeks ago when I had the chance on the destroyer, and fucking castrate that son of a bitch?" I suggested, only half joking.

Nate snorted, that wry kind of amusement exactly the reaction I had been going for—but didn't offer up anything else. When I raised my brows at him a few seconds later, he finally deigned to answer me. "I can't find it in me to tell you not to go for it," he offered, but talked right over me when I tried to interject. "But—and I don't have to tell you that—I don't think it would be wise."

"When have I ever done the wise thing?"

Another amused sound left him. "You're usually smarter with the big decisions that could end your life within seconds."

"It won't kill him," I reasoned. "And you heard what Elle said. Her doc's terribly bored at the moment. With her on standby, they'd have a tourniquet tied within seconds and have patched him up in under half an hour. Judging from my own experience, he'd bounce back within a day or two if he didn't lose too much blood."

"I love how reasonable you can sound sometimes," Nate wryly surmised.

I left it at a bright, albeit fake, grin before I made myself back off the warpath. He was right. It wasn't Bucky who I was concerned about, but his men. I hadn't just spent half a day slaughtering zombies to show them how much I was one of them only to turn all that around for a moment of endless satisfaction. Even though I really wanted to, with my mind, body, and soul. That realization scared me—and it wasn't the only one. It was easier to close the lid on the roiling pot of anger now than it had been back when I'd almost lost it after my fight with Hamilton, but it wasn't easy. Damn fucking hard was more like it.

"Exactly how much is that serum screwing with my impulse control?" I more mused than asked, but the knowing look on Nate's face told me he had an answer for that. "And I'm way too trusting toward the French. I can't remember the last time I just waltzed into anywhere and didn't feel like I constantly needed to watch my back." And my, didn't the idea of something screwing with my brain on a more permanent level than those booster shots make me really, really happy.

Nate's mouth took on a wry twist. "You can't completely take a soldier's fear away and still expect him to perform at top-notch level. But you can make him feel invincible once he's overcome that initial bout of fear."

My mind skipped over several options until it settled on the most obvious—and quite disturbing—one.

"Does that shit affect my amygdala?"

He shrugged. "You read the documentation on the project."

"Yes, the genetic side of it," I grumbled. "They didn't include a 'this is you now' instruction sheet."

"Your guess is as good as mine," Nate offered. "But it's been known to happen that a lot of us are more prone to take risks and head into certain danger without a second thought. Seeing as that's usually your MO, anyway…"

He trailed off with a smile when I made a face. "That explains why I thought it was a good idea to go zombie slaughtering. Not why I feel like Elle's my best friend."

"I think you're mostly projecting on her because you spent almost a month in what you perceive as the most hostile environment known to man—men. And your mind might still be basking in the afterglow of one hell of an adrenaline rush. Hence your need to also tear my clothes off."

"That's not always connected," I harped.

"Experience says otherwise," Nate succinctly provided.

Okay, maybe he had a point there. "I've never heard you complain about it."

"Far be it from me," he offered, but the following pause was quite the sobering one. "I'm not one hundred percent sure about the trust thing, but it's likely your subconscious knowing that you're an apex predator now." At my confused look, he smacked his lips. "You may still be somewhat off because of your injuries, but what you did today down in that valley was beyond what you could have done at the bat of an eyelash two months ago."

I felt like that was pushing it, but I got his point. "So what you're saying is that, deep down, my mind knows I'm awesome." I got a blank stare back, making me laugh. "Oh, come on! Would it really kill you to, this once only, admit that I'm amazing?"

"I'm more concerned about what it would do to your ego," he snarked.

"Seeing as survival means modeling myself after you, overinflation might be an issue," I shot back.

The smile Nate had been fighting finally broke through, and he leaned in for a second to push his forehead against mine, making us share a breath. "You should stop constantly seeking my—or anyone else's—approval."

"Not seeking anything," I claimed, although it wasn't entirely true. "I just want my husband to admit that I'm a good catch."

The pause on his side that followed was downright insulting, but finally, he folded, mirth lighting up his eyes. "You're awesome. Happy now?"

The way he was looking at me made me chuckle, and I did as much of a victory dance as possible, which wasn't a lot seeing as I was still pretty much trapped between his body and the door.

"It was the 'awesome' part that hurt, right? You could have just said amazing. Or wonderful. Spectacular. Unsurpassable."

"Are you done yet?" he grated, pulling away to create enough space between us so he could properly glower down at me. Like I gave a fuck. As much as I wanted to continue goofing off—and loving that I felt both physically and mentally up to it once more—we still had a mile to go before we were done.

"Why didn't you tell me what was going on with you?" I asked, trying very hard not to sound as disappointed as I felt at him not letting me know that, well, he was having some issues as well. And I wasn't even talking about the currently impacting physical limitations that was causing.

Nate gave that some thought, but his gaze never wavered from mine. "And when, exactly, should I have done that? When I was halfway convinced you wouldn't live through the night? Or when it took all the strength you had left to heave yourself onto unstable feet? When you were so weak that hobbling around was all you could do? When you finally started to recover but it took everything you had not to scream your head off at your own reflection? You had a lot of shit to deal with that was way more important than my shit. I'm smarter than adding to it when you're just barely hanging on as it is." He paused, then spilled the rest of the beans. "I know you're doing a damn good job convincing yourself that you don't hold any of that against me, but I do. Rationally, I know it's not my fault. But that doesn't change a thing about the memories that haunt me. I couldn't put this burden on you while you were still recovering."

"What changed your mind? Besides obvious necessity, I mean."

A hint of annoyance crossed his features. Obviously, I'd used up all the goodwill he'd allowed for because I couldn't handle shit.

"You got better. And watching you down there today, moving with strength and stamina you've never had before, was glorious."

"Ha, I knew it! You only stayed back so you could watch my scrawny ass!"

Nate chuckled softly at my triumphant crow. "And someone had to keep the undead at bay while you idiots took forever to get to the French," he pointed out.

"Yeah, I guess our grand gesture wouldn't have been so useful if they'd gotten eaten in the meantime."

Silence fell, both of us considering. I could almost see the gears grinding in his mind, and I didn't like how he started to tense, ready to pull away—emotionally and physically. This was not how I was going to let my first—and maybe only—chance for us to have some alone time go down.

"So, what are we going to do about this situation?" Withdrawing my right hand, I poked his stomach, trying to be at least a little circumspect. "Correct me if I'm wrong, but when I pulled you in here, you weren't exactly opposed to bumping uglies with me. And while not quite there yet, you were definitely getting there. Until, you know, your mind started getting in the way."

I got a wry, if somewhat sad, grin back. "How many times do I need to tell you that I get off on getting you off?"

"You do love rubbing it in my face that you're quite proficient in said aspect," I groused, then flashed him a bright grin. "What are you waiting for? Worst that can happen is I get off. I think I can deal with that."

Nate went as far as rolling his eyes heavenward in a silent, "What did I do to deserve this burden?" if there ever was one but didn't resist when I grabbed his head to pull his mouth down to mine—and then, with determination, grabbed his hands and put them on more interesting places than my cheek. He knew what to do, and thankfully did rather than continue our conversation. I may have exaggerated my reactions just a bit, but within minutes, that wasn't exactly necessary anymore. Lo and behold, when my hand traveled southward once more, things were looking a lot better. Better still after some well-meaning manipulation. And absolutely great when he picked me up and hauled me over to an abandoned workbench that was close to the perfect height for all things involving bad lighting and the odd giggle in between. If it took a little more time than our usual record-setting be-done-before-the-zombie-eats-us thing, I so wasn't going to complain.

It must have been close to the allotted time Elle had promised she could get me that found us both panting heavily, sweating somewhat profusely, and equally less wound up than when we'd entered the room. I couldn't wipe off the stupid grin that had taken hold of me and didn't even try. "You could have told me that this is another unexpected side effect of the serum," I prompted, having to stop halfway through the sentence to catch my breath. My, but I might even be a little sore later—ignoring all the scars and bruises and whatnot that had built up too much of a background noise to ignore, even when I was feeling thoroughly... satisfied.

Nate snorted as he stepped away to look for something to clean up with, but I didn't miss that small smile that he was trying to hide. Three, two, one—scathing remark about to come. "And have you hound me about not getting you shot up over a year ago? Fat chance." Seeing as there were only oil- and grease-stained rags to be found, I pelted him with my thick thermal to use instead. I was hot enough that my tank top would do for now, and the corridor outside had been surprisingly cozy deeper into the base. Seeing as the wall behind me wasn't ice cold, I figured they must have had some kind of heating system run through the entire complex. Geothermal springs, maybe? Nate expertly caught my shirt, then watched me as I started putting the remainder of my clothes where they belonged. After spending weeks bundled up, it was downright weird to only be wearing a layer or two.

As I straightened, he caught me in a last, lingering, bordering-on-sweet, kiss, but I already knew that what he was about to say next would make me want to punch him. Time for admitting I was awesome was obviously over.

"Bree, promise me one thing." I raised my brows at him, prompting him to let me have it. "Never, ever even think about producing a sex tape."

I burst out laughing, incapable of holding back. Of all the things he could have said, that was the last I'd expected. It took me a few seconds to get a grip on myself. "Okay, I'll bite. Why should I never, ever make a sex tape?"

"Because the sounds you were uttering were the absolute opposite of what anyone would find titillating."

That got me braying all over again. "Well, it worked, didn't it?"

"Because you were annoying as fuck, which served as a distraction," my dear husband let me know.

Pursing my lips, I wondered if I should tell him that this was not the impression I'd gotten, but left it at something between a leer and a smile. "That's on you then, isn't it? Whatever floats your boat."

He made as if to come after me but—sadly—thought better of it. The frown appearing on his forehead reminded me that the fun time was over now.

"How are we going to play this once we walk out of here?" I asked. "There are only so many ways they could have found out who I am, and while I'm very happy to bank on their goodwill, I'm not going to trust the French unless they give me a very good reason to." It was kind of funny to realize that while I was convinced that Elle had no ulterior motives besides thanking us for helping her people, I just knew there was trouble brewing on the horizon. If it wasn't going to come from the French, I was sure Hamilton would jump into that breach.

Nate looked positively nonplussed. "They seem to have taken a liking to you—"

"Unexpectedly, you mean?"

"Unexplainable with what we know right now," he corrected. "Until we know why, we have to play it by ear. I say we do what's worked so far."

"You mean, I do all the talking and you do all the sulky glowering?"

I was surprised that my barb hit home, but probably shouldn't have. Bucky's revelations about what had been going on behind the scenes in his camp had had a sobering effect on me. I could only guess at how much that had upended Nate's plans.

"It only makes sense you take the lead for now. Weasel all the information you can out of them. Then we'll decide together what we do with it." He hesitated, then added, "As much as it pains me to say, don't deliberately antagonize Hamilton unless you absolutely have to. Until we know what his mission is really about, all we can do is flail blindly in the dark, hoping to get a lucky hit in. I know you are tempted to use any leverage you could gain here for payback. Don't. Be diplomatic and kill his people with kindness. They've had years seeing you as my plaything. You did a lot over the past few days to show them that you're a force to be reckoned with. Force them to reckon."

That left a bitter taste on my tongue, but I nodded my agreement without protest or hesitation. "Anything else?"

Nate was already shaking his head when someone started banging against the door to our little hidey-hole, or kicking the living shit out of it from how it sounded. "Time for you cockroaches to scuttle back into the light!" none other than my beloved Capt. Hamilton shouted, loud enough to make me hunch my shoulders. As soon as I realized that I was doing it, I suppressed the impulse. Nate and I shared another look, the anger in his gaze nicely mirroring my own. Had he always been that bad about keeping a lid on it and I just hadn't realized it? Or was that powder keg about to blow?

"Coming!" I shouted, then couldn't help but giggle when my gaze fell on the stained thermal in Nate's hand. "Or I have been, repeatedly," I added more levelly, garnering myself another flat stare. "Oh, come on! That was funny. Actually…" I trailed off there, considering. "Do I look freshly fucked? Because for maximum impact, I think I should."

While generally not one to rebuke my advances, Nate preferred to play it more low key than that. I expected one of his usual barbs, something that would leave me just exasperated enough that it was easy for me to cut down on my apprehension on coming face to face with Hamilton and let me appear cocky and without a care. What

I didn't expect was for Nate to come for me, slamming me against the still-shut door, to start downright devouring my mouth while shoving his hands down my slightly loose pants. After getting off only minutes ago, I was sensitive enough that it really didn't take much until I was screaming against his lips, no more than a muffled moan making it out. That Hamilton continued to throw a tantrum outside barely registered.

So worth it.

Leaning back against the door—quite contentedly—I donned a grin in between my slowing pants. "Or, you know. You could go out there and stop holding back. Take control. Be the guy again who told me not to be stupid and let my quest for tampons be derailed by political-correctness-motivated stupidity."

Nate answered with a wry smile that turned sarcastic within seconds. "So that's the part you're never going to let me live down?" When all he got was a blank stare, he shrugged. "Yes, I could do that, but it would be so much smarter if I didn't. Because the first thing I would do would be to kill Hamilton. Then I would have to kill the four or five of his people who'd take grave offense, ultimately leaving us with too few people to complete whatever his mission is, I'm sure."

"Who says we should complete it?"

Now Nate's expression turned condescending. "Oh, come on. We both know that we both have too much bloodhound in us to just quit now, even more so after losing five or six good people to the cause already."

"That you had to kill," I stressed. "And not sure that 'good' moniker befits anyone lurking out there in the corridor right now."

Nate ignored my barb. "I gave my word, and even if you seem to value you doing the same less than I feel comfortable with, I saw how excited you got when Cole dropped that little snippet about why we're here. You wouldn't miss the chance to find out if my brother actually found a cure for the side effects of our untimely expiration or not."

The accusation in his voice irked me more than I liked to admit—and also more than the hint of gloating he couldn't hide as he revealed that last observation.

"I would keep an oath that I felt wasn't forced at gunpoint by people I only trust as far as knowing I can't trust them," I insisted.

"You don't even try to deny that I'm right."

"Why should I? Yes, if there's a chance your brother found a cure—and, likely, by extension a cure for the zombie plague—I want to know. I doubt they would have carted us halfway around the world on a wild guess." I paused there, thinking—and also wondering if that was a byproduct of the serum screwing with my mind as well, but doubted it. If it furthered my knee-jerk reactions, I doubted the reinforcing reflection would help. I was likely just mellow because I felt really good right now—and a little high.

Nate snorted, but that typically male, I-just-thoroughly-satisfied-my-woman look he gave me mollified me somewhat. "And there she is again."

Which was to say, thoroughly confused me. "'She?'" I echoed.

"The woman who knows that the entire world lies at her feet and there's nothing she can't conquer," he explained. "Last time you were looking at me like this was when we hit Dispatch and the Silo for the first time. Before the factory—"

"And everything went to shit," I finished for him, exhaling forcefully as the usual pang of pain twinged through my heart. "I can't believe that's only been, what? Seven months ago? Eight? Feels like a lifetime." Nate didn't protest my assessment. "Guess I had a lot to work through." Again, no contest to that. I couldn't help but mull that over some more—which got increasingly harder when Hamilton assaulted the door once more, his shouts muffled into unintelligibility. The door behind my back shuddered dramatically, my weight not quite enough to keep it entirely shut. It stopped moving when Nate sagged sideways against it, both of us leaning into the sturdy material with our shoulders now. "I'm so not going to miss this," I noted.

He gave a mirthless bark of laughter for an answer, but his expression remained surprisingly calm. "This will pass also," he reminded me. "It's only for a few more weeks, until we're done here. Once we're on the destroyer, we can easily avoid each other, and after that…" He trailed off there, reminding me that neither of us had a clue what to do once we were back across the ocean. The only thing that was sure was that we weren't going to stick around, and not just because of Hamilton. That latent unease that had started clinging to my soul since Bucky's reveals about Decker—the ghost he and Nate both had assumed was a thing of their past—returned, making my skin itch all over.

"I want to go back to how things were back then," I found myself voicing my thoughts without much intent, but the words rang truer than I'd expected. "I want to be that woman again. I don't want to give a shit about anything or anyone outside of our group. Fuck helping people who don't even want our help or only if they can abuse our gullibility. Who fucking needs a job anymore? We just do our thing, and that's it. We can easily fortify our hideout and get whatever we need to keep it going forever. That's what we should have done in the first place."

It wasn't the first time I'd come to that conclusion, and Nate didn't protest. The next bang against the door just seemed to underline the necessity of acting on that plan.

Taking another second to ground myself—for all the good that would do me as soon as I got face to face with that asshole outside the door once more—I pulled away, mentally giving myself a shake. Nate was right—nothing we could do about our situation now… except that wasn't true. I couldn't control Hamilton, but I sure as hell could control how much I let him goad me on. Maybe it was simply because I felt more self-assured now—and with the edge of my anger quite dulled due to residual feel-good shit pumping through my veins—or maybe it was Nate's reminder about how things had been last spring, but I sure as hell wouldn't let Bucky continue to rain on my parade. If I really missed feeling like I was the queen of the world and could do whatever the fuck I pleased, why not try getting back into that mindset? Super strength and endurance certainly didn't hurt.

"So, play it by ear?" I asked once more, getting ready to face the music.

"The same as usual," Nate agreed, picking up the soiled thermal and getting ready to shut off the flashlight while I got the door handle.

"Then let's do this."

My pull on the door was a little too hard, making it open in a dramatic motion that almost jerked it out of my hand before I could let go. I used the momentum to propel myself into the corridor, ending up smack in Hamilton's face, who'd been getting ready for the next round. He didn't seem particularly pleased seeing me waltz right up to him, but I did my best to keep my shoulders down and body relaxed as I slipped past him—the fingers of my right hand wrapping around my Glock where it was once more stashed in the holster at the small of my back. I didn't draw, didn't even tense that arm, but it was damn reassuring to have my gun ready should I need it.

"Are you finally done?" Bucky sneered in my face. It was unclear what reaction he expected to get from me, but the easy—and still a little winded—smile he got seemed to enrage him further.

"What's the urgency?" I quipped, more lighthearted than I would have managed earlier. "Just because you can't find anyone to bump uglies with doesn't mean that I can't get laid."

A day ago—heck, a few hours ago—I would have cringed at what seemed like just the next instance of my constant foot-in-mouth issue, but unlike before whenever we'd skirted any issue even remotely alluding to anything sexual, I felt my confidence surge rather than falter. Over the past weeks, I'd given Hamilton way too much power over me because of that, and this was going to stop now. I might have felt a little ridiculous at the notion of wrapping myself into a security blanket made out of my own sexuality, but really, why shouldn't I? It was about time I owned my shit once more, and stopped letting anyone, least of all some limp-dicked asshole like Hamilton or Taggard, take that away from me. And seeing the anger in his eyes let me know that, somehow, he realized what was going on.

It was also impossible to miss the confrontational expression on Nate's face where he ended up just inside the door, not bothering to step around Hamilton to physically shield me with his body because, lo and behold, I didn't need that anymore.

Keeping my smirk in place, I slowly withdrew my hand from my gun, relaxing into an easy stance. Let Hamilton see that I wasn't afraid of him. And yes, having a few of the French at my back now that I was facing Hamilton helped, a little. It also reminded me of my recent trust issues, which took some of the glow from my mental triumph, small as it was.

Bucky seemed more than ready to sneer his misgivings at us forcing him to wait for us to join him right into my face, but Elle, stepping up next to me so the three of us could see her without having to stop our childish glaring game, spoke up first. The look on her face had a bemused quality to it but was lacking some of the previous leniency. Peachy—we were already wearing out our welcome.

"I'm sorry that I have to interrupt your conversation," she offered, pausing long enough to let her neutral tone be as chiding as it was intended. "We have finally established satellite connection, and, at best, that gives us a fifteen-minute window."

I had a certain feeling where this was going, and quickly nodded for her to go on, hoping that neither Nate nor Bucky would take this chance to have at it and make us all look bad. Another missed golden opportunity to take Hamilton down a notch, but Nate's assessment had been right: if we killed him, we might as well consider asking for asylum in France, because getting back to the States would likely be short of impossible.

A slight woman with light brown hair behind Elle gestured further down the corridor. "Gabriel Greene wants to talk to you."

Chapter 3

My first reaction was to want to crow in victory because my guess as to who was to blame for our surprisingly warm welcome had been correct. I cut down on the impulse quickly, also because riding shotgun with that sentiment came the almost-missed sense of paranoia that always shut me up. So the black, fat spider in his New Angeles web had flung his reach right across the ocean—answering one question and posing a hundred new ones. Rather than dwell on it, I gave the woman a nod, starting forward.

Elle fell into step beside me, ignoring our two hulking, glowering followers. "We have time for introductions later. The weather is clear tonight so we should have good reception, but you're well-advised to get your important things stated first," she iterated.

I acknowledged that with another nod, a little absentminded as I tried to sort my suddenly buzzing thoughts. There I'd had weeks with a lot of mental downtime to make up theory after theory, and suddenly found myself with seconds to decide which one to go with.

The turn the woman had indicated before led into a large, dome-shaped room, full of the remainder of our people mostly scattered around the perimeter, and a handful of not-yet-introduced French. The half closer to the door was dominated by a table that was large enough that ten people could have easily lain down on top of it. Red was leaning against it, facing the opposite wall but just now looking back over his shoulder at us, his expression carefully neutral. On the wall, there was a bank of monitors connected to three workstations, all but one dark. I couldn't help but compress my lips in not-quite irrational misgivings at seeing Greene's face on screen, leached of color and with static because of the less-than-stellar connection pixelating the image every few seconds. No surprise that Gita was busy talking to him, Tanner lurking at her side as if to ensure nobody would keep her from giving her status update.

As I passed by the table—on the free side, to avoid bumping into Richards—I caught a few odd smirks but did my best to ignore them. I could tell that my face was still flushed and I was obviously not cold although I was only wearing a tank top on my upper body. While it had sounded like a neat idea to in every possible way rub it in Bucky's face that any sway he held over me was slipping fast, I hadn't exactly considered who else would see me like that. Well, no avoiding that now, and I refused to feel weird about it.

Leave it to Greene to make that impossible.

As I stepped up to Gita—and not so incidentally to where Burns was lounging against the wall next to one of the computers—

Greene's attention shifted to me, and Gita shut up after finishing her current sentence, a recount of what we'd found at the conservatory, from what I caught. I rocked to a halt trying to still look relaxed, but as I crossed my arms over my chest I was suddenly reminded that, unless I stuck my hands into my armpits, my fingers would be in plain view. So I quickly continued the motion and dropped my arms to my sides, putting my fingers onto the tops of my thighs where they would hopefully be out of the focus of the webcam, wherever it was mounted. If that meant I was idly fingering the holsters of my Beretta and knife, that was pure coincidence.

Rather than greet me like any normal person would, Greene squinted at me, and I could tell that he didn't miss any of the scars now in plain view due to my state of undress. His eyes returned to my face, yet not quickly enough to keep me from gnashing my teeth. "Is that your freshly fucked face? I really didn't need to ever see that."

Irritation burned away any thread of self-consciousness left from feeling like a mutilated freak-show, forcing me to fight for composure for a moment. Rather than snap at him, I donned as pleasant a fake smile as I could. "Gee, it's so sweet of you all to always be up in my business and worried about the state of my marriage," I drawled. Greene's mouth snapped open as if to refute that, but I talked right over him. "I hear we're pressed for time? I'll make it short then. I assume it's because of you that the French not only were expecting us, but have done so with the notion that I'm somehow some kind of savior-level VIP?"

From the corner of my vision I could see Bucky make a face where he'd stopped next to Red, while Nate—having settled just out of his reach, next to Burns—didn't hide a snort. Oh, the overflow of support was melting my cold, dead heart. I had to admit, the situation was kind of funny, and not just because it irked Hamilton to no end. Elle, to my other side, didn't react, clearly content to observe rather than judge prematurely.

Greene's obvious mirth about the truth of my observation surpassed his gloating at my obviously flushed state from moments before. "That is correct. I will leave the explanation of the details to the lovely Madame Moreau, and Gita should be able to fill in the blanks on our side." At the mention of her name, Gita hunched her shoulders, looking slightly uncomfortable—a reaction I couldn't quite place. It couldn't be because she'd figured I hadn't worked out yet that she was along because she was Greene's spy—that had been obvious from the day we'd set out on the journey north to the Silo, and then so, so far beyond that.

"Instead you're going to tell me why we're here?" I ventured a guess, then turned to give Richards a blank stare. "Told you the time was running out where you giving me a bone to chew on would make a difference. Clock's officially stopped ticking." Richards didn't react, and Hamilton doing the same confirmed my guess that Red playing "good cop" to his "bad cop" had been going on since we'd come to that damn Canadian base of theirs.

Greene's response made me focus on him instead. "I sure hope so. If you'd like to fill me in on what you already know so that I don't have to repeat everything?"

Exhaling slowly, I rocked back onto my heels, buying myself a moment of time to sort out my working theories. Well, there went nothing.

"My guess is that we're here because Raleigh Miller, while working on the serum project, made more of a breakthrough than we previously thought or was in his personal notes. That means, someone else was doing the actual experimenting, likely in a lab not too far from here or else it wouldn't have made sense to leave a trail of breadcrumbs right from the coast to wherever it is we're headed. Call it a cure." It took some strength of will not to look over my shoulder and single out Cole for divulging that little detail. "What I'm not quite sure of is why we're on such a tight schedule that they had to pack me up before I could heal at least somewhat, but I doubt it will be notes we're here to pick up, and while most labs have nitrogen tanks to store biological material for long times, I can see why being over a year and a half into the apocalypse might make things rather pressing."

Greene snorted. "It's the fuel." When I eyed him askance, he leaned back in his oversized swivel chair, a bout of static turning the motion into three choppy intervals. "The fuel for the plane that dropped you off at the ship, and the ship also. Even if they found reservoirs that were full and untouched after the shit hit the fan— which I doubt—what's still available is slowly rotting away. You must have gotten into the same trouble with refilling your cars more than once already. A year from now, or five? Who knows if any of that fuel is still useful for anything except gunking up the engines. We're heading right back into the stone age, so any fast travel over long distances has to be done before the last drop has spoiled."

That was a sobering thought—and a better explanation than I'd come up with myself. I was sure that if I admitted that, either Hamilton or Cole would laugh in my face again like they'd done with my short-sightedness about possible radiation issues from nuclear reactors. They could all, collectively, go fuck themselves for all I cared, so I took Greene's explanation with a nod and went on.

"So, possibly secret lab it likely is. I know France had a couple of BSL-4 labs but I somehow can't see anything connected to this shit being done in an official site. I'm still not quite sure how your father's company managed to pull off doing that kind of research while pretending to be just your run-of-the-mill biotech company." I cut off there, making myself stop rambling. Time, right, I reminded myself. "I still don't quite understand how you could have anticipated that we'd end up here without knowing of Raynor's invitation for me"— and I sure as hell hoped he'd been as oblivious as me, or else our next meeting would not be a peaceful one—"but you obviously sent Gita along because you expected that her hacking skills would come in handy. I like to delude myself into thinking I'm along because of my superior intellect and the fact that I am one of the last surviving people who has the scientific knowledge to do anything with the material and information we might recover, but I'm not that naive." I allowed myself a small chuckle there. "The security system of the lab is likely the same that you used at Green Fields Biotech, and while my access has never been activated, it's likely in their system. A generator and a few minutes of time are likely all Gita needs to change that. And my, aren't we all happy you decided on iris scans rather than palm prints?" I couldn't help myself and shot a gloating look at Hamilton. Oh yes, my guess had obviously been right from how he was grinding the enamel off his teeth. Turning back to Greene, I waited for his answer.

"Gee, and there I thought I could dazzle you with a fountain of new knowledge," he grumbled, but it was only a momentary one. Picking up a file, he briefly looked down at it. "You're heading to Paris, more precisely to La Défense, the satellite city just to the east of it. The lab is situated underneath one of the towers, a good twenty levels below street level. As for your guess why you're along, I think you hit the mark spot on."

"Why's everyone always so disappointed that I'm a smart cookie?" I couldn't help but complain. "I didn't get my PhD for being pretty or land any job because I was boinking the boss. Just his brother, and years after his death, but who's counting?" Burns gave the appropriate chuckle to that while Greene chose to ignore me. Really, this was no fun!

"I'm sure that Emily Raynor in particular will be delighted if rather than get your head bashed in, you use it to help her analyze whatever you find," Greene proposed.

"You think that's a likely possibility? I'm rather attached to the integrity of my cranium, and while we've had some fun moments involving light evisceration, things haven't really gotten to the point where I was actually afraid anyone would kill me."

Now Greene looked properly curious, but a somewhat stronger burst of static made him ignore the point. "As much as I'm sure that you all had a great time with bonding exercises, I'm actually referring to what might be waiting for you in that lab."

"And here I thought it was mere coincidence that almost all of us wouldn't have passed that weird glowy-eyes test." I paused, considering. "Did you know that there's something in the serum that makes our fluids, including fresh scars and eyes, glow in what I suppose is some kind of near-black light frequency?"

Greene looked rather nonplussed. "How do you think they quick-test their own soldiers?"

That made more sense than I'd expected. "Then why go through the hoodoo blood screen they forced on all the scavengers?"

I knew it was a stupid question when Greene smirked at me. "To see how much you've been screwing the pooch?" he suggested but went on before our conversation could derail any further. "I'm sure that by now either your husband or one of your other higher-ranking illustrious companions has told you that the Esterhazy base has, for a long time, been one of the experimental labs of the serum project? That was late-stage, almost-ready-for-mass-production testing. The lab you're heading to now? That was all first-stage alpha testing. Rumor is, nobody ever came back out who was sent there. They pretty much used their test subjects until there was nothing left that could have walked out."

My, wasn't that a sobering thought? It certainly put a damper on my latent need to snark. Not quite a surprise, but something I could have done without knowing. And it offered a possible answer to another thing I'd been wondering about.

"Do you know if they've had their own version of the serum in Europe?"

Greene seemed surprised at my question. "Not as far as I know, but it's likely that a few hundred individuals who had been inoculated were on the continent when the shit hit the fan. Why?"

"Because we've encountered a former security guard who was packing quite the punch. Literally, as in hitting me heavily enough that it must have burst some hidden pocket of infection I've still had in my torso that then caused some issues. Was a really bouncy fellow, too." I knew Greene couldn't do anything with that information and I mostly dropped it so I wouldn't have to explain to the others once we were done here.

Greene considered for a moment. "No clue, really, but it stands to reason that if they developed something, they would have shot up their security staff with it. I presume it wasn't a random encounter?"

"No, it was at the conservatory where they had a safe full of papers with serum variants in the triple digits printed on it, presumably the backup location for some of the data from that secret lab." Again I sent a gloating look at Hamilton over my shoulder that went ignored just like the previous one. Spoilsport.

"Probably expect more of that when you get down there," Greene advised unnecessarily. "Another bit of information you will find interesting: the lab went silent two weeks before the outbreak happened in the States."

I could almost hear the screeching sound of my thoughts grinding to a halt. "Wait a minute. The virus hit Europe weeks after it had already wiped most of us off the earth." We'd found plenty of old newspapers propagating that.

"Exactly," Greene agreed with me.

"Shit." I could tell from the way that Nate shifted that he hadn't made the same logical jump as I had. Half-turning to him but speaking loud enough that everyone in the room could hear me, I tried to explain. "However they managed to get the weaponized virus into the damn syrup and distributed all over the US, they must have manufactured it somewhere. There's a good chance that part of that lab was a bank of bioreactors so they could manufacture whatever they needed for their experiments in bulk. The lab likely went dark when whoever these whack-jobs had planted as a mole or recruited had to shut down the entire facility so they could harvest the virus and get it out of there. Think several truck-loads of material." It must have been a logistical nightmare, and no idea about the details. Then, something else occurred to me. "This was the lab that went dark that prompted Emily Raynor to push the doomsday clock button, right?"

"Must have been," Greene agreed. "Because it was the only facility working on the serum project that went offline until we were neck-deep in undead. It's anybody's guess what you will find down there, but if your theory is right, you'll also have a chance to harvest the raw version of the zombie virus. Enough to waste the fuel for one last return trip with the Navy's last remaining, still-operational destroyer, wouldn't you say?"

So much for thinking about what might happen if we missed our rendezvous at the beach for pickup. Something told me that whoever was there would wait—but only once.

"So we're here to get what might be the cure, and the cause for the end of the world. Sounds very poetic."

"A heroic quest," Greene jeered.

"I'm sure our people back home will be cheering us on. Or they would if they knew. Never mind."

Greene stared at me for a second, obviously considering—never a good sign. "If the news that you'll only have one chance to come back across the pond wasn't enough to make you worry, there's more. Turns out, Raynor and her people have been quite busy over the past weeks, since we last talked. You likely didn't hear it yet but you and your husband, you're best friends with the Army and the reconstitution effort. Everyone knows that you're working with them, all in good faith and the spirit of unity."

If he'd slapped me physically, it would have had less of an effect on me than hearing that. "Excuse me? And people believe that bullshit?"

"Why wouldn't they?" Greene offered, nonplussed. "His old buddies. Your career before the apocalypse happened. Nobody really knows shit about what went down at the Green Fields Biotech building, and who really got your motives for leading your crusade in late summer? They all just heard you claim that you were ambushed, and then you suddenly turned up to lead the rebellion to a surprisingly easy truce. Makes a lot more sense that you're a plant, and it was all staged to make everyone believe you were fighting for them while, really, you were helping sell them the story they needed to hear."

"That's—" Preposterous wasn't even coming close, but Greene had another word instead.

"—what people are already believing, and with you not around to try to refute it, it's already become the truth." He paused, watching my reaction, which was probably more amusing than anything else. And the fucking hypocrite didn't even sound heartbroken. "I'm not saying I believe it, but a suggestion, if you will? As it is right now, the people in France might be a lot more positively inclined toward you than those on this side of the ocean. I hear Normandy is lovely in the spring."

A stronger, much longer burst of static followed, oddly befitting how I felt hearing that. Why was I even surprised? Five minutes of feeling superior because, for once, I was ahead of the game, and, of course, karma had to knock me right back on my ass, where I belonged. So much for hoping that I'd have until we were back at the US coast to decide what to do—if we even survived.

I should probably have seen that as a warning and shut up, but when Greene's face came back into focus, I just couldn't hold back. Trying to appear casual now, I cocked my head to the side. "Say, does the name Decker ring a bell?"

Someone behind me—likely Bucky himself—gave a chortling huff, but I ignored it, instead trying to look for the smallest of tells on Greene's expression—but there was none.

"In what context?" he asked, genuinely perplexed.

"Army context, what else?" I offered, trying for levity. "I've been hoofing it across the country with a bunch of whiney old wives who love to drag up the most cozy campfire tales of camaraderie, every damn night. Gimme a break. They're name-dropping like it's a competition, and I know that in this one thing, you're likely drawing a blank just as I do. Humor me." A deliberate pause. "A recruiter maybe?"

Greene continued to think, restoring some of my faith in humanity—until his face lit up. "Might not be the same guy but my dad knew a guy named Decker, an old friend of his from 'Nam." He chuckled. "Never liked the guy, and he sure as hell didn't like me. Called me a waste of genetic material on more than one occasion. Meant it, too." His smile let everyone know he couldn't have cared less, and that I believed. It also made a lot of sense why a civilian biotech company was involved in something that I was sure USAMRIID wouldn't have let out of their grasp easily. Another piece of the puzzle falling into place.

I was already turning away, my mind still churning on so many levels, when Greene's question made me pause. "Why?"

More static followed, as if on cue. I shot Nate a glance and only got a shrug back from him that could have meant anything. Right. Play it by ear.

"Sorry, what did you say?" I overly loudly called toward the screen. "You're breaking up!" I then turned to Elle. "I think we got everything we need."

"And more than you were asking for, it seems," she surmised, then nodded at the guy manning the workstation below the single working monitor. "Cut the feed." She then continued to talk to him—in French—so I turned away, which incidentally made me face the table. No surprise there when I found Hamilton smirking at me.

"Just had to keep digging, never knowing what's good for you," he jeered.

I told myself to drop it, to simply ignore him, but Greene's recount of the propaganda scheme going on at home just made my blood boil.

"Why, afraid who might be listening in? I have to have the name from somewhere."

Bucky seemed unperturbed, but I wasn't buying it. I would have loved to discuss this further, but when I heard a deep, male voice clear itself behind me, I dropped the point, turning around.

Three men had joined Elle, only one of them taller than her. I bet he was in charge, his bright gray eyes trained on us now. With a full beard and shaggy, sandy blond hair in a bun at the back of his head, only a flannel shirt was missing to turn him into a hipster, but he certainly looked like he meant business—as did the tree-trunk thick muscles on his arms.

"I presume introductions are in order?" I guessed. "Since you mostly know who we are by now."

He held out a hand to me, introducing himself. "I'm Alexandre Bernard." I hesitated for just a moment, figuring that it was way too late to get self-conscious about my fingers now. His grip was strong yet not crushing, a quality handshake that immediately acknowledged me as his equal. He let go and nodded at the man to his left, who shared the strong build and hair color with him, yet had dark brown eyes and an easy smile rather than a stern expression fixed on his face. "This is my brother, Antoine. My XO, if you will. Elle, our chief of security, you have already met. And this is Raphael." He nodded at the last man, who was more the Mediterranean type, and a little slighter and younger than the other two. I vaguely remembered him being one of those who'd observed our little strip-down affair before. "He is the head of our scouts and will likely know best how you can get to whatever destination you are headed to."

I couldn't quite place a finger on what about my talk with Greene had smoothed over my ruffled feathers, but I easily resisted the temptation to be a bitch to Bucky as I did our rounds of introductions, doing my very best to sound as neutral as Alexandre had. I could only guess what they were making of the obvious bickering that was going on between us, yet none of them gave a clue of it now. A momentary lull in the conversation made me wonder if it was too soon to ask about that, but I decided that not knowing wasn't in my best interest, so I turned to Elle. "I presume it was Gabriel Greene who told you who I am?"

Her slight smile seemed to hold more knowledge than it had a right to. "He confirmed your identity, yes."

I wondered if that was a translation error, but that sounded too cryptic to just let it slide. "But you already knew?"

Her smile grew. "Of course. You're the woman from the video." She paused. "You're the one who saved millions of lives."

Chapter 4

Before my talk with Greene, that statement alone would have made me want to gloat. Now, it made my skin itch all over. What was it with people telling tales about me?

"You saw the video?" I'd heard the same mentioned from a few people along the way, particularly in the very early days, but it had been a while. I hadn't expected to hear the same on the other side of the Atlantic ocean.

"Of course," Elle responded, seeming a little irritated at my obvious doubt. "We'd heard that communications were already breaking down on your continent by then, but we had another week of working internet and television, and a good two months before radio communication turned patchy." She and Alexandre traded glances, and after a few seconds Elle resumed. "There were debates, of course. A lot calling you a raving lunatic. But then the virus started spreading in the cities, and more people listened than doubted. We were able to evacuate before it was too late and build and hold defenses over the summer. We lost a lot of good people, but we were able to save many more."

"How many did you save?" I was surprised that Nate would speak up, but probably shouldn't have been.

"A good twenty million," Antoine responded, his voice a warm baritone to his brother's more rumbling bass. "In France. That is a little less than one in three. All over Europe, particularly in the eastern countries, the numbers are closer to one in two point five. The winter was harsh and claimed more lives, but we persevered. Of the seven hundred million people, a good two hundred million are still alive."

The answering silence was deafening, the lot of us stunned into silence until low murmurs began to break it. I couldn't help but stare at them, hard-pressed to keep my mouth from gaping open. "How?"

Elle offered a slightly triumphant grin. "We did what we've been doing for centuries when faced with foes coming down on us in superior numbers: we went into the mountains. They are easy to defend, and we had time to build shelters and homes in the abandoned bunkers from the World Wars and mines to provide for everyone at first. By autumn, we had many mountain valleys reclaimed and secured, forcing us to only abandon the cities to the dead. We had to give up a lot of luxuries, but in parts we still have electricity and running water, at least until the power lines come down. The reason why you haven't encountered more of us is because for the winter, everyone has withdrawn to the strongholds. Less active people consume less food."

Her answer made me want to ask for details—so, so many details!—but I refrained, instead zeroing in on something else

Greene had dropped. Turning to Gita, I gave her a blank stare that was enough to make her hunch her shoulders once more. "And what exactly is your part in all this?"

I could tell that her discomfort at getting all that attention wasn't an act, but the heap of bullshit that Greene had so casually dumped on me—again—made me less than sympathetic for anyone else's plight. Plus, he had pretty much told me—and thus, her—to spill the beans. Tanner inadvertently took a step closer to his charge, resembling the big, protective brother even more than usual, and I couldn't help but feel a hint of disdain ghost through my mind when I realized that move made her relax. I raised my brows, urging her on to speak, and with a sigh, Gita did.

"I guess it's common knowledge that the video was released by the group who we all think is responsible for this?" She didn't pass up the chance to glance in Nate's direction rather than mine, but he gave her nothing. None of the soldiers said anything.

Alexandre eventually inclined his head. "We have heard mention that you blame a group of, what did Gabriel Greene call them? Eco terrorists? For contaminating high fructose corn syrup with the virus and releasing it at strategic points all across your country." I nodded. He looked as doubtful about the story as Hill had professed to be a few days back. That, more than anything else, made me wonder if I'd never doubted it myself simply because it sounded so convenient, and hit very close to home because of Nate's involvement with that very same group—only that he hadn't known about their motives. "We never found out what made the outbreak originate, but the theory most people believe is that, all across Europe, around a thousand sick people arrived and started spreading the infection."

Elle waited for him to fall silent before she interjected. "There have been reports that infection exploded in a few larger cities so it's possible that the contaminated goods had reached us as well, but there have been virtually no new infections from food registered in the past year. But to be sure, we have switched to consuming our own produce where possible in favor of preserved and processed food originating before the outbreak. We've had some issues with starvation at the end of winter, but over the summer we should have managed to upscale production to feed everyone well into spring this year."

"Then you're lucky," I offered, incapable of keeping my mouth from twisting. "We have tons of contaminated food. A candy bar is all you need to turn yourself into a walking bomb." I'd never forget Bailey biting that bullet to give the rest of us a fighting chance at the factory. Too late I realized that this could turn into a touchy subject, but Hamilton left it at a contemptuous snort. Like he wouldn't set up a contingency plan like that. I was sure that if I dug into any of the packs of his people, I'd find similar precautions than we'd carried around for most of the year.

"Well, it's true," Gita pressed out, her level of unease rising. "And I know because I've, ah, kind of been one of them."

I wasn't the only one who tensed and went still, staring at her. That explained her unease all right.

"Well, isn't that just wonderful?" Hamilton drawled, but didn't make a move. I felt a tad torn between my knee-jerk protective reaction and being a little on guard, but his sneer decided it. I'd have given her the benefit of the doubt, anyway, but now more than ever.

"I'm sure there's more to this," I insisted, earning myself a belligerent look from Hamilton.

It wasn't that much of a surprise that Nate was the one to try to defuse the situation, now that he'd found his voice. "We all make mistakes based on not enough or the wrong kind of information sometimes."

She shrugged. "They didn't tell us they were going to kick off the zombie apocalypse. I doubt they'd have found so many volunteers to help."

"Where did they find those?" I just had to ask, curiosity again overriding common sense.

"Craigslist," Gita admitted. A few of the soldiers chuffed, and Elle shared a look with Alexandre that spoke volumes. Yup, stupid yanks. So much for good impressions.

"Seriously?"

Gita gave a noncommittal grunt at my accusing question. "Not just there, but that was where they started recruiting. It sounded all good and well, too. Stick it to the man, fight against the mega corporations, you know the drill. Their objectives didn't sound that dangerous, more like guerrilla activism. Hack into a few servers, nix quality control checkpoints so evidence could be fabricated, although they titled that as keeping the corporations from continuing their lies and deceit. I didn't even really believe in their message about Mother Earth needing a reprieve. Guess I was just bored, and jonesing for a challenge." She paused, still hedging. "That was, until things suddenly started turning really weird and what had sounded like harmless blathering turned into fanatic creeds. That's when I decided that, just maybe, I should back off. But it was already too late."

I really didn't know what to make of that. "When was that?"

"Weekend before it started up on the East Coast and Seattle," Gita professed. "I tried to ignore the nagging feeling I had that something really bad was about to go down, but what could I have done, all on my own? And who would have believed me?" She paused. "Believe it or not, if you go to the FBI and say, 'Hi, I'm a hacker. I may have done some very illegal stuff but those other guys are worse,' they don't offer you a plea deal like they do on TV. Monday rolled around and nothing much had happened, and I told myself to relax. Then that video from that guy going crazy after eating ice cream hit the web, and I told myself it was just coincidence."

"But it wasn't."

She nodded at my statement. "No, it wasn't. On Wednesday morning, I had no internet connection at home anymore, nor at the coffee shops down the street. That's when I knew that something really, really bad was going on or else they wouldn't have taken control over the media." She swallowed uneasily, idly scratching her arm. "I tried calling a few friends, but half of them were too sick to pick up. Same as my roommate. I tried getting her some cough drops from the drugstore but they were already out of them."

"Where were you?" I asked—a valid question, not just for the timeline.

Gita hesitated. No idea why she suddenly got so evasive. "East coast."

"So the riots started—"

"On Wednesday evening," she offered. "I knew there was a local liaison for the group, so I tracked him down. He was stoned out of his gills and very obviously not well anymore, but he let me use his laptop—that miraculously still had a connection—when I feigned interest in checking up on what was going on. That's when I found their dark web forum where some of them were cheering on the progress—and posted videos they'd made." The unhappy look on her face was impossible to misinterpret. "I recognized a few of the names and did my best to remember them, but the dude got high-strung when I overstayed my welcome, so I went back home. Made it there just before the looting started."

She paused, as if to give us a chance to ask questions, but when the uncomfortable silence continued, so did she.

"My roommate and I, we barricaded ourselves in our tiny apartment when we heard the sirens start up outside. Someone tried to break in during the night, but it was obvious that there wouldn't be anything interesting here so they left us alone after that. On Thursday morning, one of our neighbors knocked, asking how we were doing. My roommate, she was barely breathing by then, her fever so high that not even cold compresses did anything to lower it, and she'd started vomiting blood during the night. I told him to go away, but he returned a few hours later." This time, her halting had a decidedly painful quality to it. "I didn't want to go. I was afraid of what was out there. But she... she died at just after three, and staying in the apartment with a dead body wasn't how I wanted to spend the weekend, you know? So when he dropped by again, I packed up a few things and we left."

Richards, so far silent, spoke up. "Why would you? With looters out there and everyone getting sick, why leave?"

Gita gave him a look that spoke plainly that she wasn't that much of a coward. "For one, I needed to know what was going on, and chances were, that guy's laptop might still be working. And Mark, he said we had to leave, and if a former marine tells you that you should beat it, you leave. He wanted to hightail it right out of the city, but I convinced him that I needed that laptop. So we went to fetch it. Middle of the day, Mark built like a tank, nobody bothered us. Until we came to that guy's house." She exhaled forcefully as she made herself go on. "Long story short, we got the laptop, but not only had the dude turned, he came right for Mark as soon as we got the door open, chewed right through his jugular. I was so stunned, I would have been dead if Mark hadn't gotten a lucky shot in. I know I should have tried to help him, but I just grabbed the laptop and portable modem and ran. I hid on the roof of the house, figuring nobody would go up there by accident, and reception might be better. And it was."

Forcing herself to slow down to where she didn't skip over half of the words, she resumed at a somewhat slower pace. "Nobody was active on the forum anymore but I found leads to another. They were coordinating, still busy suppressing media coverage, only letting through what they deemed appropriate. They'd somehow managed to take out part of the electrical grid on the Eastern seaboard."

I didn't know why that made me glance at Nate, but the deadpan stare he returned made me want to draw up short. He gave me a warning look when I opened my mouth to inquire, shaking his head ever so slightly. No to the asking, but that was pretty much a confirmation that this was his doing. One of these days I really had to ask him what he'd been doing leading up to his mission. I vaguely remembered that a week from that, he's shown up covered in bruises and cuts. I hadn't asked then, and probably shouldn't ask now—if I ever wanted to sleep again. But talk about regretting your decisions.

Gita, oblivious of our silent exchange, meanwhile droned on about some hacking stuff that sounded to me like what my scientific explanations must sound to the others all the time, until she realized half of us were zoning out. "Anyway, I managed to convince some of the people who were still online that this was a crazy, fucked-up thing that was going on," she explained. "So we rallied, found whoever else we thought might be able to help, and started systematically tearing into their defenses and whatever we found that led back to them."

Elle had followed the story with interest, but that made her perk up. "While you were still sitting on that roof?"

"Pretty much." Gita nodded. "I had a power cord with me, and there was electricity, at least for minutes at a time, until Friday afternoon. By then we'd rallied over two hundred people, most of them sitting in the midwest and south where the virus was spreading at a slower rate. I knew the closest of the others was a good twenty miles away from me, and with the city full of screams and gunshots, I didn't really want to chance it. But then the electricity died, and three hours later the modem as well, so I had to chance it. Still don't know how I made it out there but I got to his house just after sunrise on Saturday morning." Which was just about the time I grew some balls, destroyed the viral stocks from the vault in the hot lab, and thought the worst that would happen to me that day was either dying from a possible infection, or Nate's wrath from having gotten locked in the decontamination shower. Fun times.

"Was your friend still alive?" Elle asked, having taken over from me to urge Gita on.

"He was, but he was sick. By then we had a good idea of what might happen so he made me promise to, at the very least, lock him inside his bedroom once things got bad. He gave me a brief update what they'd done during the night, and we jumped right back in, just in time to help take down their main server that they'd used for the media blockade. They only wanted to share the files and videos they'd compiled for their own archive, but we threw it all out there to see for everyone who still could." Her gaze flitted over to me. "That included that video where you explained what the virus was and what it was doing. For most people in our corner of the world it was too late, but turns out, overseas they still had a chance to use that knowledge."

That all sounded nice—and very edited down. "So what aren't you telling us?"

She shrugged, although now that the cat was out of the bag and nobody had broken her neck yet, Gita seemed a little more relaxed. "We're hackers. Of course we tried to hack into anything we could get our grubby little hands on. When someone managed to blast into one of the military networks, we found out that someone had started powering down the nuclear reactors, which at first we thought was sabotage because it killed the grid state by state. But then we realized that loss of electricity might not be the worst that could happen, well, compared to nuclear fallout, so we checked what reactors were still online and hacked into the controls of those. We also might have taken half of South America off the grid. And someone may or may not have published what he claimed was the President's browser history on Reddit."

I couldn't help but snort, even though the rest wasn't exactly funny. "Well, God bless your priorities."

Another shrug. "It is what it is. By Sunday evening, my buddy was too weak to help, and on Monday morning the last battery pack ran out. Last thing I read on the 'net was someone going bonkers about the sugar thing after your warning on the radio. That was the last connective bit that I'd still been missing. I'd found their distribution network info and shit, but not what they'd been spreading exactly, and how, or we could have warned people days earlier."

"Do those files still exist?" I figured it was a valid question.

Gita hesitated, but then answered. "Greene has them. And I'm sure they do, too." She cast a sidelong glance at Hamilton, who, of course, didn't confirm or deny anything.

I turned to Elle. "And that's how you got the information? At least about the virus?"

She inclined her head. "That, and warnings about what we were about to face. We could have saved more if we'd listened better, but it made more of a difference than any of our own contingency plans could have done, taken together. Whether you want the fame or not—and I can tell that, at best, you're a reluctant hero—you've earned it." Her gaze dropped down to my fingers, still splayed across my hips. "A lot might have happened since then, and a lot more that we can only speculate about, but know that you have our gratitude. We will support you on your quest however we can. Should you decide you want to stay, you will always be welcome here, as is everyone else who wants to stay with you."

I'd never thought I could be that conflicted about anyone offering their—seemingly—unconditional support. Maybe I simply wasn't used to it.

"I'm honored by your offer. Thank you," I assured her. "As for what we need…" I turned enough so I could cast a brief look at Hamilton, who caught and held it easily. "As I already told you, I'm just the technical advisor. Far be it from me to want to lead this mission."

Hamilton let out a low chuckle under his breath as he took over from me. "We need maps, and any intel on how we can reach our destination, if you have it. Food and shelter for three days. We likely won't bother you again on the way back but move right on to our pickup point at the coast."

Alexandre gave a small nod, at which the diminutive woman who'd shown us the way in the corridor outside stepped up, drawing attention to herself. "We have three empty rooms just across the hall that you can use for quarters, if you don't mind sleeping on mattresses on the ground. There should be enough bedding for all of you to get comfortable in. You can grab whatever food or drink you need from the kitchen or pantries. We have enough to feed ten times your numbers. If you need anything else, please let me know. You can go outside to your gear anytime you want. You're all cleared with the guards."

With everyone in uncustomary hygienic condition after the hot showers, a few of the soldiers were only too happy to tramp off to go foraging for food or catch some sleep, although my guess was that most would try to add some socializing as well. Cole, Aimes, and Hill remained yet grouped together where they were keeping to the wall by the door. That left Hamilton and Richards, plus the five of us. Raphael disappeared only to return with an armload of maps, half of them hand-drawn.

"La Défense, right?" he reaffirmed what Greene had said.

Richards inclined his head. "Tour Coeur Défense, on the north side of the plaza."

Gee, not even getting a destination helped clear anything up. All that my mind had snagged on was what sounded like an endless labyrinth several levels underneath the ground floor to me. "If the first thing we encounter down there is the computer projection of a little girl telling us that we're all going to die down there, I'm out," I grumbled as I watched Raphael spread out the maps all across the table, pretty much covering the entire top of it. Burns laughed. He was the only one.

Antoine watched the scout with a similar expression of doubt that I felt well up inside of me when Raphael put his finger down on a spot that was way too far inside the Paris metropolitan area than I felt comfortable with. "It's a suicide mission," Alexandre's brother drawled. "Ajou is the closest base we have been able to hold since the outbreak, and that's over a hundred and twenty kilometers out."

Hamilton gave him a cool look. "We're not amateurs, and we will find a way. We've come this far without losing anyone."

Antoine didn't seem impressed, yet before he could retort anything, Red spoke up. "We appreciate your warnings. We have encountered more of the undead than we anticipated, certainly more than we are used to from back home. You said you still have a population of over twenty million alive? As many undead as we saw out there, that's hard to believe."

Elle had an answer for that. "From what Gabriel Greene has told us in our previous conversations, a lot of your initial infected died and stayed dead?" Richards nodded. "Ours didn't. We had a conversion rate of well over ninety-five percent."

I couldn't help but whistle through my teeth. "That's... a lot."

Elle nodded. "It's what cost most people their lives—the inability to cut off a loved one's head just as they expired. People are smarter now. That's why we had less than ten percent losses from infections since four months after the outbreak. A lot more have died from accidents and diseases since then. We've managed to keep the dead out of the mountains, but our cities are still overrun, and a lot of the flat land as well."

Richards looked less than happy. "So of the over two million inhabitants that Paris had—"

"Most of them are still there," Raphael finished for him.

Didn't that sound great? Considering what a few thousand zombies had done in Caspar in the spring—and twenty times that in Sioux Falls—that sounded like a shitload of trouble.

"There might be a way," Elle proposed as she looked at the maps. "It's been unseasonably warm this week. The Seine's not completely covered in ice. We could use the boats. La Défense is very close to the river."

"Boats?" I echoed. "I presume you don't mean to row upriver?"

"The noise will be an issue," Elle acknowledged. "It only works if the ice has receded far enough that the undead cannot jump onto the boats. But if you go by day and far enough up the river, then let yourself drift back, they might have quieted down enough so you don't get eaten right at the riverbank."

"It's a good start," Hamilton said before anyone else could protest. "Maybe we will come up with an easier solution, but I've heard worse. Let's sleep on this first, and I'd appreciate fresh intel from you tomorrow morning. That should give us plenty of time to work on something solid."

He and Red started discussing in hushed tones then. I didn't even try to listen in. Boats on a partly frozen river, surrounded by very cold water, the ice around teeming with shamblers—what was not to love? Compared to dwelling on that, I downright welcomed Gita sidling up to me.

"You're not mad at me?" she asked, sounding small enough that whatever residual misgivings her reveal had left in me—most of which resonating with my usual misgivings toward Greene, I had to admit—quickly dissipated into thin air.

"We all have our secrets," I offered—and wasn't that true. Just because most of mine had gotten freshly aired over the past weeks didn't mean I didn't know a thing or two about regrets and guilt. "And you didn't have to try to help. You didn't have to risk your life, and that of your friends." Whoever that Mark fellow had been, he must have meant more to her than just a random neighbor, and I remembered from our past conversations that her roommate hadn't just been an acquaintance, either.

"But I did nothing until it was too late!" she insisted with vehemence that I was also all too familiar with. "If I'd said or done anything a week earlier—"

"They likely would have killed you," I finished the sentence for her. "These people had no qualms killing billions. Even though some of that was accidental, they knew there would be a hell of a lot of collateral damage even if they just hit the super soldiers and made them insta-convert. You've seen what damage we can do when we still try to act human. Without that? You've seen enough of that as well." After what I'd done in that ravine today I felt like I'd earned the right to consider myself part of that faction, whether I liked it or not.

She nodded but hung her head. I hesitated, but rather than just patting her on the shoulder, I gave her a quick hug. Part of me needed that as much as she did. Damn fucking Raynor, signing my death warrant—and I hadn't even been aware of it…

Hamilton's voice grating across my conscience brought me back to the here and now. "Oh, she's big on forgiveness. Don't forget, she married the reject that not only betrayed every single value he ever stood for, but also used her life like any other poker chip in the game."

Letting go of Gita, I did my best to hold on to that residual glimmer of warmth inside of me, trying hard not to let the anger seeping back consume it all at once. "Well, I haven't killed you yet although I had a good three chances. I must be really big about forgiveness of late."

Hamilton snorted but didn't add anything that made me want to hurl myself across the table at him. He left it at that—which made me instantly suspicious—and instead bent down to get something from below the table… only to resurface with a stack of manila folders, dropping what looked like a few hundred pages in three neat piles in front of me. "The documentation of the project that you left on your bunk. All the update notes that Raynor had of the lab before it went dark, dating up to two days before that. And a list of the viral strains she thinks might be the most interesting. If your new friends here have a working printer, we can add the decrypted files we got from the conservatory; else, Cole will hook you up with a laptop so you can review them digitally. That is, if you find the time between screwing your brains out. After all, we have you along to be our scientific advisor."

My first impulse was to shy away from the stacks of paper as if they were poisonous snakes, but my curiosity won, making me pick up the folder in the middle—presumably the notes from the lab—after a moment's hesitation. I refused to react to Hamilton's barb, even less so as I still felt mellow enough that it was more of a glancing blow than a direct hit. "How much time do I have for this?" I asked absentmindedly, already soaking up what felt as close to the Holy Grail as anything I'd ever come across in my life. I sure as hell wasn't going to look that gift horse in the mouth, not after weeks of going insane from not knowing what was going on.

"Depends on how long we're welcome to stay," Hamilton said, his gaze skipping to someone—presumably Elle or Alexandre—behind me. "Two days, maybe three. We need to recuperate before the next leg of our journey, and if it gives us an edge, we have a day or two to spare."

"So Greene's assessment was right. You are running out of fuel," I surmised, momentarily looking up from the data.

Hamilton didn't answer, but that was saying a lot in and of itself. I suddenly felt a little stupid with my constant resentment clouding my judgment; I absolutely didn't put it past him to annoy me for the heck of it, but it made a lot more sense that he'd been closed-mouthed because desperation wasn't always the best motivation, particularly when getting stranded in a foreign country was suddenly also a very real possibility. It sure explained why he'd been pushing onward as if we had flames licking on our very heels.

As if he'd read my mind—a truly disconcerting idea—Hamilton offered, "Before yesterday, you hardly seemed up to reading two consecutive sentences, let alone understanding anything that's in there. No one's expecting miracles from you, but it will make our job a hell of a lot easier if you can point at things or rattle off numbers rather than spend hours searching. This is not a computer game where you just have to run up to the blinking quest icon on the map. We have no idea what's waiting for us in that lab. The sooner we're done, the better."

My, didn't that sound nicely cryptic? "I presume you know a thing or two about what might be lurking in there?" Greene's hint was enough to make my blood run cold, but human experiments were one thing; juiced-up super zombies quite another.

Whether it was that he wanted to appear diplomatic now that our French friends were listening in, or he'd gotten tired of being an obtuse ass to me all the time, Bucky surprised me by giving an answer. "Know? No, and I doubt they would have marked these things in their update notes. But if I was head of security in a super secret lab that suddenly found itself shut down because of a security breach of some kind, I would unleash hell on whoever caused that incident. If that meant shooting up a kennel of test subjects with the latest version of whatever fucked-up shit that had been part of the ongoing research, I would do it in a heartbeat. Or if someone was about to kill us all by unleashing a deadly gas or other agent, I'd make sure something was set free to avenge us." He paused, offering me a humorless grin. "I'm sure your husband told you a few of the old wives' tales the men like to tell about the serum project headquarter that Raynor has taken over? Most of that's just stories. Because where they actually originated, that's where we're headed."

This was getting better and better. I was almost happy when he shut up, clearly done with the question-and-answer session. Picking up the folders, I briefly inclined my head. "I'll see what I can find in this."

Hamilton acknowledged that with a nod and without the usual verbal abuse, already turning back to the maps. I hesitated, wondering if I should stick around for planning, but I was the first to admit that I knew next to nothing about how to best find a way to infiltrate a zombie-overrun city. So I left, Gita the only one trailing behind me as I made for our new living quarters.

Chapter 5

I briefly considered claiming one of the two smaller rooms that the French had set aside as our quarters, but then ended up joining the others in the much larger room that sat in between—partly because one room had already been allocated for the contents of our packs and weapon maintenance, and the other was claustrophobically small, barely wide enough to fit two mattresses next to each other. Burns would have had trouble stretching out lengthwise across them. It also felt weird to be closeted away from the others, a fact I only grudgingly admitted. The entire last week I had been happy for every single moment away from them, but there was safety in numbers, even if the French hadn't given us even a hint to be concerned about anything.

Or maybe it was that, given the news Bucky had sprung on us, I really didn't want to be alone right now.

I ended up parking my tired ass in the corner by the door that had, so far, not been occupied. All along the walls of the room lay mattresses dressed with fresh sheets, and haphazard stacks of pillows and blankets in between—in short, luxury I hadn't expected to ever find again anywhere on the road but so very appreciated. Gita moved a little farther into the room down the left wall, leaving me the corner including two mattresses that quickly got covered in stacks of papers as I started going through the files Hamilton had so graciously handed over. Cole came in shortly thereafter—probably an hour or two later— and stopped short at the other side of my paper fort, another stack of papers, smelling tantalizingly like fresh printer toner, in his hands.

"Just drop that somewhere," I told him, not bothering to look up from the table I was perusing.

He gave a short laugh. "Don't tell me there's a system behind this mess."

"Sure is." Focusing on him, I was ready to tell him to stop screwing around, but then realized that I'd managed to cover my entire vicinity with paper, leaving nothing but the very end of the mattress to my right free, precariously close to the door and prone for anyone walking by to accidentally kick things over. "Gimme," I said instead.

Bemused, Cole idly pushed papers aside with the tip of his boot until he could reach me, dropping another three hundred odd pages into my lap. And a sandwich—well, baguette, to be precise—filled with what looked like roast beef and brie, wrapped in a threadbare cloth. "Miller says you should eat this, unless you want him to stuff you like a goose. I was considering not telling you because that spectacle would sure be entertaining."

Glaring at the food first, then Cole, I nevertheless unwrapped it and started digging in, not bothering to close my mouth as I chewed. "I've seen at least seven women since we came in here, and that was without visiting any of the common areas deeper inside the base yet. Don't you have anyone else you can annoy? Or, you know, do more entertaining things with?"

Except for Davis, still nursing his hurt leg, and McClintock, who seemed to have pulled an extra long shift last night, the rest had fled the sleeping quarters quickly enough. Even Gita had abandoned me after she realized I meant business with the files.

Cole made a face. "Hamilton warned us not to antagonize the natives. So unless a buxom French mademoiselle is going to plunk her ass in my lap, I'd better keep my hands to myself."

I couldn't help but snort. I was sure that the warning looks Elle had taxed the lot of them with had done more to scare them straight. "So in the meantime you've set your sights on annoying me? Get lost. Unlike you, I have actual work to do." Cole inclined his head, still grinning, but paused when I held him back. "Thanks for dropping that hint on the trek over," I offered, meaning it. "It sure helped not to sound like I was bumbling in the dark with the powers that be—or rather, wannabe—all knowing."

Cole hesitated but then relented. "You're welcome. And it was quite funny to see both Greene and Hamilton fed up that you'd pretty much figured out everything by yourself already."

"Helps to have friends sometimes." I knew it was a cryptic statement and I didn't even know myself what exactly I wanted to say with it, but Cole took it as the olive branch that it was.

"Sometimes it does." He left me to my baguette and notes, looking as bewildered as I felt.

Dropping the section I had been perusing before, I quickly leafed through the file Cole had brought me, now a little less at a loss of what I was reading than when the files had still been encrypted, and I hadn't had the full documentation spread out all around me. A lot of it was the same information as in the notes—weekly update reports for the most part, and a monthly summary of each project, from what I could tell—but there were a few nuggets of gold strewn in between endless tables of experimental conditions and raw data. As much as my curiosity still burned bright, what I'd read so far had done a few things to make sure I wouldn't be able to sleep well going forward. They'd been doing experiments on human subjects all right, and while they'd used assigned numbers rather than names, it was impossible not to cringe at what was evident if one simply read between the lines. Twenty-three numbers had been mentioned so far, five of which had expired. Considering that one of them had been assigned dates more than twenty consecutive months, I wasn't sure if those five hadn't been the winners.

Another hour passed, and while I would have loved to be able to taste the food I devoured, I didn't mind not losing the appetite I didn't have anymore to what I kept finding in the files. Yet it wasn't the superficial dread of compassion for the victims of the trials that made me uncomfortable, no. It was the almost certain knowledge that if Thecla and her maniacs hadn't killed Raleigh Miller when they did, I would have sooner or later ended up connected, on some level or other, with the research that had been going on at that lab—and very likely managed to justify it, somehow. I really didn't want to contemplate what that would have done to me. From that point of view, Raynor's utter lack of compassion and empathy looked more like a survival trait than a trade secret.

And there I'd thought Hamilton would be the worst thing I'd have to deal with on this trip.

Burns dropping by to claim one of the remaining mattresses—next to the ever-spreading piles of papers—was as good an excuse as I'd get to drag myself back to the here and now, and I was more than happy to let him physically pull me up and along toward where dinner had been set up in one of the larger rooms of the complex that I hadn't visited yet. I still took one of the reports with me, but mostly so Hamilton wouldn't have any ammunition against me and my purported lack of interest in helping with the mission.

The room—or hall, as it turned out—was about five times as large as the communication center, or war room, that we'd been in before, housing two long lines of tables and benches, haphazardly cobbled together to form some kind of a banquet setup. Both tables were covered in more food than I'd seen in one place for a very long time, and buzzing with people dropping in and switching places to grab a bite but mostly to shout on top of each other in good-natured conversation. I stopped right inside the door, the general level of noise making me draw up short. Burns, as usual, grinned at my obvious moment of overwhelm before he pushed me on toward the right of the tables where I saw Elle and Alexandre talking animatedly with—or rather, at—Nate and Red among a lot of unfamiliar faces. Bucky sat farther down the same table, stuffing his face while Aimes, Russell, and Parker were bickering among themselves. I ignored them in favor of squeezing in next to my dear husband, not quite sure what to make of the fact that both Hill and Cole dropped down on the bench opposite us when a few of the French vacated the premises.

Before Nate could get cute and pile food on my plate, I set to the task myself, going mostly for fat and protein-rich leftovers that others seemed to have avoided—or hadn't gotten to yet. It all looked delicious, but after a week of hearing the guys complain about the MREs—that they always devoured right down to the very last crumbs—almost anything would have. There was also an abundance of steamed and grilled vegetables that I made sure to get a heap of as well, much to Nate's amusement. While I started stuffing my face, Elle and Red kept a conversation going about 19th century French literature that was only fascinating because of the people having it. I welcomed Antoine shooing a cute girl away so he could sit down next to his brother, much to Alexandre's apparent dismay—and Elle's continuing ignorance. Far was it from me to speculate, but as far as I could tell, the French weren't exactly prudes.

Or circumspect, as I was about to find out.

"What's up with that," Antoine asked, gesturing with a piece of bread in my direction. At first I thought he meant the now somewhat stained report that sat mostly forgotten next to me except for Nate idly looking at it once in a while. When he saw my confusion, Antoine clarified, "Your fingers."

"Ah. That. Well," I started, chasing some peas around my plate to come up with a good answer. "It's kind of a long story." And not necessarily one that I wanted to recount, in present company, when both Hill and Cole visibly perked up and even Red took some interest. It wasn't like they didn't know the details.

Antoine leaned back as far as his perch on the bench would allow. "We have time. There's still food on the table, and lots of wine for when it's gone."

I wondered if I should have told him that alcohol wouldn't do a thing for me anymore, but eventually gave in.

"Long story short, I got infected by the virus but because dying would have been too easy, I survived, yet what I thought was full immunity I'd gained was only immunity to the virus, not the secondary bacterial infection I got from the zombies gnawing through my hip right down to the bone. Not the most sanitary thing, rotten undead mouths. The infection spread slowly enough that it took me months to realize that I had it, and then there was nothing else to do but scrape and cut all the necrotic bits off. Even got my left femur partly replaced with titanium because the fucking critters ate away everything down to the bone."

Alexandre and Elle both looked fittingly impressed—and more than a little skeeved out—but Antoine barely batted an eyelash. "How does a virologist—no less the woman who knew all about what was going on just as it was unfolding—end up getting bitten by zombies? Shouldn't you have been sitting safely tucked away in a lab or bunker somewhere?"

I didn't much care for his openly chiding tone, and less so for the obvious agreement from the peanut gallery next to him.

"Not quite my style," I offered when telling him to go fuck himself didn't sound like the smartest answer in the book. "I spent my first year out in the apocalyptic wilderness and being locked inside didn't sound that appealing anymore after that. They even offered to let me run one of their labs, but that would have come with more fine print than I was happy with at the time. Plus, I didn't quite agree with the direction they were going at that lab, and all over. Some of us do still take that 'land of the free' thing more seriously than others." Cole looked less than impressed with that statement while Hill chuckled into his beer. Red, awfully neutral, reminded me more and more of Nate when he didn't want to let me look into his cards.

"So rather than help your people, you chose to get eaten by the undead," Antoine surmised, continuing on that train. I wondered if he'd already spent too much time with Hamilton and his flunkies.

"Well, I wouldn't have gotten eaten if some assholes hadn't set up a trap for us and decided that it was worth getting killed just to annoy us," I pressed out, maybe a little more harshly than warranted. Then again, maybe not.

Elle didn't miss the baleful glance I sent the soldiers, in turn scrutinizing them before she turned back to me. "And yet, you are working with them now?"

I shrugged, feeling strangely chastised by her statement. "Why, just because I lost two of my friends, almost my own life, the life of my unborn child, and a good fifth of my semi-vital body parts doesn't mean I have to hold a grudge, right?"

While Hill kept nursing his beer, Cole had about enough of my snark. "That might explain the chip on your shoulder, I give you that. But don't forget the part where you rallied a good thousand of your miscreants to kill anyone who might be disagreeing with your kind of frontier outlaw lifestyle."

That made me laugh out loud, but likely for a different reason than he expected. I couldn't tell whether it was the food—or having the French as a buffer between us—but rather than anger me, that assessment was strangely amusing.

"There's that," I agreed, gifting Cole the sweetest smile I could manage. "If some of you hadn't spent the summer killing scavengers and kidnapping and raping women, I wouldn't have been able to rally anyone. So, there."

Cole and I kept glaring at each other across the table, prompting Nate to assume the role of commentator. "We've had quite the interesting summer, if you were wondering." Red toasted his silent agreement, making Burns laugh.

"That we did," I agreed, trying to step off the soap box once more before the French could start thinking about taking sides. "Lots of misunderstandings and some bad eggs that needed to be cracked. Why are we here now? You heard what Greene and Hamilton said. If there's a chance that we can find some kind of a cure or whatnot, it would be a waste not to take it." There was no need to stress that our agreement had pretty much been forced at gunpoint; the more time I spent around the soldiers, the more I started to believe my own half-lies. Part of me still felt like a traitor, even more so now that Greene had told me the reaction most of the scavengers seemed to have when they'd heard the news. For the first time it occurred to me that Raynor's carrot-or-stick offer kind of absolved me of any direct guilt in a sense—at least to myself.

Antoine, still riding the blunt train, honed in on that. "Doesn't seem like that made you incredibly popular to your own people."

I shrugged, still not quite sure what to make of that myself. "Nothing I can do about that now. I first have to survive this suicide mission before I can worry about what someone I've probably never met thinks of my motives."

For whatever reason, that response mollified Antoine somewhat, and got me a nod from Elle. "You're welcome to stay with us," she repeated her previous offer. "Whatever happened in your country, you will find that people here don't much care about it."

"My friends are back home. My family," I corrected. "As much as the idea rankles that my attempt to ultimately help people might get me their anger, I'm not afraid of a possible lynch mob waiting for me back in the States. It's a huge country, and as you've probably guessed from our reactions, we've lost a lot more people than you did. That also means there are entire states with close to single-digit inhabitant numbers. That's a lot of opportunity to keep from inciting another witch hunt."

"Fair enough," Alexandre offered, breaking his silence. "We would never want to keep you from your family. But if you decide that living between a rock and a hard place isn't the end of all things, there's a reason the Germans coined the saying, 'living like God in France.'" True to that sense, the French toasted each other and thankfully moved the conversation into a different direction.

"Mountain fortresses," Red inquired a while later. "That's enough to feed that many people?"

Alexandre, his tongue loosened by wine quite a bit, shook his head, laughing under his breath. "Without a lot of the valleys that we managed to wall off, we wouldn't be able to get enough food for half of the people we need to keep alive. We have no predators left in those regions so breeding livestock is what helps quite a lot. And we've secured most of the islands in the Mediterranean, particularly in Greece and what used to belong to Spain."

"We've had to give up on Ibiza," Elle said with true remorse swinging in her voice. "The outbreak hit hard there, and with no survivors it made little sense to try to reclaim the land. Cyprus and Malta were a close call but the hard winter helped, made the undead sluggish enough that the defenders managed to push them back enough to eventually get rid of them."

"Fishing has helped as well," Alexandre picked up from her once more. "We've struggled, but people learned to adapt quickly. Our biggest losses were our first responders and hospital staff. Those we cannot easily replace."

The same was true for the US, although with the company I kept, I hadn't felt the sting of it much—and now likely never would, I reminded myself.

"How did you manage to stave off the zombies in the first place?" Cole wanted to know. "Without weapons, it must have been a bitch."

Alexandre and Elle gave him blank stares that were somewhere between insulted and confused, until Antoine let out a loud guffaw. "You really think we have no weapons just because we're not Americans?" His almost-accusation made him laugh all the harder. "You maybe couldn't buy them in a supermarket here, but we've all had proud traditions of hunters. Maybe not in the cities, maybe not in the media, but when the need arose, we knew how to defend ourselves."

Kris, the slight, brown-haired girl from the war room, agreed with him, her German accent getting stronger the more drunk she got. "Don't forget all the old weapons left over from World War II. For a while I ran with a guy who claimed his neighbor kept a tank in his barn. A fucking tank!"

Elle gave her a soft smile that disappeared when she turned her attention back to Cole. "Besides, guns are not always the best. Shots are loud. They attract attention. We've had quite some success setting spear traps and using javelins and arrows for ranged attacks. And nothing recovers from a smashed-in skull. Noah told me that except for your sniper, you barely used guns when you helped our people this afternoon. I see that you've come to a similar conclusion as we did very early in the fight. Attracting attention is the last thing you want." She paused to let her statement gain the weight it deserved before she turned to Nate, Red, and me. "You need to keep that in mind when you go into Paris. A shout might be enough to bring tens of thousands of undead down on you. If you open fire with an assault rifle, you're as good as dead."

"Duly noted," Nate supplied more wryly than I thought was appropriate.

"We don't always go around shooting at everything," I tried to defend myself. Nate cocked an eyebrow, making me snort. "Okay, not exclusively. Just whenever we can get away with it. But we have larger hordes of shamblers at home as well. We've started calling them streaks because you can usually tell at a glance where they passed through. Not a lot because they don't seem to congregate without someone making them—"

Richards heaved an exasperated sigh at my barb. "I told you before, it wasn't us."

"And yet, I don't believe you," I harped, yet rather than pursue this, I continued my explanation. "Be that as it may, particularly when it's just a handful of us, edged weapons or anything that does massive blunt force trauma is the way to go. Or, you know, just good old running away until they can't keep up with you anymore. I had the pleasure of having to resort to that for almost an entire day when I was out there on my own."

Elle looked impressed while Cole and Hill traded glances—a little too curious yet at the same time too knowing for my comfort—while Antoine guffawed in disbelief. "Nobody survives a day out there alone, whether you have less of the undead roaming the country or not."

"Did, too," I insisted. "Guess I'm a lot tougher than I look."

For the umpteenth time, Antoine glanced at my hands. I wondered if he and Hamilton shared a common ancestor somewhere down the line. "Not that tough."

I had no clue why I cared, but with present company, I couldn't very well let that slide. "Wanna bet? I may only be a month out of my deathbed—for the second time in under one year—but I can easily take you on in a fight."

Antoine looked ready to accept the challenge, but Alexandre put an end to it before things could escalate. His brief remark to his brother in French sounded less than friendly, and I could tell I was trying his patience with my antics. I couldn't help but feel a little chastised, but at the same time strangely vindicated that none of the strong men at my side had felt the need to jump in to defend me. Well, they had watched me almost eviscerate Hamilton, and that was before my body had started working properly once more.

"I would appreciate it if you didn't," Alexandre told me. "Please excuse my brother. He gets like this when he's drunk."

I waited for Nate to offer up a remark that would get him to sleep all on his own tonight, but Cole was quicker. "She's always like this," he offered, miming the informed character witness. "At least she's been like that since we left the base, and considering the events of the last summer, it's not a new development. If you ask me, we lucked out, considering she's one of our chief scientists who's still alive. None of the others survived out there, and when some of those hiding away in a bunker got presented with a recently deceased infected, they ended up getting eaten when he reanimated. I feel a lot safer knowing that our squint isn't necessarily someone we have to take extra care of protecting."

I blew Cole a kiss for that, then turned to Nate, giggling. "See, he thinks I'm awesome, too! I think I could get used to that."

"Then again, sometimes she's just fucking annoying," Cole added, looking very satisfied with himself. Nate appeared less than threatened in his masculinity. Oh, well. You win some, you lose some.

"Oh, come on! You'd all be bored as hell if there was no friction, no in-fighting, just lots and lots of shamblers day in, day out," I claimed. "Keep it at 'we lucked out' and be done with it."

"I'll drink to that," Nate offered, raising his cup that contained water rather than anything stronger. The French were quick to toast, as were Burns and I, and the soldiers obviously didn't want to be left out. I couldn't help but smirk. That was too easy—but I'd take easy over complicated any day.

I figured conversation would veer off to something ridiculous next, but Elle clearly wasn't done with the bits and pieces of interrogation she'd snuck in all evening. "Do you actually believe you can find a cure in that laboratory?"

I'd kind of been waiting for that question, but still hadn't found an answer that was satisfactory—so I kept it at the truth. "I don't know. But we won't know unless we try, right?"

I was surprised at the somber nod she gave, but even when I kept looking at her, she didn't volunteer anything further.

When I asked Nate the same question a few hours later, curled up on our corner mattresses under a heap of blankets as we were, the room around us filled with the soft—and not-so soft—sounds of snoring, he took his time answering. When he finally did, what he said wasn't what I'd expected.

"Part of me wants it to be true, simply because that would mean my brother hasn't died for nothing. But I'm not sure that there should be a cure."

"Not even if it means that there won't be any new infections?" I proposed. "Whatever might keep us from insta-converting will likely be the same thing that keeps everyone else dead, infected or not."

Even in the near dark of the room, it was impossible to miss his stony expression. "Every last one of us who got the serum did unspeakable things. We don't deserve salvation."

He waited for my reply, and when I didn't give one, he turned onto his back, staring at the ceiling yet kept his arm outstretched so I could continue to abuse it for an extra pillow. Part of me wanted to get angry at his claim—and what sounded too much like accepting defeat—but eventually I snuggled into his side and closed my eyes. Maybe he was right. I certainly didn't feel like I deserved anything except a bullet between the eyes, eventually, after a hopefully long, long life. Yet at the same time, this was a possibility for redemption in so many ways. And it wasn't like either of us had to accept a cure even if we found something that could, further down the line, be used as such. Maybe it was just the unease and resentment roiling in my stomach at the idea that, once we got back home, we wouldn't be celebrated as heroes but instead regarded as traitors, but redemption? That sounded pretty sweet to me.

Chapter 6

Three days passed quicker than I would have thought possible. Back on the destroyer when sleep had been impossible and every motion hurt, hours had stretched into eternity. Now, I was barely through all the documentation Hamilton had dropped in my lap before it was time for one last strategy meeting on what was reportedly a cold, early dawn back in the war room, and then the comfort and warmth of the bunker complex at Ajou would be a thing of the past for us. Everyone was present, including Elle, Alexandre, Antoine, and Raphael, but also their doctor, two of the people we'd helped rescue, and Kris, the German with the contraband tank neighbor friend. The table was once again covered with maps, but also a stack of blueprints that I presumed was of the lab we were about to break into. I didn't know as I hadn't been a part of any of the previous strategy meetings—that had been Nate's job. My days had been filled with numbers, and consequences that I forced my mind to back away from. Pretty much the only times I hadn't had my nose stuck in the reports was getting fed—and even some of that had happened with some extra reading material on the side—or when Nate and I had been getting it on. The latter had taken more time out of my days than the former, which was rather telling of just how much and how strongly my libido had roared to life. Far had it been from Nate to protest, and last night I'd finally voiced my suspicion: that had been a side effect of the serum as well. Not even the idea that he'd likely field-tested that theory with Rita back in the day put a stop to that. It wasn't like we'd get another chance until we were back on the destroyer. His only response was a shrug, but that was in itself very comforting—as was the fact that previous, recent issues seemed to have become a thing of the past.

But now play time was over, which was further underlined when Hamilton passed up the chance to comment on Nate and me being a little late to arrive, both of us still a little flushed. My mind was clearer than it had been thirty minutes ago, but I figured most of that was due to the fear and anticipation rather than taking the edge off.

Bucky welcomed everyone to our powwow, then turned right to me. "So what do you have for us, doc?" It occurred to me that he hadn't called me "Stumpy" since the ravine—or maybe Elle's latent glowering kept him in line. I didn't know for sure, but there had been some altercation the morning of the second day of our stay, and since then Hamilton had rarely left the war room.

Looking at my hastily scrawled notes, I then regarded Bucky and Red calmly. "Did either of you read this?" I pointed at the entire documentation. Red shook his head, and after a moment, so did Bucky.

"We got a brief overview," Red explained.

That could mean anything. "You are aware of how many test subjects they had stashed away?"

Richards remained silent, leaving the reply to Bucky. "Far as we know, it was over fifty during their last months," he offered. "Raynor didn't have the specifics."

Some murmurs rose in the background, quickly silenced when Hamilton cast a glare around.

"So that's potentially fifty, at the very least juiced-up super zombies waiting for us in there," I summed up what everyone was thinking.

Hamilton gave me a less than impressed look. "Why did you think we brought the heavy hitters?"

"They should all be dead," Richards interjected. "The lab has extensive protective measures. One of them is to gas everything in the experimental wing." I could tell that he tried to sound convincing, but it didn't quite work.

"Anything else than the obvious?" Hamilton asked.

Forcing my anger down, I inclined my head. "I think I've found the scientist Raleigh Miller was working with. Dr. Rosamie Andrada. I ignored her at first because she's a biochemist but then I remembered seeing her name attached to a few papers I'd read for my thesis. Her specialty is cell division and checkpoint control." As expected, I only got blank, bordering on bored, looks for that. "Whatever. If she has been working on something, we'll likely find notes in her office."

"Do you know the room number?" Red asked.

Rather than wait for my answer, Hamilton whipped out another list. "312," he rattled off after a brief scan. "Second floor, south side."

Red was quick to pinpoint the location on the blueprints. I looked them over, getting turned around just from a quick glance. This was about to get really interesting. At least the room wasn't that far from the central area between the offices and normal labs, and the BSL-3 and -4 labs in the other wing.

"Any other possible connections?" Richards asked.

I shrugged. "Nakamuri and Dale might be interesting but I don't have any real leads, just going from what I've been able to decipher of the reports. Very wild guesses."

Hamilton still got the office room numbers. "248 and 115," he rattled off. "Top floor both."

While Red marked the locations, I continued to peruse the blueprints. As far as I could tell, the central part of the lab was situated across five levels, only the top and bottom most connecting to what looked like a sequence of weirdly separate squares to the side. "I presume those are the bioreactors?" Levels one, three, and five would be waste and air management, only levels two and four containing any actual floor space.

Richards nodded. Burns, so far silent, spoke up. "What's up with that? Some kind of bio-fueled energy source?"

The idea made me laugh until I realized that he couldn't know. "No, it's got nothing whatsoever to do with energy. Those are pretty much huge tanks filled with bacteria or yeasts in suspension, and you harvest cells or whatever you have them produce. At least in a setup like this, that's what's happening. My guess is that if the eco warrior terrorists have taken over the lab, that's where we might find samples containing the activated virus."

Another red circle went on the blueprints.

"You have the version numbers of the serum batches interesting to us?" Bucky asked next.

I handed him smaller notes—in triplicate—where I'd written them all down. "Depending on what we find in Dr. Andrada's office, there might be more, but those are the latest stable versions they've been working on." I hesitated before adding, "If we find any deceased specimens in the experimental wing, we should take tissue samples from them as well. Make sure they at least died for something." None of the soldiers present reacted, making me itch to scream in their faces to show at least a hint of humanity. "You all realize that this could have been you, right? I have no idea what those unlucky bastards did to end up there, but fifty's a little high to be just the chaff that dropped through the grid. That's a good one percent of people who got shot up with the serum." Still no reaction.

Nate pushed away from his position by the wall, the motion drawing Red's interest. "So that's the lab," Nate surmised, changing topics. "The much harder part is, how do we get in there?"

"After wading through seas of zombies, you mean?" I offered wisely.

Red pointed at a small maze of corridors at the southern side of the complex. "Electricity should be shut off, and the external generators must have run empty during the last year so the outside defenses should be down."

"Defenses?" I asked. "Should?"

"Mostly heavy steel doors," Burns provided, joining Nate by the table. "Nothing that a little C4 shouldn't take care of. We'll still try brute strength first to keep the noise level as low as possible. The emergency exits might be problematic but once we get into the building, forcing our way into the elevator shaft shouldn't be that hard. Then it's just a twenty-level drop, and we should be in."

"Twenty levels?" This was getting better and better.

"Don't worry because of your grip," Richards, ever helpful, offered. "We'll get you down and back out, no problem."

I glared at him, hard-pressed not to hide my fingers in my armpits as I crossed my arms over my chest. "I can rappel and pull up my own weight, thank you very much. Just not too fond of the distance, or the fact that we have no way out if anything happens to that shaft."

"There's still the emergency exits—here, here, and here." Richards pointed to them on the blueprints.

"I still don't like elevator shafts," I protested. "Last time I was in one, I got shot. First scar I got when the shit hit the fan."

Burns seemed a little confused; I was sure he hadn't noticed. It had been barely more than a scratch, anyway. Nate, ever supportive, leaned in and whispered, "I'll make sure to not blow the building up all around us this time." My answering glare made him smirk.

Cole spoke up next. "Depending on what we find down there, we'll have to bypass the security system so it will let us in. They have three layers of reinforced steel and concrete cages around the entire complex, then again around the hot labs and experimental wing. The generators down there should still be operating but we have enough fuel for our portable ones to gain us around five hours to work with. I've been coordinating with our wiz kid here." He nodded in Gita's direction, who was still keeping herself in the background. I hadn't seen much of her during the last few days. "Together, we should hack through their system in less than thirty minutes. That should give the rest of you four hours. I don't think we should overstay our welcome. I'm not sure we can shut down the automated security measures that will start up as soon as we breach the system, but they have a countdown set for emergency operations like this, giving us four hours and forty-five minutes leeway. Four hours is on the safe side."

"Four hours it is," Bucky declared. "Next step—how we get to the location." He turned to Raphael. "What's the latest intel saying about the weather and ice on the river?"

Raphael, scratching his stubble, didn't look too euphoric. "The last confirmed data we have is months old. We haven't gotten anyone closer than a fifty-mile radius from the city. Our stations upriver and closer to the sea said that the Seine is only partly frozen over. It's your best bet, so you should risk it. You won't survive if you try to get to La Défense over land." He turned to one of the larger maps then. "Ajou is here. The shortest, if not quite safest, route is to head east until Mantes-la-Jolie. We have three fueled-up boats hidden away there that we will take up the Seine, at least three kilometers past the bridge crossing over into La Défense, or as far as the river is clear. There's an island there, bisecting the river, so that might or might not be a problem. We'll try to drop you off there, and if there aren't too many undead close, we'll stay there until your return. Else you'll have to wait until we can pick you up, likely downriver."

I liked that even less than the elevator shaft exit, but I trusted his assessment.

"The weather should be clear for the next few days," Kris provided, checking the notes she'd brought with her. "With luck, you should be in and out before the next snowstorm hits us. Two of the stations on the Swedish and German coast have called in that bad weather is coming, but as you're leaving today, you should be good. Might not even get here until the end of the week."

Hamilton acknowledged that with a nod. "Anything else?"

"Raphael, Antoine, Noah, and Ines will come with you," Alexandre stated, not even reacting to Bucky making a face. "They are our best scouts, and they know the territory you need to traverse. They will find you the best route to the boats. They won't come into the laboratory with you, but they are more than capable of holding the position by the boats until they get overrun."

"I wish I could go with you," Elle stated, regret heavy in her voice. "I would have loved seeing Paris one more time. But my job is to defend our position here and that doesn't allow for gallivanting through the winter wonderland."

"We appreciate your support," Richards offered, even making it sound honest.

"You're welcome," Alexandre responded jovially, if with a certain smirk. Elle inclined her head, but the way she smiled my way made me guess that, without my presence, their cooperation might not have extended this far. Gee, way to make me feel appreciated by my own people.

"We haven't been able to re-establish connection to your people back home in the States," Elle continued. "We will try hailing your ship to update them on your ETA plus a week's travel back to the coast. You will likely be there sooner with the boats drifting downriver. Most of the beaches are clear so you should be able to find shelter until you can rendezvous with them."

And decide whether to change our minds and stay with them, but she didn't add that, which I appreciated.

Red thanked her before he cast one more look down at the maps and diagrams. "Anyone got any questions that we can't discuss on the march? Get ready. We move out in twenty."

I felt weirdly at a loss at his declaration, not quite sure why. When I'd dressed this morning I'd done so for harsh outdoor conditions, not another day of lazing away in comfortable warmth, yet now that it was time to take our leave, I felt like we'd only just gotten here. It wasn't even trepidation because of what I knew—and had gotten spelled out to me just now—lay ahead, I realized, but more a latent resentment of leaving friends that we'd only just made and would very likely never see again. I didn't need a shrink to know that was a lot more about being afraid to be stuck here without a chance to ever see my friends back home, but since that wasn't a pressing concern at the moment, it was easy to ignore.

Priorities, I told myself. First, I had to live through what was to come. Once that was behind me, I could worry about the rest. Somehow I got the feeling that was the only thing that had kept me going since Dom and Sunny at the Silo had confirmed that I was rotting from the inside out. One of these days that house of cards would come crashing down on me, and I wasn't sure how I would be handling that.

Taking our leave turned into the somewhat orderly chaos I'd expected. As much as I hated to admit it, Bucky's people knew how to pack and get ready so it was mostly last-minute holdups that made us ten minutes late. Although they were happy to help us with the boats, I got the sense that the French weren't heartbroken to see us go. My pack was as large and heavy as I remembered, and while those two and a half days of rest had helped my body heal further, I wasn't exactly pain free once everything was strapped back in place. More than once I asked myself why I was doing this as I got ready and let Nate do a last check that everything was stowed away neatly. I reminded myself that I hadn't been lying when I'd told the French that I kinda, sorta believed in what we were doing here, and I didn't think it beyond Hamilton to gag and tie me up to drag me along if I put up a fight. Being able to defend myself was much preferable to that.

Raphael held us back before it was time to head from the large entry hall into the cold outdoors, making us all repeat the names of the five checkpoint towns that were close to the route we were about to take, wincing his way through us slaughtering the pronunciation. He insisted on the practice should anyone get lost. If we encountered even halfway as many zombies as they had all claimed still roamed the area, anyone who got separated would likely die before being able to reunite with the rest, unless he turned around and walked back to Ajou. Four hundred million undead all over Europe, and a shit-ton of them clustered together in the central low regions outside of the mountain ranges—my mind still had a hard time wrapping itself around that number. How we'd managed to survive this far, stumbling more or less blindly through the countryside, was a miracle—and one I was afraid would come to a bloody end all too soon.

The sun was only a few inches above the horizon as we climbed up the stairs and through the reinforced steel doors, the air cold enough to make me want to draw up short as it hit my face. Right, more of that. At least my entire body wasn't frozen solid in under a minute, but I wasn't exactly feeling cozy.

Red was about to split us into our previous marching order of fire teams once more, but Antoine would have none of that. "One team forward, led by one of us," he insisted. "The rest of you follow, together. If anyone gets in trouble, strength in numbers is the only way to go."

"You mean like what happened to your people that we rescued?" Parker asked, the medic's sunny disposition without a doubt hailing from the balmy conditions.

Noah, who'd been the leader of said group and the one I, and later Bucky, had been talking to, looked less than impressed with that accusation.

"We underestimated how frozen the ground was, yes," he admitted. "But if we'd been walking all spread out, none of us would have been alive for any of you to notice us."

Hamilton considered for a second. "One recon team at a time it is," he declared. "Everyone, keep radio contact." His gaze zoomed over to me without hesitation. "And I mean absolutely everyone."

I held eye contact easily but didn't otherwise react. As far as I knew, the French didn't have a com system and we hadn't brought anything except spare batteries, yet with three or four others someone would manage to report in, I was certain.

So we set off, the recon team in advance, the rest of us following in a slightly drawn-out line, East, on our quest to get to the boats on the hopefully mostly ice-free Seine.

Chapter 7

We were up third to do forward recon, and I wasn't heartbroken that Ines joined us rather than Antoine. She didn't seem to want to talk to anyone and didn't comment the few times I misplaced a step and struggled a little, which was fine with me. As much as my body had appreciated the time resting to heal further, it hadn't done anything for my balance. Before long, I was hurting all over again but not enough to mobilize the full extent of my stored-away energy and stamina. At least I was in moderately good spirits since sorting through the research notes had given me an unexpected purpose I hadn't realized I'd been missing. One could say I even felt a little loopy with excitement, with only the residual discomfort holding me back. So when Nate wasn't looking, I punched myself in my remaining kidney, not quite sure if I wanted to whimper with pain or high-five myself when the world around me suddenly snapped into sharp focus.

Ah, much better!

What I'd thought was a measure of stealth turned out to be anything but, as I was still staring transfixedly at a patch of ice glowing brightly in the sunshine when Nate trudged into my field of vision, glowering at me. "What the hell?"

I tried giving him the most innocent, "Who, me?" look I could muster but cut the crap when the ebbing waves of pain made it impossible for me not to make a face. "I need to learn how to control this," I offered. "Even more so with what's up ahead. Stop babying me." Besides, I so didn't mind the added hint of euphoria slithering through my brain.

Burns, a little farther ahead, ignored us, but Ines was less than amused by our bickering. "We need to stay quiet," she reminded us. "Stealthy. Keep the foreplay to when it's no longer my life on the line as well."

It was impressive just how venomous the look was that Nate sent her, making me smile where he couldn't see it. It was less amusing when he turned that exact glare on me next, but we would have long ago killed each other if I always took him seriously. Putting one foot in front of the other wasn't easier with a more acute sense of agony radiating through my body—euphoria notwithstanding—but having a slightly better sense of my surroundings made a difference. I could always wallow in my misery once this was over and we were safely back on the destroyer, en route home, I reasoned. Now I needed to stay sharp. I was sure that Hamilton wouldn't do anything in the meantime to jeopardize that outcome of us blissfully surviving this mission.

It turned out, we didn't need Bucky harassing me to turn life needlessly complicated once more—the resident undead population was more than happy to step in. We were less than ten miles east of Ajou when we had to stop and backtrack for the first time because our chosen route was blocked by the undead, shuffling this way and that in the freezing cold. How they could still move, let alone be a menace, was beyond me, but the five we had to do away with had looked dead for good, half frozen in a ditch—but weren't, as we found out as we passed. They were hard enough to kill as it was. Back to the other side of a low, sloping hill, where we ran into another obstacle, this time a pack of wolves. They didn't attack us but didn't back away far enough to be out of shooting distance, either—which we couldn't do as it would have drawn the attention of the hundreds of zombies that had forced us to take this route. By afternoon, I was so keyed up from watching anything and everything like a hawk that I repeatedly jumped at boughs swaying in the light wind or leaves crunching under a badly placed boot. Maybe making myself that keyed up hadn't been my brightest idea, but I was loathe to admit that. And I wasn't the only one, judging from the many wide-eyed looks I caught all through the day.

With our provisions freshly supplemented by the French, there was no need to go foraging, nor to stop before it got too dark to move on. Red led a team that cleared out a small cottage in the middle of what had been a vineyard, and it took us another hour to drag all the corpses of the previous residents far enough away not to draw too much attention to our hideout—and those we encountered while establishing said perimeter. Our home for the night still reeked of spilled zombie guts, but it was so damn cold outside that being on watch detail wasn't much of a relief. Feeling the difference now, I couldn't delude myself anymore—I'd been damn near in a constant stupor until Parker had cut me up, only that I hadn't realized then how much my mind had been running on autopilot. I told myself this was an improvement, but a debatable one at times.

The cottage had a single large room, and once the group up for first watch had exited, it only made sense for me to dump myself in the next available spot as close to the makeshift fire we had going in the middle of the room, right between Cole and Hill. When they both eyed my pack curiously, I smirked. "What, afraid my girl cooties will rub off on you?"

"Still debatable whether you've stopped being contagious yet," Cole grumbled under his breath but shuffled to the side so I could park my ass on one of the makeshift benches—a couple of still-frozen logs we'd dragged inside—next to him. It was a valid question, but nothing I felt like worrying about.

"Not like you could catch it," I offered. "Nor will you get any chance to."

Hill guffawed at that—or the face Cole was making—and watched with amusement as Burns, Tanner, and Nate found their own places not too far away but for once not clustered around me. While Burns didn't seem to mind, Nate was sporting that awfully neutral look once more that he had been donning since the beach.

"Just weird that you don't keep that cliquey thing up you've had going until now," Cole pointed out.

I shrugged, digging into my pack for some jerky. "The last few days I've slept in the same room with you all, with not a single weird comment from anyone, and now you complain about the lack of segregation? Just be happy I don't ask for cuddles to warm up quicker."

"Thanks for the offer, but I prefer to keep my hands and dick." He didn't need to glance in Nate's direction to underline who he seemed to be afraid might make him part with the aforementioned body parts.

That made me laugh in earnest. "Trust me, I'm more than capable of doing any required dismembering myself."

Everyone was too busy to continue talking as the beans and rice were passed around, but as soon as he'd treated himself to seconds,

Hill got chatty. "So, what's the deal with you and Gabriel Greene? Considering how the French were salivating all over him, you did a moderately good job acting like you were happy to hear from him, but I've seen that same level of resentment come off you in waves whenever something ruffles your feathers. He's your closest ally and still you can't stand him?"

Hamilton was lurking around outside so I didn't get the chance to offer any nonverbal comparisons, but I wasn't opposed to the other kind, either. "Does it come as such a surprise that I'm able to work with someone even if I absolutely can't stand them?" I didn't even try to make the fake smile on my face look anything but.

Cole snorted, but Hill wasn't satisfied yet. "There's gotta be a story in there somewhere. No need to spill all your trade secrets; we know that bunch at the coast like to keep their cards close to the vest. Just dish on your personal dirt. There's got to be something. People you just don't like don't draw that level of ire from you." He pointedly glanced at where Russell and Parker were hunkered down a good distance from our cozy little corner.

I waited to see whether Nate or Burns wanted to offer up something, but Nate had gotten busy mending a tear in the side of his pack, while Burns—and, surprisingly, Tanner—were all ears. I signaled Burns to hand over a tea refill, cradling the cup in my hands more for warmth than sustenance.

"Not much to tell, really. He tried to bash my head in and strangle me, and I'm known for being a vindictive bitch."

That got me some surprised looks, Hill choking on his beans for a moment, eyes wide. "And you didn't kill him for that?"

Strangely, his surprise felt rather satisfying. I allowed myself a small grin to go along with the sentiment, even though the memory made me want to frown.

"I did dump a bucket of shit on him for that," I offered. "Literal bucket of shit," I clarified when I got more odd looks. "Long story."

"We got all night," Cole remarked.

"It's a good one," Burns chortled under his breath. At my less than nice glare, his grin spread. "Not sure I ever got the full version. You weren't quite that talkative in the early days."

"Suddenly finding myself in the middle of a zombie apocalypse kind of took precedence," I harped, but his continuing grin worked to mollify me, as usual. Several of the other soldiers had stopped pretending like they weren't listening in, so I heaved a theatrical sigh and resigned myself to my fate... until I caught Nate's smirk. "It's all your fault, asshole," I griped.

I got a very bland look from him back. "It's a good story," he insisted. "And my plan worked better than I could have set up on my own."

A few of the soldiers looked surprised, among them Aimes and Rodriguez, so I decided why not put the blame where it belonged? But Greene first.

"You all know that Greene was the CFO of the biotech company I used to work for? Daddy owned it, that's why he had the job." Although, knowing what I knew now, I wasn't quite that sure about his lack of qualification, yet I didn't need to tell them that. "Until the day before the shit hit the fan in that part of the country I never really had anything to do with him. We had a weird company policy going on, enforced by our HR hag, where it was the women's fault somehow that the sleaze ball that was the boss's son was oozing his charm all over them. Spending most of my time in a lab coat and scrubs, or T-shirts and jeans, kind of kept me off his radar as long as he had the office staff to harass." I briefly wondered what had become of that woman, until I remembered that she'd been eaten by shamblers. Or had she stepped on a mine? Almost being buried by a detonating building will do that to your short-term memory, I figured. "Anyway, I clashed with the HR hag a few times but I don't think Greene knew I was working for his father's company until that day."

Surprisingly, Aimes was the first to interrupt my merry tale. "You and clashing with authority figures? Who would have thought."

The sentiment behind that statement made me feel all gooey and warm. "I was wearing shirts she deemed as inappropriate. That's the most offensive thing I ever did."

Nate was trying to hide a smile, probably for the very same reason as me. Ah, how things had changed. When he caught me looking, he saluted me with his mug. "They were borderline questionable shirts."

"They had funny slogans on them," I insisted. His smirk let me know that he must have seen more than one of them, although I'd made sure that I'd dressed a little less dorky—most of the time—on the few occasions of our clandestine meetings. "Do you still remember which one I was wearing that fateful Friday? Because I sure as hell don't."

"Sure do," he drawled, spiking my ire some more.

"It was the periodic table of elements one, right?" That flicker of a memory came up for a second.

Hill looked downright confused. "Nerdy, sure, but that doesn't sound like a dress code violation to me."

Nate's smile was a bright one. "It had the periodic table printed on it, but the script was the questionable part. 'Chemists do it on the table—periodically' might rub some people the wrong way."

I suffered through the round of laughter with as much grace as I could muster, which wasn't a lot. "Har, har, I get it. At least I'm not a stuck-up prude." The general amusement continued, also spreading to Burns and Tanner. Couldn't let that fly. "Well, at least I gave those yahoos a run for their money when they tried to round me up. More than anyone else, far as I remember."

Cole, if anything, found that statement hilarious. "You tried to hide in a supply closet?" he ventured a guess.

"Nope, I escaped into the ventilation ducts. Twice, I should add. Made them chase me all across the building, including Zilinsky shooting me out of the ducts. And if I hadn't managed to run into the wrong staircase that ended on the roof, I might have escaped you altogether."

More laughter, but this time semi-appreciative. Burns in particular found that part hilarious. Cole was still a little doubtful. "How did that shark of a woman miss you?"

"On purpose, I'd guess," I had to admit. "She was trying to scare me, not actually kill me. I wouldn't be sitting here otherwise. She changed her mind after I bashed Greene in the head with the bucket full of shit and tried to kick the living crap out of him. Start of a wonderful friendship."

It was weird to see the round of nods now after they'd made fun of me just moments before.

Aimes scrunched up his face, confused. "I feel like I'm not getting half of that. You two were screwing around before he blew up the building? And what exactly is his fault?"

Nate had abandoned his busywork in favor of the conversation so I let him fill in the blanks. "Yes, and she blames me for Greene coming after her."

That version was way too edited. "First off, we weren't just 'screwing around,'" I clarified. "He had the bright idea of befriending me first because he thought he might need my help to pull off that mission."

Cole's answering grin was bordering on nasty. "And then you just slipped and ended up on his dick, or what?"

"Pretty much," I said, not giving him the satisfaction of flinching. "Went on for a couple of weeks before, one Friday afternoon, he strolled into my workplace just as I was getting coffee, and minutes later, they blew up all of the possible entrance points and let everyone except a choice few people go."

"While you were hiding in the ducts," Aimes filled in, still sounding skeptical.

I didn't try to hide my vexation. "Exactly. One of the new security guards tried to fetch me and when I got suspicious, I figured I might as well be a little cautious. I overheard a few conversations, then made the mistake of not being stealthy enough and they caught me.

They threw me into that damn glass cube of a temporary prison with the others—the previous company reception. After the only other scientist qualified for the high security labs blew herself up—"

"Wait a minute," Hill interrupted. "How did that happen?"

Nate responded this time, scratching his head. "I left a bunch of grenades lying around. One of my guys insta-converted when he ate a contaminated chocolate bar and she used the moment of distraction to kill herself."

"She was the one who murdered his brother," I helpfully supplied. "We think she was part of those idiots who caused all this. When she realized her plan was working, she chose to absolve herself of her guilt. Coward to the last second."

Glances were exchanged until Cole picked up the thread. "So Greene realized that your Missus was your backup plan, and to avoid playing into your hands, he came after her."

Nate nodded. "I made that rather obvious."

"And you beat him up," I added. Nate allowed himself a small, satisfied smile that made me roll my eyes at him. "You provoked him. He reacted. And I ended up having to scrub shit and piss out of my hair."

"A true modern love story," Burns enthused between bouts of chuckles.

Nate made a placating gesture that I ignored. "As I said, couldn't have planned this any better. Admit it. By the time you realized what was going on, you were already convinced that helping me was the right thing to do. I just added a dash of self-preservation to your motives to make the bitter pill a little easier to swallow."

I didn't give him that point, instead continuing my recount, jumbled as it had gotten. "Long story short, I did help him. Also to place the explosives down in the hot lab to make sure that any material stored down there would be destroyed for good. Then it occurred to me that I actually knew how to get into the vault where they stored the frozen viruses, so I locked him in the decontamination chamber, manually destroyed what remained of the shit his brother had been tinkering with, and that's that."

Cole looked less than enthusiastic about my deeds than they still made me feel. "You do realize that if you hadn't done that, we might not have to be freezing our asses off here?"

"Doubt it," I opined. "The woman who was helping him likely destroyed anything of value of his current research seeing as she was actively sabotaging it all. And from what little I've seen of what they were doing, none of that would have done anyone much good. It was child's play compared to what they did where we're headed now."

A few glances were exchanged, lending Burns time to drop another bomb. "You left out the part where you tore one of your gloves pulling that last stunt, and that's why you went all YOLO on his ass and fucked him right outside that decontamination shower and the shit ton of C4 that you had planted all over the place."

While I waited for the laughter—some of it disbelieving—to die down, I snorted at Burns. "It's disconcerting sometimes how much you know about my sex life."

"It's entertaining," came his answer, making me shake my head with mirth. He kind of had a point, I had to concede that much.

Yet Aimes still wasn't done. "Pardon my French, but I still don't get what the huge deal was about you."

"Gee, you're so sweet," I shot back.

"Seriously. Anyone can walk into a lab and blow shit up. You don't need expertise for that."

It was only then that I realized that I'd hashed over too many details. "Not a normal lab, asshole. A BSL-4 lab. That's biosafety level four, as in, everything in there will kill you. That's where they keep shit like ebola. You know, with the funny-looking positive-pressure suits? Even though they'd tried to clean it all up beforehand, he was shitting his pants having to go in there alone, on his own. He wanted me along because I'd been working in such environments for a long time, and I knew exactly how to get everything right to keep him from accidentally killing himself. I wasn't just some random trained lab monkey. I was a superhero lab monkey, damnit." Something else occurred to me as I looked at the faces around me. "You guys realize that the lab we're headed for is one of those labs, too? Yes, they need my retina scan to make it easier to get through the front door, but the reason Richards out there is playing good cop is because he knows that it will be his ass on the line with me right next to him when we go in there. At least I presume he'll come with me to collect what we need, because I don't see Hamilton being stupid enough to risk being in there alone with me."

Silence answered me, and it was a heavy, uncomfortable one. I got the sense that, somehow, their briefing hadn't contained all the specifics. That even Aimes seemed to back off now made me mad rather than happy—I'd spent the last year being a huge pain in their asses, and it was that detail that made them suddenly respect me?

Nate, for once, turned out to be the mitigating voice of reason. "I think they knew that. It's just easier to ignore it when what might kill you isn't something you can stare down and actively fight."

"Is that supposed to impress me?" I huffed.

His silent warning told me to back down... and for once I decided to heed it.

"It's not like they'll make all of you walk into the high-risk zone," I explained with a throwaway gesture of my tea mug. "My guess is, they'll test that the air isn't contaminated, and leave the potentially hot zone for me. Whatever may be lurking outside of that is definitely something you can shoot and kill, if it doesn't kill you first. Those labs are built to withstand pretty much everything shy of a direct hit with a nuke, maybe even that. That's why we needed several bags full of explosives just for the inner shell of the hot lab to make sure it would be completely destroyed, including any possible contaminants." It wasn't lost on me that I now freely associated myself with Nate and his lot, and although it still felt like a lie, considering what other lines were drawn here, it made the most sense.

I almost laughed at the relief that I saw on their faces. It absolutely made me want to criticize their mission briefings but I could see where, maybe, it had made sense to hash over details that they needn't concern themselves with—and it wasn't like the way over there wasn't more likely to kill them than anything that might be lurking in the hot lab. The serum would probably prevent them from catching most, if not all, lethal bacteria or viruses. It certainly eased the flutter low in my stomach.

Just then, the door opened, admitting Richards. Apparently, whatever he and Hamilton had to discuss was done. More than one pair of eyes avoided him as he scanned the room, without a doubt picking up on the shift in mood from twenty minutes ago when he'd left. I would have asked the bunch of assholes what was going on; he seemed content with getting some hot chow and ignoring it.

I figured that was it, but Hill spoke up after most of the others had turned their attention elsewhere. "So that's why you never flipped and joined our side, at whatever opportunity you had. Whether directly or not, Miller got you convinced from the start that what you're doing is the right thing to do."

I considered that for a moment but eventually inclined my head. "I didn't really think that much when it was them or you back after they'd blown up the building. I was tired and scared, and just went with the familiar over the people who were there to smoke them out. When they offered me to take over the lab in Kansas, I was tempted but it didn't make any sense to abandon my family. I knew there wasn't a cure to be found." I couldn't help the sarcastic smile creeping onto my face. Thought I'd known, rather. "And at the factory, or Taggard's tiled prison, or the Colorado base—I was a hundred percent convinced that I was deciding in the interest of my survival, not that I ever really had a choice to begin with. Your side really needs to work on your sales pitches."

"But you still think we're the bad guys?"

I gave that some thought, coming up ambivalent. It was easier to focus on the facts. "I didn't have a choice to come with you. You would have killed my friends if I hadn't agreed. Your esteemed leader has done nothing but be a complete and utter asshole to me, and I don't believe for a second that it's only that hypothetical cure that we're here to fetch. Tell me what about all this should have changed my mind, huh?" Leaning closer, I stared deep into his eyes. "Yes, I take my clues on how to orient myself toward unknown entities from my husband, but I've had opportunity aplenty to build my own opinion going forward. If you're afraid I will just up and kill you, or sabotage the mission out of spite, rest assured—I won't. I'm better than that."

"I'm not afraid," Hill said, and with enough conviction to sound like he really meant it. "But if all of that's true, I don't have a reason to trust you."

"Fair enough," I admitted, then glanced in Burns and Nate's direction. "You trust them?"

He hesitated but then offered, "Mostly."

"Then trust me mostly, too," I advised. "I'm no more or less of a wildcard than they are."

I was about to consider that point over and done, but Hill leaned closer still, pretending to fiddle with something on the side of his pack. "I trust them more because I know Hamilton won't fuck with them. He has orders to bring them into the fold if possible. You're likely still on the kill list, whatever bull he told you a few days ago. And it's obvious that if he fucks with you, you will react, and I'd prefer not to get caught in the middle of that."

I blinked, partly irritated, partly perplexed. Had he just warned me to watch my back? He had already turned away, joking with Aimes about the subpar quality of the food, making it impossible for me to question him—not that I felt the need to. Fuck. Just when I felt that I'd finally gotten a sense of how to play this game and come out alive, the rules had to change. Unless, of course, Hamilton had set Hill to screw with me.

Nate picked up on my sudden change in mood, eyeing me askance but I shook my head ever so slightly—nothing he needed to concern himself with. I was sure that he wouldn't let his guard down around Hamilton either way. That bridge was burned for good.

Not for the first time I wondered what Red's place in all this was. He made it really easy to trust him, which was my main reason of why I didn't. And I couldn't just get up and ask him, right?

At least mulling that over gave me something to distract me from the cold, and how much my body was still in recovery mode. Only one way to find out, right? I hoped that it wouldn't be too late by then.

Chapter 8

I barely got any sleep because I remained cold and jumpy as hell through the night, which didn't turn me into a ray of sunshine the next morning, the endorphin high of the previous day having worn off for good. We were up and moving by first light of pre-dawn again, trying to maximize how far we got before night forced us to hunker down once more. Food helped, even if I still couldn't taste a thing—as did after-hours conversations. I hadn't forgotten about Hill and Cole both stressing on different occasions that they didn't quite trust me, but even those of the soldiers who clearly didn't like me had so far done nothing to stoke the fire of my latent paranoia. Maybe what Burns and Tanner had been doing—trying to forge connections beyond ideological issues—had paid off. Or maybe the other shoe simply hadn't dropped yet. It shouldn't have made me feel safer but knowing that Bucky actively depended on my help alleviated some of my fears—and finding ourselves constantly neck-deep in undead helped in a sense as well. That was a danger that was familiar, and while deadly, it was easy to see them as an obstacle that we'd managed to deal with for long enough to, just maybe, get a little complacent about.

We tried to push forward at the same speed the following day, but our progress got slowed to a crawl—sometimes literally—as we found more and more convenient routes blocked by the undead. It was obvious that Ines and Raphael knew where we were headed; more than once I saw them check on what I realized were old marks left behind from previous trips, but that didn't help much when we were trying to go one way only to find every direction except where we had come from swarmed with shamblers. Most of them looked docile and self-occupied enough, but every single time we inadvertently drew their attention, they came after us with the fervor of the horde of starved predators that they were. Most of them were well-fed enough to be a real menace, and once they identified us as food, there was no letting up. Even though we tried to be silent, the fight usually drew even more in, which in turn forced us to eventually retreat, hacking and bashing at anything that came after us. By the end of day two I was tired enough that I fell asleep with my gear only partly cleaned of gore, my senses so accustomed to the stench that it didn't make a difference anymore.

Day four promised to get worse as we woke to dense fog that cut down visibility to less than a hundred feet at times, making it impossible to see what was lurking out of sight but still remained close enough to hear and smell us. I doubted the stench of our gear would completely masquerade whatever sounded the dinner bell.

"How much longer until we reach the river?" I asked Raphael when we paused mid-afternoon to refuel and get some hot tea into us to try to stave off the cold. While perky at the beginning, the French scouts were as tired and weary as the rest of us now. Compared to this, last week had been a piece of cake.

"Not much longer," he said, but I didn't quite buy it. He read that right off my face, giving a small shrug. "Before nightfall. Without the detours, we would have reached the river this morning but you can see for yourself now why we've been delayed. It should be smooth sailing once we reach the golf course. The boats are hidden in the shed right where it meets the riverbank."

I thought about offering a quip about whether he planned to work on his stroke but then paused. "Not many people died on the golf course, I presume?"

Raphael gave me the hint of a smile. "And they had the river access cordoned off," he said, finishing my train of thought. "Unless there's an incursion on the grounds itself, we shouldn't have too much trouble. We've used the main house as a refuge a time or two to wait for the undead crowds to thin out or pass."

That still left a lot of potential for issues but considering the alternatives—like towns—it made sense to stash the boats there. Or so I hoped.

It took us the rest of the day to finally make it to the golf course. By then I was tired enough that even standing still was hard while Ines got busy undoing the cable binders they'd secured the part of the wire-mesh fence with they'd cut out last time they'd come this way. My attention was wavering, making it impossible to concentrate on anything for more than a few moments at a time. I'd given up trying to hide it an hour ago, and the way Nate was watching me rather than our surroundings wasn't very comforting. I'd tried fueling up on the go, snacking on beef jerky and nuts, but lack of nutrients didn't seem to be the issue. I was exhausted, plain and simple, and that didn't bode well for what lay ahead.

And after pretty much crashing the morning after I'd had the bright idea to key myself up with pain, I wasn't ready to do that again just for fun. I was sure that if push came to shove, I'd find plenty of volunteers to punch me into that enlightened state of consciousness.

"Maybe we should camp on site tonight," Tanner proposed when Red ambled close. It was only then that I realized that Gita was swaying ever so slightly on her feet.

Richards hesitated, but rather than shake his head he gave a shrug. "Let's see how overrun the territory is first."

"Might be our last chance before we head into the city," Nate offered, his tone saying quite plainly that doing anything else would be foolish.

Either drawn by our conversation, or wanting to check on Ines's slow progress, Hamilton joined us, barely glancing my way. "She can sleep on the boat. We'll spend hours going upstream; even if we have to take care of some enterprising undead, I doubt we'll need everyone available on lookout."

Nate seemed perfectly annoyed by that rebuke, mirroring my feelings, but kept his tongue. I hated how Hamilton's remark made me stand up straighter, as he'd no doubt intended. I once again entertained myself with the question of whether I should have tried to castrate him when I'd had the chance, back when we'd been sparring in the makeshift gym at the destroyer. Definitely yes.

"Done," the French scout whispered as she straightened, pulling a flap barely large enough to let a grown man, without his gear, through. Some shuffling and rearranging ensued as everyone got ready to crawl through. Donning my pack on the other side once more was more than annihilating the brief respite of not having it on my back for a few moments. Damn, but I really missed our cars, and not just for sentimental reasons.

Once everyone was through, Ines used fresh wire to close up the hole in the mesh once more, a quick solution but still taking more time than I was comfortable with. We'd spent a good thirty minutes killing shamblers to clear the vicinity of the fence so we could remain in the open, undisturbed, but while I couldn't see the corpses we'd left back in the trees anymore, I could hear the unmistakable sounds of something tearing into them.

"Spread out. We advance together," Red ordered, taking point himself with Russell and Hill. I hung back a little but not far enough to be part of the rear guard. Nate seemed to consider hovering but then trudged forward, leaving Burns to watch my six—just like the good old days. Noah, the guy from the group we'd rescued, ended up to my right, repeatedly looking back over his shoulder. While the other three were more relaxed now that we were inside the fence of the golf club, his anxiety seemed to increase.

"Did you notice anything?" I whispered, making him jump momentarily.

He shook his head, but the frown never left his face. "Too quiet. I don't like it."

"But shouldn't the course be safe?"

He looked out over the rolling, overgrown meadow, the brown grass high enough to make it impossible to tell where the former green had begun. "We always had some trouble. No trouble means more trouble, usually," he offered in broken English.

"How many times have you been here in the past?" It seemed like a valid question.

He continued scanning our right flank for a good thirty seconds before he replied. "Three times. Always ran into trouble."

The ground started to slope down toward what I realized was a small pond at the very bottom of the hollow. That's when it hit me— not exactly a whiff of decay, but something that made the hairs at the nape of my neck stand on end.

"Wait," I called out, just loud enough that Red and Bucky could hear, maybe thirty yards ahead of me. To my surprise, Red halted, giving the signal for the others to pause as well. I continued to stride forward until I was next to them, inhaling deeply.

"Saw something?" Red asked, momentarily focusing his attention on me rather than our surroundings. Hamilton shot me a look that was shy of condescending, but also held a certain kind of anticipation.

"Not sure what tipped me off, but I have a bad feeling about this."

Someone to our left—Hill, I thought—chuckled under his breath, but I ignored him. The light current of air—too light to be called wind, really—came from the west, not helping much. The last rays of the setting sun were partly obscured by the fog, casting parts of the landscape into stark relief while others completely disappeared in darkness, the residual light impairing my enhanced low-light vision considerably.

Rustling of gear spoke of the general restlessness spreading through our group, but I continued to scan the lightly moving grass ahead of us. We hadn't found a single corpse or gnawed remains yet, but I just knew that the golf course wasn't as deserted as it seemed…

"We can't stop every time you get twitchy," Bucky grated out. "Move—"

I interrupted him yet refused to look at him directly. "We should backtrack and head toward the river outside of the fence. When they come for us, we'll be penned in like sheep. I know that they are hiding out there somewhere."

All rustling around us stopped, and I could tell that the group collectively held their breaths. Red cleared his throat, and I didn't miss the warning glance he cast my way. I ignored that, too.

"What, you the zombie whisperer now?" Bucky joked, offering up a small laugh that made it plain how ridiculous that notion was. In spite of my annoyance with him, that term made me smirk for a second. And that had been way before I'd joined the ranks of the no-longer-quite humans…

I knew it was an exercise in futility but I closed my eyes for a second, attempting to give my senses a boost, as if trying to actually sense them was something I was capable of. Maybe without the visual clues, my nose would pick up something… but to no avail.

"I'm not wrong," I insisted as I snapped my eyes open once more, finally deigning to give Hamilton my full attention. "They are out there. I'm not saying I have some supernatural zombie sense or something, but we've had a few close calls since you didn't manage to kill me at the factory, and we've always avoided them because I was right to trust my gut." I didn't mention the weird town I'd stumbled into after escaping Taggard's white-tiled prison with all the stashed converted shamblers that had almost gotten me. In hindsight, if I hadn't been starved and half insane with thirst, I would have known not to sneak in there.

As expected, my warning continued to be met with deaf ears. Hamilton's lips twisted into a sneer, and I so didn't care for the gleeful glint coming to his eyes, promising violence. "You about done disobeying a direct order? Don't think that just because we might need you alive until we breach the labs that I won't lay down the law right fucking now. And trust me, you won't like that any more than my previous attempt to appeal to your common sense, obviously lacking as it is."

My teeth clacked together as I forced my jaws to close on the slew of profanities I wanted to hurl at him, but I forced myself to put a lid on the wave of anger that surged up inside of me. The world around me snapped into sharp focus, my body following my mind in gearing up for a fight—and not a verbal one. At the very edge of my conscience, the nasty voice always lurking there reminded me that Hamilton likely believed me and had said that to get me into top fighting form, but that didn't help me much right now. Not even the lick of fear that followed managed to cool down the heat surging into my cheeks. I continued to stare straight into his eyes, letting my silence be the only affirmation he'd get.

Hamilton's lingering smirk at getting a rise out of me morphed into a more neutral expression as he nodded once at Red, who followed suit and gave the "move out" signal.

"Just don't cry later if only half of us make it to the river alive," I grumbled as the first soldiers stalked past me, Hamilton joining Russell after a few more tense seconds passed.

I'd thought he'd been out of earshot but apparently not so, as Bucky hollered back over his shoulder—low enough that his voice barely carried—"Not your choice. Welcome to the joy of following orders."

I was sure that it wasn't a coincidence that Burns bumped into my shoulder, gently pushing me into motion rather than passing by me. I let my body pick up the momentum, trying to focus on the grass around us more than the rage churning in my stomach. "Don't believe me, either?" I snapped, ignoring the smile I knew was coming.

I was wrong. When I turned to glance at Burns, I found him alert and tense—ready for the attack I'd predicted. "Nah, I know you're right if you get like that." He relented, giving me the hint of his usual bright grin. "Zombie girl." I couldn't hold back a snort, ruffled feathers or not.

"This is going to bite us in the ass—quite literally,"

Burns continued to grin but made sure to give me enough space that we wouldn't hinder each other once the shit hit the fan… any second now.

I was almost disappointed when we reached the pond, frozen over as it was, and still no attack. Rodriguez tested the ice first, and when it held her, the others followed. I didn't care for how dark the scratchy ice looked once we got away from the bumps of frozen reeds at the shoreline, half-expecting one of the undead to float up from underneath. I still couldn't smell anything, but the sense of unease kept increasing to the point where I was asking myself if this was something akin to an anxiety attack. Could it really just be in my head?

Sadly, no shambler chose that moment to come crashing out of the reeds at the other side of the pond to alleviate my doubts.

Up the slope on the other side of the hollow we went, Red signaling us to spread out further. Burns followed suit but he was still close enough that he could be on anything that might jump me in under five seconds. I itched to switch my tomahawks for the M16 but forced myself to keep it on its sling instead. Yeah, ringing the dinner bell with shots fired, not the brightest idea.

The sun set, and still no attack. Also no foxes eyeing us suspiciously from a distance or mice scurrying away, a dead giveaway if there was one that indiscriminate predators were out and about. What were they waiting for?

We crested the rise, reaching what I figured was the very middle of the golf course. A little under a mile away I could make out the buildings that must have entertained the not-so-sporty clientele in the past and, beyond a small strip of a parking lot, the broad band of the river—our destination. Rather than be relieved, I could practically feel my paranoia run up my spine like a colony of ants. Any moment now...

It was more coincidence than planning that I looked back the way we had come as I caught my foot on a twig hidden in the leaves and grass. The trails we'd left, about fifty yards wide altogether, were easy to follow back to the pond and continued on the other side. I was about to turn back and keep scanning what lay in front of us when I noticed the grass moving a little to the east of where we'd passed. Sure, it could be nothing, but...

"Shit," I more whispered to myself than anything else, then, louder so the mic would pick it up, "They're behind us."

I didn't stop and neither did any of the others, but I saw several of the soldiers scan as far back as their position would let them. I checked again but the small trails, almost invisible next to ours, were gone, the momentary motion that had created them halted.

"Don't see anything," Munez declared, but he sounded far from certain.

I already had my mouth open to insist that I wasn't seeing ghosts—much more preferable, really, but sadly not the case—when I realized that Nate had started falling back to my position, walking more slowly until I'd caught up to him. His eyes kept skipping over the terrain, letting me know that he hadn't found anything to latch onto yet, but there wasn't a hint of doubt in the tense set of his jaw.

"Shouldn't we stop and maybe come up with a tactic of how not to get swarmed from behind?" I proposed, mostly asking him but not muting the mic. That had been fun when I'd felt good about pissing Bucky off in the past, not when it might mean nobody heard me call for help later.

"Keep going, and keep up the pace," Bucky ordered, still striding forward with purpose. I must have inhaled loudly enough to voice my protest for him to pick it up because he added, "What do you think will happen to us if we stop now, Lewis? Single us out as prey in the predator's eyes?"

Grudgingly, I had to concede that point to him—at least until he started calling out names, among them mine and Gita's, for who was to take the lead. "What, frail womenfolk can't hold our own in an attack?" I grumbled, again loud enough that the mic caught it. Nate shot me a glare that made me shut up for good, but I didn't miss Burns still being highly amused, the rising tension notwithstanding.

Hamilton ignored me as he continued calling names—this time for who'd bring up the rear guard—and I kind of saw his reasoning when I realized that he was holding the heavy hitters back, quite literally, among them Hill and Burns. He still took a moment to gloat back at where I was slowly catching up to his position while he fell back. "If you need to know, it makes the most strategic sense to position our light, fast runners up front and those who can hold back the tide in the back so we force the attack to split, giving us a better chance not to get overwhelmed." His pause was a pregnant one. "Afraid you can't run fast enough, Stumpy?"

That fear wasn't quite unfounded—and I hadn't really had a chance to test my full-out sprinting capabilities since we'd set foot in Europe—but I did my best to sound cheerful. "I just have to run faster than you, right? And that I can do any day."

I ignored the mocking expression on his face as I passed by him, instead forcing my senses to better focus on what lay ahead. It wasn't easy, exactly, as all I wanted to do was glance back and find any possible hints where the attack might be coming from. Gita looked scared as shit so I signaled her to join me, the nasty voice at the back of my mind—sounding awfully like Nate's—assuring me that I'd probably get a head start if the shamblers ate her first. Realistically, I'd hang back and get mauled instead, or so I told myself. Maybe. Probably. Fuck.

On and on we went, and still no attack. The French scouts ended up between the two groups we split up into, Ines inching toward me while the three men hung back to where Cole and Carter were maybe twenty yards behind me. Rodriguez and Munez were in front of us, both twitchy as hell. I couldn't help but feel like the shamblers must have been really stupid not to attack yet because according to Hamilton's claim we were already more like the deer caught in the headlights than the driver.

I didn't see the shambler rear up—one moment Rodriguez was striding forward, setting one foot in front of the other, and the next she let out a muffled cry and simply disappeared. Two more tried the same move on Munez, but alerted by her shout, he reacted quickly enough and managed to keep his footing, with the undead suddenly clinging to him, trying to bring him down.

And then they were on us, strong hands reaching, finding ample purchase on limbs, packs, and gear.

Instinct took over, my body kicking into overdrive before fear could fully clog my thoughts. Anywhere I felt pressure, I blindly hacked at, twisting my body in a different direction. I didn't give a shit about how ridiculous I probably looked, happy to quickly dislodge the zombie suddenly clinging to my left thigh, strong fingers digging into my mostly numb flesh. The wet sound of the tomahawk embedding itself in a shoulder that got the arm to drop away was most satisfying—not that my mind had the time to process that. A kick, and the zombie tumbled back into the cover of the thick grass it had been hiding in, making it hard to track as one of its brethren came for me from the left.

"Vanguard, disengage and head for the river!" I heard Bucky's order. Part of me wanted to bark that I was a little busy here, but when I managed to twist around and look back, I saw that the ones behind us had even more shamblers crawling all over them. Carter and Hill were down as well if still putting up a fight. I barely had time to check that Burns, Nate, and Tanner were all holding their own before a cry from Gita got me casting around for her. She'd managed to somehow disentangle herself from the shambler trying to come for her, but that left her barely able to fend off the reaching arms now.

Taking two steps in her direction, I went down when another, yet-hidden shambler went for my knee, pretty much yanking my leg out from under me. I kicked and hacked as soon as I got my bearings, landing twisted sideways, partly supported by my pack. I managed to dislocate its lower jaw, making it hang by a few tendons on one side only. The shambler screamed at me, but no sound came out beyond a guttural exhale. It was only then that I realized that all the evident shouting and grunting from around me came from those still alive. What the fuck? But no time to dwell on that now.

The shambler reared up the same moment I managed to roll over onto my knees, sparing me having to come for it as it met my ax in mid-swing. The sharp blade sheared off its nose and flesh from the side of its cheek, adding more disfigurement to its face but not doing much damage. The other tomahawk embedded itself deep into the scrawny neck, getting stuck for a second before I managed to tear it free once more. Gooey blood and bits of flesh came along but I ignored the gore. The next swing went right through its spine, severing the head for good.

Staggering to regain my balance, I looked around, finding Gita and Munez busy helping Rodriguez to her feet. What was visible of her face was covered in blood, but she was able to stand unsupported so it couldn't all be her own.

"We need to head forward!" I called at them, making sure that no new attacker was about to come for us. Another shambler reared up to my right but I kicked it in the face before it got close enough to tackle me. "Run!" And because it was sound advice, I followed it myself.

It worked for exactly ten seconds. When they realized that their prey was about to escape, the shamblers hidden in the grass came for us in earnest. I figured that was a blessing in disguise as we could at least see them coming for us—or I could, the last rays of the sun finally gone to make my low-light vision work as it should. For the others, not so much.

Gita tried to support Rodriguez while Munez surged ahead of them, but a few staggered steps and they were swarmed again. I was closer than Munez so I took over shoving the undead away where possible, but they came right back at us as soon as they regained their bearings. I wasn't strong enough to try to punch them out for good, and with nobody around who carried a sledgehammer, the tactic didn't work as it had in the ravine days ago. But that wasn't the only problem—the undead we'd encountered there had been sluggish and on the stupider side. Those here were crafty, sneaky, but also strong fuckers. This wasn't looking good.

"Vanguard, what's the holdup?" I heard Bucky grate over the open frequency. Looking back, I saw that the rest of our people were doing only marginally better.

"Rodriguez is injured," I offered. "And we're just as overrun as you are. We could use someone who can smash in heads."

"You sure could," came Hamilton's response—yet despite his jeer, it only took a few moments for Hill to break away and try to close up to us. Apparently, he wasn't one to stay down, which I found myself oddly happy about. Munez and I managed to hold the shamblers back until Hill arrived, and a few tiring moments later, we could finally break away forward. Munez and Gita took the lead while Hill grabbed Rodriguez under one arm to support her, leaving me to fend for myself.

I ran, or tried to, as much as my exhausted muscles would let me. My legs felt like lead, and it wasn't just obstacles hidden in the grass that made me stagger. Damnit!

"Switch?" I asked Hill when dispatching another shambler forced me to fall back to them. He gave me a weird look that I was sure he thought I wouldn't catch, but then let me take over supporting Rodriguez so he could clear the way ahead for us. Rodriguez wasn't much taller than me but her sluggish body seemed to weigh a ton. Up close, the scent of blood tickled my nose, making my stomach roil. Glancing back, I saw Cole maybe twenty yards behind us, the others another hundred behind him. The sea of grass was moving all around us but the shamblers seemed to hold back now that we'd broken free of their first wave of attack. It was easy to believe they'd lost interest but I didn't buy it.

"We need to move faster," I told my semi-responsive burden. "Once they realize what's slowing us down, they'll try to overwhelm us again, and this time it will work."

She didn't answer but the tension in her body increased, the load she had to put on me lessening somewhat. We continued to hobble forward, right behind Hill's swinging sledgehammer, until I almost went down once more when a shambler grabbed my ankle. Rodriguez let go so I didn't drag her down with me, and Hill managed to dispatch the shambler before it became an issue for me. I grabbed Rodriguez again, but this time she sagged against me, no longer able to carry her own weight.

"It burns," she pressed out between gritted teeth, her eyes impossibly wide with what I realized must be pain. "Why does it burn? Why is there fire in my veins?"

I wasn't sure if she was actively asking me for my opinion, but I chose to refrain. My own body hurt enough as it was, but I could feel the serum doing its thing, the increasing concentration of adrenaline in my veins making it all easier to ignore, my body singing with the need to burn any residual energy off rather than slow down with exhaustion.

"Just ignore it," I pressed out as I pushed myself forward, looking toward the river as if seeing it would bring me closer to my destination. The buildings of the club would have been easier to reach but I doubted that we would find a warm welcome there.

As if he'd read my mind, Munez drew up short after veering slightly toward the houses. "Can't be sure but looks like they are overrun," he reported, glancing back toward me for a second. I couldn't help but smirk, although Rodriguez's increasing weight on me quickly wiped it off my face once more.

"Head for the river," I repeated Hamilton's previous order. "At least they won't be able to follow us into the water."

The sounds of our voices were enough to bring another wave of agitated undead down on us, making me shut up for good. I had to let my burden slide off my shoulder so I could use both arms—and effectively—to fend off the shamblers, doing my best to kick them away from me so I wouldn't fall over the dead ones. None of them even glanced at, let alone fell on, their dead, obviously preferring us for a food source.

Cole finally caught up to us, grabbing Rodriguez while I was still hacking away at my latest undead victim.

"Go!" he hissed at me when I still hesitated. "The others won't get rid of them, but if you ready the boats, we can flee into the river. But for that to work you need to create more of a distraction."

I was about to follow his advice when the deafening roar of an assault rifle going off right next to me made me jump. Shamblers all over came surging out of the grass.

"How's that for a distraction?" Rodriguez panted, giving me a bloody grin. "Stealth doesn't work with those sneaky assholes. We need to waste some ammo to get through them."

She was right, even if I didn't like the fact that she'd rung the dinner bell before alerting us to the fact. I didn't waste another moment on yelling at her and instead switched weapons, the weight of the M16 alluringly comfortable in my hands. While unable to hack at anything while being carried before, Rodriguez could very well still shoot, and we actually made better progress now. I hated how fast I chewed through my magazines, even using single fire only— but it worked when Gita and Munez joined in, leaving only Hill to continue bashing in heads. We finally broke through the wave, and then it was down the last sloping mile toward the river, gravel paths intersecting the long, brown grass until it ended in a haphazard belt of reeds. Tightening the grip on my rifle, I ran as fast as I could, hoping that I wouldn't kill myself by breaking my neck this way.

Eight hundred yards.

Five hundred.

Three hundred, and I could make out the shed that Ines had told us to find so many times that I was disappointed that the glorified lean-to didn't look quite like the mental image her words had conjured up.

Two hundred, and a look back over my shoulder verified that the others weren't all dead yet, as if the constant cursing on the coms hadn't alerted us to that yet. My lungs burned, as did the muscles in my legs and back, but with our goal so close, it was easy for hope to rise inside of me—

Until another wave of shamblers came out of the reeds, heading straight for us.

"Veer to the left!" I called out to Munez and Gita—more to her than the soldier running by her side—while I kept on going straight, getting ready to fire into the undead horde. Hill cursed and finally switched weapons so he didn't have to wait for close-quarter engagement. Turning to Cole, I jerked my head toward where Munez was following my order. "After them! Hill and I will join you in a few secs."

Lo and behold, Cole didn't protest but instead lumbered after the others with his burden, leaving Hill and me to make our stand. No coordination required—as soon as we were close enough, we both came to a halt and opened fire, strafing the entire line coming toward us. Zombie after zombie fell yet I knew that it wasn't enough. At fifty yards distance, their lines finally broke but that still meant over a hundred of them, and only two of us.

"Fire in the hole!" someone—I thought it was Davis but couldn't be sure—hollered over the com, and a moment later, a grenade went off roughly where the first gravel path had crossed the grass farther up the slope behind us. Two more explosions followed, close enough that I could feel them but they didn't force me to take a balancing step forward. The zombies in front of us staggered, if not to a halt then with confusion. That was all the distraction I needed. Making a quick motion down when Hill glanced my way, I let myself fall to the frozen ground, using the same technique the undead had used on us before—and prayed like hell that it would work. And because I had no intention of getting trampled by zombies, I started dragging myself in the direction the other three members of our vanguard had run into, trying to make as few sounds as possible.

Our plan didn't work well, but it was enough. Only a handful of shamblers noticed us as they passed, and they found their timely end in a much quieter way than what the others were heading toward as Hamilton's group opened fire on them. As soon as I was sure that we were in the clear, I pushed myself up into a crouch, then ran as quietly as I could for the shack.

I found the others huddled on the ground a good hundred feet away from the shed. A quick look around confirmed that Gita looked spooked but okay; the same couldn't be said for Rodriguez. Cole had let her slide off his shoulder and onto the ground where she writhed, her eyes open impossibly wide from what looked like pain and panic, blood frothing at her nose and mouth. Over the noise the others were making, her moans were low enough not to draw any attention. I tried to check her body for injuries, but except for the blood smeared all over her cheek—and now pretty much the rest of her face except for her forehead—I couldn't find anything. Most of that seemed to come from what must have been a bite mark below her chin, where sharp teeth had torn a chunk of flesh out but it wasn't enough to hint at a severed carotid.

I was just about to ask Cole for his opinion when she let out one last gasp before she sagged in on herself, her stare turning vacant.

I didn't think as much as react, plunking down next to her so I could start CPR. New bubbles appeared at her nose but I knew that was just the air being forced out of her lungs. I should have stopped right there but my brain wasn't up to rationality right then, the thought stuck that it wasn't possible for her to just die with no real injuries other than a flesh wound. None of the others stopped me, which was enough for me to continue. My mind was racing too fast for me to count—and I absolutely didn't remember how many compresses were required—but when I felt too frustrated at her lack of a reaction, I stopped, hesitating only for a second before pinching her nose closed so I could breathe air into her lungs—

And that's when she lunged at me.

It. I really should have been long enough in this game to stop having issues with the pronouns.

There was no warning. No sound, no tensing, no nothing. A very small part of my brain reminded me that I'd made the very same mistake as Nate when Taggard's people had blown up our guys and it had been too late to save Campbell. But at the same time, that wasn't true. We might call it insta-conversion, but even when Bailey had sacrificed himself and had eaten that contaminated chocolate bar, it had taken over a minute for him to turn. Bates, hacked to pieces by the cannibals, had been dead several minutes. I should have had enough time for a TV-drama-worthy performance of cursing and going on until Rodriguez reanimated—which was underlined by the fact that everyone else was as ill-prepared as I was.

Tough luck that I was the closest.

And damn, for someone who weighed maybe ten pounds more than I did, she packed one hell of a punch.

Because she started out prone on her back, her momentum was off, and while her blind flailing hit me hard enough in the side of the head that I saw stars, she didn't manage to break anything. Pain made me withdraw instantly, which likely saved my life. As she came off the ground, she managed to grab on to my shoulders but not enough to pull my face right into her snapping jaws. Unbalanced, I staggered, slipping on the frozen ground, dragging her right along with me so she ended up sprawled on top of me. A low, rumbling growl left her chest that made every single hair on my body stand on end, and I did the first thing I could think of—using the momentum of my fall, I managed to get my legs properly between us, and before she could go for my face or neck, I kicked her right off in an almost perfect maneuver, sending her body flying. It all happened in the span of seconds but was enough to kick my entire body into overdrive.

I came vaulting to my feet as soon as my body completed the roll, but she was still faster, mad eyes casting around for a victim. Her gaze landed on Gita but Cole was smart enough to step in front of the girl, drawing the former soldier's attention to him. I had no intention of getting anywhere close to her again so rather than step into her reach, I hurled one of my tomahawks at her, hoping against hope that it would do some damage. In a one-in-a-million moment, the blade of the ax imbedded itself in her chest with a wet "thunk," but all that did was make those mad eyes snap back to me.

Probably not the best idea I'd had all day.

The grass rustled behind Rodriguez, and for a second, I hoped that it was more shamblers, making a run for the body that was still fresher and warmer than anything else they'd sank their teeth into for ages. Instead, the two figures materializing out of the foggy gloom turned into Carter and Davis. Rodriguez's head snapped around, focusing on them, and in the blink of an eye she went for Carter. He had just a moment's warning when Cole shouted, which was likely not enough time to make sense of the blood—and the ax embedded in her upper chest cavity. Carter didn't even have time to cry out before they went down as she collided with him, once more going for the face.

More shouts, and as if through water I heard Hamilton demand a status report in my ear, but I ignored all that. Focusing on the fresh zombie—that was very successfully tearing Carter's face off, his high-pitched screams going well with its wet sounds—I drew my Beretta and shot Rodriguez in the back of the head as soon as I was sure the angle was right that I'd miss Carter, whether he'd appreciate that or not. Three successive shots because double-tapping wasn't cutting it with one of those. The back of her head turned into a spray of gore, the left temple pretty much exploding where the bullets exited the cranium once more. Almost as fast as it had started, it was over, leaving me panting raggedly, my gun wavering not an inch—now pointed at Carter.

"What the—" Davis pressed out, his face frozen with shock. I tried to silently check in with him by holding his gaze but his attention snapped right back to Carter, writhing on the ground, a bloody, torn mess where his face had been. Already, his groans and whimpers ebbed off, and I had a pretty good idea what would happen in, oh, thirty seconds from now—so I shot him, too. I waited for my soul to start wailing with guilt, but all I felt was panic receding as relief flooded through me. No, that one wouldn't be the end of me, either.

"Status!"

This time, I was more aware of Hamilton's demand, yet Cole replied, voice cold and calm, before I could.

"Rodriguez turned. Lewis put her down as she went for Carter. Lewis put him out of his misery before he could turn as well." As he responded, Cole's gaze found mine, and the way he regarded me was different from before. If my head hadn't been pounding hard enough from Rodriguez's blow to still make it hard to focus on anything now that I was calming down, I might have said something.

Burns's harsh mirth was unmistakable, even over the static-filled line. "Damn, girl, you're cleaning house."

Hamilton sounded much less amused. "Confirmed dead?"

Hill kicked both corpses in what remained of their heads—in Rodriguez's case his boot went right through the remains. "Confirmed," he called in.

"ETA in less than four minutes. Get your asses over to the shed and secure the boats."

I was a little disappointed that no barb at me followed, but he couldn't very well threaten to court-martial me for disobeying orders and then be equally unprofessional himself.

Cole acknowledged for all of us, but I didn't miss the pause as he waited for me to do it first. So it wasn't just Munez. Interesting.

I waited for someone to inquire about my health, although of course neither Burns nor Nate could know that I'd gotten a little banged up in the process. I was glad when they both kept their traps shut. When nothing followed, I walked over to the corpses to retrieve my ax, gritting my teeth when it remained stuck even when I put my foot on Rodriguez's chest—my grip kept slipping even though I should have had enough leverage. Hill nudged me aside and—quite easily—pulled my tomahawk free, switching his grip so he could offer it to me handle first. I snatched it from his hand without comment, hesitating before I bent over and cleaned it on Carter's left leg. I was sure he wouldn't mind anymore.

I was surprised when Hill and Cole started to methodically strip both corpses of first their weapons and packs, then everything else that was easy to retrieve. Cole still had that weird stare going on, and when he saw me watching, he frowned for a second. "Anything else you can use of hers?"

"Like what?" It was a valid question, and I couldn't help but feel like there was an underlying accusation in that gaze, even though he must have known that if I hadn't killed her, he likely would have had to.

Cole shrugged. "Boots, jacket—you name it. She's the only one roughly your size."

I didn't correct him about the slip in tenses and shook my head. It made sense to take what we could carry considering our very limited resources, but I would have felt weird about rummaging through her pack for her lightly used bras. Besides, that came with us, anyway.

"Nah, I'm good." While they continued their gruesome duty, I made sure that no more surprises were waiting for us, but then hesitated. "Gimme one of your trash bags," I told Cole, almost in afterthought. He followed suit but grunted when he realized I was turning it inside out to be able to grab Rodriguez's blood and gore-drenched scarf, and what bits and pieces were easily removable from Carter's ruin of a face. "Samples," I told Cole when I secured it all and handed the knotted-up bag back to him. "Don't tell me I'm the only one weirded out by this. She shouldn't have turned, not like that. Whether she got the serum or not—"

"She was one of us," he affirmed my not-quite guess.

I nodded. "We are a lot harder to kill than this. And we don't come back like that." It was only then that I realized exactly how lucky I'd gotten when she'd socked me a good one—or not. "That blow should have shattered my temple. Sure, she was crazy strong, but not insta-converted going on nuclear strong. This doesn't add up. Even if the samples degrade, I'm sure someone will want to take a look at this."

Cole gave me a humorless smile but packed the bag away without protest.

"You mean someone like you?"

I shrugged, happy that the approaching rest of our group gave me a very good reason not to respond. I didn't know how they'd managed to slay all the shamblers, but they'd done a decent enough job, giving us ample time to find the boats and get them into the water before the next enterprising shamblers tried to come after us. By then I was safely huddled at the bow of the boat, using one of the spare blankets that had been stored with them for a cover, right next to Nate. He didn't say anything, nor did he appear to do anything except check that everyone else in the boat with him was secure before we cast off, but once we'd settled and Ines engaged the engine, his arm reached underneath the blanket and pulled me back against him, anchoring me to his side. At first, I thought it was a quiet show of support—after all, he was aware that, quite often, I wasn't as stone-cold a killer as I liked to pretend—but it was only after a few minutes of leaning into him that an alternative motive occurred to me: he was likely damn glad that I was still alive after not just one, but almost two of the people who'd been inoculated with the serum died and came back right next to me. Considering my obvious—and decidedly severe— physical limitations, I should have been dead.

But I was still here, alive and kicking, ready to die another day. And considering what lay ahead, that was a damn fine perspective on life.

Chapter 9

The plan with the boats was a good one—ignoring that it had remained the only option that didn't guarantee our untimely and imminent demise—but it came with some considerable drawbacks, the first among them the attention the boat motors drew. They weren't just noisy, they were loud, too loud to allow for communication between the boats without our coms. Even in the pre-apocalyptic world they would have been considered that, but now it was even worse. Getting them ready hadn't really been a problem, but from the moment on when all three had been in the water and Antoine gave the signal to start the engines, it was on.

And "on" meant pretty much every shambler in running distance of the river seemed to congregate at the riverbanks, at some points so many that they were pushing each other into the water—and soon the ice that had formed where the currents weren't strong enough to sweep it away.

Of course we'd known that would be a problem, but once again, being directly confronted with something made it way more real than concepts had managed to convey. Lack of sleep and still being weirded out about Rodriguez turning didn't help.

Antoine was steering the lead boat, Raphael the second, and ours—in the very back of the short line—had Noah in control, with Ines standing by for later. Hamilton, Richards, and a few others had donned their night vision goggles while the rest tried to get some sleep, which was impossible between the whine of the motors and the howls floating across the river from all sides. Judging from the terse chatter going on, they were aware of what was going on over there, but not to the full extent.

"Exactly how long do we intend to do this?" I asked a good thirty minutes after we'd left the golf course behind. "Because I'm not sure if you're aware of this but we are causing a hell of a lot of a racket. If we keep this up, we won't need ice on the river for them to reach the boats. They'll simply drop down on us from the bridges that are still intact." Sadly, no adventuring shambler demonstrated that move, but I'd seen plenty of them reaching for us from perches up high.

I waited for Hamilton to—again—shoot me down cold, but it took him a few moments to respond. "How would you know? It's pitch black out there and you're not wearing your night vision gear."

I did a mental check—no, I'd never had watch the same time as he'd been out, and his men must be less chatty than I'd presumed. I was tempted to point out that with snow covering parts of the landscape it wasn't actually that dark, but he had a point. Kind of. I couldn't hold back a smirk as I responded.

"Looks like they didn't give you all the details about me in what must have been an amazingly titillating briefing." Maybe I should have kept that to myself but the fact that I could one-up him in this was worth giving him a look into my cards. There was no response, but I was sure that if I just listened hard enough, I'd catch the sound of Bucky gnashing his teeth. "Ever since I got infected, I have stellar low-light vision. It's not as good as it was when I first woke up from what should have been my deathbed, but it's still pretty decent. Actually, way more useful now after Raynor fixed my eyes and toned down the bright light sensitivity somehow. I'll likely be blind as a bat in a dark room underground, but out here in this? I see plenty."

To me, the pause that followed seemed to be lasting forever, but maybe that was just because I enjoyed my not-so-silent gloating too much for my own good.

"Exactly how good is 'stellar'?" Richards inquired.

"Cast-over day bright at midnight?" I tried to find a good comparison. "I obviously don't see colors, but to me it's rather obvious that we're the main act for thousands of shamblers right now—and we're not even close to the city itself." More to Nate than the others, yet without muting the com, I mused, "Think that would shift my chances further toward survival if Decker ever got his claws into me? I think I'm what you'd call an asset for that quirk alone." Nate didn't respond beyond giving me the flat stare I deserved, but Hamilton's lack of an answer sounded like delicious agreement to me.

"We knew this was going to be a problem," Red offered. "That's why we need to go further upriver before we float right back."

"If we make it that far," I pointed out, looking back to Noah and Ines. "Have you guys ever done this before? Or do you generally only use the motors from the coast up to where the boats were stashed, and float different ones down through Paris?"

Ines remained quiet while Noah gave me a similarly pinched look as he had as we'd entered the golf course. Perfect. Just perfect.

"It's a sound plan," Antoine insisted from one of the other boats, arrogance more than certainty in his voice. "And it's the only plan."

"We won't make it in the dark when they're active and have full visual advantage on us," I voiced what I was sure was on everyone's mind. "It's the only plan, but not under these conditions. We stand a much better chance if we go by day where half of them will be too cautious to be out in the open, and we can see them up on the bridges."

Hamilton didn't even protest, which instantly made me suspicious. "We'll lose a full day if we stop now and set out in the morning."

"Still better than losing a third or half of our people. Or what do you think will happen if one of them does manage to drop into a boat? They'll either smash right through it or cause it to capsize, and that water is ice cold. In full gear, we'll sink and drown before we can even get paranoid about whether their bites can make us convert or not."

I hadn't expected him to, but that got Nate joining the conversation. "She's not wrong with that assessment. And you just lost two people because you didn't listen to her concerns."

That made me snort. Hamilton sounded a lot less pleased. "Aren't you obliged to always agree with her? I think there's a word for this… right—"

"Smart," I offered before he could rain on my parade. I thought it was Burns who laughed but couldn't be sure; he was in one of the other boats.

"Do I have to remind all of you that this is not a democracy?" Hamilton ground out—but before I could continue with my wisecracks, he doused my gloating effectively. "If you see that much better, it only makes sense you should be our lookout. Just tell us if things don't go as planned."

That wasn't what I'd wanted to hear, particularly as I was really fond of trying to sleep—but he kind of had a point. My bad, after having to brag how good my vision really was. I didn't miss Nate's soft laugh—or misunderstood how it was meant. I glared at him for his trouble and made sure to plant my elbow in something vital as I shifted to grab some binoculars from my pack.

"If you insist—"

"I do," Hamilton confirmed. "Unless you absolutely need your beauty sleep, princess?"

I didn't reward that with an answer. The lead boat started falling back behind us, and while I knew it was simple imagination, I felt twice as exposed as before. This was going to be one hell of a long night— and I had a certain feeling that tomorrow would only get worse.

"You good?" Nate's question—and quite questionable wording— made me snort.

"Do I have a choice?"

"You always have a choice," he murmured, the words almost drowned out by the barking of the motor.

A few wrecks of what must have been river cruise ships came up ahead, drawing my attention to them. They looked deserted, rusting hulls that they had been reduced to, but I didn't trust that assessment. My late reply was absentminded at best. "A little sleep deprivation won't kill me. You've put me through worse last year—both incidentally and quite deliberately." I'd remember that week for the rest of my life where he, Pia, and Andrej had set their minds to not letting me sleep until I fell over from exhaustion, both proving to me that I was stronger than I thought, and exactly how crappy I'd feel when it was about to happen. Ah, fun times that we'd had in that bunker last winter. Considering my current circumstances, I felt a strong pang of homesickness come up inside of me. Things hadn't been exactly rosy back then, but the company had been much better—and I'd still had all my fingers to try to count the hours I'd already been awake for.

Nate remained silent until we'd passed the wrecks. "That's not why I'm asking. And you know that."

True, but if Hamilton's order for me to turn into a bona fide pathfinder now had one advantage, it was that my mind had something to occupy itself with other than itself. "I'm good."

"You just killed two people," he pointed out, still speaking low enough that the din of the engine easily scrambled what his mic would capture.

"Not my people."

No response followed, and I spent a good five minutes scanning the river before glancing back to Nate. He was watching me in turn, the look on his face a long shot from blank. Yeah, he wasn't buying that. Mostly to avoid his, I let my gaze skip over to the other boats following us, catching Hamilton staring my way as well—as did a few of the others. Should have cut the coms ahead of that conversation, maybe, but now it was too late. I considered what to say, but nothing came to mind that sounded anything other than apologetic.

"What I did was necessary," I amended, more to them than myself. "Rodriguez killed Carter in under twenty seconds, and it wasn't just surprise that got him. Something was wrong with her, and I couldn't exactly ask her what. We caught a lucky break as it is, because if she'd turned later on one of the boats, our number of casualties would be much higher. Or the shamblers could have overrun us while we were distracted with her. Did I enjoy ending her life? No, but you know since Smith that I have a knack for killing people others care about. Martinez forgave me for that; I'm sure they'll get over it, too, seeing as none of the big strong men could accomplish what the weak cripple did." If the last part came out bitter, there was no way around it.

Nate looked tempted to get in my face but refrained when I absentmindedly touched my gear over where the mic was hidden, telling him silently that this wasn't my first rodeo, and I could play the manipulation card as well. I knew he was burning to berate me for actually feeling worse than I let on, but the damage was done, and crying over spilled beans wasn't doing anyone any good. It sure made me miss the Ice Queen even more not to get snapped at for throwing myself a pity party.

Leave it to Hamilton to make me feel much better. Try as I might, his muttered, "Freak," came over the frequency audibly enough not to be an accidental uttering. I still chose to ignore it.

"How much fuel does this thing eat up, anyway?" I asked Ines, not just as a welcome distraction. "Do we need to refuel? Do we have a place where we can? Because that over there doesn't look too inviting." I jerked my chin at the riverbank, shamblers still popping up everywhere.

"We have a safe spot two thirds of the way there," she offered. "We likely won't need it but if we can stop there, we will. We should be there in about an hour or so."

"That soon?"

She nodded. "We still need to go farther upriver so they quiet down and forget about us, but we could be at Pont de Neuilly in about two hours from now if we go at maximum speed. That's the bridge leading to La Défense," she explained when I just stared at her. "We could go slower but it wouldn't save much more fuel, and if we float back, it won't be a problem."

Again I asked myself why the rush but didn't bring up the point. I certainly didn't mind not having to be on the lookout for the entire night. Speaking of lookouts, what I saw up ahead made me frown. "Is that a fork in the river?"

"Islands," Ines clarified. "The Seine meanders in these parts. We've already passed two larger ones." She paused, looking over her shoulder to Noah. A brief exchange followed before she turned back to me. "Up ahead, after the next, what do you call it? Riverbend? Sling? There's another lock at Andresy. It's across one of the smaller islands, forest for the most part. The larger ones, closer to Paris, they have houses on them. We will need to get out of the boats and drag them over the lock, anyway, but with luck the island is empty so we could camp there for the night, or at least a few hours. We can test the theory there that the undead will quiet down if we're silent. Just upriver of La Défense is also a lock, and while we likely can't stay at that island, if it's just a few minutes until they lose interest, we can remain in the water and don't have to traverse the dams in both directions."

I wasn't quite sure whether I understood, but not wasting idle time sounded great—as did catching a break. "Sounds good. How much farther until that first lock?"

"Twenty minutes, if there aren't any more obstacles here," Ines explained. "Not too many bridges here, either. But there are plenty in Paris. We should avoid them, going upriver." Making so much noise, she meant, I was sure.

There were obstacles aplenty ahead, among them what looked like several houses that had been torn away by flooding, but we made good headway as forest replaced towns on the riverbanks. A little later than expected, I saw the river split up ahead of us around a larger island, and then another, with an additional canal on the northern side. Noah steered right for the smaller, left fork, where trees grew right up to the waterline. Tentative moans and the sounds of something moving beyond the trees came from that first island we'd just passed, hinting at more habitation between the few houses that I could see.

"Anyone else wanna take point?" I asked Hamilton and his merry men. "The island looks deserted, and I'm not catching anything landside, either." What must have been the smaller part of the lock, leading toward the canal, was maybe a hundred yards from where Noah let the boat idle to a halt, the whine of the engine turning into a low rumble.

Hamilton gave the order that his boat would land first, with us keeping lookout on the river. Noah let the boat get dragged along by the currents until we were at the very peak of the island once more and I could see across the larger river fork. "Still got movement over there, but not much," I reported, not sure anyone was listening. Even over the engine noise, I could hear the soldiers tear into the forest underbrush, sure they'd attract any attention there was to attract. Ten minutes later, Richards and his boat landed, and we followed after that. I didn't need help to drag myself out of the boat and onto the cement blocks that made up the sides of the lock, but thanks to my limitations I was exempt from boat-dragging duty. From up there I could see the other side of the dam—lock, whatever—where a lot of driftwood had piled up, forever shutting down the mechanisms that had before allowed ships to be lowered and raised to accommodate the artificial elevation level of the river.

Aimes and his fire team returned from their brief scouting mission, reporting that this part of the island was indeed deserted— no wonder, since it was only reachable by boat. I would have loved to just sit down and rest now, but wasn't really surprised when Richards called Nate, Burns, and me to go ahead and scout the northeastern part while Munez, Davis, and Murdock got the western side. Nate let me take point as it made the most sense, seeing as I had the least trouble finding my way through the trees.

The island was maybe two hundred yards wide but over a mile and a half long, all forest except for the middle part where we found what looked like some kind of park and an abandoned restaurant. Ines had warned us that there were some houses on the northern, narrower part but since we didn't encounter any undead in the southern half—and no remains whatsoever—we returned to where the others had in the meantime finished getting the boats over the lock and back into the river.

"The urban sprawl of Paris starts north of here," Ines explained to Hamilton just as we got back. "If you decide to rest, this is it. You won't get another chance."

Hamilton considered, still scanning the adjacent island on the other side of the lock where a few shamblers had found their way to the artificial barrier. "Two-man watch at the boats, the rest on rotation," he decided. "Lewis is off the rotation because we'll need her fresh and perky once we set out again, at oh-six-hundred."

That order made me frown. It sounded like he'd planned this all along, so why make me think I'd have to pull an all-nighter? My consternation must have been rather obvious as when Nate bumped into me to make me turn around, he whispered, "Because he's winging it."

While the others got our late dinner started, I did my best to clean myself up. Rodriguez hadn't managed to inflict any cuts— only some great blunt-force trauma—but she'd done a stellar job bleeding all over my shoulder and torso, and considering what had happened, I really wanted that shit off. I tried to tell myself that it must have been a fluke but didn't quite buy it. I didn't want to bring up the point, though, as there was no sense in that besides drawing even more ire from the others. No one was stupid enough to debate whether killing her had been necessary, but the way Aimes glared in my direction had now reached almost the level of balefulness he usually reserved for Nate. I got it—they'd spent a lot of time together, probably had been friends, not just comrades in arms, but it wasn't like I'd had a choice.

The fact that Gita also eyed me cautiously was weighing way heavier on my mind. I wondered if I should have tried to clear up whatever that was all about, but decided that with what loomed ahead tomorrow, I could take another day for that conversation. Who knew, maybe we'd both be dead by then and that was one uncomfortable talk I didn't need to have.

I slept like crap, and not just because the howls in the distance never quite died off. Ines had been right in as far as the shamblers who'd directly been drawn by the noise of the engines had lost interest eventually, but on the northern side of the river in particular there was obviously more going on than we'd encountered this far. Not being able to see them didn't help, although I was glad that the air here, in the middle of the trees and the river, was clear once more. I knew I should also have been bothered by what we would find down in that lab tomorrow, but my mind refused to dwell on that. First, we'd have to get there, anyway. And then, well. Then I would do what these idiots had dragged me along for—if we were still alive.

It was after getting up and fetching some quickly downed breakfast that Cole ambled over to me, still a little bleary-eyed from having had last watch. His mood was somber but a far shot from

Aimes and Wu's open hostility. When he saw me glaring their way before I focused on him, he allowed himself a small smirk. "Didn't you spend the entire time griping that everyone was doubting your competence? Well, congratulations—that's cleared up now. Deal with it."

It was the kind of backhanded compliment that could have come from Nate, and went down about as smoothly as if it had. I found myself staring after Cole as he walked over to his boat, considering, but we were off before I found a conclusion for myself—had it been a blessing in disguise or a colossal mistake on my part to prove to them that their misconceptions about me had been just that? Time would tell.

Chapter 10

The sun didn't rise as much as the gloom surrounding us lightened gradually, fog hanging like a thick blanket over the Seine. Any advantage my good low-light vision might have conveyed me was instantly nixed. The undead didn't care that they couldn't see us or we them—they still made a racket as soon as they heard us. And hear us they did; just under an hour later of slow weaving around partly submerged obstacles found us nearing our refueling point, and it wasn't as deserted as I would have liked it to be. I'd expected another island, but Ines steered right at where three larger ships—river cruise ships from the looks of them—had collided around the massive pylons of a bridge. And said bridge spanning the river, slowly emerging from the fog as it was, was teeming with zombies.

We weren't even in shouting distance yet as the first already lunged over the rails and plunged down into the dark depths of the river, or thumped onto one of the ships, only to spin on and disappear into the water. The first time that happened it made me laugh from how comical it looked—but that laugh had a decidedly hysterical note to it.

"No way that we can avoid that, right?" I asked Noah, sitting next to me. The French scout silently shook his head. "Do we have to syphon the fuel from the cruise ships?"

Again, he negated my guess. "We have portable canisters stored on the blue one, just above the waterline," he explained. "Just need to grab them."

That sounded easy enough, but considering that another ten shamblers plunged to their wet death while we spoke, I had a certain feeling this was going to be everything but.

"Why choose this point? Wouldn't one of the islands—or literally any other spot—be better than this?"

Noah gave a shrug that wasn't exactly disagreement. "Two of our boats sank right there and the ships were close enough to salvage most of the canisters we'd brought. As long as there's no flash flood that tears the wrecks loose, it's as good a place to store the fuel as any."

At least his fatalism was admirable.

"Has anyone ever tried to retrieve fuel from your strategic hidey-hole?"

His smile was more of a grimace, really. "Didn't need to yet."

So much for that.

"Do we really need the fuel?" I asked more loudly, addressing our asshole-in-charge. "We might need a few more days if we simply float down the river rather than run the engines, but we're just over the midway point to our deadline. Do we really need to risk this?"

Hamilton didn't seem pleased that, yet again, I dared think for myself. "In the field, you never pass up a chance to get resources if you can," he barked back. "And we have to cross under the bridge either way."

"But there's a difference between playing Frogger and zapping through, and halting in the very middle of it to try and get fuel from rusting wrecks."

Even over the screams of the shamblers, Hamilton's growl was audible, but he chose to ignore me going forward, instead calling out the order of the boats in which to approach the wrecks. Ours was last. He ended with, "And Miller? Shut that bitch of yours up unless you want me to drown her right this fucking second."

I sent the brightest smile I could manage across the water toward the other boats. "Gee, you should wait another, oh, twenty-four hours with that. So close to your mission objective, would be a shame if you ruined it all right here and now."

Nate seemed more annoyed than amused, but for the most part ignored us both. "The canister depot is on the right-most wreck, you said?" he asked Noah.

The scout nodded. "You can climb in through that hole in the hull. Impossible to miss once you've made the jump."

I scowled toward the mangled ships. None of them looked exactly stable, and even ignoring the shamblers on the bridge above, it wasn't an easy maneuver to get close—and that was ignoring how someone vaulting over, and presumably returning, would upset the balance of the boats. Suddenly, I was overly aware of the fact that my grip strength, both to hold on to something or pull someone back onto the boat, was shit. I hesitated for a moment but then looked at our designated driver. "Move over. I'm taking over the wheel."

Ines looked at me as if I'd grown a second head—or claimed she had. "Do you even know the first thing about steering a boat?"

"Can't be that different from other vehicles," I shot back, trying not to appear the least bit worried. "Besides, I'll be the least useful in retrieving the fuel. Let me free up some resources for that."

I could feel literally all eyes on me as I traded places with her. I took a moment to glare toward Hamilton before I got my crash course in boating, or whatever you wanted to call it. Meanwhile, our boat got caught by the currents and started drifting downriver, giving me a good many yards to familiarize myself with the controls as I caught up to where the others were still idling. Davis and Munez, also in the same boat with us, looked a little green around their noses from my first attempt at a smooth bank which felt a lot more like a weird swerve.

"What could possibly go wrong?" I murmured to myself as I finally got the hang of it, steadying the boat for good. Someone snorted on the coms, making me glance up at the others. "What? I'm a hell of a good driver."

Burns didn't disagree with me, but his mirth had a darker tone than usual to it. "Last time I checked, you wrecked two cars in under four months."

"The Jeep wasn't my fault," I grumbled. "None of us saw how unstable that bridge was. And considering how high I was when I sent the Rover down that collapsing mountainside, I'd say that speaks for me, not against me." I didn't miss the handful of smirks that last bit drew, making my ire rear its ugly head. "Raise your hand if you had the guts to do something insane like that? No one? Well, too bad." Looking at the others in my boat, I did my best to put a lid on my ego, focusing on where Nate and Ines got ready. "I'll do my best to get you as close as I can. Promise."

"Never doubted you," my dear husband enthused, then jerked his head toward where the first boat was starting its approach. "Simply avoid any undead dropping down on us. We'll take care of the rest."

I still didn't like the entire concept of this, but having a little more control now that I was behind the wheel helped somewhat—even though I still wasn't sure about half the controls of this thing. Oh well. What could possibly go wrong?

Antoine did some impressive swerving around dropping shamblers as he cut underneath one side of the bridge, where he executed a tight turn that made water spray up behind the boat, and several of its inhabitants cling on for dear life—making me doubly glad I'd traded places with Ines. Cole and Russell jumped across, making the maneuver look easy, although the wreck gave an impressive metal groan at their landing. They reappeared within moments, tossing several red canisters across before they returned to the boat. Russell landed perfectly, but Cole miscalculated, making the boat almost capsize as he went too far, only Richards quickly grabbing and pulling him, keeping him out of the water. The combined cursing was audible even over the screams of the still-dropping shamblers. As soon as the boat stopped rocking, Antoine gunned the engine, and with an impressive swerve away from the wrecks brought the boat out into the open of the river, plowing right through two zombies that were still splashing in the water, not having gone under yet.

The second boat set out, Raphael steering it with a lot less aggression and aplomb. He tried a slower approach that got the zombies really agitated, entire clumps of them coming down over the railing of the bridge. They all missed, but while he steadied the boat so Aimes and Wu could get their canisters, several of the shamblers managed to drag themselves over to the boat and wrecks alike, requiring some improvised pest control. I watched with a roiling stomach as Hamilton and Burns stood side by side, throwing shamblers back into the river as soon as their rotting hands could grab the boat. Raphael was much quicker in his retreat, leaving behind some nice waves that rocked our boat as well.

And then, it was my turn.

Looking up where the stream of zombies jonesing for a good ice bath still wasn't ending wasn't such a bright idea so I concentrated on how I'd have to maneuver to get the boat to where it needed to be. I almost called for Noah to take over for me, but I knew he was needed to catch the canisters, and maybe Ines and Nate as well. Timing the droppers was impossible as well—so I just went for it.

Speed was of the essence, so I allowed the boat to float back a few yards before I accelerated, making the bow shoot out of the water in a tight turn. Left, right, and then I sent it into a wide, long turn, almost sliding sideways underneath the bridge. Corpses dropped left and right, narrowly missing the boat, yet I ignored them in favor of getting closer to the wrecks, letting the boat drift the last few feet. As soon as the side bumped into the rusty hull, Ines leaped across, Nate following a moment later. He kicked off hard enough to push the boat away, forcing me to micro-steer it back to where it belonged. I felt the currents, irregular and strong where they broke around the wrecks wrestle with my control, making the boat waver and pitch to one side, then the other.

The first canister came soaring out of the wreck, Munez snatching it up more by chance than plan. I concentrated on keeping the boat level instead, my gaze every so often scanning for swimmers. There was a lot of splashing going on to my right side, making me wonder if they'd manage to build up from the river bottom until they could reach the boat from underneath. The current should have been too strong for that—and the Seine too deep—but in my paranoid mind's eye, I saw ghostly white, rotten hands reach for the rudder—

"Keep the boat steady!" I heard Nate's call, forcing my mind to snap to attention. As soon as I got it back where it should be, Ines hurled herself back across, landing in Noah's waiting arms. He steadied her, then got ready for Nate. Our eyes met across the short distance, and I didn't miss the grin flashing across Nate's features as he pushed off—

And landed safely on deck, the boat rocking hard.

I gunned the engine, sending the boat into another turn as it accelerated, heading right for the other two boats—

Until a dropper managed to clip off the left side of the bow.

The boat lurched out of control as the impact tore my hands off the controls, if only for a second, acceleration dropping away to zilch. The howling above us increased immediately, and a new slew of shamblers came down all around us. Grasping blindly, I hit the accelerator, making the boat shoot forward, aiming straight for the stern of one of the wrecks. Cursing, I tightened my hands on the wheel, forcing it into a controlled hard turn—and away from both the bridge and the water.

I may have laughed maniacally—and by the time the boat shot by the others that were idling in the middle of the river, I meant it, adrenaline making me loopy and stupid. Oh, it was a great feeling to be alive!

"You like cutting it close, no?" Noah remarked as he joined me at the controls, still looking a little harassed—and making no attempt to take over once more. Fine with me—sitting around was just making me stir-crazy, anyway.

"Sometimes," I quipped back, grinning at my admission. "Life's too short to always play it safe." It was impossible to tone down the exuberance in my voice, and I didn't really try.

He kept his opinion to himself, instead conversing with Antoine and Raphael for a bit, then pointed to the left riverbank. "After the next bend, make sure to stay on this side. There are canals, but the next island is several kilometers long, and the lock on this side is easier to traverse. And watch out for the wrecks."

"Wrecks?"

His smile turned forced. "We're close to the city now. You'll see."

I was still confused as I steered the boat around the long, slow bend, making sure to stay in the middle of the forking waterway that he'd indicated—until the next bridge loomed up ahead. Doing a quick calculation in my head, I figured it was likely the extension of the same road that the previous bridge had served—only this one was no longer intact. And if I wasn't completely wrong, it hadn't collapsed on its own.

"You detonated the bridges?" Nate guessed as he surveyed the wreckage—including what looked like hundreds of cars, busses, bikes, and small river craft—that surrounded what remained of the concrete that had once spanned the Seine.

"We had to," Noah declared, his voice somber. "Elle told you that we had weeks of warnings, over a month to prepare to evacuate? Many didn't listen. Many didn't believe. And when the sickness swept through the doubters and killed them one by one, we knew we had to try to contain them. It was futile, of course, as Paris spans both sides of the Seine, but evacuation was still going on. The only thing we could do was make sure that the dead couldn't follow us across the river. The official order was to head north. The Resistance decided to make a stand toward the south. I think you know who had the better idea."

Considering they still called themselves the Resistance, I did. Why did the sudden feeling creep up on me that Elle and Alexandre had fed us a rather edited version of the events?

But then that was one sin I was equally guilty of myself.

"How deep do the wrecks go?" I asked, forcing myself to concentrate on the immediate danger over the horror of the past.

"The boats are light enough that they should get over everything you don't see," Noah explained. "But it would be wise to stop driving the boat like a racing car." Also more fuel efficient, I was sure, but I didn't offer that up, and instead slowed down to a more sedate, cautious pace.

So we watched in silence as we glided past the burnt-out wrecks that spoke of the dying pains of one of Europe's largest cities, the layers of fog only adding to the ghostly horrors of it. And we were far from alone. If before we'd drawn the attention of hundreds of shamblers, it was thousands of eyes following our progress now—and that was only those we could see in the less than clear morning air. The sounds of movement, interspersed with harsh shouts and guttural grunts, echoed from all sides, only partly lost in the fog. It seemed like they were one immensely huge pack of hungry, patiently waiting predators. If we hadn't been so far removed in the middle of the river, we would have long since died. I wondered how many others besides us had ever become witness to this; the scouts, obviously, and by their stoic ignorance I could tell that the knowledge of what had happened—of what they'd had to do to survive—cut deep.

Only they'd been smart enough to stay outside the city for the most part, and none of them seemed to have tried to leave the boats. Trust us not to be that intelligent.

And then, several bridges—and another harrowing climbing and dragging tour across the next lock—later, a few miles farther, at one of the straight passages of the river, Ines pointed at one more partly destroyed bridge looming ahead. "That's Pont de Neuilly. La Défense is right there on the right riverbank. We're here."

Chapter 11

Getting to our destination was one thing; getting off the boats, quite another. The only positive thing about our situation was that, even up here, the Seine hadn't started to freeze over—not really a lot we had going for us.

I barely caught a glimpse of the skyscrapers where Ines indicated, having to pay more attention to said bridge and another river island splitting the stream in two. As the French had told us, the island had been a place for leisure activities, and unlike most of the previous islands, it was inhabited—not heavily, but I could make out a good fifty shamblers eagerly following the roar of our engines as we sped by, partly hidden between the trees. Trees were good, as was the fact that the island was large enough to completely obscure the other fork of the river—and the center of Paris that loomed behind. Most of the attention we got was from the side where we were going to embark on. "Should we maybe switch to the other side and hope we can better sneak in that way?" I suggested what seemed quite obvious to me.

As expected, Hamilton shot me down. "If we don't have to cross the bridge, we won't. The roads leading up where we need to go start at the quay. So that's where we start as well."

I wondered why I still tried but couldn't find it in me to shut up. "And the boats we'll leave at the island so they can pick us up later? Won't they get eaten in the meantime?"

Ines seemed to be the only one still amused by my protest. "There are more wrecks in the other fork because a lot of boats were moored there," she explained. "We can easily go there, wait, and then swoop in and pick you up. Don't worry about us."

The end of the island was up ahead with the piled-up mess that was yet another dysfunctional lock creating a natural barrier. I cut the engine as we reached the massive cement structures that cut the river into several smaller parts, waiting for the other boats to join us. Ropes were cast to tie the boats off so the current wouldn't drag them downriver too soon—and then we settled in to wait until we became all but invisible.

"No talking, and no sounds unless you cannot avoid them," Hamilton reminded us. "You all know your fire teams and the order in which we will disembark. You know your destination, and you know the contingency plans." I craned my neck to look past the structures of the lock to the road that ran right by the river. It wasn't exactly packed with shamblers, but there was no way I'd survive up there more than five minutes. Was dying a quick, horrible death really a contingency plan? Whatever else we found in that lab, getting out of the city would be the worst part if anything went wrong. Hell, jumping into the river and hoping not to drown or freeze to death was the best chance we had. I really fucking hoped that it wouldn't come to that.

Nate nudged my elbow, making me look at him rather than at the resident population. He gave me a pointed stare followed by the hint of a smile. Right. Getting locked inside my head now wouldn't do me any good, so why bother? It was much better to enjoy the late morning air, full of fog and the stink of millions of decomposing bodies all over. Ah, Paris!

And so we waited. And waited. And waited some more. I went through a bottle of water—cold enough to hurt my teeth—and a bag of jerky. I knew I'd need the energy, and it gave me something to do. Two hours passed. Then a third. The shamblers were still staring at us and the boats, slowly bobbing up and down in the river. Every few minutes, one of them had the great idea to tumble down the steps that led from the street to the river walkway, and a handful of those down there in turn splashed into the water as they tried to reach us. They were swept beyond the next bridge before they stopped resurfacing, a few hundred feet downstream of our position. To say I was bored right out of my mind was an understatement, but unlike Noah and Munez, I didn't manage to catch some shut-eye. Knowing that the worst was still before us really didn't help. But I seemed to be the only one antsy with tension, making me wonder if the others were somehow more used to this. Were military missions usually like this? Brief bouts of terror interspersed with immense stretches of utter boredom? Nothing we had gotten up to had ever went down like this. We'd all been about action, action, and then lots of reaction, including some timely running away or chasing down the stragglers. I couldn't say that I was very impressed.

My mind started drifting off but I forced myself to remain focused and instead repeated the version numbers of the serum variants to myself that we were looking for. After that, the room numbers I should be looking for. The highlighted routes on the blueprints that Nate had, late one night, drilled into my brain, visualizing the exit routes from all points of interest with me until I felt like I'd walked them a million times—or got so annoyed with him that I'd claimed I'd gotten it. Now, I wished I'd done the exercise a few more times on the way over.

It wasn't so much sound as motion to my left that jerked my attention outward, just in time to see Bucky motion to the French scouts to get ready for cast off. To me, the shamblers at the riverbank still seemed way too interested in us, but I doubted they'd actually quiet down—and I really had to relieve myself. If anything, that would be easier once we had dry, solid land underneath our boots.

Antoine jerked the rope free first, and as soon as the boat started to get swept away by the current, attention ran like a wave through the zombies—but only a single one of them went into the river; the others just stared. Nate was just as tense as I felt as he watched the boat make it through the first bridge—ours was the next after that—still without causing too much of a fuss. The second boat went next, Raphael looking tense behind the wheel that likely let him do only minimal steering without the engine on. Hungry eyes followed their progress but still no agitation. Hope flared up inside of me, although I tried to quench it immediately. This wasn't even the real first step; we were still twiddling our thumbs with the prep work.

Then it was time for us to float down the river. I tensed as first one, then a second shambler tumbled into the water, but they were far enough away not to get anywhere near the boat as they were carried downriver the same as us, eventually disappearing underneath the black waves. There was some grunting and moaning coming from the road by the quay but no sounds of direct pursuit. Maybe this was less of a stupid fucking plan than I was still afraid it was.

We followed close enough behind the second boat to see when Raphael started inching it toward the riverbank, away from the island. Ahead, the first boat reached the destination, jerking to a halt as grappling hooks on ropes caught and anchored it for now. Hamilton and two more figures climbed onto the quay, still too far away to clearly identify them. The rest remained in the boat, waiting. Boat two joined them, the boats quickly fixed to each other with more rope. We did the same when it was our turn, my fingers itching from being useless as fuck—and ice cold from hours of inactivity. Above us, it was eerily quiet, the sounds of the river muting anything else that was going on.

It was a good twenty minutes after the first boat had anchored itself when Cole suddenly appeared on the railing above us, giving us a silent go-ahead. There was blood and gore on his gear but none of that seemed to belong to him. I didn't protest when Nate unceremoniously helped me don my pack, and as the boats got more empty, pulled me along until we were next to climb up the ropes to get up on land. Rather than force me to scramble up, my fingers likely too weak to do a good job pulling my weight and my gear, Nate and Burns boosted me up so all I had to do was grab onto the railing and swing my leg up and over it. Hill was waiting for me, helping along so that I dropped to the sidewalk with barely any sound, quickly casting around for danger.

There were a good thirty heaps of rags on the ground, more leading toward the road branching off perpendicular to the one following the river. Everyone was alert going on twitchy, loud and heavy weapons stowed away in favor of knives and good ol' hands. Car wrecks had piled up all across the two lanes of the road plus the sidewalks and everywhere else available, giving us plenty of cover. I didn't need Cole's signal to duck behind a blue minivan, making sure to move with deliberate motions not to cause any unnecessary noise. With strength in numbers not in our favor, stealth it was instead.

Nate lightly tapped my shoulder as he crouched down next to me, and we waited until Burns joined us before I slid to the other side of the car and studied the road. A handful of shamblers were already invading the zone that our vanguard had cleared but they took minimal interest in the corpses, instead dragging themselves on almost aimlessly. Almost, as their heads jerked around in unison when a metallic clang sounded from further up the road. I used the opportunity of distraction and eased over into the other lane and onto the sidewalk, behind an overturned truck. Only for a moment, I looked back to see whether Nate was following and got a death glare from him for my effort. I gave him the finger for that but kept my attention forward, picking the best route to keep us as covered as possible, dutifully waiting for his light pat on my shoulder before moving on each and every time. I caught sight of Munez moving ahead of me a few times but except for him, the ramp we went up could have been deserted. Judging from the sign and width, it had been a pedestrian path but three cars were still jammed together at the top, giving me a good place to rest for a second to stare up at the massive skyscraper to my left. It had been the one that Ines had pointed out to me on our trek upriver. It must have been at least fifty stories tall, most of the windows looking marvelously untouched. The ramp led up to roughly the height of the third story, a pathway to the right leading to some kind of park deck—that was crawling with shamblers. They were nesting, as in, had dragged all kinds of debris inside and built huge piles of it that looked like primitive shelters. A few of them stared out into the foggy daylight but none of them made a move to come out. I gave myself a visible shake and moved on.

The ramp took a sharp left turn at the top, ending in a flat, open space that was the centerpiece of the entire satellite city of La Défense. I'd seen the maps, and Elle had described it to us in detail when prompted at dinner, but the view opening up in front of me took my breath away for a second—and not just because, like most causeways, it was dangerously open and devoid of good cover.

For the length of almost a mile, and well over a hundred feet wide, the plaza ran from where I was crouching behind the remnants of what had likely been some coffee shop furniture, up over several stages of gentle steps, to a giant geometric arch-like structure, roughly the dimensions of a cube. Left and right, skyscrapers stretched seemingly endlessly up into the clouds and fog, most too tall to see their tops in the abysmal weather. And as I looked the other way, I could see the center of Paris at the extension of the plaza, the road that ran across the bridge, and on into a straight line to the fabled Arc de Triomphe. Back in the day, it must have been quite the inviting spot. Now, it was a great place to get a really good look at all the undead clogging the broad road that disappeared underneath the structure we were standing on now, the dark spaces below likely their usual daylight hideout. A few of them must have been out and about before we'd come close, but I was sure that we'd woken up quite a few more.

Up on the plaza, there were fewer shamblers, but still plenty enough that I didn't dare venture out into the open where a large pool, frozen over, with weird sculptures placed in it took over most of the space. I waited for Nate to give me the signal before I started inching forward, using two of the sculptures for cover. Next to us, the gaping maw of a Metro entrance yawned, giant holes ripped into the flimsy grates that had closed it off telling of something rampaging there to get out. That didn't look very comforting.

No cars had made it up onto the plaza, but there was debris aplenty from the shops and restaurants that must have already had outdoor seating ready when the shit hit the fan, and a year and a half of seasons to let the carefully arranged vegetation run wild. Even with obvious signs of destruction, it all had a rather peaceful, quiet air to it.

I absolutely didn't trust that, and that false sense of security was setting my teeth on edge.

I took my time picking my way through lots of dry leaves that had gathered in the corners and lower edges, going for minimum exposure wherever possible. All that glass, steel, and concrete made this seem like a business district but I had no idea how many high-rise penthouses had been here, and whether the hotels had been deserted. The memory of the stealthy, conniving undead at the golf club was still too fresh on my mind not to distrust the momentary quiet, although the lingering scents of decay—mostly of plant matter—were comforting to a point, familiar.

We reached the first flight of steps where Red was waiting with Tanner, Gita, and five more soldiers. Two more teams were behind us, a total of five people. Red silently signaled me to proceed further up the plaza. The next part was in more disarray, several of the trees that had grown there lying this way and that. I considered going around them to hug the side of the buildings, but I didn't like how deep the shadows were around there. More than one glass front had been destroyed, and I was sure that something must be lurking in there. Better not risk it. As I slowly advanced down the steps, I saw movement up ahead, but it was just one more of our teams going the same route I'd decided for, also avoiding the buildings for now. I looked back briefly, trying to see if any of the shamblers from the garage had come out, but what I could see of the ramp was still deserted.

I really didn't trust this.

The section with the trees in the middle was bisected by a small garden and some restaurants, followed by another open space, then more trees. The second half had more room on the sides, and to the right loomed the corner of our destination, a double-towered building as fantastic and tall as all the others yet with curves rather than straight plains as the central architectural motif. It looked like the last place where I would have expected an underground lab to be housed, but that must have been the reasoning for the location. Ahead, I could see another shallow, huge basin, and then the plaza opened wide, leading up to that oversized cube arch. I was quite happy that we didn't have to go that far, the expanse of all that exposed space making my skin crawl.

As we got closer to the tower we were aiming for, I saw Bucky had already arrived, waiting next to the entrance. None of the ground floor glass panes had remained intact so getting inside wasn't exactly hard. That he was hesitating to get out of the open made me guess that he was waiting for backup to do some preliminary cleanup. That seemed to be the case as he disappeared from sight as the fire team in front of us arrived. I strained my ears but couldn't hear a sound besides the wind howling through the maze of buildings.

Nate held me back before we made the mad dash across the open space in front of the basin, taking point himself and signaling Burns to come right after him. I didn't hang back but they made it a full ten seconds ahead of me, leaving me frowning as I followed inside. The cloud of stench that met me told me everything I needed to know. Before I could look for the others, Cole signaled me over to where he was crouching next to the huge elevator banks in a defensive position. I joined him, reasoning that I still had the actually useful work ahead of me that only I could do—I could take five now where I wasn't strictly needed.

The other fire teams followed in quick succession. When Red made it in, he sent Gita to Cole and me before he joined the cleanup effort that by now had turned into a barricading effort. I knew that there were two exits deeper into the building but our chosen main entry point was right here, so it made the most sense to concentrate on this one—after making sure we could still use the others. I didn't like standing by idly, watching the gloom outside deepen by the minute. I knew that was due to the weather worsening, not yet night falling, but the undead weren't too picky about what kept the sun away from them, as long as it did. Suddenly, the four-hour window that we had to explore the labs sounded like a hell of a lot of time. Even if we were quick—which I highly doubted would be possible— it would likely be dark outside by the time of our return. I knew the plan was to make it to the river and onto the boats, anyway, but I wouldn't put it past Hamilton to decide that it was best for us to wait out the night in this building—and hope the French would still be around the next morning. What we'd do if that wasn't the case I didn't want to consider. What would happen if they tried to check on us after dark made me taste bile just the same.

Hamilton reappeared in the foyer, surprisingly silent for a man of his bulk and gear load. He nodded at Cole, who, rather than turn to the elevators, went over to a small maintenance door and started easing it open, Hamilton and Russell covering him. It squeaked god-awfully, making me hold my breath as I listened. Nothing. Five tense seconds later, the soldiers disappeared inside and the lot of us followed, everyone with their night vision goggles ready.

Let the fun begin.

The staircase behind the door was barely worth the designation, just a shaft with a decidedly flimsy set of stairs leading down. The entire construction shook and vibrated under our combined weight, the beams of a few flashlights not enough to make much of a difference as I didn't exactly want to see through the grates at what was below me. I didn't count the steps but the number of turns made me guess that we went down three levels, where the stairs ended at another small door. Unlike the one above, it didn't make a sound as it opened. I patiently waited my turn but from the low, even sound of steps the soldiers up ahead didn't meet with opposition.

Behind the door was a corridor that mirrored the foyer upstairs in layout, including the elevators, but only a single one—the second on the right—had a call button for "down." Where upstairs there had been glass and granite, here it was all unfinished concrete. There was another maintenance door at the other end of the corridor but after making sure it was locked, Hamilton—loudly—declared that our mission was a go. Within moments, the doors to that special elevator were pried open and blocked with a bar to remain that way, Davis looking down the shaft with one of the stronger flashlights, then up. "Cabin is somewhere in the upper floors so the way down is clear," he reported back.

In short order, climbing ropes were unpacked, and down we went—not my favorite part of our expedition, although I noticed on the way down that the shaft had ladder rungs on two sides for manual climbing. Down and down we went into what felt like the very bowels of the earth, every additional foot making me more nervous. There were no other doors—or in fact any markings indicating other floors—in the shaft until we reached the very bottom, the heavy doors there already pried open like the ones above.

While I tried to swallow the distinct feeling of nausea that had taken hold of my stomach, I watched as portable generators and batteries were unpacked, soon crowding the dark granite hallway that ended in a small, empty room. The only distinct feature was a black security camera in one corner above the heavy fire-safety door leading further into the building, as-of-yet sealed. Cole was already booting up his laptop; Gita hovered behind him, vibrating with tension, watching him pry a wall panel loose and pull what looked like a random bunch of cables out that they connected to their workstations. I eyed the dead display next to the door, the iris scanner both oddly familiar and so far removed from what had become common in my life that it could have been alien technology. Everyone else was shirking heavy packs and exchanging them for lighter ones, only taking weapons and as much ammo as they could carry with them. There was a general air of quiet anticipation going on, except for Parker, who was so white in the face that I was tempted to say "boo" to him and watch him faint. It was only when Hamilton pried open a panel in the wall that I hadn't noticed until then and started taking handfuls of gas masks out that I got a little queasy myself.

"You are aware that anything that could be lurking in there will likely get right through the filters in those masks?" I remarked, not really a fan of my own doomsday message.

Hamilton gave me a smile that was bordering on sweet—as much as he was capable of that—but never stopped in his task. "Standard decontamination protocol is UV light and formaldehyde, right?" I nodded. "And what do we need to breathe through that, should Cole not manage to shut it all down?"

"Right," I murmured, letting Richards push one of the handed-out masks into my hands. "But the offices and common areas shouldn't have those decon measures installed."

"You going to bet your lungs and freak eyes on that, Stumpy?"

I didn't need Nate nudging me in the side to ignore that dig. If my attempt to be helpful went ignored, I could very well keep all that knowledge to myself—but I made sure to check the filters on the mask. Never hurt to be cautious.

"Progress?" Hamilton asked Cole as he stalked over to breathe down the geek squad's necks. If I couldn't make sense of the rapidly scrolling lines of code on screen, I doubted Hamilton fared any better.

Cole ignored him for a full twenty seconds. "We're in, but the system's not meant to be fiddled with so this may take a little longer. But good news, the backup generators are still running so we should have baseline electricity inside, and access to the logs." He paused to look up, first at Hamilton before his gaze skipped to me for a second. "That means we at least have a chance to check what went down here."

"Get us in," Hamilton grunted. "That's top priority."

Cole was already focusing on his monitor again, mumbling a barely audible "Yessir," under his breath.

For what felt like the millionth time, I checked that I had enough backup magazines for my M16 ready—no stealth approach for this. I couldn't help but fidget with the assault rifle, nerves I hadn't realized I was feeling suddenly making me jittery as hell. Hill eyed me cautiously, but it was Burns who addressed the elephant in the room, nudging me softly. "Still not trusting the rifle that's literally the most used weapon in the armed forces?"

"Figuratively," Nate admonished, making Burns flash him a quick—and very unapologetic—grin, as usual annoying me—which worked as the distraction it was supposed to be.

"What can I say. I miss that kicking mule like hell."

"What is it with you and shotguns?" Hill wanted to know, seeming calm as fuck. Asshole.

I shrugged, wishing my fingers weren't quite that stiff. Hell, still having all of them would have been even better. "It's kind of my thing, I guess? First weapon I got to use often enough that it became second nature. Great for busting down doors and shooting anything in the face that's been hiding just behind said door. Hard to miss at arm's length."

He still didn't seem to get it. "I've seen you do target practice. You're not that bad of a shot."

I waited for the punchline, but when none came I realized he was serious. Exhaling slowly, I tried to choose my words wisely—not something I usually did, but with everyone so close together in the same room it wasn't like this was a private conversation.

"I just like my shotguns, okay? Last year, I started out from zero knowledge, surrounded by, well, you know what kind of people. To say I was useless as fuck is an understatement. At best, I was a distraction, but I was very aware of the fact that I was absolutely a burden; someone that had to be taken care of rather than an additional member of the group to fully rely on."

As I'd expected, the conversation didn't remain between us, Aimes only too happy to interject. "I'm sure they could have thought of some way to put you to good use," he offered, not quite daring to leer at me, but the message was impossible not to get.

Snorting, I plastered a fake smile on my face. "And that was part of the problem. Maybe it was just luck that the first thing Romanoff grabbed to explain to me after a handgun was one of the shotguns they'd liberated from a squad car. Maybe he figured it wouldn't be missed as much as a rifle if I somehow managed to ruin it. Maybe he thought it perfectly matched my winning personality. Who the fuck knows? Anyway, I learned how to use it, and the next time I got a face full of zombie, I blew its face off, and that made a difference. I didn't need anyone else anymore to finish it off. I could do it myself. I could have someone else's back, and I could help keep up a defensive perimeter. Sure, it was easier in the long run seeing as we didn't have enough ammo to waste to teach me how to properly shoot at longer distances with a rifle, nor did we often have the chance to be somewhere truly deserted where we didn't draw too much unwanted attention to us. None of that was necessary because I could do what needed to be done with my shotgun. We started switching things up once we got to the bunker and bare necessities survival turned to foraging and seeking out training opportunities, but by then, the damage was done."

Aimes looked ready to offer something that would make me really yearn for my Mossberg, but Hill, wisely choosing a good-natured tone, surmised, "So the shotgun's your comfort weapon? Cute."

I would have loved to say something acerbic to wipe that grin off his face, but Hamilton cut through our little trip down memory lane with his announcement. "Everyone, buckle up. Parker, if you would hand out the candy now?"

I wasn't sure if that was meant more literally than I was comfortable with but didn't exactly feel relieved when I realized that the medic produced a small case filled with syringes. It was rather obvious what that was about.

"Oh, hell, no," I muttered—and realized that the reason Nate was hulking at my back wasn't coincidence, or because he wanted to guard my back, but to effectively keep me from backing away. The blank look he shot me held enough warning to make me deflate before I could even work up a temper, the silent promise in there that he would hold me down and do what was necessary, whether I consented or not.

Parker ignored me, already busy with uncapping needles and ramming them into any presented neck close to him, but Hill—again—gave me a weird look. "Just your garden variety booster shot," he explained. "I thought you'd had some before?"

I forced myself to lock my muscles in place to keep from bolting. Not wanting that shit in my veins was one thing; being humiliated after being handled like a small, petulant child quite another—and my ego really didn't need that experience today.

"Yeah, and those aren't my fondest memories." Hill seemed to wait for further explanations but when none came, he was happy to get his own dose—as did the others, including Burns and Tanner.

Then it was just Nate and me, and the way Parker looked my way as if he was about to approach a rabid animal ready to bite his arm off almost made me smirk. I didn't make a move to bare the side of my neck, and neither did Parker step closer, until Nate let out a half-defeated but mostly annoyed sigh, holding his hand out to the medic. "I'll do it." I tensed, but didn't move a muscle to defend myself. It burned like hell, then burned some more, but almost immediately I felt my body kick up into a state of alertness—and that wasn't the only effect. Meanwhile, Nate got his shot as well, giving me another warning glance, likely to keep me from pulling that kidney-punching shit again. I wasn't really tempted, my intentions getting derailed in an entirely different direction. And this was decidedly not how it had been before.

"Isn't this a little, you know... distracting?" I asked no one in particular. "I mean, I get how the endorphin high would keep you going when you're a breath away from dying, but you'd think this could get the wrong kind of distracting." Hill looked at me as if I'd gone crazy—not so different than usual—but even Burns didn't seem to get what I was going for, which made me draw up short, mentally. Smirking, I looked over my shoulder at Nate, but he didn't give me anything, either—which could have been silent confirmation as well. "You'd think any of the women in your ranks might have mentioned this, but I guess not. Obviously, Zilinsky would die before she'd admit—" I cut off there, laughing softly. Yeah, that idea was hilarious—but I could totally see her charging into battle, first to hurl herself into the enemy masses, laughing wildly inside. The Ice Queen had a wicked sense of humor, just well-hidden and seldom displayed.

But I couldn't quite see Rita keeping this from Nate, particularly considering their... history.

"Is any of that supposed to make any sense, or are you just annoying as fuck on purpose?" Aimes complained.

Smiling at him now was easy, so very easy. "Maybe a little bit of both? Scratch that—lots of both. And you have no idea what you're missing." Speaking of missing, I was sorely missing a moment of privacy here but even with my pulse spiking and adrenaline eroding my common sense, I could tell that it wasn't wise to ask Bucky if we had time for me and Nate to disappear for a couple of minutes. But damnit, I needed to get my hands on another dose of that shit—for research purposes, of course.

A metallic clacking sound, followed by a low drone starting up behind the still-locked door distracted me, silence falling in the before noisy room. "That's the ventilation system," Cole needlessly confirmed. "I'd say we're ready to roll in five."

I waited for Hamilton to ooze his charm all over me but when nothing came, I had to speak up. "So how exactly are we going to do this now? I presume you'll need my iris scan to open that door, and likely a few more?"

Bucky remained silent, but thankfully, Cole had an answer. "We're trying to reactivate the access profiles right now. If we can get yours working, things would be a lot easier. Else, we'll have to make a new one, and it looks like we'll need to do that from the central console in the security station. Hell, even rewriting an existing profile would be easier." He suddenly drew up short, going as far as sitting up straight before he looked from his console to me. "Didn't you mention something about knowing his brother's access codes?"

Nate didn't react, but no one had expected him to. I shrugged. "I know Raleigh Miller's password, but it's useless without his actual eyes to scan. Iris patterns are more unique than fingerprints, so no luck with that, even if they kind of do look similar."

Cole was already shaking his head, grinning. "Yeah, we can't use that profile to get inside. But we can use it to verify activation of yours if we're lucky." His attention snapped back to the laptop, his fingers perfectly flying over the keys. "Almost got it…" he murmured to himself, then, "Code, please?"

I prattled off the sequence, feeling like it had been a million years since the last—and only—time I'd needed it, when I'd broken into the viral vault of the Green Fields Biotech hot lab.

"And your access key?"

I offered that as well. The previously unlit panel by the door flashed white for a second before a single red light started blinking at the top of it.

"Is it supposed to do that?" Red didn't look too comforting, really.

"Only one way to find out, right?" Cole was way too enthusiastic for his own good. "Step up to it. If it works, your iris scan should open the door."

"With a potential formaldehyde cloud waiting on the other side." Really, did Hamilton have to put that bug in my ear?

The asshole in question gave me a sneer as he readied his own mask, everyone else following suit. "Only one way to find out," he echoed Cole's sentiment.

Dropping the M16 onto its sling, I got my own mask ready yet kept it up on my forehead as I stepped up to the panel. Worst thing that could happen was that the scanner blinded me, right? Or set off some other security measure like spraying the room with corrosive acid or sarin gas. Or engaging built-in flame throwers. Endless possibilities!

I realized just how much the booster shot was screwing with my mind as I felt myself grinning at the idea of evading that challenge, should I have to. Sure, who needed caution if you could just accidentally kill yourself from believing you were invincible?

We didn't, it seemed.

Even though my mind blared at me that we were all going to survive this, I was still tense as I stepped up to the panel, blinking a few times to make sure my eyes were well moisturized before I stared at the scanner panel, willing it to do its thing. At first, nothing happened, yet just as I wanted to turn away and complain, I more felt than saw something cross the right side of my field of vision. Not exactly a red beam of light, but something was triggering the more sensitive bits and pieces of my freak eyes, something I likely hadn't been equipped to notice in the past.

The red light went out and flashed green once, the locks of the door disengaging with an audible "clack."

I quickly pulled my mask down and made sure that it was fastened securely, not letting in air anywhere around my face. Aimes, Wu, and Davis were the first through the door as soon as Hamilton wrenched it open, the bright beams of the flashlights fixed to their rifles lighting up the long, white corridor opening up in front of them. For a second, I had a really unhealthy kind of déjà vu as the hallway reminded me of Raynor's lair, but my mind quickly snagged on all the differences. For one, there were more doors, most of them torn off their hinges, and debris littering the floor. I'd never been so happy to see what looked like someone had rampaged through a break room.

I remained standing to the side of the door until most of the soldiers had filed through, happy to take my place toward the back. It was only a matter of time until Hamilton would need me for the next barrier he couldn't barge through, and if anything in there was actually out to get us, I'd rather it got them first. Nate seemed to subscribe to a similar doctrine as he paused next to me, waiting until I looked at his face, then down to his hands. He silently gave me the signal for "save yourself first," making me smirk under my mask. Yeah, I had zero intentions of laying down my life for this mission, scientific interest and morbid curiosity be damned.

I was a little surprised when Cole and Gita grabbed all their equipment to take inside with them. Not my place to question, and I absolutely couldn't concern myself with everything, so I simply didn't.

Hill and Tanner brought up the very rear, and into the lair of evil we went.

Chapter 12

The corridor behind the door was just that—a corridor, and not yet part of the real complex. Sure, there was a station where a security guard would have been sitting, bored out of his mind, and locker rooms for the personnel to change into their most clandestine work clothes; also a small break room—where the splintered tables and bent chairs came from that had ended up in the corridor—and doors leading to maintenance panels, but all that could have been part of any lab—or office building, really. There were no corpses—long dead or still quite active—but also no blood or remains anywhere in sight. I figured it would have been creepier if it had all been in pristine condition, but not by much. I wasn't sure what I had expected, but this was still too clean, too neat. None of the doors showed any signs of anyone trying to get out. While the one behind the scanner lock was massive enough that it wouldn't have budged, even if assaulted with said chairs or table legs, that still would have left some scratches or chipped paint. Yet something must have destroyed that furniture, and suddenly, not knowing what was a bigger concern than I could ignore.

Richards and Munez quickly checked on the locker rooms, coming back out after declaring them "clear." There were two vending machines in the break room, their glass fronts still intact, half full of snacks and sodas. The fact that nobody had tried to get to them made the destroyed furniture even more suspicious. If I'd found myself locked in here, knowing I was about to die, the least I would have done was stuff my face with candy.

As expected, Hamilton was cooling his heels at the next security door, waiting for me to work my magic—which I was reluctant to do as that gas mask was as comforting as it was uncomfortable to wear.

"Who's gonna play guinea pig?" I asked, not pointing out that until we were done here, I really wasn't expendable. I was surprised when Russell of all people—one of the few I was certain hadn't been inoculated with the serum, and hadn't received a booster shot as well—pulled his mask off, his face pinched with anticipation. We all waited with more or less bated breath. Nothing happened, until Richards did the same, experimentally sniffing the air. "Stale but could have been worse with the ventilation system on standby for so long. Not a hint of a chemical smell—or decay."

One after the other, the soldiers removed their masks but kept them on the outsides of their packs where they were easily retrieved. I waited until the absolute last moment—after getting an exasperated look from Hamilton—before I pulled mine off and stepped up to the scanner. Again, it tickled my eyes before the door locks disengaged.

On the other side, a corridor led deeper into the building, yet another one was crossing it just after one more—equally abandoned—security station. After they'd made sure that nothing lurked in the vicinity, Cole checked on the dead computer while Hill got out a spray can and, quietly humming to himself, left four arrows on the walls of the straight corridor, one on each side of the intersection, all pointing the way we had come. When he saw me watching him, he shrugged—after making sure not to inhale the fumes. "When you're on the retreat, it's easy if you don't have to guess which way is out." He then proceeded to paint two red Xs on the floor of the crossing corridor.

"Station's dead," Cole reported. "We'll have to get to the main server room. That should be on standby."

Hamilton took that with a nod. "Aimes, Wu, check left. McClintock, Williams, right. Meet up with us at the main level common area once you've secured the rooms back here." Apparently, now that we were at our objective, the asshole-in-charge was doing just that, being in charge. Red didn't seem to mind, although I got the sense that he was keeping an eye on me. Or, which was less likely, he was eyeing my ass. I preferred to think he expected me to either run off or do something exceptionally stupid. My weird mind supplied that both was easily possible at the same time.

The rest of us went down the main corridor, stopping at the few doors that were unevenly distributed along the way. The first few were offices and a library, the rest labs and the assorted rooms belonging to them. Nothing interesting, although I noted that all the machines were on the high end of state-of-the-art, even though the equipment wasn't much more complicated than you'd find at any college's basic chemistry labs. While Hamilton was moving forward, I hovered in one of the labs for a bit, randomly pulling one of the black lab journals from where they were neatly stored above a desk by the door. As I'd expected, only basic-level prep and analysis work, nothing interesting. Any lab, even the most secret, clandestine one needed the facilities where the lab monkeys mixed the buffer solutions and ran endless series of PCRs.

None of the lab spaces looked out of the ordinary, and only in a single one did I find a smashed glass bottle on the floor, likely having slid off the shelf as it had been placed too close to the edge. I had no idea if earthquakes were common here—or how the lab had been sealed off—so it really might have been a matter of gravity. Hill continued with his arrows, appearing way more relaxed than any of the others, making me wonder if that was his tell. Not that I cared. It was just something to occupy my mind with while I got more bored by the second—and really wanted to do other things than stand around and look at broken bottles.

From remembering the blueprints, I knew that we were coming close to that recreational area that Hamilton had referred to when Nate sidled up to me—or probably just took one more step than necessary. It was hard to tell. He stopped scanning the white walls and instead looked intently at my face, his gaze skipping all over before it settled on my eyes. I stared right back, widening my eyes just a little as I continued to hold his gaze. It was tremendously hard not to smile.

"Are you high?" he whispered, low enough that the mic probably wouldn't pick it up.

I shook my head, but that damn smile escaped me. "Nope. But a different word starting with 'h' comes to mind."

Steps behind us alerted me to our four explorers returning to the fold, and Aimes didn't waste a golden opportunity. "Horrendously annoying comes to mind," he offered as he pushed past us. I glared after him for a second before I looked back at Nate, pursing my lips. He was biting his, hard-pressed not to laugh. Oh, he'd definitely gotten that message. And speaking of hard—

I forced that train of thought to derail and followed the others. "I'm good. Just give me something to do and I'll be great."

"Keep that thought," Nate murmured, still amused. It was highly unusual for him to be so easy around me in situations like these, but maybe that was the lack of the burden of command. What did I know?

Up ahead, the corridor opened into a huge room, and just before that, another corridor branched off. Hamilton waited at the intersection, sending Richards and Tanner forward to check. They returned maybe a minute later, both looking strangely quiet. "It's empty," Red reported, his eyes skipping over the lot of us, evaluating. "But I wouldn't necessarily call it 'clear.' No hostiles."

Hamilton set four people to guard the intersection and had the rest of us move forward. At first, I didn't get Red's cryptic remark, but then we got deep enough into the room to see the opposite wall—and the massive, dark splatters on it. I couldn't see any bullet holes—and the dried blood looked more like it had sprayed in arcs rather than the patterns exit wounds might have caused—but it was impossible to deny that these were signs of violence. Instantly, everyone seemed more alert, their motions more precise, eyes never stopping as they roamed over every available surface. There were no other signs of disturbance; not even one of the sofas or chairs was misaligned. Or so I thought, until I looked up to where the upper floor ended in a room-spanning balcony, and noticed that a single ceiling panel wasn't quite matching up. Probably whatever had smashed that bottle in the lab had been responsible for that as well, I told myself. Hell, if I hadn't had my own adventure of crawling through ducts, I never would have noticed. But I did notice, and there was no ignoring it now.

Once the room was secure, Hamilton sent a few teams of two to check on the two corridors that led away from the area—one to the more interesting labs, the other to the animal facility—and set a guard at the stairs to the upper level. As soon as they got the okay, Cole and Gita scurried into the first room on the right on the animal facility branch—the main server room, as Cole explained.

And three minutes and a whoop later, the emergency lighting came on, green signs glowing ominously along the corridors. It hurt my eyes a lot less than the bright flashlights and let me see more of the upper floor—and the ceiling, with the dislodged panel.

Nate flicked me an inquiring question with his fingers, finding what irked me himself when I pointedly stared at the upper corner of the room. There must have been barely enough light for him to see without shining his light directly at the panel, but he gave the slightest of nods as he looked in my direction once more. He didn't really look concerned but also didn't tell me to forget about it.

With nothing else to do, I followed Hamilton when he walked into the server room, finding Cole and Gita quite busy in there. I'd expected a small room, crammed top to bottom with hardware, but the space was easily as large as the recreational area outside, and warm enough that I felt sweat bead on my forehead within a minute. Gita had already shirked her jacket, and Cole looked like he wanted to yet was too busy typing to bother. One of these days I had to ask him how he'd acquired those skills, and not ended up working for a Fortune 500 tech giant instead of Special Ops.

"So nobody's going to mention that huge blood splatter out there, eh?" I drawled, mostly to amuse myself than expecting a reply. "And still no bodies. Doesn't look good."

Cole ignored me, and so did Hamilton. Too bad.

"Do you have access to the security logs yet?" Hamilton wanted to know.

"Just a sec," Gita mumbled, hammering away at the keyboard of one of the resident workstations. "Got them right here." She briefly scanned the many, many lines appearing on screen. "Pretty much matches the info you already got. The shutdown sequence was started at 3:49 in the afternoon. No further entries after that, except the automatic switch to standby once power failed two months later and nobody manually disengaged it. The next entry is us hacking into the system." She briefly glanced at Cole. "We should probably delete that."

"Too much work," Cole muttered. "Just leave it."

I studied the entries before the ones she'd indicated. "Do they log every single access?"

Gita hesitated, as if asking permission from Hamilton. "That's the main system log. It's admin level entries plus who passes through the outer door by the elevator."

"So nobody left after the shutdown?" She nodded at my observation. "Anyone leave just before that?"

"Not in the last six hours leading up to the shutdown," she noted. "But that doesn't seem unusual. I briefly checked the days before that. Almost nobody left during the day, and most stayed for ten hours minimum. If you consider the decontamination protocols, it wouldn't make much sense to just drop by for an hour or two."

I was burning to tell her that I was very aware of that myself from years of practice but swallowed the remark. "How many people were here the day of the shutdown?"

Another window went up, more endless lines and columns. "A hundred and thirty-eight," Gita reported, then hesitated. "Plus twenty-one in the other wing."

"Other wing?" Nate inquired from beside me.

I gave him the answer with a fake grin hurting my facial muscles. "Bipedal animals, you could say. They actually housed them in the animal wing. No kidding."

Looking at the numbers once more, I quickly did the math. "So that's, what? How many calories does the average human body have? Let's say we have a more sedentary lifestyle than the average population, and a few fitness freaks to balance that out. How many supercharged zombies can one hundred forty snack boxes feed for twenty-one months? Plus some lab animals as well, I guess. I don't think they would have ignored a less savory snack after a week or two."

Hamilton gave me a level stare that was dripping with condescension. "You done with that nonsense?"

I now beamed that same smile at him that Nate had gotten before. "Just calling it as I see it. No sense in deluding ourselves that we're not the second helping. Or how else do you explain that we've been down here for half an hour and checked on a good tenth of the facility and we've found not a single sign of any of those one hundred and thirty-eight bodies? They must have ended up somewhere."

Sadly, my keen observation went ignored, Hamilton instead turning to the screen Cole had pulled up. "Those are the secured doors?" It was a neat diagram with lots of green lines, only the two we had traipsed through glowing red since we'd kept them propped open.

"All others still locked," Cole reported. "Any I should disengage?"

Nate cleared his throat, not bothering with checking the data. "I wouldn't. The great thing about a door that locks is that you can slam it shut. Unless you want to set up some kill zones, I'd leave them to manual operation."

"Gee, so I'm the only one who can go wherever the fuck she pleases?" I summed that up. "Neat."

Nate and Bucky had their momentary staring match going on until the idiot-in-charge inclined his head. "Keep the doors locked. Except for these two." He pointed at a spot next to the animal facilities.

"Why, wanna make it extra easy for them to get us?" I jeered, but only got a flat stare back.

"You have your tasks. I have mine," Hamilton offered, a hint of nastiness in his tone as if the fact that I wasn't in the know would drive me crazy. Well, it just might, but I did my best to stomp down on the instantly sparked curiosity. But what I couldn't prevent was me taking a step toward him, thus invading his zone of privacy, which forced me to look up way past what was comfortable, but there was no avoiding that.

"Good. Because you don't really know what mine are, do you?" He continued to smirk at me but I didn't miss the hint of doubt that crossed his face, making me grin. "And you don't, trust me," I continued. No idea why I was yanking his chain, but I wasn't in the mood to hold back now.

"I do," he insisted, putting extra emphasis in his claim—and leaning closer so that his elbow brushed my arms where they were crossed over my chest, as if that would intimidate me. I briefly considered turning this into a real physical altercation but the rules of our previous encounters were still true, the booster making me stupidly aware of shit or not. He was taller and heavier, and had reach and number of fingers on me. Too bad, really.

"You don't," I disagreed. "Or did you listen in to the entire time Raynor cut me up and put me back together? I know for a fact you didn't, else you would have stormed into that room and beat her up, I'm sure. Or in the hangar, when you held your little speech—did you follow the conversation she had with me and Gita? You didn't. So, yes—I can't look into your cards but you also can't look into mine. And considering I'm the only one in here who understands what she's dealing with, that puts me miles ahead of you."

"So what?" Bucky jeered, slowly getting his groove back, yet the fact that I'd gotten under his skin, even for a second, made me feel terribly vindicated. "It's not like you can actively do anything with that knowledge."

"I can't?" I posed the logical hypothetical question. "I can grab the newest version of the serum they've been developing—or whatever else they've been researching—and inoculate myself with it. That's such a fancy word, now, isn't it? Simply swallowing it will do the trick. And I even got my backup here with me should one dose not be enough." I took a moment to pause and look dramatically at Nate over my left shoulder before focusing on Bucky once more. "You still think they'd waste a dose of the updated serum on him just so you can pull your little mind control stunt? Oh, please, don't be so naive. You know just how much each dose of the stable serum is worth. Enough to fund this entire mission, waste so many resources, and possibly so many people that cannot be replaced. And you know that Raynor can't stand you. So why should she trust you?"

Sadly, no more doubt followed but I hadn't really expected to get a second hit in. "Isn't it the opposite of smart for you to tell me that now?" Hamilton drawled. "You're bluffing."

"Maybe I am," I conceded. "Or maybe I'm telling you so you think I'm bluffing while I'm really not. Maybe someone else is going to do it? Who knows? How sure can you be about everyone's—" and I meant Richards with that, obviously "— loyalties? So many possibilities, and only three and a half more hours to waste. Tick, tock. What are you gonna do about it, Bucky?"

He didn't give me the satisfaction of reacting to his nickname that he loved as much as I did the one he'd pinned on me, but I could tell that he didn't know for sure if he hadn't misjudged me. A stupid move of me, and one that I couldn't explain why I'd felt driven to go for it, but hey. What could possibly go wrong?

What he settled on saying was a semi-grumbled, "You have your tasks, I have mine. We both should get going."

Before I could reply, Cole interrupted our grandstanding conversation. "I got the camera feeds up, if anyone's interested? Only from inside the BSL-4 cocoon, the others are fried for good. But it's better than nothing."

I pointedly continued our staring match for another second before I broke eye contact so I could round the desk and look at the display Cole was pointing at. Everything looked like it was supposed to, I realized after a moment of dreadful anticipation. After all, we'd been breathing that air for thirty minutes now—too late for any measures to save us, and nothing I could have done about it in the first place; but security was security.

"Does the decontamination system still work?" I asked as I continued to check what I could see of the rooms as the camera feeds cycled through them every few seconds.

"Check on the lab," Cole reported, looking at a different display. "And on the decontamination showers, too. All systems green, and zero breach attempts." Since the other logs had said the same, I wasn't terribly comforted by that last statement, but it was something.

Looking at Hamilton, I considered. "We do whatever each of us has to do next, and then we go in there, I presume?"

"Correct."

"So I have, what? An hour until then?"

Hamilton checked his watch. "One hour and twenty minutes. We go into the hot lab at exactly two hours after breach."

I didn't ask whether he'd calculated the insane amount of prep work we'd have to do, but figured that was his problem, not mine. And we did have those extra forty-five minutes on top of the four hours, if push came to shove. "Great. Can you engage the decon cycle from here? And when was the last one?"

Cole nodded. "I can, and just over three hours ago. Next one is scheduled in nine hours." He paused. "Isn't that a little paranoid even for you?"

I shrugged. "If it's my life on the line, I like everything as squeaky clean as I can have it." Casting another sidelong glance at Hamilton, I patted Cole's shoulder. "Run the cycle. I'm not going to be the one who breaks his neck slipping in a puddle of formaldehyde."

I didn't wait for Hamilton to add anything to that as I walked out of the room, Nate following me, a slight smile playing around his lips. I rolled my eyes at him, as if he was the petty one. Burns was waiting for us outside, clearly having watched the spectacle from there, next to Richards, Munez, and Davis. "I presume you're coming with me to search through Dr. Andrada's office?"

Red nodded. "And the other two scientists' as well," he reminded me. "That is, if you're done here?"

"Quite."

Although we knew exactly where we were headed, Richards and Nate still checked on the blueprints once more before we set out, me and Burns trailing behind the others. As soon as we were at the top of the stairs leading to the upper floor and outside of the downstairs view, I let go of the relaxed demeanor I'd tried so hard to keep going, letting my body snap to full alertness. The chuckle coming from behind me let me know that Burns had noticed the difference. Well, good for him.

With only six people, it was impossible to secure the corridors and offices as we passed them, but since the space here was only reaching as far as the area we'd passed down below, not the wings to the sides, it was less of a worry than it could have been. I still strained my ears for any sounds coming from anywhere that weren't caused by us, but the echoey hallways remained unremarkably so. Within ten minutes, we'd made a quick tour through the entire area and returned to door number 312—Dr. Rosamie Andrada's office.

Nate did a quick sweep before he let me in—not much work seeing as it was just a desk, a chair, a cupboard, and all available wall space filled with shelves, no place to hide for anything that was larger than a mouse. It wasn't even a large office as those went, making me guess that she'd been a junior among the senior scientists. There were a few personal items, among them a photograph of a large, beige dog, but everything screamed professional and tidy.

I didn't even check on the laptop, simply signaled Richards to pack it up. Her lab journals were next, but after the third I checked I shook my head. "We won't find anything in there that's not typed up if it's important. That's all the official documentation, and you already have that." I still rifled through two more in another section, then turned to Davis, who was trying to pay attention but seemed really bored. "Can you look all these over? Just check if you find anything out of the ordinary, like a piece of paper that doesn't belong, or whatnot."

"Think she hid something in there, in plain sight?" Davis guessed, already setting to the task.

"Got anything better to do?" I asked, then turned to the others. "Do the same with her books. We have another hour, and this is the best place around." Then I turned to Red and silently pointed at my mic before giving a questioning shrug. He considered, raising three fingers—switch to channel three. Munez and Davis looked puzzled at the order but did so just as Nate, Burns, and I did. There was still a chance someone might be listening in, and we'd get the general alerts on the main frequency, but I didn't need to make it easy for Hamilton. The fact that we hadn't heard a peep from him and the others made it obvious that they were doing the same thing, only with a different frequency.

"What do you hope to find, anyway?" Richards asked as I started going through the things filed away on top of the desk.

"I'll know it when I see it," I replied, mostly focused on my work. "Not sure there is anything to find here. Her home address would make a lot more sense for anything she might have wanted to hide from the powers that be."

I checked the desk drawers next, but again, nothing. The only moderately interesting item I came across was a bottle of ink, which made me laugh for the simple fact that it must have been the most useless item in the entire post-apocalyptic world. Fucking ink! Richards meanwhile poked around the cupboard where I could see more files neatly put away. I wondered how a woman that pedantic had dealt with dog hairs.

"That's old school," Red muttered, making me look up from my drawer.

"Say what?"

He held up a bundle of envelopes. "Letters. Actual handwritten letters. I didn't know anyone did that anymore."

I shrugged, not quite sure what to respond. The only remarkable thing about them was that she'd stashed them in her office, but considering the work hours she must have kept, she'd probably not had time for private correspondence at home. Unless…

"Who are they from?"

"Doesn't say," Richards offered after checking the envelopes, then went as far as pulling one out and scanning it. "Signature says, 'Lee.'"

I was ready to forget all about that but Nate suddenly stepped up to Red, looking at the letter in his hand. "That's my brother's handwriting."

I immediately dropped the inventory note I had been looking over and joined them. "You sure?" I asked quite needlessly. Raleigh. Lee. Close enough, and you'd think that Nate would recognize his brother's scrawl. Or penmanship, rather, I corrected myself as I got a glimpse at the letter. I couldn't have written anything that curly and plain legible if I'd tried. "What does it say?"

Nate continued to read the letter while Red started on a new one, leaving the rest of the envelopes on the cupboard. I pulled another one out, checking the date first—a few months before Raleigh Miller's untimely death. This could be good. Like really good...

Only that it wasn't.

"What the fuck is this? Some kind of code?" I asked as I finished the first page—of six. It read like a school assignment, What I Did In My Summer Holidays, only way more boring because Miller hadn't been on vacation. He didn't even passingly mention his work, or anything else that might have been remotely interesting to us. And it wasn't a love letter, either, the only other valid option that came to mind.

Nate shrugged, frustrated himself. "No fucking clue. If it is, I don't think we can decipher it."

Grunting, I put the letter back, ready to continue searching... but then paused. Something tickled my mind. Something... I'd seen. Just where? And when?

"Gah, I hate this," I muttered, looking around mostly to distract myself, hoping to jump-start my memory this way.

"Life in general, or just working with people you can't stand, to accomplish something you don't believe in?" Richards snidely observed.

He got a brief, sweet smile for his trouble but I talked to Nate instead. If anyone could jog my memory, it would be him. "Do you ever feel like if you could just concentrate hard enough, you'd remember something you really needed to know?" Far be it from me to hope that the reply I had coming for that nonsense would help.

Only that, for once in my life, he didn't make fun of me for waxing platitudes but instead looked at me with interest. "Booster."

"Huh?"

"Cognitive enhancement can be a side effect of the booster," Nate explained. "If you feel like your mind's going off on something, it probably is." He glanced at the letter I'd just dropped. "Anything you read in there?"

I shook my head. "No, it wasn't connected to the contents. Just in general. Like—"

I glanced at the desk, but to no avail. It wasn't like that cursed woman had left anything out there that could be inspiring, except for those two fancy pens she'd likely written her responses in—

"The ink!" I called out, already making a dive for the bottom drawer. Seconds later I resurfaced, a triumphant smile on my face. "Anyone got any blacklight? I'm sure I saw it in the logistics files at the destroyer for the decontamination protocol in case of getting mauled by something untoward." Which was exactly what had happened with Rodriguez—and what the French had done when they'd scanned us for injuries.

Richards held out a small stick to me that he fished out of a pocket in his pants. "Here."

Grinning, I picked up one of the letters and switched the light on. Nothing—until I turned it over, and the seemingly blank backside of the page was covered in softly glowing script. I only needed to read over two lines to know that I'd hit gold. "Gotcha."

Nate and Red both craned their necks to see. Even to the uninitiated, the mention of "virus" and "serum" was a dead giveaway, as were the experimental setup conditions that followed. I started reading the letter from the top, more slowly this time to try to commit the contents to memory. Hey, if my mind was running at one hundred and twenty percent right now, I was getting the most out of that for sure.

Davis seemed absolutely flashed by my congeniality. "How the fuck did you get the idea that anyone would write with invisible ink?"

I shrugged, not quite sure how to explain. "She had two pens. There's only one bottle of ink in her drawer. Made me wonder with what she'd inked the other pen."

"She could have simply liked the color."

"Dumb luck, I guess." I couldn't help but laugh. "That got me this far. Not going to let that hold me back now."

While I continued reading the letters, Nate and Red got busy sorting them by date, and handing me the next one as soon as I finished the one I was occupied with. The earliest dated back almost three years before Raleigh's death, and they had made quite a lot of progress—if not quite in the direction I'd expected.

I didn't even notice that I had started rubbing my side absentmindedly with my free hand until Nate's grunted, "Just don't," made me look up, confused. He caught my gaze, perfectly scowling. "Don't," he repeated. "The booster will start screwing with your mind if you key up but don't have anything to burn off the adrenaline. Might be scintillating reading material but not that scintillating."

I ignored him with a slight snort to myself—but dropped my hand to my side instead. My foot started tapping a few seconds later of its own account, and I realized that I was now rubbing my left thigh where the massive scar tissue from the zombie bites was, with the titanium parts that kept my femur together right underneath.

Red noticed, prompted by our conversation, no doubt. "Are you always this hyper when you're physically inactive?"

Snorting, I shook my head. "Still not the h-word I'd be using." So much for that. Back to reading.

Everyone was looking at me expectantly as I finished the last page, my mind churning with possibilities. "And?" Richards asked simply, but I was sure he was ready to wring my neck if I didn't spit it out the very next second.

"They didn't find a cure," I offered, choosing the simplest version first. "But they were close to finalizing a version of the serum that came with most of the benefits yet without the final conversion." I paused, tempted to keep my trap shut, but then barfed up the rest. "They also managed to, accidentally for the most part, generate a super-charged version."

Davis snorted at the face I was making. "You say that like it's a bad thing."

"None of the subjects they tested it on survived past sixty hours post inoculation," I explained. "And they all went crazy way before that. Not really a good trade if you ask me."

I got several solemn nods for that. Nate latched on to a different part of my statement. "I take it they didn't test it on rats?"

I shook my head, grimacing. "Five test subjects, five negative results. There's also a side note that makes me guess that they kept them afterward and put them in a single cell and watched which one would be the sole survivor, if you want to call it that. Number three, if you were wondering."

"That means—" Red started, but I finished for him before he could.

"That means that whoever was running this facility was very aware of the trials, and likely also the materials used and took samples. There's a chance that none of that made it out of this facility, but it's not something that remained between Miller and Andrada. Hell, part of that could be the reason why it's possible that we convert if you get in contact with the original activated virus. I also have no clue what she did after Miller died. I'd love to believe that she continued trying to hunt for a cure but the fact that they turned it all into a deathmatch makes me think that whoever funded this was way more interested in weaponizing it. Without the human trials, they might have kept this on the down-low, but not like this." And who knew who else was aware of this? After all, Bucky had pretty much told me to my face that I didn't know everything about what he was here to get.

Maybe I would do the world a favor if I somehow managed to shut us all in here and drowned us in peroxide and formaldehyde? The answer was likely a resounding "yes."

Richards looked less disturbed than was good for my psyche. Nate gave me a considering look that let me know he was considering where to plant the explosives, right on track with my own reasoning. Burns tried hard to pretend he wasn't considering the ramifications but the way he kept inching toward the door made it obvious that it only took a breath from me or Nate, and he'd help us do away with the other three to enact whatever plan we were hedging.

"So not exactly good news?" Red summed up what I'd said.

"It's not all bad," I admitted. "Actually, I think they were closer to finding the cure than they thought. I'd need to check her notes—if they are on that laptop—but I think that Miller was right with his initial assessment."

"Which is?" Finally, a thread of exasperation appeared in Richards's voice. So he was human after all.

I shrugged, but there was no sense denying it—and who knew, maybe this would turn into an extension of my lease on life? "That if he hired me, I'd be able to fit that last missing piece into their puzzle." That sounded way less modest than it had in my head, making me smirk. "I'm not blowing my own horn. They both were experts in their own fields. I was beginning to be one in mine. Miller never confirmed it, but I got the job offer from Green Fields Biotech after I'd shared the later stages of my thesis with him—sounds realistic that he figured my knowledge could complement theirs."

"But you can't tell right now what's missing," Red stressed.

I couldn't help but cock my head to the side and regard him suspiciously. "And I probably wouldn't tell you if I did. Not as long as we're pretty much stranded in the middle of a shambler nightmare on the other side of the world. But I'm feeling generous right now so here's an honest answer: Not right now, but I have some ideas from the notes Hamilton gave me to go over when we stayed with the French. And right there in these letters are a few more clues, ones that are missing from her official notes. Given enough time, I might come up with some theories. One of them might just be the one."

Richards nodded, ignoring how exactly I phrased my answer, talking in suggestions rather than absolutes. He looked at the stack of letters next, considering.

"Are you going to take them to Emily? I'm sure she'd be extra nice to you if you dropped those in her lap," I cooed.

I got a look that was shy of an attempt on my life for that—almost worthy of Nate but not quite getting there—but Richards finally grabbed the letters to store them away in his pack. "I'm sure that Dr. Raynor will appreciate getting a look at them," he agreed, very levelly.

"Oh, come on! I've been horny as fuck because of that damn booster you shot me up with. The least you owe me is no more bullshit like that. We all know you two are a thing. No worries, nobody's gonna judge you for having a thing for strong, older women who could eat you for dinner if they wanted to."

If I'd sprouted a second head, Richards would have looked less taken aback. Nate allowed himself the hint of a grin but gave me a warning look, silently telling me that Red wasn't necessarily the one I should antagonize. Burns was grinning outright, and Munez had a hard time not choking on his chuckle. Davis bit back a bark of laughter before turning to Burns. "Is she always like that? Because I'm starting to feel like I've missed out on a lot since deciding not to go with you bunch of idiots." He had been one of Nate's guys for his mission to avenge his brother but had decided to throw his lot in with Bucky when given the choice.

Burns was only too happy to enlighten him about his loss. "Pretty much. She usually doesn't accept anyone's authority, but that's Miller's fault—he pretty much beat his standards into her, and more often than not he can't hold to that himself. She doesn't accept authority, and don't even think about pulling rank on her. I'm not sure she even has a clue how ranks and hierarchy work."

There, I had to interject. "I'd think twice before antagonizing Zilinsky."

Burns guffawed. "Yeah, because you're not suicidal, and she's as much of a role model for ruthless behavior as you're ever going to accept." No objection there, so Burns turned back to Davis. "Usually, it's pretty fun. Until some asshole or another gets cute and abducts and locks her up, and then it's all bloody murder on the warpath."

Again, I couldn't let that slide. "That wasn't entirely my idea, either," I pointed out. "And I didn't hear any of you big, strong men object."

Burns shrugged as if that was all the same to him, continuing with, "Actually, I don't remember the last time she was as agreeable as she is nowadays. Might even go as far as saying that I don't quite buy it, but hey, I could be wrong. She can be a highly reasonable, logic-driven woman. And it's not like someone shot her up with a chemical cocktail that's been known to give her delusions of grandeur and gets the adrenaline junkie in her to take over the steering wheel. Then again, Lewis without a filter is always worth it, so I say, who cares if we're all going to die down here. At least we'll do so laughing."

Davis looked more concerned than I'd expected. "Don't worry," I told him. "I'm sure that Hamilton was well aware of any side effects. Well, not all of them, but those that I've openly exhibited in the past. But he must have reasoned that it's all the same and he needs every ounce of strength any of us can muster so anyone will survive what's coming for us, so it's all good."

His eyes only got wider. "Do you know something the rest of us don't?" Munez and Richards had mostly listened in silently until now, but that question made them look up sharply. Nate himself seemed a little disturbed, which made me want to laugh him in the face. Did no one ever listen to me?

"Know? No. But didn't you just hear me tell you about the experiments they do down here? I don't know for a fact—because how could I?—but I'm telling you, they had some other experiments going on when they shut down the facility, or they started a last round just for the hell of it, and the test subjects of those experiments are still very much alive. They must be really, really hungry by now, even if they went after each other. Every single shambler we've encountered out there has been a pack hunter, and those super freaks they've created will be, too. They are hungry, and they've culled down their pack to the strongest ones, and the moment we let our guard down, they will be coming for us. The only question is, will any of us survive so I can tell you that I told you so?" And just for a second, I was sure that he believed me.

Richards cleared his throat, making all of us look at him. "Paranoia's also among her strongest character traits," he observed.

I smiled, letting all of them make of that what they wished.

Red seemed poised to say more but then tensed, not reaching up to his ear like people did in bad movies, but it was obvious that he'd gotten a message over his com. I hadn't, and from what I could tell, neither had the others. "Why do they have a command frequency and we're not on it?" I harped in Nate's general direction.

"Because we're not in command," he repeated the statement that Bucky so loved to rub in my face, his voice flat.

My possible answer got cut off when Richards reported, his eyes straying to me for a second, "No, we didn't find anything, just a laptop." Pause. "We're about done here. Proceeding to the other offices now." Another pause. "Copy."

I waited until Richards looked to me once more before I observed, "My, my. Lying to our most esteemed leader. I wonder what he'd think of that if he knew?" Then I turned around and gave Burns a nod. "Lead the way, big guy. If you want to keep laughing your ass off at my shenanigans, you better keep me alive."

"Yes, ma'am," Burns offered with a huge grin but his attention was already on the corridor outside—and I didn't miss that he not only checked twice, but also looked at the ceiling far longer than he had on the way over here.

Well, here was hoping that I was really only rocking a tad too much paranoia—but I really didn't think so. And damnit, I'd hate to be right this time.

Chapter 13

As expected, the offices of Drs. Nakamuri and Dale were a bust, but at least they were close to the common area in the level below so we didn't have far to go once the order came to haul ass there. I didn't bother asking what Hamilton and his group had been up to in the meantime although I was burning to know. My body was singing with the need to burn off some energy any way possible, but physically attacking that asshole to try to beat the answer out of him didn't seem wise—not even now when I felt like my chances were five percent higher than before at managing the feat. Not for winning, but doing some real damage.

That still didn't mean that I was looking forward to what was next on our agenda.

But first, a detour to the bioreactors.

"Do we have any confirmation yet why the lab shut down?" I asked Hamilton as I followed him down the corridor leading toward the labs, but taking a straight at the intersection where the left turn would have brought us to the security checkpoint behind where the more interesting labs were. Someone had already gotten busy spraying arrows and Xs all over the hallway, and it felt just a little foreboding that we stepped over one of the "no go" signs.

Hamilton didn't deign to look my way as he shook his head. "Cole is still trying to recover some backup files. He said the primary logs have become corrupted."

"Or someone deleted them, manually," I opined.

Now I did get a sidelong glance. "You mean your super-juiced experimental lab monkeys who are about to eat us alive?"

I wondered who else had been listening in to our conversations in that doctor's office—or whether Munez or Davis had tattled on me. Munez, probably; Davis had looked sincere in the slight regret he'd shown when he'd asked about my usual MO. That alone wouldn't have been enough to chalk him up as still sympathetic to Nate—and us, by extension—but it had only been the latest moment in a string of more moments, going on Burns's assessment. I still didn't quite understand why he had started trying to judge the soldiers' reactions to us—knowing their allegiance was nice, sure, but wouldn't make a difference in the end.

"Very funny," I grumbled, then went on, artificially upbeat. "Or it could have been those eco warrior terrorists who, you know, kicked off the zombie apocalypse two weeks later, yay! Would make sense that they cleaned up after themselves, including deleting all data on the central servers. Might also explain what happened to any dead bodies in here. I don't think they would have left anyone alive."

Hamilton was still smirking—of course he didn't believe me. "And not leave the bodies for the super-juiced experimental lab monkeys to dispose of them?"

"Well," I started, considering. "They could have managed to delete the files, and then gotten killed. Sounds like a good compromise to me."

"Will you finally shut up if a super-juiced freak comes charging at you?"

I considered that for a second. "I'll likely scream like a girl when that happens."

"When," Hamilton echoed, derision dripping from his voice.

"Yes, when," I repeated. "Do I get a cookie when that happens? One of those contaminated, sugary ones?"

Hamilton left it at a grunt, but I could tell that he wasn't taking me seriously. Nothing I could do about that, but since we were at the security checkpoint for the bioreactors, I had other things to do, like let my eyes be tickled once again.

"I think I was wrong," I mused as I waited for Munez, Davis, and Russell to clear the corridor up ahead. "I don't think we'll find anything useful left over in the tanks." That Bucky didn't jeer right in my face kind of underlined my guess. "I mean, there's no evidence that anyone breached or took over this lab. And I don't quite see how they could have gotten anything out after it was sealed. So the contents of the tanks are likely whatever's in the log. But then you knew this already, didn't you?"

Hamilton regarded me evenly before he extended a hand toward the door. "After you."

While the others filed out and checked for any hostiles, I went over to the terminal by the door to check the—bona fide paper—logbook. As I'd expected, all three tanks had been full of yeast, doing... yeasty things. I couldn't make sense of the designations of the strains and what they had been producing but one thing was obvious at a glance—this had nothing whatsoever to do with our objective. When I told Hamilton as much, I got a raised eyebrow from him. "And you're sure about that?"

I nodded. "They were likely producing large-scale stuff for other experiments in here. What we're looking for is all viral. I can, of course, waste half an hour to get into a suit and directly check on what's in those tanks, but that's thirty minutes of time we'll be missing for whatever is actually your primary objective. You only went in here to humor me, didn't you?"

The look on his face was surprisingly unreadable, but for once not hostile. "Negative confirmation is still confirmation," he said rather cryptically. "We need to make sure."

I was burning to object, but instead went on the com. "Cole? Does the bioreactor lab have electricity?"

A few seconds later I got confirmation. "All systems are on standby or down, and there's an entire log full of warnings, but everything is still operational."

I nodded, mostly to myself, and went over to the other workstation by the window that, were the lights inside switched on, would let us see the massive steel tanks in their level-spanning space. It took several minutes for the station to boot up, and a few more for the system to be operational. Then it was just a few clicks and some mechanical whines that made everyone currently lazing around really alarmed, and my work was done. Grabbing a plastic bag from besides the station, I went over to where the automated system had deposited the three 50ml samples full of what looked like puke, containing the long-overgrown and dead yeast cultures that had last been cultivated in the tanks. Hamilton looked at me weirdly as I handed the bag to him. "What, disappointed that I didn't have to strip naked? Here are your samples. I wouldn't open them outside of a containment box. That shit will stink to high heaven, but it's likely safe."

"Likely?" Munez, next to Hamilton, asked, highly concerned.

"Well, there's flesh-eating yeasts as well, but from the log those should all be your garden variety lab yeast. You could also use it to brew beer or bake a cake, but I wouldn't use that batch." I glanced at the bag that was right now disappearing into Hamilton's pack.

Done—and still not giving me an answer—Hamilton called everyone back who wasn't already securing the endless maze of corridors between the single labs. They were all biosafety levels one and two out there so minimal barriers—for anything moving in there on two legs. I lingered at the log for another moment, quickly checking on the previous entries but—of course—finding nothing suspicious. This was getting weirder and weirder by the moment, and that was ignoring the blood splatters outside and the general state the facility was in. Something was wrong here, and I absolutely didn't want to find out what.

We retraced our steps to the last intersection before we turned toward the BSL-4 labs. The sample collection had taken just over twenty minutes—plenty of time for ten people to make sure nothing was lurking in the roughly fifty rooms around three hallways, the central one being that of the most interest to us now. It looked just like the others; the security station at the end of it did not. It was a three-component checkpoint that needed not just my iris scan but also a manual override from the local console, and some five-minute server-side magic Gita finally managed to pull off. I tried to remain outwardly calm but couldn't keep my pulse from picking up as we stepped into the airlock. This was it—the reason why we were here. One of the last remaining treasure troves of scientific advancement. Potentially, the keys to the kingdom. Then why did a part of me pray that what we'd come here to fetch simply didn't exist?

The locks finally disengaged and let us pass into the blast-proof shell that the high security labs were situated in. It was an eerie sensation walking into a setup that was so familiar that it gave my heart a pang—and that was even before the lights suddenly came on and revealed that they'd even used the same tiles here as in the Green Fields biotech hot labs that Nate and I had ended up destroying. It didn't have the same layout as the labs here were a good four times larger, but still. This was what I'd trained years for to do—and now it made me want to vomit and run, but not for the reasons similar sentiments had been haunting me the last time I'd donned a positive pressure suit. Back then I'd been afraid because I'd almost accidentally killed myself in the lab. Now it was a deep-seated knowledge that I didn't belong here anymore—and never would again. Those endless hours on that operating room table had sealed that deal forever. I'd been aware of this, and until now I, quite frankly, hadn't given a fuck about it. But seeing that door with the changing rooms behind it, and beyond that the room where the suits were kept by the decontamination shower made it impossible to ignore.

And I really didn't care for how much it hurt.

It was easy to hide my feelings behind the comfort of my usual display of misgivings toward Hamilton as the others swarmed out to secure the wing. There were maintenance rooms, a small break room, and offices to secure, and guards to post outside the security station as well once they realized that our coms didn't work well inside the cocoon of concrete and steel that was built to ensure that no earthquake or nuclear hit topside would let anything escape down here. Hamilton was busy shooing his people around but Richards was watching me intently—analyzing me, I realized. Just what I needed. Turning my back on him, I caught Nate's gaze when he returned from securing the offices, and gave him a quick, "this sucks!" hand signal. I'd expected scorn but got a heartfelt, "I know," from him, judging from how he glared at Hamilton's back. We all had our burdens to carry—and it was about time I shirked mine.

"Any chance you'll let me do that on my own?" I asked Hamilton when he returned his attention to me.

Rather than answer me, he nodded at the door to the labs. "Get on with it."

To the absolute surprise of no one, he and Richards followed me inside while the rest waited in the hallway by the connective corridor where viewing windows let them see into three of the rooms inside the lab. I didn't bother with being modest or circumspect as I dropped my weapons and pack in one corner of the changing room and set to peeling myself out of my many layers. I didn't check if either of the two idiots was ogling me, and neither did I care. A tiny part of me was revolting that I didn't go looking for scrubs to change into; I didn't intend to strip down to my skin, also not on the way back out. The spacesuit would do its thing, and that was enough—or so I prayed. Stripping down left me in a tank top, thermal leggings, and socks. I couldn't bring my com unit with me, either, not that it would have done me any good in here. I hated how disconnected from the others that made me feel. That I hadn't expected, but nothing I could do about that now. I barely checked to see that the men were also down to their long johns before I stalked into the next room, hunting for the positive pressure suits. The bright lights were making my eyes tear up but that wasn't why I was gnashing my teeth. This was wrong. Just plain wrong.

"I presume you expect me to do all the prep work?" I called out as I grabbed some gloves, absolutely hating how there was no way to make them fit on my hands.

"We'd be much obliged," Bucky drawled behind me, following me into the prep room. He was carrying a huge steel canister that I hadn't seen before but must have been hidden in his pack. Richards dragged in a second. I guessed they were for sample storage. Judging from their size, they'd easily hold hundreds of the small tubes currently stored in liquid nitrogen. The very idea how much destruction those could yield made my mouth dry up. I'd never have agreed to help Nate if he'd attempted something like this. Yet here I was, and I wasn't even going to get a good fuck out of this—but I was sure that, somehow, I'd end up getting screwed.

I didn't explain—or talk at all—as I meticulously went through the motions of selecting and prepping three of the positive pressure suits. My brain still remembered all the steps but my body had forgotten half of them, and had issues with a few more. It took me a good twenty minutes but Hamilton for once held his tongue, letting me concentrate. I considered sabotaging his suit but wouldn't put it past him to force me to take that one instead, so I didn't. Really, if I killed him I wanted it to be with a knife or a gun, not gear failure. Then it was time to don the suits after taping our gloves on—which Red helped me with—and get into the boots. While I waited for the others to be done, I looked at the viewing window, finding Nate waiting right outside, watching me mutely, a look of quiet confidence in his eyes that I knew he wanted me to see. "You got this," it said. Also, "don't do anything stupid." Oh well. Time would tell which of that was good advice.

And then I was all out of excuses and tasks to do, and after a last check that my suit was working, feeling the air from the connected hose caress my sweaty body, I disconnected the line and slowly walked into the lab proper, Hamilton and Richards following with their containers.

More than any other part of the facility, I'd memorized the floor plans of the hot lab, so I knew where to turn to. The security feeds hadn't shown any disturbances inside but I was still surprised that neither of my two burdens chose to bring a gun with them. I felt naked and exposed without a weapon but I knew that in here was likely the safest place on the entire earth—at least as long as I stayed in my suit. That would even withstand the next decontamination cycle easily. The air from the connective hoses tasted as it should— clean with a hint of something chemical—proving that the HVAC system was still doing what it was supposed to do, and likely would do for another year. If I wouldn't have starved to death within five days or so, I could have stayed in here forever.

We had to make our way through seven rooms until we got to the vault where the storage tanks waited, requiring a code. As in the past, I used Raleigh Miller's code—my birthday—again feeling weirdly sentimental. That nobody had deactivated it was beyond me. Last time, that had felt like a stroke of luck. Now it made my paranoia surge, the conviction that someone had intended me to use it too strong to ignore. Richards pulled the door open as the display flashed green, and endless rows of nitrogen-filled storage tanks lay before us.

"I presume we get all the serum version numbers I've compiled from the notes you gave me?" I asked when Hamilton still hadn't said a thing.

"We'll start with that," he replied. My stomach sank. Of course.

Exhaling loudly, I snatched a hose to connect to my suit so I wouldn't suffocate or die of heat stroke in here and waddled over to the bench by the door where I found the inventory logs. And my, there was a lot of inventory to go through. And no, they hadn't filed it alphabetically.

"What's taking so long?" Hamilton grunted a few minutes later.

"Wanna help? Then shut the fuck up and let me concentrate," I snapped back, not even bothering with looking up. "You try finding a hundred vials in a haystack of several million." Of course, just as I turned a laminated page, I found a batch of samples labelled with the serum project variants, and just a little more effort produced the right boxes as well. Then it was just a matter of checking the tank orders, and I made my way over to the first—but gave up after five seconds. "I can't get this open," I ground out between gritted teeth. "You want this shit? Then help me."

Richards joined me, still lugging his container along, setting it on the floor next to the tank I was glaring at. I had to show him how to disengage the lock, and of course he sloshed liquid nitrogen everywhere as he pulled the suspended rack inside the tank out way too fast, not considering that the liquid was also between the boxes inside the racks. Nitrogen evaporated as it hit the much warmer air inside the room than the tank it had kept cool, clouds of vapor surrounding us. I would have smiled at Richards cursing and trying to avoid the ice-cold liquid hitting his suit, but we really didn't have time for this. As soon as he stopped dancing around, I reached for the rack and pulled out the fifth box from the top, quickly finding the vials we needed. More nitrogen came sloshing from the tank as Richards let the rack slide inside too fast, drawing another derisive grunt from me. Amateurs.

"We'll take fucking forever like this," I complained when I realized I'd have to get back to the inventory log now. "Hamilton, work for your money and find us the next tank and box. Richards, you open the tanks for me but I get the racks out. And keep that container open, the samples won't thaw that quickly, anyway."

To my never-ending surprise, neither of them even gave a peep of protest. Hamilton was disappointingly quick to find the next tank, and off we went. Dragging the heavy rack out of the tank didn't agree with my sweaty, aching fingers but even lacking a lot of my former alacrity, I didn't get nitrogen all over us and had the samples out in a fraction of the time Richards could have managed. Now that we were at the right tanks, it was easier to find the next samples. And the next. Soon, the entire container was full and Richards went to fetch the other one. This wasn't so bad, I told myself. So far, all of the samples had been serum variants that had been in the documentation. Maybe they'd sent Hamilton on his super-secret side mission to get someone's handwritten notes of his semi-embarrassing erotica project.

Hamilton sent me over to the next tank, yet rather than tell me the version numbers of the samples, he left it at a snide, "Box four, samples ten to fifteen." As I balanced the rack on the rim of the tank and pulled the box out, I figured he'd switched to what he thought was a more effective system—until I read the label of the first vial. My stomach knotted up as I realized where I'd last seen it—the invisible ink letter from Nate's brother. I swallowed thickly and checked the next label—the same series as that one. Those were the trials that had ended in that death match, literally.

"You sure that's the right box?" I asked, my voice pressed even though I tried to make it sound casual. "Just give me the version numbers."

Hamilton looked up from the log and stared at me. Even through the visor of his suit, I could see his smirk firmly in place. Oh, he knew what he was asking me to fetch, and it must have become obvious that I knew just the same.

"Just get the samples," he told me, his tone flat.

I hesitated, wondering what to say, or if it made any sense at all. I considered dropping the samples into the tank, but he'd only have to turn it over to get them out. He was watching me closely now so switching them out wasn't exactly an option. Richards had noticed my hesitation and was giving me a curious look, not getting my reasoning—so he hadn't tattled on me. Not that I thought he'd had time enough to read, let alone remember, the numbers. Unless he was a very good actor, that was, which was entirely possible. And why did I even care?

Because it could be me who got that shit injected next. Or Nate. Or someone else I cared about. Hell, I'd even think twice subjecting Hamilton to this, although he kind of had it coming after the shit he'd pulled on Nate.

"Lewis, just do it," Hamilton told me, his voice taking on a dangerous edge. I looked at the samples, then back up to Hamilton, still undecided. "Or is there any particular reason why you object?"

"Those numbers aren't on our list," I offered, the weakest protest ever.

"They are on my list," he stated, as if that was reason enough.

"They're not the cure," I said, trying to reason with him. Why was I even playing this game?

Bucky's eyes narrowed. "Put them in the container. We're running out of time here, and you're needlessly wasting it." Again I considered—and when I looked at him once more, Hamilton had a gun pointed at me. So he had come in armed, I just hadn't noticed it. Swallowing thickly, I stared at the barrel, then back at his face. "I'm not afraid to use it," he told me in no uncertain terms, and with more than just a hint of glee in his voice. "You became obsolete the moment you got us into this vault.

We can grab the rest of the samples and leave without you. Consider it a token of professional courtesy if I don't put a cap in your crown." His mirthless grin widened. "Or better yet, just your leg. Cleaning cycles or no, with a ruptured suit and an open wound, chances are very high you'd catch something in here, and you're terribly afraid of that. And without the ability to run, you'd be dead outside long before you could choke on your bloody vomit. So do yourself a favor and stop screwing around, or I will put a permanent end to it. Put the damn samples into the container."

I wanted to believe that, deep down, I was still operating by a strong, moral codex, but he was right—and I could tell that he was silently counting down, and maybe even looking forward to shooting me. So I did the only thing I could—and put the samples into the container.

"Sheesh, calm your tits, dickwad," I mumbled, quite proud that my voice wasn't shaking. "What's next?"

He took his time before turning around, his glower definitely on the gloating side. The second his attention strayed from me, I tilted the box, still in my hand, to check the other labels. And there they were, second row from the bottom—the last-mentioned variants that had very reduced drawbacks, most of the advantages, and didn't come with a homicidal countdown.

My tongue was burning with the words that this was what we needed, what we'd come here for—but again, I reconsidered. I had no idea who would get these samples. Maybe Hamilton would drop all of them off with Raynor; maybe just some and he'd keep those select special few to himself. Richards had the letters, and although the notes in there were vague, I was sure that Raynor would be able to piece the information required together. And Hamilton had stressed in very plain words that my only obligation was to do exactly what he told me to, absolving me of all guilt and responsibility.

But.

It was that very moral objection that had, time and again, gotten me into shit often deeper than I could shovel. It made me care about what happened to the traders; to the women Taggard and his boys raped and killed. It was the reason why we weren't safely tucked away from everything somewhere up in Canada or Alaska, or happily dozing under some palm trees on some tropical island only accessible by boat—the perfect post-apocalyptic fortress. This was the very last chance of anyone to get their hands on these samples, I was very aware of that. Already, the liquid nitrogen in some of the tanks was close to no longer covering the top boxes, meaning that the tanks that automatically topped up the liquid were running on empty. A few months—heck, maybe a few weeks might be enough—and the samples would thaw, their contents forever lost to the world. That was the real reason for the timing of the mission—Raynor must have realized this was about to happen any day now. Yes, the labs were built to last forever, the ventilation system and electricity to run it guaranteed for three years or more, but nobody had expected that the easiest component, the cheap chemical that would keep it all at a balmy -320 Fahrenheit, wouldn't regularly be topped up. It wasn't even a huge security risk as the vials would do their thing to contain the material inside as it slowly degraded, and anything that might leak out or otherwise escape would get sucked or washed away—destroying it for good. The containers we were dropping the samples in were likely kept at equally low temperatures with some kind of cooling system that would keep them safe for the month or so until they could be submerged in nitrogen once more. Even the thawed, degraded material, if fresh enough, would be good enough if processed by the right people—but not once it was destroyed for good.

I couldn't let this go to waste, even if it ended up in the wrong hands. I simply couldn't.

"There are some more samples in this box you should take with you," I told Hamilton, briefly glancing at Richards but mostly focusing on the other man. "I found some mention of them in Dr. Andrada's notes. This is as close to the cure as she and Raleigh Miller got."

Hamilton paused, and I could practically see the gears in his head grinding. Turning around to face me, he didn't look very happy.

"And you forgot to mention that until now because…?"

"I didn't forget. I lied when I said I didn't find anything." I wondered if he'd shoot me now after all—or threaten me into revealing every last thought I'd ever kept from him. Not that we had that amount of time, but I was sure the idea of beating me to a bloody pulp was an appealing concept. The positive pressure suit killed all body language that I might have exhibited but I did my best to appear calm and collected, even if I was far from it as I challenged him with my gaze. "You claim we're here to find the cure? Well, that's the closest we'll get. Unless you're ready to 'fess up that it's not even a minor objective, take these samples as well. Everything you had me grab is in there in redundancy, even if you have every single sample space planned out, we can easily make room for five more vials." There were more in there but that would suffice.

Hamilton considered, his hand close to where he'd put the gun down next to the inventory log. "Do it," he said after giving himself a visible jerk. "And hurry. We still have more samples to find."

I forced myself to stop thinking after that, going through the motions as quickly and efficiently as possible. It didn't matter what I did or said anymore—the best and worst I could have done was already behind me. Short of grabbing the gun from Hamilton and shooting him—and likely Richards as well—there wasn't anything I could do now. I considered that for a few moments, weighing my options and chances of success. Could I do it? The answer was yes, even if it left a bad taste in my mouth. Neither of them was an innocent bystander, and if the last year had taught me anything it was that I could reason everything away if it led to my survival. It was kind of a greater good thing, too, although I really wasn't convinced anything connected to this would do anything good either way. I could claim it was an accident. It wasn't like anyone would be able to simply check on the bodies if I claimed we'd gotten attacked. Sure, there were the cameras, but Cole struck me as one of the people who might fold and follow Nate's leadership if he acted quickly enough—and he would, the second he realized what I'd done. We would still complete the mission, just minus a few vials that nobody except Hamilton had known to get, anyway. Right now was the only chance I'd get—as soon as we were outside the decontamination shower, we were back to the old rules.

So, could I do it? Yes. But the real question was, should I do it—and with lots of annoyance at myself I decided that the answer to that was no. My ego absolutely wanted to, but the analytical part of my brain—often buried and mostly ignored—told me not to. Who knew what we might need Hamilton and Richards for in the future? In the end the fact remained—like Nate, like me, they were resources that might one day be sorely missed and direly needed. If I was choking on my decision, that was an easy price to pay if it maybe meant someone would live who'd otherwise have died.

"That's the last one," Hamilton stated after I slid another rack into a tank, making the liquid nitrogen slosh gently. "We're all set. Let's go."

Richards closed the lid of the tank and grabbed the sample container while Hamilton picked up the previously filled one. I quickly disconnected the air hose from my suit, and because I was a nice, caring gal, I did the same to theirs, seeing as they didn't have both hands free. I didn't miss that Hamilton left his gun next to the inventory ledger, although he waited for me to exit the room first, which I did with a smirk on my face. Ah, trust—not something we'd ever establish, I was afraid. I didn't have access to my watch but the small timer I'd taken with me from the board at the entrance showed that we'd spent just over seventy minutes inside the lab, which left us a comfortable pillow of time for decon, and then to get the hell out of here.

I patiently waited for Hamilton to close the vault before I set off down the corridor that would bring us back to the decontamination shower, a vague feeling of sentimentality mixing with my reluctance of not having at least tried to kill that asshole. It was kind of ridiculous how many last times I'd spent in labs over the past years, but this time I was sure it really would be the final one. I couldn't properly hold, let alone use, a pipette anymore; couldn't one-handedly unscrew a bottle; couldn't do any of the many fine motor functions required to operate anything inside a laminar flow hood—motions that were so deeply ingrained in my brain that they rivaled autonomous things like yawning or blinking. I'd for years prided myself that working in the lab had turned me ambidextrous to a point, a skill that had certainly served me well in compensating for the parts I'd lost. But there was no going back. This was it.

I couldn't be out of here a moment too soon.

I was the first to round the corner and get to the corridor with the viewing windows to the outside, expecting to find Nate there, waiting not-so patiently but showing no outward signs—but the window was empty, what little I could see of the hallway outside the cocoon of the labs deserted. Disappointment tickled along my mind but I quickly shoved it away—they were likely bored out of their minds, standing around, pretending to guard, and eating jerky all the while.

Checking back on Hamilton and Richards, I paused, reaching for another air hose mostly so I'd have something to do until they caught up with me.

Out of the corner of my vision, I saw something whizz by outside, so fast my distracted eyes couldn't latch on to it. It startled me, old reflexes catching up in milliseconds—nobody did anything sudden inside a BSL-4 lab. Grumbling under my breath, I chalked it up to one of the idiots outside throwing something, or whatnot. With all the soundproofing of the installation, it was impossible to tell.

The others finally made their way over to me, giving me a good reason to appear all calm and relaxed—

So when a body was flung against the outside of the viewing windows and hit with a "thunk" that was loud enough to translate through the thick glass, I not only jumped, but let out a girly shriek.

Had to jinx that one, didn't I?

Chapter 14

"**W**hat the fuck?" Hamilton grunted, having had the worst view as the farthest away from the window.

"I think that was Russell," I offered helpfully, feeling my pulse spike with fear-driven adrenaline—and a strong sense of giddiness that, finally I'd get to do something. "Told you so."

Hamilton strode forward, prompting Red to take a step aside to let him pass. "You told no—"

"Just because you like to make fun of me doesn't mean I wasn't right," I prompted, ignoring him as I stepped closer to the window to get a look outside. I could see something on the floor—a boot, still attached to a foot—but the angle was bad and didn't give me any further information about the state Russell was in. The corridor remained deserted, with no further movement.

"We should get moving—" I said—and found the hallway deserted behind me. For a moment my mind jumped to the conclusion that they'd somehow gotten inside as well, but it made much more sense that Hamilton had kept walking while I checked. Sure enough, I could hear plastic squeaking from over there. Momentarily relaxing, I made my way to the next intersection—only to see the heavy door to the decontamination room closing right in front of me. My body was still moving forward on autopilot, my gaze snatching to the display by the shower just as it came on, the ten-minute cycle starting.

They'd locked me in. They'd fucking locked me in the fucking lab!

I was very tempted to scream but instead did the stupid thing and tried the door, which, of course, wouldn't budge. There were no emergency overrides, at least none that I could see, but for good measure I still pounded against the heavy door. "You fucking assholes!"

I hadn't expected them to still have the suit communication on, but Richards's voice sounded, appropriately apologetic, in my ear. "We have orders. You have to understand—"

His voice cut off suddenly, making me guess that Hamilton had done away with our means of communication. At least Red had sounded sincere in his regret—not that this helped me one bit.

Yup, I definitely should have shot Hamilton when I had the chance. Or at least a chance, which was gone now.

Frustrated, I reached up to run a hand through my hair but of course only managed to bump my hand against the visor of the suit. I checked the display again—it read 9:43, counting down. Shit.

The easiest—and without a doubt, smartest—thing would have been to simply wait, but my body was singing with the need for action, so that was out of the question. Pivoting fast enough that my boot almost slipped on the floor, I turned around and stalked to the next viewing window, one down from the one Russell had been slammed against. I saw shadows, someone moving toward where I knew the entrance to the lab was. Against better judgment, I slapped my hand against the glass, hoping that would draw attention. Much to my surprise it did, Tanner appearing around the corner. He ducked out of sight after he saw me wave at him, and a second later, Nate came barreling into the corridor, obviously worked up and somewhat disheveled. Whatever was going on out there hadn't just started but seemed to have been going on for quite some time.

The positive pressure suit wasn't made for pantomime, even less so with the floppy gloves, and I felt my frustration skyrocket immediately as I tried to sign that I was okay but really, really fucking frustrated. I tried to signal "dick" and "locked in" but Nate just stared at me as if I'd gone insane, halfway through my routine looking away when someone must have called out to him. He looked back at me, his expression twisted with indecision and disdain, then made the universal downward motion for me to hunker down—or hold on tight—and disappeared again, making me shout in frustration for real this time.

More movement from where Nate had disappeared to, and something solid thunked into the wall—another body, I realized, leaving a bloody imprint where it slid down. Aimes, I realized, his head cocked to the side at a rather unhealthy angle, his eyes, wide open, staring at nothing. I waited for him to get up again—or reanimate—but nothing. Another figure came running into the corridor, this one still propelled by her own feet—Gita. What was she doing back here? She'd been in the server room last I'd checked, with no reason to go anywhere except straight back out of the complex. She was limping, and one side of her face was covered in blood, likely from a cut close to her hairline. She cast around frantically, backing up toward where Russell was down, her mouth opening in repeated shouts that I couldn't hear through the glass. As she continued to back up further into the bright light spilling through the window, I noticed the trail of blood she left on the floor. That wasn't a simple cut, but something had torn off half of her right ear and chunks of flesh from her temple and cheek—not looking good.

Frustration and grief just added fuel to the fire raging inside of me, but that damn display was still at eight minutes. Exhaling loudly to clear my head, I took two steps back, torn with indecision. Pounding on the glass was a bad idea because I didn't want to distract her if I could help it. Not that it mattered much—she would be dying either way, with no chance at all against the virus, not even hoping that whatever had killed Rodriguez wouldn't work on the rest of us. Because she hadn't been inoculated.

Yet.

It was a stupid idea, I knew that, but it wasn't like she had options—and neither did I. So I did what any crazy scientist would have done and sprinted back toward the vault, skidding on the floor with every step. Adrenaline surged, making me so jumpy for a second that I only hit half the keys to disengage the lock. The door opened on the second try. I was through as soon as I could squeeze myself inside, aiming for the back of the room. I'd forgotten the number of the tank but managed to visually pick it out in no time. Getting the lid off was a nightmare but I managed, need lending my fingers strength they hadn't had an hour ago. I didn't give a shit about sloshing nitrogen, trusting that the suit could easily be dunked in that shit for minutes and would survive a few splatters. I almost dropped the box as I fumbled it out of the rack but managed to hold on to it even as the rack fell back into the tank, more nitrogen boiling off as it splashed out. I barely took the time to plonk the lid back onto the tank, then headed for the door, but made a quick detour to pick up Hamilton's discarded gun. Habit had me check the magazine, not sure whether I was relieved to find it loaded and full. I hadn't expected him to bluff, but knowing how close I'd been to getting my brains blown out wasn't exactly comforting. As the box was already sitting on the workbench, I took the lid off and inspected the vials still inside. There were three left of the batch I needed, but also over thirty that I wasn't certain about. It must have been Andrada's personal research box to hold both the cure and what might be one of the most lethal weaponized versions, so there was no guessing to the other contents. I could only use those three vials so it made no sense to take the rest. And mostly out of spite than rational action I dumped the box in the desk autoclave sitting by the door, yet didn't bother trying to see if it was still operational. No one would look for anything in there so it was the best I could do.

I shut the vault door and headed back toward the decontamination showers, pausing for a few seconds by the viewing window when I felt a little woozy all of a sudden. Air, right. Snatching up one of the hoses, I let fresh—and wonderfully cool—air into my suit, using the few seconds of downtime to check on what was going on outside. The corridor was deserted, and the boot—with the rest of Russell presumably still attached—was gone, the few drops of blood from Gita leading in a haphazard line in the other direction.

Disconnecting the hose, I rounded the next corner, my gaze first skipping to the display. 1:35. Perfect timing, except that I still had ninety-five seconds to waste—and then ten whole minutes more. My entire body was vibrating with tension, and the thought crossed my mind that Nate must have felt like this when I'd locked him in the decon shower way back when. Payback never felt good, but this absolutely sucked!

The countdown finally reached zero, and I was yanking at the handle as soon as the display went off. Of course it was still locked, only letting me wrench open the door after the exit had locked itself once more, leaving me staring balefully at it, wishing Hamilton and Richards to die a violent yet slow death. I slammed my palm down on the button to start the showers, forcing my muscles to lock in place as the torrential rain of chemicals started pelting me. I'd felt a million times better the last time I'd been in this very situation, and back then I'd been halfway convinced that I'd infected myself with that damn zombie virus. Ah, good times.

What couldn't have been more than thirty seconds in, I started pacing, incapable of remaining still. I rolled my shoulders, tried stretching the long muscles in my body, getting my fingers to be as nimble as they would be—without dropping the vials. I knew I shouldn't take them out like this without a containment vessel but I honestly didn't give a shit.

And most of all, I needed to get out of here and do something!

The gush of chemicals started tapering off and I knew my last ten seconds of captivity had begun. So I closed my eyes, gritted my teeth—and slammed my fist as hard as I could into the softer flesh just above my kidney. The black of my vision turned red with pain, then white as agony continued to explode through my body, but I didn't care. I hurled myself at the door as soon as the lock disengaged with a clicking sound, stumbling out of the shower with my suit still dripping shit nobody should ever inhale or come in direct skin contact with.

The prep room lay deserted, two discarded suits on the floor to the side. I didn't lose a step as I grabbed the zipper of my suit, tearing the plastic around it as I opened it too fast, yanking too hard. Cooler air hit my sweaty body as I fumbled with the tape of the gloves, quickly transferring the vials to the inside of the latex glove I'd just torn off. A last kick and my feet were free of the boots, and I was flying into the changing rooms, ignoring the showers. No trace of Hamilton or Richards, but at least they'd left my pack where I'd dropped it.

"Bree?"

I almost jumped out of my skin when I heard Gita's voice coming from behind me. It took me a second to force my body to relax and not karate-chop her on principle. She sounded scared out of her mind, and when I turned to look at her, I found her huddled in on herself, her face white and sweaty where it wasn't caked with blood, trembling all over. The carbine she was clutching was more for moral support than anything else from the looks of it.

"They came out of nowhere," she panted out, her voice hoarse from panic, and likely pain. "We had no warning. No screams, not even a thump or anything. Fuck, we still don't know how many of them are out there!" A pause as she gasped for breath. "Hamilton shoved me in here. I didn't see you anywhere but when I checked the other room, I saw that the shower was on, so I figured you were still in there."

"Yeah, the assholes locked me in the hot zone," I grumbled, searching my things for my com first. When I switched it on, there was the typical low-level static but nothing more than the odd squeak or whine. "Lewis here. Anyone, copy?" I asked, feeling my stomach knot with anxiety. They couldn't all be gone yet.

"It's not working because of the shell around the lab," Gita supplied, sounding just a little more like herself now that my presence served as a welcome distraction—or she knew she hadn't been completely abandoned. I could relate, even if I tried hard not to show any of that. "It will… at least I think it will work again once we're back at the other labs."

I ignored her stutters as I shoved my feet into my boots, then grabbed a pair of latex gloves as I hastened over to her so I could grab her head and inspect the damage. The fact that she didn't flinch although I must have been touching her way too close to the wounds not to hurt told me all I needed to know—spreading numbness was one of the early signs of infection, didn't I know.

Tremors ran through her, and I noticed that, already, she was burning up. "They got me back in the server room," she whispered, her voice losing strength. "I was just sitting there. And then I wasn't. I didn't even feel the pain at first, just a sense of vertigo as something pulled me out of the chair and to the ground."

Done, I let go of her head in favor of grabbing her shoulders, forcing her to focus on me.

"Take a calm breath," I told her with authority that I absolutely didn't feel.

"I'm dying," she continued to whisper, her eyes darting all over me but without latching on to anything. "Bree, I'm dying."

"Dying's overrated," I snapped back, immediately regretting my tone. "Here, hold this." I fished one of the vials out of the discarded glove I'd stashed them in. "Until the frozen core is all liquid. And then I'm going to inject you with this. Do you understand?"

She took the vial but rather than nod, she simply stared at it. "What's that?"

"Maybe the cure," I said, hating how much I hoped that I wasn't wrong. "I'm running on theories here but that's all we got. It's the same batch that I found mentioned in the letters. I don't know if it will help you, but it's worth a shot, right? It won't kill you faster than what's already killing you."

She nodded but there was no hope in her eyes, not even a glimmer. I really wanted to hug her but we didn't have the time. Getting into my gear wasted another handful of minutes, but I couldn't go out there in my underwear and hope to survive. All my extra magazines suddenly didn't sound as much like overkill as the soldiers had made fun of back when we'd landed at the beach. But Gita first.

"I need a hypodermic needle," I muttered, looking around. There had to be supplies here somewhere, likely in the suit room. Until backup arrived—if it arrived, and I really didn't count on it at the moment—we were likely safer in here than outside, seeing that the door was secured with a scanner. That was, if it was still secured. "Did you disengage the locks?" I asked her, unable to keep the anxiety out of my voice. If Hamilton intended to strand me in here, it would make sense—and might just have exacerbated the problem that we had now. No wonder everything could move freely around right now. That was exactly what Nate had tried to prevent.

Gita nodded, but quickly explained. "We had to. They already move around as they please, using the ducts and connective tunnels they seem to have dug into behind the maintenance panels—into the maintenance floors. It was only us who got cornered and couldn't run away when we needed to. Cole and I can both remotely engage them again." She tapped something in her jacket pocket. "Got everything I need right here."

I really didn't like that answer, but nobody cared about that. "Watch the door for a sec until I'm back," I told her and went back into the prep room. Sure enough, after digging my way through a stack of plastic containers and empty vials, I found what I was looking for, grabbing an entire blister of needles and two syringes. One would likely have been enough but I got the sense that we wouldn't have much time left for finding spares. Gita looked relieved as I returned, but that changed when I took the by-now thawed vial from her and prepped one of the syringes with the entire contents of it. "You sure that won't kill me?" she whispered, eyes impossibly bright.

I had already given her the honest answer, so she got the one she needed to hear right now. "Yes, I'm sure. I'd inject myself to prove it to you, but I only have three or four doses, and I have a feeling we might still need them. If not, I'll give you the rest once we're back outside. Trust me." I flashed her a quick grin. "I'm a doctor."

Her hand shook as she pulled her jacket to the side so I could reach the less bloody side of her neck, barely whimpering when I—not very expertly—stuck the needle in and pushed the plunger. "I'd say not that kind of doctor but I guess in this case you are," she muttered. "Shit. That burns."

"That's a good sign," I lied.

Momentary silence fell, both of us listening to our own breathing for a few seconds. I knew that we really needed to get going but I figured that if anything dramatic were about to happen to her after the injection, it would happen now—and I needed to take that time to check. "So what exactly did I miss?" I asked, my eyes now trained at the door rather than my patient, yet watching her closely from the corner of my eye. I should know what I was up against before I went running out there blindly.

Gita, now leaning against the wall next to the door, shrugged. "You called it when you said they're not dead. Whoever they experimented on, that is. At least it sounds like that's them. We don't even know how many of them there are—maybe fifteen? Could be less. They're strong, like, freakishly strong. I saw one barrel right into Burns and fling him across the room. I know you lot can pack a hell of a punch, but not that much." She grimaced, reaching up to scratch her neck at the injection site. "They don't look like the shamblers we're used to. Not sure they're dead, for one. They bleed when you shoot them, and they're quick as fuck. Gaunt going on emaciated, but don't let that fool you. The one who got me was heavy enough that it took Cole kicking it off. He couldn't pull it loose." Her gaze found mine when I briefly glanced at her face. "I don't wanna die," she said, her voice dropping to a whisper again. "Not like this. Not today of all days."

"Today's always a bad day to die," I told her, smiling sadly. "But you won't die, so chin up."

I couldn't wait any longer. She wasn't insta-converting—obviously not, her body would have needed something first to initiate that—or dying at a much quicker rate, and that was all I cared about now.

Looking through the small window in the door gave me nothing, so I nodded at the handle. "I take point. You cover my back. Switch over to the other side and open it. We secure the corridor outside, then we see what we can do about the checkpoint." That came out confidently enough. I even felt I would be able to hold the corridor on my own—and that right there was a problem. I still gave her a nod so she'd go ahead, and then eased myself out of the lab.

At a first glance, the hallway was clear—except for Aimes's dead body. His weapons were gone, but he still had his pack strapped to his back. I didn't exactly grieve for the asshole, but he hadn't really done anything to deserve to die. I'd kind of expected him to be a constant pain in my ass for much longer. Ah well. I was sure he hadn't expected this, either. There were some drag marks where Russell had been flung against the viewing window, but either he had gotten up himself or he was gone for good. Then there was the blood Gita had lost—and that was it. Holding my breath, I listened, trying to pick up anything, but all I could focus on was the hammering of my heart in my chest.

"I didn't see any of them when I hid, right there around the corner," Gita explained. "The one that killed Aimes and banged up Russell came through the open doors, not from behind a wall panel. Miller shot it down but it fled back into the main part before he could finish it off." That must have rankled—and I sure hoped that thing was still gone.

I was tempted to ask why Nate hadn't hung around for me, but the answer was obvious—no order from Hamilton could have made him leave me behind, but the knowledge that there was danger ahead that prevented us from exiting sure would have done the trick. I thought I could hear faint noises from the direction of the main lab complex, but nothing close enough to identify it. Even outside of the hot lab the air recycling system was running on full, making my work so much harder than was necessary.

"Stay here," I told Gita, nodding at the middle of the corridor. "If anything comes through the airlock, shoot it and go hide in the lab. The toilets off the changing rooms have locks on them. I'll check around the corner. Be right back."

I felt my neck itch like crazy from what I hoped like hell was just paranoia of being watched as I slowly made my way toward the left part of the outside section of the labs where I knew some of the maintenance rooms were housed, responsible for air and waste management. Here, that system spanned all the levels of the complex, unlike beyond the airlock. The flaw in my plan became obvious immediately as I realized that there were doors leading away on both sides of the hallway, and I'd never be able to establish any kind of anything, let alone a perimeter. This simply wasn't working.

I felt marginally better when I returned to where I could see Gita, and judging from how relieved she looked, she felt the same. I went right past her and did a similarly half-assed check on the mirror section at the other side, and decided that it would have to do.

"What do we do now?" she asked as I came back.

"We need to find the others. We're at close to three hours and fifty minutes since breach. Our first countdown is up in ten minutes from now so we have just about fifty minutes left in here until the air becomes unbreathable—if the security system still works, and I'm not risking my life on the guess that it doesn't. We need to get out, and stat. I say we go through the checkpoint and then—"

I was still trying to find the right words when something slammed into my side, dragging me to the floor as we both rolled, the impact driving the air right out of my lungs so I couldn't scream—

Shit just got real.

Chapter 15

I t took me only a few seconds to realize that the jaws that were snapping for my face belonged to Aimes, not one of the duct-crawling, super stealthy former lab rats—but that didn't exactly improve my mood. I'd walked by his body twice, and besides considering what there might be left to loot I hadn't thought about it much. I'd certainly not done what should have been my first move—to put a bullet between his lifeless eyes. Well, now I was paying the price for that, and feeling like I kind of deserved this really didn't help. He—it, damnit!—may not have had the strength to fling Burns around, but considering he still had a good thirty pounds on me, that helped me only so much. That I was super fast and super strong now didn't count for anything against something that had the same advantages, plus a healthy dose of rage and bloodlust that I couldn't match. But it wasn't like I had a choice.

Our quick roll-and-tumble ended with me on my back and Aimes perched above me, as these encounters so often went. Anticipating that, I didn't try to punch up but instead threw my body to the side, breaking the lock it tried to put me into before all our momentum was gone. I got to tear myself free with one knee underneath me, pushing up into a crouch. I'd managed to hold on to my M16 but there was no time to position myself right, let alone aim, yet it was something to slam in the zombie's face, stock first, as it came for me again—if not enough to get any distance between us. It was right there once more, dripping blood and saliva, and all I had for my effort was a nasty twinge in my left wrist.

Two shots went off in quick succession, the shambler howling with rage as the bullets bit into its ass and thigh. I didn't have the air in my lungs to congratulate Gita on not shooting me, and used the seconds that bought me to properly grab the assault rifle and pull the trigger myself. The bullets tore right into its torso, sending more blood spraying, but didn't do much actual damage that would keep it down. I aimed up, trying to get a headshot in, but the shambler knocked the rifle away with a powerful swing of its arm, making me stagger along with it as I wasn't going to just give it up like that. It pounced, slamming into me a second time, but now I was prepared— at least enough that it forced me into a crouch but didn't manage to pull me along. My entire side where it hit me exploded with pain but I forced myself to push through it, the instant kick of adrenaline that came out of nowhere letting me act fast. Using the stock of the rifle once more, I bashed at its face, hitting and breaking its nose and several teeth. A normal human would have reared back from the pain; the zombie came right after me as soon as I took a step back to get more room to maneuver. It was fast—but I was faster.

I didn't count the bullets I sent into its jaw and neck but it must have been around seven to ten. It may no longer have felt pain, but it sure noticed when it was suddenly lacking a lower jaw, greatly impeding any potential biting action going on. It blindly flailed in my direction, but a well-aimed kick in its middle sent it staggering back, finally putting it in reach of a killing shot—

That I didn't get to take because right when I had my rifle up and ready, something at the edge of my vision moved. Not by the door to the lab where I knew Gita was standing, likely more terrified of accidentally shooting me than getting chewed up, but coming from the maintenance corridor where my half-assed check had obviously not been enough. I had a split second to decide, and no time for regrets.

Following instinct more than thought, I swung the rifle toward that blur and fired, sending a barely aimed burst into the corridor. I didn't hit the thing that was coming for me, ducking low in a move I'd never seen in any of the undead, but at least I got a glimpse of it before it rammed its shoulder into my hip and toppled me over backward.

Gita's assessment had been a good one—it didn't look like the shamblers I was used to. It was pale, the skin mottled with bruises and lesions but none appearing to be actual decay, more like a rash or a barely healed-over fighting wound—or what I'd had a week before Raynor had cut me up. There wasn't much padding to speak of to the muscles that moved underneath the skin, hinting at malnutrition, but they hadn't more than started to atrophy. All of that was in plain sight as it didn't wear any clothes, but that was the last detail I found interesting right then. It may have been thin going on gaunt, but it sure packed a punch as it hit me, taking me down effectively. Bright, intelligent eyes stared into mine, calculating—there was definitely something still home in that almost-bald head, not just the simple need to feed.

I didn't think that trying to reason with it would yield positive results.

Instinct and training took over as I used the M16 as a hard, physical barrier between me and the thing that, whatever it was, still tried to take a chunk out of me. Gita shot again—what, I wasn't sure—and the zombie halted for a second. I used that moment to wrench the barrel of the assault rifle underneath its chin, and pulled the trigger. Resilient fuckers they might be, but nothing survived getting their brains scrambled like this. Blood sprayed everywhere. I didn't wait to get drenched in it. A kick and roll, and I was back on my feet, panting heavily as I tried to orient myself. Gita must have hit the thing in the leg as it was bleeding all over the floor, the amount of blood way more than I was used to seeing. Hell, even the shambler that used to be Aimes hadn't bled like that, and it had still been warm enough for the body to almost react like humans did. Then again, I'd gotten the chance to kill one of the super juiced ones several times in a row back in Sioux Falls—I knew that they weren't exactly reacting like humans should in general.

Speaking of Aimes—the shambler was back, and it obviously saw me as the easier meal, ignoring Gita for the moment. At the end of my patience, I swung the M16's barrel around and sent a burst into it, making it stagger but not fall. Exhaling hard, I forced my mind to snap into focus, and when I pulled the trigger again, three bullets bit into its forehead, making the zombie jerk—and that was the end of it.

Glancing to Gita, I allowed myself a brief smile—we were still alive after all—but it froze on my face when I saw yet more movement behind her shoulder, coming from that same corridor once more. She whipped around when she saw the alarm on my face, but I didn't give her the chance to react—or, worse yet, freeze. "We need to get out of here or we're toast," I pressed out between gritted teeth, not taking my eyes off that mutant thing slowly stalking into the light spilling out of the lab viewing window furthest from our position. "Get behind me and start backing away toward the airlock at the security checkpoint. And as soon as we're in that hallway, you turn around and run, do you understand?"

"But they love to give chase—" she started, stopping when I gave a loud grunt.

"They love to beat us to a bloody pulp as well. And eat us. We need strength in numbers if we want to survive." I hated admitting this, but she was smart. She knew that neither of us counted for full compared to the others. I'd been insanely lucky to kill the first two zombies, but luck wasn't anything we could rely on.

"Okay, got it," she said, moving out of my field of vision, her footfalls almost silent. The zombie kept stalking forward just as I started easing back, blindly following the sounds Gita inevitably made. Stalking, stalking...

I was maybe ten feet away from where the hallway narrowed into the airlock when Aimes gave a twitch, then another one—and started to get up. I wasted a second to check—yup, I had hit that undead asshole square in the forehead, and there was plenty of blood and brain matter where it had landed on the floor. Just as my mind was catching up with this, the pale, gaunt freak also started to move, rolling onto its side so it could—slowly but surely—drag itself up into a crouch. This wasn't right! It wasn't fair. But sadly, I couldn't exactly cry foul for them suddenly changing the rules on us.

"Gita? Haul ass, because those undead fuckers didn't get the memo that headshots should kill them," I called over my shoulder.

I didn't get an answer, and I realized that she'd stopped in the small space between the doors of the lock. "I just saw something moving up ahead," she more whispered than said. "I'm not sure but—"

"More of them," I offered, agreeing with her unspoken assessment. "Look, we need to get closer to the others. As soon as I'm through the airlock, I'll try to seal it off. I'll try to create a diversion, and then we both run and hide. We split, that way we have a higher chance that one of us makes it to the other end of the labs."

"Yeah, because that's always such a great idea in horror movies," I heard her chuff under her breath.

"I'm not telling you to be an asshole and abandon me," I told her tartly. "They stalk us, and they will try to corner us. As long as one of us gets away, she can create another diversion or get help. I don't like this, either, but all the big, hulking fellows have left us behind so it's up to us to get us out of this shithole of a situation. Any objections? Then get ready to run."

All three zombies were now up and moving, slowly drawing closer. I tightened my grip on my rifle even though I knew I'd have to let go of it any second now as I stepped into the airlock. In the past, I'd always felt weird in those relative tight spaces; now it felt way too wide and easy to breach.

"Way ahead is clear," Gita muttered from right behind me. "Wanna go left or right?"

"Left," I decided in a split second. Not that I intended to go far at first—I needed to know whether the airlock sealed, and more importantly, remained locked. "Okay. On my mark." Taking two more steps backward, I started counting down, feeling my entire back light up with perceived itches as I made it into the much larger lab space corridor with not a glance over my shoulder yet.

"Mark!" I called and slammed my hand down on the red button that would make both sides of the airlock snap closed and engage the locks. Air hissed, parts moved—and the freak zombie I'd shot in the head jumped forward, powerful legs propelling it faster and farther than I would have thought possible. I heard Gita take off next to me, but rather than whip around and do the same, I held my ground, shooting at the zombie instead, hoping that the impact of the bullets would somehow slow it down or throw it off target. I hit it in the abdomen and chest, more blood spraying its torso but not doing much else.

The outer side of the lock was slightly faster in closing and I hit it three times as it blocked my way, chunks of plastic and glass ricocheting everywhere—but the door closed. The zombie hit the other side a moment later, flattening against the barrier with an audible "thump." Panting hard, I waited for it to somehow grab it and tear it free, but it held—so I did the smart thing and ran.

As soon as I whipped around, I caught a glimpse of something pasty white ducking through a doorway halfway down the left corridor, but it was gone before I could focus on it. Not wanting to get too close, I ran past the first door but wrenched open the second, finding a dead end behind it—a centrifuge room. There were labs right opposite so I turned around and jumped in there. Moving too fast, my trajectory sent me crashing into a bench, making bottles and bottles of buffer solutions crash onto the bench they had been stored above. Nothing I could do about that except crunch through the broken glass and try not to slip in the spillage. As fast as I could, I crossed the room but rather than tear through the connective door and small storage area into the next lab, I ducked underneath one of the benches, waiting and listening.

For the first few seconds, all I could hear was my own breathing and the pulse thundering in my ears. There was the dripping I'd caused, and some residual crackling from the glass I'd disturbed. Faintly, I could make out the freak in the airlock trying to break through, which also served as a good point of orientation. Nothing from Gita—which I presumed was good—but also no sounds from whatever else was lurking here with us.

Groping blindly for my com, I switched it to the limited frequency I'd shared with the small team while looking over the offices—Nate and Burns were the two people I'd need to reach. Chances were, Tanner would be somewhere close by. "Lewis here, anyone copy?" Nothing for several seconds, so I switched back to the main frequency and repeated, before adding, "Any of you assholes still alive?"

Silence stretched long enough that I felt my stomach sink, but rational thought cut down the rising panic. It was unlikely that the freakish zombies would be able to kill all the members of our illustrious group that fast, and even considering the ten-minute head start Hamilton had on me, it was unlikely that he'd made it through the entire complex yet.

Then the dulcet tones of my husband's voice sounded in my ear, making me feel a wave of instant relief. He was speaking barely loud enough for the mic to pick up his words. "They hunt by sound, so keep it down as much as possible. Auditory diversions work best." Rather than respond, I blew out a puff of air in confirmation. Nate laughed softly. "I presume you're still back at the labs?"

"Outside the airlock in the general area," I pointed out, trying to speak as softly as possible. "Gita's with me, a few rooms over. I managed to get the airlock closed but not sure how long it will hold. Oh, and not sure if you noticed, but they don't stay down just because you blow their brains out."

This time, his responding sound of mirth was a harsh one. "Yeah, we noticed. How many do you have breathing down your neck?"

"Three in the high-security labs. Well, two, plus Aimes. None of you cared to shoot him when you still could, and I doubt it would have taken when I later had the chance. Tried to rectify that, but... yeah."

"Just like with Rodriguez," someone else chimed in—Cole, I realized after a few seconds. "McClintock's down as well, just the same. He didn't reanimate right away or convert so we thought he was dead for good, but he chewed right into Parker's arm ten minutes ago."

"Forget the usual rules," Nate went on. "Hide, and sneak away when the air is clear. The only way we get out of here is by getting out. Not sure we can kill them all even if we try, and trying's not a good option."

Looking around, I assessed my surroundings, my gaze halting on the duct grate directly above me. I discarded the idea immediately— it hadn't really worked with humans, and if they used those regularly and hunted by sound, they'd have me pinned in there with no exit route in moments.

"Anyone wanna come get us?" I asked with more levity than I felt. "How many of us are left? Aimes and McClintock are down, and I presume Parker as well—"

"He's still moaning and bitching as usual, so he'll be useful for a little longer," Cole interjected. "No further casualties but we're pretty banged up as is. Pinned down in two spots—Miller's at the central hub on the lab side, and we're in the animal wing, two fire doors down from the hub. We managed to blow up one with grenades, but they're damn resilient fuckers."

I considered trying to build some chemical bomb—or a flamethrower—from what I knew must be all over here, but I didn't remember any recipes, and doubted we'd have time for this.

And just as if I'd jinxed it, suddenly the soft lights turned off, switching to red lighting instead—emergency mode.

"The fuck?" someone I couldn't identify asked, but Cole's soft cursing was answer enough.

"Security turned on panic mode," Cole explained a few moments later. "We tried switching it off, but it was impossible. The system's built with some back doors like the ones we used to get in for events like this, but we overstayed our welcome."

Nate sounded calm as he responded, not a thread of nerves in his voice. "That still leaves us forty-five minutes—more than enough to get out. Cole, get your guys over there ready for a push in fifteen if you don't catch a break earlier. I'll see that we have our two stragglers with us by then. We'll be out with minutes to spare."

A round of acknowledgements chimed in, including me, but I couldn't let that sit on me. "Stragglers, huh? Hamilton locked me inside the lab to strand me there; straggler, my ass. Where is that conniving asshole, anyway?"

I waited for Hamilton himself to respond, but both he and Richards remained silent.

"We don't know," Nate finally responded when no one else did. "And fuck if I care. We don't need him to get out of here." I heard him cluck his tongue, for a moment thinking that he'd uttered some derogatory curse under his breath but then realized he'd switched to the other frequency. "Bree, listen to me. You need to haul ass and get to us," he whispered, now a lot more urgency in his tone. "We can't hold this position much longer if we want to get into the corridor leading to the exit. There are at least twenty of them out there at our last count, which already puts them at a numbers advantage. Maybe more. We don't know. We're not just running out of time; we're out of ammo, and soon we'll be out of people, too."

"Understood." It was the urgency in his tone that made me antsy more than the message. "How is it even possible that they're still alive? And I don't even mean the impossible to kill part."

"They have access to the outside," Nate said with the kind of conviction that made my blood run cold. "This is their lair, or whatever you want to call it, but they get food from out there. Maybe they recruit as well. You saw the park deck and Metro entrances as we got up onto the plaza from down by the river? Could be full of them." He fell silent, but then added, "They're not hunting us down because they need to feed. They're defending their home."

I didn't like the sound of that, not at all. "So there's another way we could get out?"

"Doubt it. Or I doubt we'll find it in the next forty minutes. The exit was unbreached when we got there so we can seal it again, and that's our best bet. Try not to get locked in down here. You've already done all your superhuman feats for the year by surviving this far," he reminded me.

"Gee, thanks for the vote of confidence," I grumbled.

"It's your 'hold my beer' knee-jerk reactions that worry me," Nate confided—and got serious once more. "Get over here so we can leave. Stat."

I was about to sign off but this was too important not to tell him. "Gita is infected. I grabbed some of the serum vials that I hope is what your brother deemed as the better upgrade and shot her up with that. I give her a thirty percent chance that she makes it. I have two more vials in my left thigh pocket. If you only manage to retrieve my badly mutilated corpse—well, more mutilated than it already is—grab the vials and inject anyone who has sustained a wound. I don't care if they already got the serum or not. Aimes and Rodriguez weren't flukes—they're a symptom of a loophole in the serum. If there's any chance that we can close it, we have to try."

His answering laugh was a mirthless one. "Always trying to save the world from itself, huh?"

"Just those that deserve it," I enthused. "Don't give it to Hamilton. It's a waste of resources."

I would have loved to spew more venom, but the sound of glass breaking a few rooms over made me shut my trap immediately. Whether that had been an accident or not, it reminded me that I had places to be and monsters to elude.

"See you in a few," I promised, already inching out of my hidey-hole so I could check if I was still alone, and then look into the corridor outside. I didn't get a response, but I didn't need one. Haul ass I would, yessir.

Chapter 16

The lab was empty, but the corridor wasn't. I was looking both ways when I realized what had my mind on edge—the pounding at the airlock had ceased. Deep down, I knew that wasn't due to the shambler giving up—even the stupid ones were more persistent than that. Part of me was screaming to go other way but I had to check, slowly inching toward the bend in the corridor that would let me look back the way I had come. And, sure enough, the airlock was wide open, with not a creature in sight but smears of blood on the door frame where something must have grabbed onto, or leaned against. Something bleeding. Something—

I didn't hear the sounds as much as somehow anticipated them, my subconscious snapping to attention while my mind was still searching. Craning my neck, I managed to get a look into the first few feet of the corridor leading straight away from the airlock—and there it was, half standing, half crouching, sniffing the air—and then turning right my way. I ducked back immediately, silently cursing my own curiosity. I had to act quickly, so I hastened down the hallway—past the lab I'd been in before—and stepped into the lab opposite of it, crouching low so that when I checked on the hallway again, my head would pop up at knee-level, hopefully below where my stalker was checking.

It was a smart fucker, that much was sure. It didn't stop in the middle of the hallway as before, but was hunkered down mostly inside the room I'd checked first, the one with the centrifuges. Lightning-fast—and without making a sound—it dashed across into the lab where I'd stayed the longest, following my previous route. Was it tracking me by scent? Looking down at where half of my gear was splattered with blood, I had to bite down on my tongue to keep from groaning. Yeah, and it likely wasn't having a hard time doing so. Nothing I could do about that now—except maybe confuse it.

Looking around, I assessed the layout of the lab room I was in. There was another exit back into the corridor on this side, but also one on the other, leading to the middle corridor. Trying to be sneaky, I didn't head straight for that door but instead moved along two rows of workbenches, to the first door, and only then on to the second. Another empty-seeming corridor waited outside, but seeing the open airlock right at the end of it was a good reminder not to trust that. I checked which doors were next to windows—and had labs behind them, likely—before I moved on to the nearest, trying to go as fast as I could without running. Another lab, and likely where Gita had been hiding, judging by a smear of blood at the side of a bench, and broken glass on the floor. That must have been what I'd heard before. I lingered a little longer, hoping to leave enough of my scent to maybe throw them off Gita's track, before leaving the lab through the connective doors into the next one.

This room was in much more disarray, bullet holes and shells all over hinting at quite the fight going down. No bottle had remained whole, leaving shards of glass everywhere. I did my best not to step on them, which was, of course, impossible, and hastened out the next door into the middle corridor as soon as I got there and checked—only to come face-to-face with one of the undead bastards who'd been lingering in the dark room across the hall.

I had a split-second to decide what to do. My first impulse was to try to shoot it, but I knew I didn't have the time for that. The alternative was to bolt down the corridor, hoping against hope I'd get away—or at least put some distance between us and any backup that would inevitably come. What I went for was the crazy idea instead: I jumped right at it, punching it in the face as I closed the distance between us. A predator by nature, it was used to giving chase, not so much having its prey sock it a good one. It made as if to evade but hesitated too long, letting my fist hit it right between the eyes. My hand lit up with pain but I welcomed that, using the surge of adrenaline to punch it a second time, following up with a kick in the groin that made it stagger back into the darkness of the room, a muffled sound of pain escaping the muscular torso. Only then did I do the smart thing and pulled the door closed, whipped around, and flew down the corridor, the sounds of my footsteps echoing in every direction.

I got thirty yards and across one intersection before something jumped me as I went by another open door, sending me to the floor where I slid a good five feet more from my momentum. I rolled onto my side immediately, trying not to get pinned on my front, completely helpless. The shambler on my back grabbed my right shoulder and arm, wrenching me back, incidentally helping me to regain my footing. I blindly pushed my elbow back, hoping to connect with something vital, twisting to loosen the death grip it had on me. My foot slipped, making me crash back to the floor but at least it let go of me for a second, which was all I needed to scramble up and make it through the door into another lab room. Groping blindly for the next best thing, I hurled a small desk centrifuge at the thing coming after me. It staggered back out of the door, likely more from surprise than being forced back, and I slammed the door in its face. I didn't wait for what would happen next but tore through the lab and out the other side, ending in the outer corridor—just in time for the next shambler to get the jump on me.

I didn't even see it before it tackled me, sending me crashing to the ground. I twisted, kicked, and rolled, but it stayed on me, heavy enough to drive the last bit of air out of my lungs. The one I'd locked out of the lab came sprinting through the same door I'd used myself and jumped right on top of the pile we were creating, both zombies momentarily keeping each other from tearing chunks out of me. This stealth thing? So not working.

Just as I thought that, shots went off, a spray of bullets hitting my assailants, making their bodies jerk. Grasping the opportunity that was slapping me in my face, I tensed and kicked as hard as I could, dislodging the first shambler so I could move enough to crawl out from underneath them. Gita was standing in the middle of the corridor, sending another salvo at the zombies the moment I was free. I pressed myself against the wall, praying that she wouldn't hit me. She didn't, but as soon as the second salvo ended, she had two enraged freak shamblers coming for her. They were smart, but not smart enough. Gita quickly ducked back into the maintenance room she'd been hiding in, letting me shoot at them unhindered. Normally, I would have tried aiming high, hoping for a headshot, but this time I went for their legs—if I couldn't kill them, I might still cripple them if there were no bones left intact to keep them running. Blood, gore, and bits of bone sprayed everywhere, painting the walls and floor in grisly colors—and I was a fucking surgeon at this range with the M16. I'd have given a lot to have a shotgun now that might blast through everything at close range, but seeing both zombies crumple to the floor as their legs disintegrated was rewarding as hell.

"Come on, let's go!" I called to Gita—a few words wouldn't do more damage than the deafening roar of the assault rifle had already caused. She was back out and running to me as I quickly slammed a fresh magazine into the rifle, dropping the empty one to the floor. I simply didn't have time to stow it away anywhere so I didn't bother. I'd have to survive now to rue not having one more magazine to refill later.

"Are we done with stealth?" Gita asked as she whipped by me. I didn't hesitate following her, our boots pounding the floor tiles loudly.

"Yeah, it's not exactly working as planned!" Looking over my shoulder, I saw the downed shamblers still trying to get up, and, failing that, start to drag themselves along the floor after us. Up ahead, one of the doors was a reinforced one for a cold room, and as soon as we got there, I pulled it open and dragged Gita inside, shutting us both in as utter darkness enveloped us. She was panting just as hard as I was, but there was a pained, wet quality to the sounds coming from her. "How are you holding up?" Maybe a stupid question, but I hoped against hope that forcing her to pretend like she was doing better might facilitate the same.

"I'm okay," she lied. I heard her fumbling for something; the next moment, the light affixed to her carbine came on, the sudden glare, small that it was, forcing me to screw my eyes shut.

Changing the topic was so much easier than digging deeper now that I had done everything I could—aside from trying to keep us both alive. "That's two down. Mostly. One of them is the one I thought I killed on the other side of the airlock. No idea about the other. I still don't get how they made it into the labs."

Gita gave a semi shrug that could have meant anything but looked like confused agreement. "Aimes is down for the count, I think," she added as I was still blinking.

"Did you manage to kill him?"

She shook her head. "Nope. Whatever kept him reanimated after you capped his crown, it seems to be losing its grip. I thought he was stalking me into one of the labs, but then he just stopped, staring at a wall. He was still standing but didn't react, even when I almost fell over a chair. Not exactly responsive." She coughed, the sound making me wince from how painful it came out. "That shit's so fucking freaky! I know, it probably shouldn't make a difference because, duh. Zombies everywhere! But this? This is fucking scary."

I nodded—nothing I could add to that. "Must be some shit they did with the serum."

"Like what you shot me up with?" she asked, her voice trembling.

"That's supposed to be the stable version," I reminded her. "But if it's not, do me a favor? Keep chewing on Hamilton if you get to him. Even if it makes him harder to kill in the long run, I'd love to see him realize what's happening to his presumably immune ass."

"You bet," she joked, but it was impossible to ignore the fear in her eyes.

"It's going to be okay," I said, patting her shoulder to try to lend my voice the conviction it was likely lacking. "There's a good chance they killed Nate's brother exactly because what I shot you up with was the next upgrade for the serum. Just... it's gonna be okay." All out of platitudes, that was all I could give her.

I saw her look around briefly, taking in the assortment of plastic material everywhere. The temperature control had long since stopped working, leaving not a trace of cool air in here, but probably a lot of mold in petri dishes thankfully locked away in refrigerators. "Think that was all of them?"

"I saw something moving out here before they came through the airlock. We're not alone. We still need to get to the others." I made sure that I had the next spare magazines in easy reach before I turned to the door. "You open that. I shoot everything lurking on the other side. We run. Sounds like a plan?"

I got a dejected stare from her but she reached for the handle after slamming a fresh magazine into her M4. "Sure does."

I was ready to empty my entire magazine at a moment's notice, but the corridor outside was empty. Well, not empty—the two shamblers I'd mutilated were about halfway down the hallway, but I ignored them. As much as I might strain my ears, I couldn't hear anything but them, either. Gita hesitated but then hastened along the corridor to the next lab door that would lead us through that room to the central corridor once more. I followed, using slow, deliberate steps, my focus snapping to the downed shamblers every few seconds. She effortlessly wove through the workbenches but halted at one of the doors—and, instead of aiming for the middle corridor, went back to the outer. I was about to jump forward and hold her back, but she stopped inside the door frame, pointing. Joining her, I saw what she'd found: one of the panels in front of a maintenance space was knocked loose, revealing lots of lines and cables—and enough space behind all that for us to squeeze through.

I only hesitated for a second, then stepped outside and checked up and down the corridor. The downed shamblers had been aiming for the door we'd disappeared through before but immediately switched course now that they saw me again, but that was it. I gave Gita the silent signal to follow me and went to inspect the tunnel, hating having to stick my head in first. Barely any light filtered in around me as I blocked the entrance, helping my eyesight improve immediately. The back wall was made of concrete, impenetrable to anything biological, but the shamblers must have spent plenty of time digging out insulation and other layers, widening the space reserved for the power lines and other shit except for the ventilation system. It was pitch dark inside either way—and I could only see so far—so I had to trust that nothing was lurking in here. I absolutely hated that, but it was the kind of alternate route that we had been missing so far. At least nothing would be able to slam into me here—or so I hoped.

Switching the light on my M16 on, I shined it down the passage the way we had come first, then forward. Still nothing, not even a rat scurrying away, but then the facility had been blissfully vermin-free—except for the bipedal sort. I had to pull my shoulders in as much as possible to manage to squeeze into the passage and still keep my pack on—turning sideways, it would have been easier—but it was possible. Burns, or even Nate, wouldn't have fit, but Gita and I for once had the advantage here. With no time to waste, I only waited until Gita had squeezed in behind me before I moved forward, trying to make as few sounds as possible.

It was slow going, and I absolutely hated how the walls pressed in around me, making it impossible for me to even look back over my shoulder. It took me a good minute to reach the next access panel, what I estimated were three lab spaces out in the corridor. We had easily five times the distance to travel so I kept going. And going. I stopped at the next panel, waiting until Gita caught up with me, her movements almost silent but in here they were easy to pick out. I was just about to suggest dislodging the panel and checking on the corridor when I heard something—right on the other side of the panel. Both of us froze, Gita's hand barely touching down on my upper arm, her fingers squeezing me tightly for a second.

I let out my breath slowly, then inhaled through my nose, ignoring my lungs as they were screaming for more air. The air back in here smelled dank but the entire complex had that latent chemical stench I'd long ago come to associate with labs. Aimes had smelled of gunfire and blood; the zombie I'd thought I'd killed, of blood and something more animalistic, yet not the typical scent of decay—which was usually more like an olfactory bomb than mere hints. I hadn't exactly had the time to get more than a whiff of it. Now?

The sound repeated itself—a soft scratching, but I couldn't place it. It was definitely coming from beyond the panel. I was itching to shoot right through the wall, sure I would hit whatever was lurking out there. But then I hesitated. I really didn't want to give away our presence—let alone position—if I didn't have to. Maybe whatever was hunting out there would go away if we just waited—

Something grabbed me, from above, and I knew that I'd hesitated that one second too long. Strong fingers dug into my arms and shoulders, heaving upward hard enough that I lost my footing—and my balance—flailing around uselessly. My hip collided painfully with the concrete wall, but at least that gave me a single point of reference to orient myself. I kicked at where I hoped the wall was, connecting painfully enough that agony exploded through my right ankle and knee. As I'd hoped, that created enough of a sideways force for whatever had grabbed me to have a hard time continuing to pull me up. Somehow I managed to get my M16 pointing upward, the light blinding me as it fell on concrete, cables, pasty white flesh—

I pulled the trigger, praying that I wasn't going to end up shooting myself somehow. My left cheek twinged with pain as a freshly ejected shell casing glanced off. Something wet sprayed my face, then my right arm was free, vertigo hitting me as I half fell, half pulled that thing down with me. Pain exploded across my right temple, disorienting me to the point where I couldn't keep up from down—and then, the sensation of being flung.

My back hit the panel full-force, driving the air right out of my lungs, but my body wasn't done being in motion. The force of my impact dislodged the panel and sent me tumbling out into the corridor, the muted but much-brighter-than-darkness lighting outside added to my sense of vertigo—and then I crashed into the floor, my leg, hip, and thigh exploding with pain that made the previous impacts pale in comparison. A small part of my mind wondered if the titanium parts of my femur had just cracked the adjacent bone, pulverizing everything between my knee and hip joint. That was how it felt, at least.

My lungs screamed for air but I couldn't draw breath, my body not cooperating. I rolled over—or tried to—but going right was impossible, so I had to roll onto the left half of my body, which was not a good idea. The pain got so bad that I blacked out for a second, gasping with anguish—but at least that finally brought oxygen back into my body. Adrenaline hit me like a freight-train, my pulse skyrocketing, my heart beating hard enough that it felt ready to burst out of my ribcage. Muscles tensed of their own volition, and suddenly I was staggering to my feet, still uncoordinated and disoriented, my body moving as if on autopilot. From the corner of my eye I saw something coming at me. I ducked, evaded, and came up again to kick, hitting squarely at the center of mass, all without my mind giving clear commands to do so. The zombie was hurled across the corridor, smacking into the wall next to the dislodged panel—that I found halfway between us on the floor, warped from my body's impact.

Rage, white hot and all encompassing, flooded my mind, narrowing my focus on the freak zombie as its sole target. I took a running jump at it, slamming shoulder-first into it, bones crunching under the impact. I reared back, my left foot slipping for a moment as my leg almost buckled under the strain after twisting the wrong way before, but I hardly felt the pain exploding up to my hip. It was easy to ignore, beyond the inconvenience of not having perfect balance. Feeling that drawback made me even more mad, and my fist came up before I could properly plan it, smashing into the zombie's temple. More pain, my fingers going numb after a second of agony, but that didn't matter. The shambler was folding in on itself, and I followed, elbow first, slamming it right into its face—and again, and again. As soon as I got control back over my fingers, I grabbed that thing by one arm, pulling as hard as I could, flinging it over me, across the corridor, where it smacked into the opposite wall and slid down into a lifeless heap.

I tried coming after it as it was still in mid-fling, but my body locked down, mental clarity returning. I half screamed, half inhaled as my lungs finally got the air they needed. As quickly as I'd lost control, I got it back now, that immeasurable anger receding into the pit of my stomach. My body snapped back into full awareness, but with that came all the neural feedback I'd been able to ignore for the past several seconds. It hurt so fucking much that I had to bend over just to make it through the next, struggling breath. My mind was still in hyper-awareness mode, and I realized that it only took a little effort to wipe all that pain away, stuff it into a box, and push it to the very back of my awareness. To dip deep into my reserves, to find the strength to not just get up but tear that zombie to shreds—but I was also aware of how much of a finite resource my energy was. Already, I was running at sixty percent at best, exhaustion like a massive storm brewing on the horizon. Only that once that well ran dry, I wouldn't be crouching on any floor, tired and still panting for breath. No, I'd be dead, and nothing in the world would be able to bring me back from that brink.

Moments before, none of that mattered. Now, it scared the fucking shit out of me, making me hesitate to even move a muscle in fear that it would burn up too much of my remaining strength. But I had to move. I had to get up. I had to—

"You need to get up," I heard a raspy voice mutter next to me, imploring, laced with dread.

My head snapped up, my body kicking into overdrive immediately, ready to physically spring into action. A quick check confirmed—the zombie still wasn't moving, and the angle of its neck made me guess I'd severed its spine. No idea if that would be enough to keep it down for long, but for now, it was. The corridor was empty in the near vicinity, the damn cripples still trying to come after us. The voice, of course, belonged to Gita, who was crouching next to me, her eyes bright with fever—and fear. Of me, the nasty voice at the back of my head supplied. Of our fucking circumstances, I told that voice, and to go fuck itself.

I pushed myself up, doing a quick check on myself. Everything was still operational, but my left leg was definitely not up for a repeat performance of this. My rifle was nowhere in sight, but when she saw me looking, Gita bent back into the hole left by the panel and pulled it out. I checked it quickly, deciding I'd have to trust that it was still working. The optics and light were a bust, but the rest seemed okay. Last, I did a check on the running countdown we were on, confirming what I'd guessed—we really needed to haul ass.

"Come on, let's go," I told her in as low a tone as I could manage and still be heard. "We're going to make a run for it."

I didn't wait for her to respond but set off instead, trying for a light-footed, even gait but probably looked like a clomping, lame horse as I made my way down the corridor. I didn't check the doors we passed but instead let my subconscious run through any clues, visual or auditory, that it might pick up. I could survive another two or three attacks like the last—but if it came to that, we might just be out of time, and it didn't matter what ended up killing me. Gita running behind me was a distraction, but also a familiar comfort. I thought I picked up more, moving to our left, far behind, but I ignored it as it wasn't an immediate danger. Maybe it was Aimes. Maybe it was an entire band of freak zombies. It didn't matter. All that mattered was to get out of the fucking lab spaces.

I stopped as we closed in on the security station at the very end of the labs, where the intersection lay that led to the bioreactors. Somewhere close, Nate and his group had to be holding down the fort. I could hear faint scuffling sounds from up ahead. Looking back the way we had come, I tried to locate whatever had been lurking behind us, but couldn't find anything.

"Can you lock the doors back here?" I asked Gita, trying to guess if the heavy fire doors would be enough to hold back what might be coming after us. With the tunnels and ventilation system, it was anyone's guess if they'd even try.

Breathing heavy from the short sprint, Gita forced herself to straighten as she pulled a device out of her pocket, blinking stupidly at it for a few seconds. "I think I'm locked out of the system," she finally replied, her voice slurring slightly. "I'd have to try from the terminal at the server room."

"Never mind," I told her, stepping past the checkpoint so I could clear the way ahead. "We're out of time."

As I neared the intersection, it was impossible not to see the signs of battle. There were cartridges littering the ground, bullet holes all over the floor, walls, and ceiling, and no short amount of blood. Someone had made a stand here—and they'd pushed forward.

I checked that my com unit was still working. Somehow, it had survived me being flung into a wall and through another. At least the LEDs were still blinking. "Lewis here. We're outside the labs now. What's your status?"

This time, I got a response almost immediately, from Tanner. "We're still locked down here. You're just in time—we're making a push from both sides to break through the main recreational area and get to the exits." He paused briefly, and I thought I could hear someone shouting in the background. "There are more of them hiding by the reactors and up in the office levels," he told me. "Your best bet is to make a run for it and get to us before they get to you. How far away are you?"

I did a quick calculation, the image of the blueprints vivid in my head. "Fifty yards down the corridor, then two bends, and then we should be in the corridor outside the rec area."

"That's where we're bogged down," he affirmed.

"Okay, we're coming to you," I whispered, giving Gita the signal to halt. I considered, then made the hand signals to tell her to take the lead—and run. I had a certain feeling that my voice had been loud enough to draw attention from everything moving around the corner, and if I went first, they'd get her before I was halfway down the corridor. If they got me, I still stood a chance to get up again. Gita shook her head vehemently, but I gave her a stern glare that made her rethink and finally nod.

I inched the rest of the way to the intersection, careful to make as few sounds as possible. A first look both ways revealed empty corridors, but I didn't trust that assessment. Closer now, I thought

I could make out the sound of someone reloading a weapon, but I couldn't be sure. Might have been wishful thinking, too.

Exhaling slowly, I forced my body and mind to quiet before I gave Gita the signal to move forward. She didn't hesitate—bless her—but even her light footfalls made me wince. Turning to face the bioreactor wing, I started walking backward, trying to keep my attention on everything all at once.

I was less than three feet away from the intersection when I caught movement down the hallway—and not just from one figure.

"Tanner, we will be coming in hot," I said as I got ready to fire. "At least three targets."

It was Burns who responded instead. "Acknowledged."

The left-most of the zombies lunged, and I fired. Rather than try to kill it right away, I strafed the entire corridor, hoping to make them pause—and buy us the time needed to get to the others. Behind me, I heard Gita's steps increase into a full-out sprint, my own mind yearning to follow her. My body, though, had other ideas, as I felt a new wave of adrenaline wash through me, making it sound much more fun to hurl myself toward the enemy rather than away from it. I continued shooting as I kept backing away, sending short bursts at each alternating target. Three became four became five, none of them looking impressed by the hits they took. The last shot left my magazine, and for a moment I was tempted to simply throw away the M16 and hurl myself forward instead. What the fuck was it with this suicide serum?

Dropping the empty magazine, I got a new one ready, still backing away. From the corner of my eye I saw that I was at the first bend in the corridor. It was the perfect point where to fling myself around and start running instead, so that's what I did—after emptying the full new magazine into the closest two shamblers, bringing them both to a halt as the wounds in their legs became inconvenient. I didn't take another moment to check whether they'd fall or not, nor to reload—I ran.

Howls and screams started up behind me, the resulting primeval fear jerking my brain stem into giving me extra speed. My balance wasn't perfect because of how banged up my left leg was, but it didn't need to be. I knew I was so close. Just sprint, turn, sprint, turn, and my people would be right there—

Only that when I careened around that last corner that brought me onto the straight leading toward the common area, there was nobody in the corridor. Also no barriers to use for cover, no nothing. What the—

Hands grabbed me from behind, not unlike inside the tunnel, but my brain didn't kick right up into fight mode. A moment later I realized that it was Burns, yanking me into one of the offices lining the hallway. As soon as we were through, Tanner threw the door closed, leaning against it, Burns immediately joining him—to keep it closed as a series of impacts made the sturdy wood shudder. Looking around, I found Gita hunched over next to a desk—and that was it.

"Where are the others?" I asked, panting softly from my little sprint.

Tanner jerked his chin in the vague direction of where the recreational area was. "Trying to break the others free. They tried to make a run for it but got pinned down. Miller figured we'd hold our own as just the four of us so he took the rest across to get the others."

I didn't ask why I hadn't heard any of that on the coms—it made sense not to distract us with chatter that didn't concern us, and might just get us killed. "Hamilton and Richards?"

Tanner winced but Burns was only too happy to respond. "Down the corridor toward the exit. Richards promised he'd keep the exit open until all of us were through."

My fingers involuntarily clenched around my rifle, so I busied myself with slamming a new magazine in and redistributing the few full ones I still had left.

"So, what, Bucky abandoned all of his people to let his arch nemesis be the hero and get them out? We sure this isn't a recruitment mission?" I jeered. It sure looked like that—the perfect bait for Nate to take, particularly after leaving me to die a lonely death at the other end of the installation with freak zombies lurking around. Suddenly, the fact that nobody had made sure Aimes wouldn't come back from the dead looked a lot less like casual negligence.

As expected, I got no response to that, not that I needed one. I had more pressing concerns to deal with. Stepping up to Gita, I forced her to look straight at me so I could check her eyes. Her forehead was burning up, and even though she tried to hide it, I could tell that she was shivering all over.

"What's the plan?" she asked, mostly to distract herself than get a response, I was sure.

"The exit's right around the corner," I offered. "If not for the shamblers out there—"

Who did a good job howling and screaming as they tried to claw their way inside the room. I only needed Burns to look up briefly to find that they'd already dislodged the panel in the ceiling that opened into the ducts. "Let me guess. We make sure they can't get inside, drop down in a different room, and take it from there?"

Burns gave a soft laugh. "Just like old times for you, right?"

I didn't particularly like the idea, even less with full gear, weapons, and rabid zombies hot on our heels, but it was a viable option—and much preferable to trying to get out of the room through the door.

"Help me with the desk?" I asked Gita. Together, we pushed it toward the door so Tanner and Burns only needed to hop aside. It wasn't a good lock—and Tanner pulled over the one shelf in the room to make it a somewhat better barrier—but that was all we had. Burns was already standing underneath the open panel, ready to boost me up, and I let him without further protest. Going first, at least nobody would blind me with their light.

After pulling myself up into the duct, I took a moment to orient myself. From what I could tell, the duct ran from the bioreactor to the common area, so the direction to go was pretty obvious. Gita was right behind me, moving with a lot more alacrity than she had a right to, considering how crappy she must have been feeling by then, but I wasn't going to complain about that. It was dark inside but not pitch black, the soft, red light coming through the vent at the next room over letting me see enough to know where to go. I moved with slow deliberation, trying not to bang my entire way through the duct, but from what I could hear coming up behind me, Tanner and Burns didn't exactly have that option.

I reached the vent soon enough, cursing under my breath when my fingers had a hard time fiddling with the screws. That punch really had busted my right hand. I even considered trying to kick the cover loose but a few seconds later I finally made progress—only to find a hungry shambler already waiting below, making a jump for me the moment the cover swung downward into the room. I jerked back immediately, banging my head and left elbow on the duct walls, but at least the shambler didn't manage to bite my face right off. It found purchase on the rim of the lid, though, immediately trying to pull itself up. Damn, but I really didn't like them when they were smart.

My grip strength wasn't strong enough to pry its fingers loose—I was more than aware of that, so I went for option B instead and contorted myself, trying to reach my Beretta.

"What's going on?" I heard Gita call out softly from behind me.

"Room's occupied," I pressed out, cursing when my fingers barely reached the holster, but not far enough to get the gun out. "Need to dissuade that fucker from coming into the ducts."

I felt Gita move behind me, for a second thinking she'd try to abandon me, irrational as that idea was. "Wait a sec," she responded, closer now. "Maybe don't kick me in the face now... got it!" A moment later, I felt the cool steel of a handgun brush my seeking fingers. Not my own, but I didn't give a shit. Grabbing it, I pulled it forward, lined up the sight, and blew the shambler's head to smithereens with a few well-aimed shots. From that distance, it would have been harder to miss, really. Blood and gore sprayed all over my face, making me wince inside, but at least the thing dropped back into the room. Two more were already standing there, fixing me with that unnervingly smart gaze. Pushing forward, I grabbed the vent cover and pulled it up, happy to feel it snap in place automatically.

"Yeah, we need another exit," I observed dryly.

"You think?" came Gita's retort. I probably had that coming.

I presumed the others had by now realized what was going on so I didn't relay any further warnings as I crawled forward to the next vent. This one was above a corridor, and I didn't even need to remove the cover to see two shamblers standing there, looking up at the ceiling with the same expectancy as cats about to receive their food dish. On I went to where the duct intersected with another. I tried to orient myself but really, it was the same where we dropped out, as long as we could do so. So I went right, mostly because the next vent was closer in that direction. Behind Gita, I heard Tanner curse softly as it took him a while to maneuver around the bend. Oops.

The next two vents were a bust as well, so at the next intersection, I turned left—and this time, it took much longer for the next cover to appear, making me guess that we were traversing the space of the corridor running by the recreational area. I waited for another left turn that might lead to the offices, but none came. It got so dark that even I had trouble seeing, suddenly glad for what little light from Gita's flashlight made it past my body. I halted when I felt a broader rim in the vents where I presumed they passed into the next structural part of the maze of rooms—which was either the exit, or the animal wing. The former would have been neat but the latter was much more likely. That guess pretty much confirmed itself when I heard hushed voices underneath me, making me halt for a second. Maybe I should have mentioned to the others that we were about to invade their hideout from above so they wouldn't shoot at us? But no shots were fired, and the next grate opened into a dark, closed-off room with lots of shelving on the walls—some kind of storage area. I listened, half-hanging out of the ceiling, then let myself drop out and tiptoed to the door. Before I could reach the handle, the door swung outward, low, red light flooding the room—revealing Nate, who was flashing a quick smile over his shoulder. "Cole, you owe me twenty bucks."

Chapter 17

I whistled, giving Gita and the other two the go signal, and turned back to my husband. "Did you know that most of the rooms on the other side of the rec area are full of freaky zombies that are very enamored with vent covers?"

"Good to see you, too," he told me instead, yet his attention was already moving on. The critical look he taxed Gita with made my stomach sink, and suddenly that damn "you're not in charge" reminder from Hamilton felt like a burden lifted off my chest—which, in turn, made me feel like shit. No way I was going to abandon her, but the fact that someone might have to make that call sucked. I took it as a good sign that he moved on to Tanner and Burns next, waiting until both men had given a curt nod—whatever that was about.

The pile of us stepped out into the hallway, finding the rest of our group huddled there, one of the fire doors creating a natural barrier at the end everyone's attention was on. As expected, McClintock was missing, and Russell, Parker, Cole, Munez, Hill, and Davis were bleeding from several wounds, barely patched up as they were. The rest also looked the worse for wear but in somewhat better shape. Since that was only Williams, Wu, and Murdock, things could have been better.

"Time?" Nate asked rather than explained what bet Cole had lost. Probably something about me and the ducts.

"Seven minutes left," Hill offered.

Nate gave a quick nod, calm as if Hill had said hours instead. "That's enough. We have two doors, along the common area, and down the exit corridor. Remember, there's a five-second klaxon before the security system snaps to sudden death status. You have those five seconds to put on your gas masks. Everyone got theirs ready? Good."

I didn't, but it was a quick grab into my pack and some fumbling to fix it to my belt where I could grab it easily. I was about to ask what exactly the plan was, but Nate already turned to us to bring us up to speed. "We try to make a run for it, using our last grenades to make those undead fuckers hesitate long enough that we can get through. My expectation is that they will retreat once the corridors get pelted with formaldehyde and whatnot, so being slower might work in our favor." While he said that, his fingers snapped a quick, "Remember what I told you," at me. I blinked once to show him that I had gotten the message—me first, and let the others fend for themselves. As much as I hated to admit it, that was the best plan, seeing as I wouldn't be able to drag someone like Burns or Hill along, but not taking away space and capacity from someone else might get them saved in the meantime. The way Tanner was plastered to Gita's side made me guess that I wouldn't have to worry about her, either—good.

"Five," Hill called out, putting an end to any chit-chat still going on.

"Get ready," Nate said. His gaze lingered on my face for a second before he whipped around, taking position at the very front of the group. "Munez, Davis, open the doors on my mark. Three, two, go!"

The moment they unlocked the doors and gave them a strong push outward, the shamblers in the hallway beyond—four of them—sprang forward, only to be met with a barrage of rifle fire. On my own, I hadn't been able to fire enough bullets in a short enough window of time to bring them to a halt, but those four were turned into sieves within seconds, joining the lifeless husks already littering the floor. Nate and Hill took point, reaching the second set of doors just as I passed through the first. The same repeated itself, only that beyond the short stretch of corridor, the recreational area lay, with lots of cover, and space. So much open space. After the claustrophobic environs of the tunnel and ducts, and spending an hour in the hot lab, I hadn't thought it possible, but I absolutely hated feeling like I had air to breathe.

At first, there was only a handful of zombies coming at us, easily dispatched just as the ones before them, but I knew that wasn't all of them. I'd seen more than that lurk in the offices leading to the other wing—and there was no way they hadn't heard us coming. But we made it out of the corridor and along the wall of the open space, passing the server room and the blood splatter—now no longer the only one—and were almost around the collection of sofas when we got a glimpse at the corridor leading to the exit. That's when my heart sank.

I hadn't expected to just waltz out of here. The entire way back from the hot lab had been an ordeal, peppered with forces that easily matched our own. My guess had been that there were a good twenty to thirty shamblers lurking in the entire complex, and considering the bodies on the floor we'd passed, that count should have been in the single digits by now—a manageable number for a dozen strong, healthy, armed people who knew what they were doing.

I hadn't expected the entire exit corridor to be chock-full of zombies, a good fifty or so of them.

Well, that likely explained why nobody had heard much of anything from Hamilton. I briefly entertained myself with the idea that he'd been torn to tiny shreds, but it was much more likely that he and Richards had painstakingly slowly sneaked and murdered their way to the exit. They'd left a trail on the floor that I could pick out even now. I couldn't see them or their precious sample containers anywhere, which likely meant our mission had been a success. But it really didn't look great for the rest of us.

We'd had a good run, I figured. So many times over, any of us could have died down here, or on the way. Hell, I should have died long before getting to Europe. Now it was time to pay up.

Looking at Nate, I expected a brief wisecrack from him. A last, "At least it wasn't your nagging that killed us," if there ever was one. No hope, but conviction to go down in one last blaze of glory.

Oh, the conviction was there—but no surprise. Only calculation.

That's when I realized that he'd known that we would be encountering this. And it made sense—Burns and Tanner hadn't tried to do anything but go into the ducts. That calm he'd been showing? That hadn't been confidence. That had been the face of a man who knew he was going to die but refused to give in to panic, grief, or anger. And it was the face of a man with a plan, it turned out. For one last second, Nate's gaze lingered on my face, as if he was committing every line of it to memory. Then he averted his eyes, looking at his men instead.

"Cole, you know what to do?" A quick nod, if no verbal answer. "Burns?"

"We'll give 'em hell," Burns responded from where he was crouching behind me.

"Tanner?"

No answer, and when I glanced at him, I could see why—he and Gita were having their own last private moment, whether it was as friends, or a little more than that. Then he glanced at Hill, giving him a brief nod before his attention turned to Nate. "Let's do this."

Deep inside of me, a part of me was screaming "NO!" but all I could do was watch, helpless, as Nate and Tanner surged forward, screaming at the top of their lungs, aiming for the corridor leading deeper into the complex. A handful of zombies went right after them, but many hesitated. Munez, Cole, Hill, and Williams hurled grenades into the exit corridor, the four detonations going off as almost one. More zombies followed, immediately to be met with fire. Given the choice between two loud, soft targets and a handful armed ones, of course they went after the former. I watched, and felt a part of me die.

He hadn't even given me a chance to say goodbye.

Deep down, I realized that it was shock that kept me rooted in the spot, if only for a moment. Yet when I sprang to my feet, ready to blindly run after Nate, Cole grabbed my arm, dragging me toward the exit. I tried to protest, but just then, the red lights increased in brightness, flashing, and an unbelievably loud wail started up, hurting down to my teeth and very bones. I scrambled to get my mask on, and by the time it sealed around my face, Cole had managed to drag me halfway down the corridor, with more people piling after us. Hill was carrying Gita slung over his shoulders, building a natural barrier behind me. And if that hadn't been enough, Burns was one of the last to follow, making sure that I wasn't going to get out of that corridor anymore, unless it was through the exit.

They'd known this was going to happen. They'd planned this. And I'd been too stupid to realize it.

Liquid started to rain down on us on the last few yards to the exit, through the checkpoint and the final door beyond. I barely noticed it. My gaze briefly snagged to one of the red spray-painted arrows, quickly washed away in a pink cloud by the liquids designed to keep the entire facility clean. Davis went down—my mind barely caught up with it although I managed to reduce one of the zombies' heads to so much gore and shrapnel. What was one more life lost? Nothing. The last few shamblers were dispatched, and just as we got to that last door, it opened, Burns making sure everyone was through before he threw it shut with a clang of finality.

Keeling over and panting from exertion that barely registered, I needed a few seconds for my thoughts to catch up with me. I tore the mask off, greedily inhaling the fresh air in the small anteroom. Hamilton and Richards were there, both armed to the teeth, all the spare magazines reloaded and at hand next to them. They'd been ready to wade back out there and help, should the plan with the bait not work, I realized. So they had been in on it.

And not just on the exit strategy, I realized, when I saw that Richards couldn't even look at me, let alone into my eyes.

Of course they had been in on it. History repeating itself was one thing, but I shouldn't have bought it, not as easily as that. There was only one explanation—either before we'd ventured into the hot lab, or just after, Nate must have realized that we weren't all going to make it back out alive. I hadn't taken my com with me into the lab, but I hadn't really paid any attention to what Bucky did beyond getting him into his suit; I'd spent minutes at a time digging through boxes of samples while he'd been standing half a room away, doing... what exactly had he been doing? Keeping up with what was going on out there? Hashing out a plan how to get as many people out alive as possible? As much as I hated that very thought, I could see how it all made sense to Nate—he was a leader who'd always chosen to lead from the front. He'd do anything to make sure that I survived, including laying down his life for me. And he'd spent that endless cycle in the decontamination shower once already, knowing exactly how long it took—how many minutes that would keep me back so they could clear the way, see if there was an alternative, and failing that, set their plan in action. Nate had trusted me to keep myself alive, given even odds. It was only the overwhelming ones that I was helpless against.

Realizing—and rationalizing—all that was one thing.

That didn't mean I'd have to accept any of it.

This time when the wave of anger swelled, I didn't keep it down. Didn't try to disband it. Didn't even try to ignore it. At first, it was only simmering like coals left over from last night's fire. Then embers turned into sparks as new wind gushing in fanned them back into flames; flames that, if left unchecked, would burn down the entire world—

I belatedly realized that someone had been talking to me—well, at me at least—for a while before I heard a single word, and it was mostly Gita's pained cough that drew me out of my stupor. She was lying on the floor by the elevators, curled in on herself, crying softly. One might have expected our medic to join her but Parker was plastered to the opposite wall, as far away from her as he could get. Burns and Hill were kneeling by her side, doing what little they could to fix what couldn't be fixed. It was Richards's voice that intruded in my thoughts, momentarily giving me something else to focus on.

"You gave her the serum?" he repeated for what was likely the tenth time. I really didn't care, but forced myself to nod.

"We'll only know if it works in a day or two," I offered my misinformed opinion. "Her progression is about double what we're used to from the normal shamblers, but might also be due to her body going to war with itself because of the serum. If she makes it out of here alive, someone should hold watch over her, just to be sure." That certainly wouldn't be me, but I didn't add that.

Red nodded, as if he'd assumed as much. "You went back for the rest of the doses." Not a question, so I just stared at him, letting him stew in his obvious guilt. Asshole.

"I still have two more left," I said, raising my voice ever so slightly—not that it was necessary. The room was small enough that none of us could breathe without all the others hearing it. My eyes fell on Parker, then Russell, Munez, and all the other injured. "No idea what this shit does, and we've seen from Rodriguez, Aimes, and McClintock that the serum might not save any of us. But if you never got it, it's better than nothing."

"Only the old version," Hamilton offered, the mere sound of his voice enough to make me tense.

I turned my head to look at him, considering. "What?"

He had no issues holding my gaze whatsoever, but for once he wasn't oozing his charm all over me. "I said, only the old version of the serum is susceptible to wearing out. The newer version— the one that I got; that Richards got; that you and Miller both got—is engineered to outlive pretty much anything, including the experimental versions." He let that sit for a second before going on. "It's one thing to create biological weapons of mass destruction. But if you could, wouldn't you make sure that your best ones are virtually impossible to put down?"

I wasn't even offended that this was another memo I hadn't gotten. At this rate, it was impossible to keep up with the bullshit they'd pulled on me.

"So when we die...?" I let him finish that sentence.

"We get up, again, and again, and again. Didn't you test that theory once on a converted one?" Another significant pause. "Didn't you die three times on that operating table?"

I continued to stare into his eyes, my mind reeling, but I quickly slammed the lid onto that can of worms before it could more than inch open. Not the time to deal with that—and, if I had my way, that right time would never come.

"And the others? Who got the serum but not that supercharged version?"

Hamilton finally broke eye contact with me, speaking to his men at large. "We knew there was a chance this might happen. We have doses of the upgraded serum on the ship. As soon as we get there, you'll all get your shots. Can't help you if you get yourself killed before that, but one little prick and you'll be fine."

I could tell that several of them let out breaths they might have been holding for the past hour or so—but not all of them. Parker was the only one looking ready to lose it, but Russell and Munez both had that brave yet knowing dead-man-walking look on their faces.

Reaching into the pocket of my pants, I pulled out the two remaining vials and syringe, briefly considering. They'd shot me up with way more than that, but then, this shit was likely highly concentrated. Neither of the men was showing signs of infection yet—not to Gita's extent—so I figured hers really was a reaction to the serum more than anything else. "It's a chance," I offered.

Russell and Munez looked at each other, then back to me, neither of them hesitating. Fumbling with the vials for a second—but more relaxed now that the knowledge that none of that shit, whatever it was, could kill me, had sunk in—I pulled the contents into the syringe.

"Make that three doses," Cole told me as he cracked his knuckles. I was still confused when he jumped into action, grabbing Parker in a headlock, subduing him within moments. Well, looked like it had been a good idea to grab that entire blister of hypodermic needles.

"You can't fucking do this!" Parker pressed out. Any further words he might have hurled at me ended in a muddled whine when Cole tightened his grip on him. None of the others moved a muscle to step in, making me wonder exactly how tired of Parker's antics around anyone previously inoculated with the serum they must have been. It was kind of sad that I didn't feel the least bit of satisfaction as I pushed the plunger on the syringe, sending a third of the dose into Parker's veins. Russell and Munez didn't even flinch. Good boys.

I looked at Gita for a moment, hesitating, but then went over to my pack where I'd left it, got my last three spare magazines out, crammed them into my jacket and pants, and pulled my gas mask back on. Burns was still standing by the door, right where he'd taken position the moment I'd shaken myself out of my stupor at Red's questioning. I held his gaze evenly, as much as the slightly foggy visor would let me. "You're not going to hold me back," I told him evenly, not making it a question or a threat.

"Was afraid you'd say that," he offered, still relaxed. "But I can't let you go in there alone."

That sentence—mostly the phrasing of it—made me want to crack a smile, not that anyone would have seen it.

"What the what?" Cole offered his opinion from where he finally let go of Parker, unperturbed by the medic's venomous looks at his back. "We got out alive. End of story."

Now I couldn't hold back a smile. "Fuck your story. I'm writing my own."

Cole gave me a look that explained what he thought of my sanity—or obvious lack thereof. "Going back in there is suicide." No protest from me. "Hell, woman, he sacrificed himself so you could live! They both did!"

"I'm not going to explain this to you," I said, biting down on my grand example of lone wolves and what they might do once their mate bit it. "I'm not asking you to come with me. Frankly, I don't give a shit. I'm not going to let him die, alone, in there. I get it, someone needed to be the bait. Someone strong enough to put up a fight to draw as many of them away so that the rest could get out. Doesn't mean I have to accept that."

"You are one crazy bitch," Cole muttered—but rather than hold me back, or walk away, he pulled on his own mask. "Then let's do it."

And he wasn't the only one, I realized. Burns wasn't really a surprise, and neither was Murdock—he had been one of Nate's people, just like Davis, who had been with Nate before throwing their lot in with Bucky. Hill wasn't shy to explain why—"I'm not doing this for that fucker. I'm doing this because you got balls"—but the real surprise was Richards.

He was also the one I had a beef with. "What, suddenly you find it in you not to abandon me?" I jeered as I watched him get ready.

He still had a hard time meeting my gaze, but there was steel to his spine when he did. "I had my orders, and they were quite explicit. It was my sole purpose in being along to make sure the samples made it out of the lab." He pointedly looked at the elevators. "That's outside of the complex, wouldn't you agree?" I might not agree on principle, but we'd need every single one along, so I forced myself to swallow my ire.

Trust it to Hamilton not to pass up a single chance to act like an asshole. "And there she goes again, killing good people for her own misguided idealism," he offered, still leaning, relaxed as hell, against the wall at the far end of the room. He also looked ready to keep Parker from bolting or doing anything equally stupid or suicidal, but that didn't keep him from dropping that gem.

The rage building inside of me devoured every syllable of that, the flames getting fanned even more from the condescension in Bucky's tone. I didn't move a mental finger to stop them—right now, I definitely was in the mood to watch the world burn. Turning to Hamilton, I stared at him, letting him see all the derision and hatred I felt for him—and now that I had no reason whatsoever to hold back, I didn't. I hadn't expected him to blanch or some shit, but the humor drained from his eyes when they met mine. Oh, he knew what was going on inside of me—and for the first time he must have been considering that, just maybe, he should have kept his trap shut.

"Are you going to try to stop me?" I jeered. Without rational thought, I felt my body kick into overdrive, gearing up for a fight that I really, really wanted to hurl myself into.

Hamilton's lips twisted into a smirk. "Don't need to. It's not like you can get in there, anyway. Security reset means that your account was deactivated. All our equipment to hack back in is on the other side of, how many were there? Three security doors. Didn't consider that, did you?"

He had a point; I hadn't considered that. But the satisfaction crossing his face made it impossible for me to back down—not that I had any intention to.

"Are you happy now that you finally managed to kill the one guy who might, deep down, still consider you his friend? And you don't even have enough honor left to see if, maybe, you can still save him?"

Bucky shrugged that accusation off like droplets of water. "I got orders, too. And they explicitly state that for no reason whatsoever am I allowed to jeopardize the positive outcome of the mission. That means no going back." His gaze dropped from me to his men, those gathered around me. "I shouldn't even allow you deadbeat assholes to try and help her."

The masks obscured all emotion on their faces, but I didn't miss how Cole tensed beside me. Ah, so he really hadn't drunk too much of the Kool-Aid yet. But none of them said anything. Guess that was my role.

"You have a choice, you know?" I said, stepping closer to him. "You can keep antagonizing me. Riling me up. Don't think I don't get what you're doing—besides being an asshole. But I'm done eating all that anger up. This time, it's going to explode. It's your choice whether that's in your face, or down that corridor as I tear apart every piece of undead ass I find. You know that's not an empty threat. You made sure that I've spent the entire time since we got to your base with my back against the wall. You took everything away from me that might have given me a reason to hold back—and now the last thing I had a reason to live for is dying in there. So either I die killing you, or I die trying to get to him. Your choice."

Deep down, I was aware that it must have been the booster screwing with my mind that made me believe those words with more conviction than was healthy—even for less suicidal notions. It definitely exacerbated my tendency to see the world in black and white only with nothing in between. My way, or no way. But that didn't mean that I wasn't right—and he had taken pretty much everything I cared about from me. My people were alienated by their propaganda that I was working with Bucky and his people; Sadie wouldn't forgive me for leaving her alone to have the baby, and now that I'd gotten Nate killed, she'd probably shoot me on sight. I couldn't join Raynor in the lab, and anyway, I couldn't risk hanging around so that Decker guy could either kill me or twist me into the perverse opposite of everything I had been fighting for. None of that had really gotten to me so far because I'd had Nate—and spending the rest of our lives together, as outcasts, in the middle of nowhere, hadn't sounded so bad.

But now that he was gone, what did I have left?

I wouldn't have called it admiration that I saw in Hamilton's eyes—we were both too stubborn to feel that for each other—but there was definitely recognition lurking there.

He held my gaze for another moment before he shrugged and turned around, his dismissal almost enough to make me go off in his face for good—until I saw what he pulled out of his pack. It was the severed head of one of those freak shamblers—and it was still alive, if one might have called it that, eyes rolling, teeth snapping, never mind that there was nothing below its second or third vertebra remaining.

"What the—"

"You'll be needing this," he said, thrusting the zombie head in my face by what remained of its hair.

Keeping my irritation in check wasn't easy. "I repeat, what the fuck?"

Hamilton's smile was bordering on gleeful. "Didn't notice that the doors don't seem to be a real hindrance for them? That's because they aren't. Their iris scans are in the system, even after the security reset. Grab one of your own once you're through that door."

Nobody remained standing in Hamilton's way as he made for the door, the blindly snapping head held out like a macabre lantern in front of him. And, true enough, the panel not only lit up as the thing got close enough for the scanner to activate—the LED switched to green.

I didn't let doubt get in my way—or common sense for that matter—so I pushed the door open as soon as the automatic lock disengaged.

Chapter 18

The lights were off but the decontamination system was still on, pelting us with more corrosive liquids for the first few yards of the corridor. Then they shut off, coincidentally in sync with Hamilton pulling the door shut behind us, killing the last remaining source of light. I hadn't considered switching my M16 for someone else's so I still had no working light on it, which didn't matter as five strobes were enough. I saw Murdock reach up to pull off his mask but I stopped him. "They likely have a multi-step system," I remarked. "Hear that low hiss? That's likely either chlorine dioxide gas, or ionized hydrogen peroxide. Wouldn't recommend inhaling either until the complex has been aired well for a few hours." Nobody tried taking their masks off after that.

The corridor looked eerily like it had at our first entry—if one was to ignore the bodies on the floor. Both the spray paint and blood were gone, and already the last of the liquid was either seeping into drains or starting to dry in the light draft I felt coming down the hallway as the ventilation system switched to a different setting. Burns checked on the first downed shambler, and it only took him a few swings with one of my tomahawks to get us our own door opener. Nobody was laughing as we left the still-twitching body behind.

The entire facility was quiet once more, the sounds we were making the only I could pick up. It was easy for me not to freak out as I was safely ensconced in my bubble of rage. Why none of the freaks tried to come after us was a mystery until we reached the point where Davis's twisted, torn body lay underneath a heap of them. Just to be sure, Hill smashed in his head—a last token of respect, but also a good idea since we had to come back this way again. Still none of the shamblers were moving, but as I glanced at one in passing, I noticed that the skin around the bullet holes in its forehead looked weird. Signaling Cole to shine his light there, I took a closer look. Yup, it was healing, the effect even more noticeable at the much larger exit wound. Still no real explanation how they kept on after getting their brains scrambled, but then it didn't take much for basic motor functions—even primitive amoebae could orient themselves along chemical trails. I vaguely remembered that one of the other doctors I'd checked up on—Dr. Nakamuri, I thought—had done research in growth factors and cell regeneration. The sick part of my mind briefly wondered how many test subjects he'd accidentally given cancer before turning them into freak zombies. The world was better off not knowing, and so was I.

On we went, Richards and I taking point as we neared the common area. Still nothing moving in sight, but as we got to where the corridor opened up, I saw something scurrying away at the very edge of the cones of light we cast ahead. We stepped over the last puddle on the floor as we left the corridor, only to be greeted by much stronger gusts of air, except in the corner where the ceiling panel was still dislodged. The blood splatter had probably remained on the wall because none of the decontamination measures could reach it.

But we didn't turn in that direction, along the trail of bodies we'd left in our push for the exit. We went down the other hallway that was looking pristine, particularly in comparison to the other one—but only until the first corner. My heart sank further as my gaze fell on several pieces of gear scattered all across the intersection between the bioreactor wing and the labs—a boot, two guns, several empty magazines, fabric that looked like a piece of torn-off sleeve. Still no blood or drag marks, but then they would have been washed away.

Then we reached the labs, and I had to squeeze my eyes shut as soon as that security door opened, low ultraviolet light piercing them somewhat fiercely. It wasn't the same wavelength as what the French had used to check on our status, but the usual UV lights used in laboratories all over the world for the most basic level of decontamination—where usually the last one out switched off the lights, we also turned on the UV lamps. The glare wasn't bad for the others—besides potentially giving them sunburn if they stayed in there for too long—but it sure was for me. That explained why the shamblers had left the labs alone—just not a good hideout if you could lurk more comfortably in the dark maintenance spaces.

Even though the glare must have been just as bad for them—or maybe worse—there were zombies still about here, in several clumps. The first were two of them eating a third, a truly macabre display as all of them were still alive, or as alive as they got. Hill kicked them out of the way, likely upsetting the power balance. None of us cared.

The second heap turned out to be what was left of Aimes—not much beyond torn-apart gear and cracked bones. Why waste a perfectly good body that might still have been lukewarm as whatever kept it going stopped working?

The third were the two shamblers I'd felled, a good ten of the more intact ones feasting on them. One or two noticed us but they were too occupied to care. I hesitated for a moment, not wanting to draw too much attention to ourselves from the sound, but Cole had no such reservations, emptying an entire magazine into any head he could reach—which was pretty much like shooting fish in a barrel. Murdock and Burns helped, until none of the freaks were moving.

The forth heap we found, in the middle corridor, was teeming with snarling, bloody shamblers, and I started shooting as soon as we were in close enough range to ensure headshots. Either alerted by the others—or smarter—they turned on us in full force. Hill had the right idea, again switching to his sledgehammer rather than a semi-useless rifle, the corridor just wide enough to let him swing unhindered. I ducked behind him, taking a knee to shoot from a crouched position whenever I had free sight. Richards broke one hand getting flung into a window, and all of us got knocked around somewhat good—but eventually, we prevailed so we could check on what was left of Tanner—or all seven major parts that had once been Tanner, in places already gnawed down to the bones.

I really didn't want to continue, but I had to. Because there was still one clump of snarling undead ahead, at the very end of the right-most corridor, inside one of the labs bathed in violet light.

My eyes were tearing up to the point where my entire vision swam, making it impossible to properly focus on anything. But it was obvious what that huddle of shamblers, crawling all over each other to be able to continue their feeding frenzy meant.

Except that there were drag marks and bloody handprints leading away from it. Across the room, underneath one of the workbenches. Across the shelves at the opposite wall, up to...

"Fuck me," I mumbled, blinking rapidly to make sure I wasn't imagining things. Nope, that was definitely a body—bloody, bruised, and beaten, but looking positively intact—that lay curled up inside the box of the laminar flow hood, blasted from all sides with UV light so bright that even squinting didn't let me focus on it.

He'd definitely put up quite the fight—now that I could concentrate on the signs, I saw them everywhere. He must have killed the two shamblers that the others were feasting on, but that wasn't everything. Two heavy desks, a shelf, and a workbench had been overturned to create as much of a maze in the room as possible. Anything light enough to be thrown—except for the fire extinguisher by the door—was upturned, one of the windows to the corridor cracked from a desk centrifuge ending up there, now destroyed on the floor below. Tanner's death must have bought him some time—and he'd made the best of that time that he'd been able to.

The sound of my voice, even drowned out by the wet squelch of tearing flesh, was enough to draw all the unwanted attention I really didn't need right then, but my body flew into action even if my mind was incapable on focusing on that right now. Rather than limit myself with a firearm in the tight space of the lab, I grabbed the heavy fire extinguisher from beside the door and used that to bash at anything bloody and snarling that came at me. And then I was past them, leaving the guys to take care of that problem. My boots slipped on the trail of blood as I careened around the corner, barely catching myself as I pulled myself along the benches. My fingers were shaking as I reached for the lid of the hood cover, yet a hand slamming against it—from the outside—made me halt for a second. Richards was standing beside me, a gun in his uninjured left hand, giving me a quick, jerky nod to go ahead. Right. There was that conversation thing that might end with me getting my face chewed off. Not that I cared right then.

Nate's body barely fit into the space of the hood, and I banged his head good as I pulled him back out, the added weight making us both topple backward to the floor. Where not covered with torn pieces of clothing, his skin was burned and had started to blister in places, but that was still better than dismemberment. He was unresponsive, but the blood slowly dripping from his nose frothed every twenty seconds or so with a shallow breath. I didn't dare take off the mask, seeing as the ionized hydrogen dioxide could easily get into the labs through any open doors, but he seemed stable enough for now. As far as I could tell, all parts were still attached, but he was bleeding badly from several deep wounds, the blood loss making the few patches of his skin that weren't burned ghostly white.

"You grab one leg, I'll get the other," Richards told me. "And grab the key."

"Key" was a nice term for our severed head, but I didn't protest. My body was still so worked up that crouching on the floor over Nate's prone body was torture; being able to move was a lot better. The others were still busy with the shamblers and gave up as soon as we were out of the lab, dragging the lifeless body between us. Burns took point, the others remained behind us, trying to keep the shamblers from following. Realizing that they'd just lost some juicy bits of warm flesh, they came after us, howling and screaming, alerting the others—and the chemical mist still diffused in the air only held them back so much.

I only realized how much when we flew out of the lab area and past the checkpoint into the corridors leading to the main part of the complex, and suddenly there were answering howls and growls coming from everywhere at once.

"Run?" I asked no one in particular.

"Run!" Cole agreed loudly from behind me before shooting down a corridor we passed.

So that's what we did, skidding and careening into corners and silently praying that we would be quick enough. My mind locked up in a litany of "please don't die"—and I wasn't entirely sure if I only meant Nate or all of us. Being brave in the face of my own suicide was one thing, but being responsible—again—for someone else's, not so much.

But we reached the exit corridor without getting torn to shreds, and while a few shamblers had wandered back in, they were much too interested in the easy food already on the ground to get in our way. Burns stopped just before the security checkpoint, waving our unencumbered runners forward before herding Richards and me along. I lobbed the head toward Hill, watching in a moment of macabre fascination as he fumbled with it. Behind us, I could hear the horde coming, the darkness so deep that I couldn't make out more than shapes. "Hurry up!"

Hill caught his burden for good and held it up to the checkpoint. As soon as that door opened, he took off, and we were on the home stretch. My shoulders and lower back were killing me, my lungs burning with exertion and lack of air to the point where I started seeing blotches all over my vision, but I forced myself to push through. Only one more door, then we were safe—relatively speaking.

Cole reached the door first, taking up a defensive position, Murdock dropping to a knee beside him. Hill didn't bother with stopping but let the door itself slow him down, pressing the head into the sensor field. Nothing happened for endless four seconds, then the lights turned green and the lock disengaged. Hill pretty much fell into the room; Cole and Murdock crawled through backward, their rifles trained down the corridor. One last, gigantic pull and Richards and I managed to trundle through, forcing Burns to vault over us as he hadn't slowed down. The others were still there, even Hamilton— somewhat to my surprise—but had been smart enough to move out of the way. Russell and Munez stood ready by the door, pushing it shut as soon as we cleared it. I hadn't planned on falling to my knees but my legs simply gave out, spilling me onto my back, just in time to see a good twenty zombies make a run for the closing gap. The door "thunked" shut not a moment too soon, the sound of several heavy impacts on the other side making not just me shudder. While everyone else was either on the floor or bent over, panting heavily,

Cole tore at the cables next to the scanner panel, putting it offline for good. It shorted out with a satisfying rain of sparks, making him yelp and jump back.

"No one's coming through that ever again," he observed, shaking his right hand, his gloves smoking faintly. I allowed myself the hint of a grin after I tore my mask off, but that was all the attention I had to spare, forcing my mind to snap out of flight mode pronto.

In the harsh glare of the flashlights, Nate looked even worse than the few glimpses in the lab had let me assess. I blindly groped for a water bottle from my pack, wetting one of my spare shirts so I could wipe off some of the blood to get a better look at where it was still coming from, easily taking off a few layers of skin that way. I winced but continued, glad when Burns held out a knife to me so I could cut through shredded gear where it made no sense to preserve it. Nate was no longer bleeding from his nose, but I figured that might just be a good sign.

"Parker, glue!" I called, not looking up from my grisly work. When no one handed me that damn tissue adhesive, I looked up, not caring to cut down on the wave of annoyance that rose within me. The medic remained huddled in the back part of the room, glowering at everyone and me in particular, not moving a muscle. I narrowed my eyes at him, my mouth opening to send a scathing tirade his way, but Cole snapped first, stalking over to Parker, towering over him. No words were exchanged but they weren't necessary; Cole returned with two first-aid kits and a satchel that he dropped onto the floor next to me, already opening them to get me what I needed.

"You know that shit's only a temporary fix?"

I nodded, taking the first syringe he handed me, tearing the safety cap off with my teeth. "One of the first things I did after the shit hit the fan was to dig what was left of the glue, plus pus and necrotic flesh in abundance, out of his chest. Martinez had to patch him up after a rebar speared him through the chest." The memory made me crack a smile. "That rebar should have gone through me, probably. Didn't because he pushed me away. You could say this is kind of our thing."

The worst-looking wounds were all superficial—and would leave some scars that could rival those on my hip and leg—but some were still bleeding enough to make me curse as I tried to plug them. One in the crook of his neck, two on his torso, and one so close to the femoral artery on his right leg that I could confirm that he had, in fact, not been going commando, and the goods looked properly tucked away still. That done, I allowed myself a simple sigh of relief as I rocked back on my heels—but that didn't mean much. In a day or two, I'd have to cut the glue out and hope I could sew him back together. Maybe after that things would look up. They had to, really. There was no alternative.

I checked on his breathing next, this time in earnest. There was some wet rattling going on that I really didn't like but he was still breathing, regularly if slowly. I could only passingly check his burns and we didn't have anything with us for that so I slapped on some gauze and moved on. I peeled his lids back next, trying to check his eyes, not sure what to expect. They weren't looking like cooked egg whites so that was good, but I knew that so much UV light would have wreaked havoc with them as well. Next came the part I couldn't do on my own but Burns and Cole were ready to lend a hand—happy align-broken-bones and pop-joints-back-in-place time! I didn't doubt that we'd have to do more of that later, once he was conscious enough to let us know what didn't move as it should.

"Are you done yet?" Hamilton asked as soon as I took a moment to wipe my bloody, grimy hands on the even more bloody, grimy rag formerly known as my shirt. "We need to get going."

Glaring up at him I found that even tired enough to keel over, I was still angry enough to be ready for a fight.

"What's ten more minutes to you? Getting bored already? It's dark outside, anyway, so what's the difference?" Dark, in a city that had given us barely a glimpse at its undead population in daylight, which had been enough already to give me nightmares for years.

"Me? I could watch you play dilettante patch-up for hours. But those undead fuckers on the other side of the door have gotten mighty quiet. Wanna bet they're smart enough to use one of their exits to the surface so they can wait for us when we finally make it up through the elevator shaft? Just a thought."

A very sobering one, and one I hadn't considered. Rather than kick myself for that, I inclined my head, if grudgingly. "That's all I can do for him right now. Do we have something we can make a stretcher out of, once we're past the shaft?" I figured someone would likely have to pull Nate up the old-fashioned way.

"Check on your other patient while we get everything ready," Hamilton told me.

I was ready to grouse at his dismissal, but then realized that he was talking about Gita. The guilt that I hadn't yet felt as we'd stumbled over Tanner's remains came crashing over me full force now as I turned to where she was hunched over in a corner, looking incredibly small and all alone in the world.

Crouching down next to her, I checked her temperature first. At least she was still responsive and hadn't seemed to get much worse in the meantime.

"You didn't find him, did you?" Her voice was weak, barely more than a croak.

I debated with myself what to tell her. I would have wanted to know the truth—but I'd gotten a second chance today that she'd never have. Adding to her obvious grief didn't seem smart, so I shook my head, hoping that none of the other idiots would later contradict me.

"Nope. I'd love to tell you there's still a chance—"

"I know that there isn't," she offered, closing her eyes for a second—and then visibly pulling herself together. "I hope he took a lot of them with him before they got him. He always said he wouldn't want to die, toothless and senile, in a bed somewhere. Just didn't think it would happen so soon."

"It's always too soon."

She let me pull her to her feet, and I went over her gear and weapons check with her. She still had two spare magazines, which was more than she'd probably be able to use. The nasty voice at the back of my head helpfully supplied that those were two spare magazines I could grab should push come to shove. I tried to ignore that knowledge as best as I could as I got myself ready before checking on Nate again. Burns was done wrapping him in his spare jacket, and the torn leftovers of the old one did a good job patching up the holes in his pants. I'd make sure to get him all bundled up once we were in the boats.

If we made it back to the boats.

That had felt like a small detail when we'd descended into the underground complex, not like the insurmountable feat it had turned into now.

Nobody was leaving here unscathed. Munez was actually the one with the less cuts, bruises, and broken bones, and considering that he was likely infected, that was saying a lot. I wasn't the only one who had trouble now ascending the elevator shaft. If not for the small electric gimmicks that helped, Richards with his broken hand—and utter loss of five of his fingers because of that—would never have been able to get out of there. Getting down had been an affair of minutes; getting everyone and what was left of the gear back out took over an hour and was far from stealthy. Somehow we managed, because what was the alternative? Exactly.

It was as we sneaked up the stairwell to the ground level that I felt the first effects of the booster finally wearing off. I hadn't kept track of it anymore after we'd ventured into the hot lab, but the sudden sensation of vertigo, followed by a spell of weakness that almost brought me to my knees, was an unwelcome reminder that I was running on borrowed resources. It passed quickly enough, but it was a warning I absolutely could have done without.

The foyer of the building was still empty, but predators—bipedal and more—had taken the last hours as an invitation to come after the corpses our cleanup effort had left. There was gore, streaks of fluids, and parts of bodies everywhere, a grisly welcome mat if there'd ever been one. But that wasn't the only nasty surprise waiting for me.

Because of my physical limitations—and this time not even those due to Raynor's precision work—I couldn't be used for hauling gear or the wounded, so vanguard duty it was. Since we had Nate and Gita to carry, and Richards couldn't shoot, it was down to Munez and me to sneak outside and find a way for all of us back across the entire length of the plaza and down to where the boats—hopefully—were still waiting for us. I hated the idea of having to leave Nate's side, but I hated the idea of Hamilton shooting me in the face out of principle even more, so out into the biting cold and darkness I went.

The last traces of light in the sky were long gone, leaving the city in utter darkness. The weather had turned for the better, the storm moving on while we'd been busy underground; only light gusts of wind were still blowing, chasing the last tendrils of fog away. It was a clear, starry night, and under different circumstances I would have loved to enjoy the view. At least there was enough light left for my eyes to work well, but that also meant the shamblers would see us, too.

I stepped out through what used to be one of the huge windows next to the grand portal, pressing myself against the cold slab of stone next to it. Munez mirrored my move on the other side, looking around nervously. My side was the one farther away from the river, toward the cube-arch thing towering above the plaza. From here, I could see the open spaces leading up to it well—and the easily over a thousand strong mob of shamblers that slowly trundled from one side to the other. There was no sense or direction to their motions so it wasn't simply a streak passing through. Why they didn't seek shelter, I couldn't say, but I didn't like how those closest to us stopped more frequently to sniff the air. I knew I was reeking of disinfectant, but to their fine-tuned senses I probably also smelled of blood—Nate's, that of the freaks I'd killed or fended off, and maybe some of my own as well. Or maybe it was something else that triggered them, who was to say?

Hamilton's orders had been clear—we needed to get to the boats, but it wouldn't do us any good if the shamblers came after us the moment we stepped outside. From their sheer number it was obvious that creating a diversion wasn't something that would work, so avoidance was the name of the game. At least the bite of the cold chased away the blanket of exhaustion that kept spreading through my thoughts.

I signaled Munez that I was going to check to the right—toward the horde. Everything inside of me screamed to go the other way, but if there was a chance that we could sneak out through the back, someone needed to check on what we might be running from if the plan went to hell. I used slow, deliberate motions to inch my way along the front of the buildings, hating how heads all over turned in my direction, eyes watching me—yet none had that focus and intelligence in them that the freaks had shown. That didn't change a thing about their immense numbers, and after watching them for a good five minutes I decided that this wasn't the way out.

Munez had returned from his brief check the other way, and when he gave me a quick nod of confirmation that the straight route down the plaza was still the better option, we started scouting that way. "Clear" was relative as even getting to the other end of the building took us several minutes and seven downed shamblers. The cold left them sluggish and easier to kill, but all that was relative.

While Munez secured the gap between this building and the next, I sneaked back inside to give the others the all-clear. I didn't get more than a glimpse at Nate before I had to go back out. Wu and Murdock would be carrying the makeshift stretcher, and Burns had Gita partly draped over one shoulder. I forced a lid on my worry and stepped out to make sure the way ahead was clear.

Our cleanup was already drawing attention, the first enterprising shamblers falling on their now permanently dead brethren. The wet sounds they produced made me sick—but they also did a good job masking the sounds my movements inadvertently produced. More and more crept closer to investigate, and I realized that they'd likely been drawn by the dead bodies we'd left on our way in. It wasn't that hard to keep adding to that, so that was the strategy I proposed in hushed tones over the com. The rescue effort ceased for a while, a small group of guards remaining with the wounded while the rest swarmed out to bash in heads and sever spines. It was a grueling, painstakingly stop-and-go effort, and more than once it was luck that my too-quick motions in downing a zombie didn't get the entire mob to come after me. Before long, I was sweating from both tension and exertion, my muscles twitching all over. I felt myself sliding ever so slowly toward that crash that I knew was coming, but I couldn't let myself succumb to that yet.

It was close to midnight by the time we'd created two grisly, bloody lines along the sides of the plaza, and none of the undead bystanders paid us any heed anymore. My leg was killing me, and I doubted I would have managed to run even if my life had depended on it. Thankfully, it depended on being slow and stealthy, instead. We finally reached that ramp by the park deck, and I allowed myself a last, lingering look across the bridge at central Paris. Even though it was twice as deadly at night, it looked so fucking peaceful in its grand old splendor.

I couldn't wait to be out of here and never see any of it ever again.

The squatters were still inside the park deck, and several of them had come out to investigate. Cole made as if to come after them but I signaled him to back down and instead wait until they had passed and joined those repurposing the shamblers we'd done away with. One group passed, giving us a few minutes respite. That was enough to get Hamilton, Richards, Burns and his burden, and Munez past them to clear the lower parts of the ramp. Up here, we had to wait another fifteen minutes to let the next group of four through, plus the makeshift stretcher. I forced myself not to follow their progress but watch the undead instead, who were still watching us. Then we caught another break and the last of us took their chance, crossing onto the ramp. Just before ducking behind the balustrade, I caught a last look deeper into the vast, open space, and that's when I saw them—an entire huddle of a good thirty of the emaciated, smart ones. Only half of them were naked, their skins darkened with what must have been fresh blood. But rather than come after us, they kept watching as well—waiting for us to finally vacate their territory. I was more than ready to oblige them.

I was one of the last to make it off the ramp and across the road between the car wrecks, all still swarming with shamblers but with enough cover to avoid them if we just took enough time to let them walk past. Everyone was already in the boats—that were still where we'd left them—and I was grateful for Cole helping me down. I was again riding with Ines although Noah had switched over to the boat that Hamilton had commandeered as his. It was hard not to notice that none of the possibly infected was in that boat—Parker and Russell were with Burns and Gita in the one piloted by Raphael, and Munez climbed in behind where I sat down in the middle of the cargo space, pulling Nate onto my lap—after drawing my Beretta. I wasn't stupid enough to expect to survive should Nate die and convert, but I sure as hell was keeping him from killing anyone else.

Once everyone was stowed away, we cast off, the engines still silent. That made steering problematic, but since it kept us from drawing attention—such as from the bridge jumpers—it was the best way to go. It only took a few minutes for the last skyscraper to fall out of sight as the gently rocking boats were swept away by the black waters of the Seine.

Chapter 19

Traversing the locks on the way upriver had been a chore. Now, it was all but impossible. We only had to make it across one barrier before we reached a small, uninhabited island where we moored the boats and crawled on land. I barely managed to drag my own weight up the gentle slope. Helping Cole and Hill get the stretcher out of the boat made me hunch over and dry heave. I found a cozy tree trunk where I dropped my pack and Nate's, and then settled in next to his prone body. No guards this time, not that they were necessary. Richards made a last round, forcing everyone to eat a few bites from their provisions before he let us crash—and crash hard we did.

I forced myself to remain awake—or at least something resembling that—but my muscles turned to liquid gelatin, not even trembling with the shakes I'd had before. Small things like blinking felt like a tremendous task. Two or three hours in, the idea of simply no longer breathing so I could die felt like a great concept, but my lungs kept expanding whatever I did. The gun in my hand started calling my name loudly, but raising that arm was too much of an effort. Besides, I had to stay alive to make sure Nate did, too. Somehow, that thought kept me going through the night and into early morning. From what I could see of the others, none of them felt much better, but most refused to show it so I very well couldn't publicly fold in on myself. I'd never done hard drugs, but this felt like the worst kind of withdrawal ever.

And that was just the physical punch to the gut. Only fourteen of us were left, and if I'd miscalculated with the serum I'd grabbed from cold storage, that number would very soon drop to nine. Eight, if Nate didn't pull through. Eight out of twenty. Except for Tanner, I hadn't exactly enjoyed the company of those no longer with us, but that number was like a beacon of horror searing into my mind. How could anything warrant casualty numbers like that?

Things didn't get better as the sun rose, but the strain on my bladder became too much, and the hole where my stomach used to be needed to be filled. On the way back from relieving myself, I checked on Gita and Munez, mostly because they were less than five steps of deviation away. Gita was still burning up but her body seemed to have quieted down—no more violent shaking, and since she hadn't started vomiting blood, I took that as a good sign. Munez was tired but since he hadn't received the booster, it was normal exhaustion and he was actually doing better than the rest of us, starting a small fire for warming water for tea and getting some rice and beans going. I left Russell and Parker to be someone else's problem, instead returning to my comatose patient.

It was still cold as fuck but I forced myself to check on Nate's wounds. The glue was doing its thing but it was obvious from the swelling and how pliable the barely healed wounds were that yes, there was pus building underneath the fresh scar tissue, and I'd get to go back in soon enough to clean them out. Some of the bites looked slightly infected—which was alarming to a point—but none got worse. His breathing was still slow but sounded clearer now. His eyes were swollen and crusty from tears constantly leaking out of them; nothing I could do about that.

Getting some hot liquid into myself helped; eating, not so much, but I would have had to keep something down for more than a minute at a time to get some sustenance. Mid-morning, Munez made the rounds, distributing bags of what looked like saline solution but must have packed more of a punch than that since I felt immediately better after a third of the infusion had made it into my veins. At first I wondered why they hadn't hooked us up to those right away, but it was kind of obvious—as long as there were still traces of the booster in our system, it made no sense to try to replenish anything if it would just burn up immediately, anyway. Nate got a bag as well, but I didn't see any change.

I would have loved to spend the rest of the day—and the coming night—on the island, but Hamilton called for us to break up camp soon after the first soldiers managed to more than simply drag themselves from one spot to the next. It was only after we got the first boat into the water that Russell broke down, hurling up rice, beans, and what looked like a gallon of blood. His eyes were feverish and bruises started forming on his neck and cheek, his wet coughing a dead giveaway that his lungs were filling with phlegm. Nobody said anything—not even Hamilton, and I wouldn't have been surprised if he'd pulled out a gun and shot Russell at the first sign of infection. What he did do was cold-cock Parker who was about to descend into a panic attack.

Two more locks, and we found another cozy island with only a handful of shamblers on it, but something we absolutely needed—

shelter. My body felt weighed down with lead as I helped clear the buildings, tasked with killing the undead so someone else could drag them to the shore and hurl them into the river. My muscles felt frozen stiff even after an hour of heavy work, and it took a good thirty minutes inside for my skin to start itching as it slowly thawed to more normal temperatures. And still no change from Nate.

Gita started getting better during the night, although it wasn't that noticeable. She remained curled in on herself, staring at the wall of the small hut, not responding to anything going on around her. Which wasn't much, at first, until Russell slid into the last stage of infection. At his request, Hamilton and Cole helped him up so he could drag himself outside. Richards and a few of the others followed. I didn't; I really didn't need to see this, and since we'd barely exchanged ten words since we'd met, it felt right not to intrude on their moment. I still felt my throat seize up as a single shot rang out through the night, answered by fifteen minutes of howls and screams from the riverbanks. Burns cast me a questioning look but I didn't respond. What was there to say?

I finally slept a couple of hours that night, but never deep enough not to rouse when anyone moved too much somewhere around me. That helped somewhat, but I still didn't refuse another infusion bag when offered. We got ready in the morning, shortly after the sun rose, to set out on the next step of our journey.

That was, until Parker started to babble maniacally about having a sore throat, and for someone to check his temperature, and oh no! We were all gonna die! Richards tried to reason with him that he was fine—he would have shown signs had he been infected hours ago, but he and Munez both were doing okay. None of the others showed any weird signs, either, but Parker wouldn't listen. Richards finally forced him to swallow a handful of pills—or rather, had Cole and Hill hold him down and cut his air off until he swallowed them— that left Parker borderline catatonic, but the game was on again once Parker pushed through the effects of the drugs late afternoon. We were past the last stretch of the river that was familiar to us, passing the riverbank by the golf course in somber silence. We still didn't use the engines, relying on the currents of the Seine alone to sweep us toward the ocean. We still had four days left until our rendezvous on the beach, so why invite trouble?

Not that trouble wasn't usually quite happy to invite itself.

Two more times Richards filled Parker up with whatever happy pills he had with him—I suspected it was part of what they'd dosed me with at first but I'd never know as I didn't deign to ask—but Parker wasn't stupid; or a different kind of stupid, rather. After we made camp the next evening, he appeared calm and docile—or only as hostile as he usually was, letting everyone forget about him. That was, until he jumped up in the middle of dinner and ran screaming from the camp, past the guards, and into the night. That wouldn't have been such a big issue—at least not for me—if not for the fact that we weren't camping on an island this time but at the northern river shore, and Parker had a lot of way to run—but chose the one trail that led him straight into a pack of shamblers that must have been sneaking up on us for a while. Bad for him, good for us—if not for the fact that they only managed to kill him, not tear him apart, so we had to do away with over fifteen shamblers and one overcharged fresh one that packed a hell of a punch. My annoyance had long since turned to rage by the time Hamilton finally put Parker down for good, several knocked-out teeth, one broken arm, two sprained shoulders, and a lot of bruises later. Hill had borne the worst of the brunt, putting one more of our heavy hitters mostly out of commission. After that, we decided to stay on the river until we hit the ocean, which meant another sleepless night with me having the honor of directing three boats through the increasingly broadening Seine.

We arrived at the river delta early in the morning, the thick fog coming in from the ocean hiding most of the towns of Le Havre and Honfleur from sight. Pretty much all we saw besides a few wrecked cruise ships was the huge bridge spanning the harbor, connecting both riverbanks to each other. We finally engaged the engines as we jetted around the town and into the ocean, then down the beach until we found a spot that was deserted enough that drop-off wasn't a required hurried five-minute job. The French scouts didn't seem too sad to be rid of us, forced as they'd been to go through the motions with us. I still got an unexpected hug from Ines, too baffled to respond. Then they hopped into their boats and took them back into the fog, never to be seen again.

The racket we'd made didn't attract much attention but because we were down to six people without major injuries, Hamilton had us scour ten miles of beach and the land behind it for the rest of the day. I absolutely hated spending hours away from where I could check in on Nate, but Gita gave me faithful if uninspired hourly updates. She didn't attempt to hide that she was heartbroken and grieving, but at least she wasn't a coward like Parker. I wouldn't have been surprised to find her gone when I returned that night but she was still there, hanging on tightly. While we'd been out and about, Hill had managed to establish communication with the destroyer, and we got the first good news in what felt like fucking forever: they were cutting short their patrol route to pick us up the next day. Considering that I doubted that said patrol duty had been more than a ruse to hide the real reason for this trip across the world, that didn't come as that much of a surprise to me.

I spent the night huddled under blankets and sleeping bags, curled around Nate's unresponsive body, trying to keep him warm. It was in the late hours of the night, when it was darkest and coldest, that I felt that veneer of exhaustion and sheer stoic will to keep going finally cracking.

"You can wake up now, you know?" I whispered into his chest, counting to five on my own heartbeats before I heard his heart beat once. "You did it. The impossible. You're still alive, and we pulled this fucking mission off. Now come back to me, will you? Because I really, really need you here, with me."

I didn't expect a response but that I didn't get one made me feel sick.

There was no sleep to be caught after that, and once I was sure that I didn't look like I was about to fall into a million pieces, I got up and walked over to the small fire we had going on, telling Cole to get lost. I half expected a pep talk from him but he beat it without uttering a single word, leaving me to my glum thoughts.

I was still tending the fire by the time everyone else got up and the final guard shift came in. Together, we waited on the beach for the boats to arrive. I heard their even drone long before I saw them, and still, the relief I had been waiting for didn't flood my mind. All I felt was emptiness, and a dash of wry humor when I realized that all of them were in full hazmat suits—both the sailors driving the boats and the two marines each they had with them for support.

It didn't take long to load us and what remained of our gear onto the RHIBs. On the way to the shore, they had been so full with people, packs, and weapons that I'd kind of been afraid something— or someone—might fall overboard; now there was empty room aplenty. They might even have crammed us onto a single boat. It was still easier this way. I didn't look back at the beach disappearing into the fog. As much as I didn't look forward to hashing out the issues ahead of me, there was nothing for me back there.

It took us maybe twenty minutes to reach the destroyer, and another few to get everyone and the boats back on board. Right there on deck, Sgt. Buehler and her marines were waiting for us, also in hazmat gear, and increasingly tense as they saw the amount of bandages our people were wearing.

"I presume we'll need a quarantine zone?" she asked while we were still unloading.

"You bet your ass we do," Hamilton told her, for once sounding more tired than out for a fight. I was sure that Richards would do his best later to smooth any feathers that remark might have ruffled, but for the moment, Buehler herself just gave a nod and pointed down the deck.

"We've cleared the gym for you." Which would be the former helicopter hangar at the stern of the ship. "Our med team is already waiting on standby."

Quarantine zone had made it sound so fancy, but no one forced us to strip down and scrub ourselves with bleach—at least not yet. Considering that we'd spent weeks in that gear without much chance to clean up, burning it all sounded like the better option, but I could see where nobody felt comfortable with that kind of waste going on. I didn't give a shit about any of that as the moment the marines brought in Nate on the makeshift stretcher, the doctors and nurses descended on him—until they drew up short after pulling him across onto what looked like the field version of a collapsible operating table.

The senior doctor cast around the room, settling on Richards since Hamilton had gone AWOL. "What's the status?"

I hadn't bothered with undressing beyond dropping my pack just inside the door, leaving my M16 for someone else to take to the armory—yet my Beretta I drew, keeping my hand down by my thigh. Burns appeared by my side, still cradling his assault rifle.

Richards looked ready to respond but then ducked away, leaving me to do the talking. "He's been unresponsive since a pack of supercharged zombies came after him. He's been inoculated with the serum before—and an updated version that's supposed to render him immune to anything else he might have caught from the undead fuckers—so his blood should be clear. I'd still try not to cut myself while working on him if I were you."

The team had obviously been briefed before and I saw two of the nurses relax—one after she noted that Burns and I were armed—but the doc wasn't that easily satisfied.

"I have been told that this serum should make those inoculated with it impervious to most damage, and what can affect them usually kills them, including the unpleasant side effects of that. Is that not true?"

I shrugged. It really was anyone's guess. "And still he's in a coma. The burns are from the UV lights in the lab where we found him. He was smart and must have realized it hurt their eyes, but prolongued exposure has its drawbacks."

He still didn't get it. "But—"

"Doc, if I knew what was wrong with him, don't you think I would have tried to fix it myself already?" I ground out, that anger coming back in an instant. I was tempted to let loose, maybe even physically, but I was sure someone would have put me down for that before I could accomplish anything. "Maybe he has a concussion. Maybe the virus those freaks were carrying mutated and somehow got around the immunoprotective properties of our serum. Maybe he's just simulating because he didn't want to walk back. I don't have a fucking clue! It's your job to fix him. So, fix him!"

The doctor's gaze dropped to my gun. "And if I can't?"

It took me a few seconds to catch on to his meaning. Right, they probably still thought I was a complete nut job because of that blender incident in the mess hall.

"If you can't, and if he dies and converts, it's my job to make sure he won't be able to hurt anyone—you, your team, the sailors, or anyone else on this ship, or off it. I know how much they can physically take once the serum has taken hold; hell, I'm the living, breathing testament to that. But there are limits, and that's why we take precautions."

"You're his wife," one of the nurses noted.

"That's why I'll be the one pulling the trigger," I told her, evenly holding her gaze. "And I won't hesitate for a second. I owe him that much."

And because he was a blessing in disguise, Burns took that opportunity to laugh softly and add, "She's probably been waiting for a chance like that for fucking forever."

The doctor finally nodded, still looking less than convinced, yet before he could get started, the door to the hangar banged open, admitting Hamilton with Buehler and two marines in tow, carrying a small case he must have retrieved from somewhere on this ship; it looked way too clean to have come with us. Bucky's gaze went to me first but he spoke to the doctor as he handed him the case.

"In here are several doses of the paralytic you might need should he wake up before you're done putting him back together. There's also a modified version of your run-of-the-mill adrenaline shot in there that might do the trick if cutting him up and sewing him back together doesn't wake him up. If none of that helps, the red-labelled bottle contains a strong tranquilizer that will ensure that he remains in a comatose state for twenty hours per dose. There's enough in here to keep him under until we reach the States if the need arises. Your call."

When the doctor nodded, Hamilton turned back to me, his focus dropping to the gun at my side before he caught my gaze again. I almost laughed when I realized that my impulse to blow out his candle was gone, instead replaced by a much deeper-seated need for vengeance. Oh, the day would come that I made Bucky Hamilton pay for what he'd done—and it wouldn't come with a quick shot or smooth cut. It might not even come at my hand, I realized—but it would come.

He must have seen that conviction in my eyes because for once, he didn't smirk or offer a goading remark, but instead gave me a small, simple nod. He knew that he had it coming, and he accepted that. In this moment he was so very much like Nate that it made me want to scream.

"Did you do this?"

The doctor's question pulled my attention back from Hamilton, and when I looked at him again, he'd joined Richards at the other end of the gym, working on getting everyone settled and eventually moved out of the quarantine zone and back into proper quarters. Nothing I felt I should concern myself with any time soon.

"You mean the glue?" The doctor nodded while his team continued cutting the pieces of bandages and fabric from Nate's body. "I patched him up as well as I could. I checked on the necrosis going on around the wounds but since it hasn't progressed as quickly as I expected, I left everything as is. You know way better what to do than me."

That had been another one of my many concerns—and one of the nurses, after checking on a few of the superficial bite wounds, summed it up perfectly. "He's healing, but not as quickly as he should, given his circumstances."

For the first time, I got a good look at Nate's body, my heart seizing up at how extensive his injuries were—and continued to be. Yet all I could do was keep to the side and watch as the medical professionals set to work. I didn't understand half of what they talked about, but then I didn't need to—nor did I care when, seconds after they gave him that amped-up adrenaline shot, a violent shiver ran through his body and his eyes flew open.

I was leaning over him before my brainstem could scream a warning at me, the medical personnel retreating to what they thought was a safe distance. It really wasn't, but one look into his eyes and I knew I could tell them to stand down—that was definitely my husband staring up at me, eyes wide and full of pain and confusion, both of which receded the moment he recognized me.

Holstering my gun, I took his face in my hands and leaned close, feeling a world of relief wash over me. "I'm right here," I told him. "Right here with you."

I could have offered a million platitudes but that wasn't what we did—neither of us. So I let the people who knew how to fix him do their job instead. We'd have plenty of time to talk later. For me to yell at him for being so stupid to try to sacrifice himself. To tell him that, except for Tanner and Davis, his plan had worked. To make him swear that he'd never ever deceive me like that—even though I knew that oath meant absolutely nothing because he'd always break it if he thought he could get away with it.

The moment I stepped away, the doctor swarmed in, trying to ask Nate a few questions, starting with his name and whether he knew where he was, but he remained barely responsive, so they went ahead and shot him up with the paralytic as well so they could get to work. They went after the wounds that I'd sealed that needed to be properly cleaned first, which took a good hour. By then, someone else had brought in a portable X-ray unit to check how his broken bones were healing—and which needed to be rebroken and realigned. I felt every cut and break as if it was happening to my own body—and vowed that I'd send a fruit basket to Emily Raynor for having been smart enough to keep Nate locked up while she took me apart. Knowing that something was necessary was only helping so much.

During the several hours that they worked on Nate, a few people tried to bring me food or take over watch for me, but I refused to focus on anything else but him. Even after the doctors had left and the last nurse gave me brief instructions on when to switch infusions, I didn't move from his side, although being able to sit down on the floor next to the cot they'd prepped for him was a lot more comfortable than standing guard. Burns eventually left, if only to take a long shower. When he returned with a tray laden with food, I finally relented on that front. The doctors had decided to let the paralytic wear off on its own, arguing that the less Nate moved, the better his body would heal. It was still a long, long night with way too much silence and self-reflection for me until he started to stir.

"Welcome back," I told him as I checked that he hadn't dislodged the infusion needle from his arm and that he was as comfortable as I could make him.

His eyes took an awfully long time until they focused on me. The swelling had gone down a day after we'd fled the labs but the nurse had told me that only time would tell how much damage had turned permanent. That had been the answer in an awful lot of instances concerning his state.

I let him drink a few sips of water when he tried to speak, but even so his voice was raspy as hell. "On a scale of one to Bucky, how mad are you about the stunt I pulled?"

I may have exaggerated the smile coming to my face. No one got hurt with that white lie. "Let's discuss that once you're well enough that I can properly kick some sense into you. Does that answer your question?"

"Sufficiently," he responded, making me smile for real. His eyes drooped closed and for a moment I thought he was gone once more but he forced himself to rouse further. "Casualties?"

Part of me was angry, bordering on insulted, that he'd care more about the others than ask about his own condition, but I made sure not to show any of that. It didn't take a mind reader to understand that the mission had ended up pulling a side of him back into the light that, in this sense, I hadn't seen before. Sure, he'd been our undisputed leader from the moment we'd set out together, even wounded and convalescing when Pia had taken over the day-to-day herding of us lemmings, but the power dynamics had been different. Everyone had been out for themselves, and we'd better play by the rules if we wanted to keep running with said illustrious group. Or maybe that had just been my assessment. Come to think of it, that seemed the likely conclusion. Maybe it had just been a thing of circumstance. Before, he'd always had to make sure he survived to keep those alive who managed as well, who might not continue to do so without a leader. Now he'd been expendable.

I really didn't like Nate being expendable.

"They got Davis in the exit corridor," I responded after shutting my anger away where it belonged. "And Tanner you probably know."

Nate's eyes drifted closed for a moment in what was obviously regret. "He pushed me forward. Insisted I could do more damage if I lured more of them further away from all of you."

I bit the inside of my cheek until the impulse passed to comment on that assessment, and instead continued my list. "The serum variant I grabbed from cold storage worked with Gita and Munez, but Russell still got infected. He took his own life before it was too late. And Parker..." I trailed off there, wondering how to put this in words. "Parker is a fucking asshole. Well, was. The serum took with him but he got even weirder about it than before, and then ran off screaming into the night when no one was looking. Just his luck that the shamblers got him, and then we had to put him down a second time."

Nate listened in silence, but the hint of annoyance crossing his face was balm on my tormented soul. Some things never change. "I'd love to say that the serum is known to exacerbate some psychological traits that are less than desirable, but I think in this case your assessment is spot on. He was an asshole."

I allowed myself a satisfied nod but the sentiment didn't take. "And that's about it. That leaves you and some of the usual. Broken bones, sprained joints. I should probably get my leg checked but there's enough time for that tomorrow." Nate didn't respond, and from how his eyes started drifting shut I could tell that now that his curiosity was sated—and he had two more names to, deep down, feel guilty about—he could get some rest. "Sleep. We got plenty of time for talking later."

He made a face as if to protest, but he was out cold a few moments later. I gently took his hand and squeezed it, a brief, silent show of support, yet when he squeezed right back, strongly, I kept mine right there. Leaning against the cot, I kept staring at him but didn't really see the bruised, patched up body. That had been close—way too close for my comfort. "Are you done yet playing the hero?" I asked him—but just as much myself. I got no response from either of us, but none was necessary.

Chapter 20

Nate woke up a few times during the night, clearly in pain and with nothing I could offer working to alleviate any of that. Just like I'd had to tough it out, so did he. He was healing and getting better but at a much slower rate than I was comfortable with. There was no biochemical equipment on board to speak of so I couldn't exactly investigate, and I sure as hell didn't want anyone else to get nosy as well. None of the nurses or doctors seemed to want anything to do with us beyond what common courtesy between the branches dictated, and both Richards and Hamilton made themselves scarce.

The gym remained in its current setup for the first week of our trek back home, if only with a handful of occupants. Nate was the most pressing concern, obviously, but Hill and Murdock also decided to stay there as their major injuries healed, claiming that it was easier to hobble around, trying to keep weight off a sprained ankle or mending femur if one didn't have to drag one's sorry ass into a bunk bed, particularly since the other half of the gym was used for physiotherapeutic purposes right now. It seemed much more likely that they were happy to occupy as much open space here as they wanted, not having to live, crammed on top of each other, with the rest.

Gita would have loved some crammed space, I was sure, but before she could take possession of our old quarters, all on her own now and even more prone to wallowing in it, I set Burns to bring our stuff into the gym to us. I got a few baleful glares from her for that, but once Hill started roping her into playing poker for the high stakes of snack food, her mood picked up decidedly. A few of the other soldiers joined in before long, making the quarantine space what it really shouldn't have been—crowded and loud at most times of the day—but since none of us was strictly contagious, it was all the same.

Hamilton came through on his promise for upgrade shots for everyone. Cole—and much to my surprise, Burns—hesitated before accepting theirs but the unspoken horror of what we'd left behind us was still breathing down their necks, so they eventually caved. I tried haranguing Burns into explaining why he'd had his concerns but he shot me down with a bright smile, and a reminder to mind my own bullshit.

I pretty much only left the hangar to hit the head, trusting that someone would see to keeping me fed. Two days after waking up, Nate was mobile enough not to need my assistance for everything anymore, but that was just as well—I had a different task to tend to. In that very first endless night on the destroyer, while I watched over his sleeping body still half afraid I'd need to use my Beretta that I didn't dare put away for long yet, Richards dropped back into the hangar, carrying a spare laptop they'd kept on the ship, the one we'd liberated from Dr. Andrada's office, and stacks of notes and printouts. I mutely stared at it all, part of me tempted to accept it, and as soon as he turned his back on me, throw it all into the ocean to be lost forever. But whatever he had gotten right or wrong about me in his psych eval, he knew that, regardless of my spitefulness, I'd never do that, so he left me to it. "It" of course being my last chance to prove that I was something more than a cripple and a knuckle-dragger.

Very soon, Nate was back to harassing me with food—excuse me, of course he was reminding me, nicely, to take better care of myself—because I couldn't be bothered to come out of my heap of notes for mere things like sandwiches and coffee. Although, for coffee I would have made an exception.

I couldn't exactly say what fueled that need to put my mark on a project that, as far as I was concerned, I'd dodged a bullet for never being directly involved in. It certainly wasn't idealism about thinking that anyone would use it for the greater good of humanity. I was hoping that Richards would deliver it to Raynor and no one else, but it wasn't like I would be there to make sure he did. Maybe it was the last dregs of my vanity and nostalgia that made me do it.

Maybe I did it because I was the only one that could—and that thought, at least, gave me a sick sense of satisfaction.

One week exactly after the RHIBs had brought us back to the destroyer, all of us gathered once more at the stern of the ship, up on the deck outside of the hangar, to say a last, formal goodbye to those that hadn't returned with us. Hamilton held a brief speech—for once not trying to be an asshole, and sadly succeeding at it—but I barely heard a word in five, and those that I did made me want to barf over the railing. Except for Tanner, I hadn't known any of them well, and if I was honest, I'd never tried befriending him, either. It was easy to blame past grief for that and call it a mechanism of self-preservation, but I knew that wasn't it. That sense of detachment sure made me feel like a shit head. Was this really who I'd become? Again, it was easy to blame circumstances—like the fact that I hadn't chosen any of this, and being forced to follow orders from one of the handful of people I'd never forgive for what they did to me didn't make it easier. But deep down I knew it was just that—an excuse. And it was time that, at least in one instance, I stopped pushing everyone away who hadn't made it his mission in life to stick it out with me until the bitter end.

Gita lingered until most others had gone back inside, and when Burns saw that I took over suicide watch from him, he beat it as well, leaving the two of us alone on the spray-slick deck. Now that I saw her in daylight—even if it was wan, the sun hidden by clouds that promised more snow—I could see that she was well on the road to recovery, her cheeks rosy not just from the cold but actually having lost that sallow tint of sickness.

I was running through the tenth line of platitudes in my head, still at a loss for what to say, when she saved me, looking at me for a second before focusing on the waves at the ship's wake again. "He always had a chip on his shoulder, you know? Tanner, I mean."

I nodded my silent assent that I'd understood. "Most of the good ones do."

That made her crack a smile, even if it was a sad one. "I guess. I certainly did a good job collecting mine." Another sidelong glance at me before she sighed. "I don't know why he was in prison when the shit hit the fan. He never told me, you know? I don't think he told anyone. But he told me something else: that he felt that he deserved it. And that he deserved to rot in there until the end of his days. Only that the zombie apocalypse had other plans for him, and he took that hint."

Silence fell, me waiting, Gita lost in memories, without a doubt.

"Did you know that he was one of the people who helped Rita build up Dispatch?"

That was news to me. "I didn't know they knew each other?"

Gita inclined her head. "He didn't stick around for long, but he helped her organize what people she'd gathered by then, and the story goes that the surviving prisoners only threw their lot in with her because he made them."

Another nugget I hadn't been aware of. "So Dispatch is literally the hub of rejects and criminals? I knew I liked it there for a reason."

That made her laugh. "Yeah, I hear it's a great place."

"You've never been there?"

"Nope. Just chatted with people who were. The story is, Tanner and a few others decided to set out looking for adventure, and that's how New Angeles was founded. That's how he fell in with Gabriel Greene, too," she explained. "But it was never enough to redeem himself, you know? I think Greene knew; that's why he tried to bind him to the city as best he could, but we did a damn good job settling in there like ticks. We didn't need another man fighting for a cause."

"So that's why he was doing duty catching caravans of new arrivals?" I hazarded a guess. "To find a new cause?"

"Your guess is as good as mine," she admitted. "But he sure got excited when you blew into town with all that talk of vengeance and your fight for freedom."

"And when I got sick—"

"Another adventure," she responded. This time, her pause was a pregnant one, as if she was considering what to let me in on. "Greene didn't know about Hamilton's mission, but he knew they were planning something. I doubt he had any clue that's where you'd end up, but, how shall I put this…"

"I'm a shit magnet?" I proposed.

She smiled. "You really are. And if you connect the dots, it makes sense, right? Your husband's not just one of them, he was literally one of their officers, on track to become one of the movers and shakers. That's someone you want back in the fold, even if under any other circumstances than the end of the world you'd never trust him again. They were holed up in a lab, and whatever you insist on being now, you were a scientist once. As for a cause, what's the one constant in all our lives? That damn virus. It was an easy guess to take all that into consideration and expect that something interesting would happen."

Viewed like that, I didn't need my rampant paranoia to come up with conspiracy theories. But since that wasn't a part of me that would ever change, I was sure she was seeing things a little too idealistically. I'd trust Greene not to have ulterior motives the day after I'd made sure he was dead and gone for good—but I didn't tell her that. It didn't matter, really.

"So Greene sent you with us because your knowledge would come in handy, and Tanner wanted another chance to redeem his unredeemable conscience."

She nodded. "Pretty much." Her next inhale was a shaky one. "I tried to talk sense into him. I really did. Told him that he deserved a better life. That no one ever needed to pay the ultimate price, that a long, long life of small chances would make a much bigger impact in the long run." A shaky exhale followed. "I tried telling him that I loved him but he shut me up before I got the words out. He told me that I shouldn't waste my life on a piece of crap like him, but who else would ever—"

The rest got lost in hiccups and sobs, all that pain and grief that was pouring out of her becoming too much to contain. And because I wasn't a complete dip shit, I hugged her, pulling her head against my shoulder, and held her while she cried, my own throat tight with emotion.

"It's okay. It's all going to be okay," I murmured, knowing that, given our track record, nope, nothing would be okay, but that wasn't what she'd need to hear now. But at least that pain she was feeling right now would fade over time—and maybe, just maybe, I was wrong this time and fate would surprise me? Who knew.

Gita eventually extricated herself from me, absentmindedly wiping her face, mostly because the biting wind was worse on wet skin than dry one. "So that was Europe. A little overrated, don't you think?"

I snorted. "Something like that. Do you know what you'll do once we get off this ship? You know that there's likely a line of people forming who'll want a literal piece of you?"

Unease shone in her eyes but she put on a brave face. "They can still cut up Munez if they want to study someone who got infected but was saved by that freak serum you gave us. I'm out of there as soon as we're in sight of dry land." She grinned to show she was joking—to a point. "Actually, Burns and I have been talking. He said he wants to swing by their base once more to pick up Martinez, and then we'll get back home together. Maybe make it a fun road trip, you know? "

"Sounds like a plan," I replied, the thought making me smile—but it was hard to keep up.

"You… aren't coming with us, are you?" she said, her voice suddenly low enough that I could barely hear her—as if, out here in the wind, anyone could eavesdrop on us.

I hesitated for a second but shook my head ever so softly. I still tried to keep my response neutral, should my guess about our privacy be wrong. "The last real choice I got to make was back in New Angeles, when we decided to head for the Silo. Maybe even before that when Nate knocked out my tooth while we were sparring and I decided not to just ignore it. Everything that came after that wasn't really up to me. I'd really like to make my own choices again."

There was real sadness on her face, but she seemed honest when she nodded. "Yeah, I get that." The grin that followed was fake, but hey, we were both doing a lot of fake-it-till-you-make-it right now. "How about we go grab some chow from the galley? That sounds like a good choice to me."

"Let's," I agreed, clapping her on the back to push her toward the door. It really was getting unbearably cold out here, and I'd had about enough of that for a lifetime.

Chapter 21

I startled awake when I heard a scratching sound close to me, disoriented for a second until I found Red crouching close to my cot where it sat next to Nate's. The hangar was dark except for the single small light by the exit, the red glow letting me know that we weren't through the night cycle yet. Sure enough, when I checked my watch it read 3am. A hint of unease tickled my spine, particularly as Richards was making sure that he was moving slowly and silently enough not to wake anyone else. He needn't have bothered; Gita was out cold since she'd been playing poker until midnight, and Burns was snoring loudly enough that people at the other end of the ship could likely hear him. Nate was still semi-comatose, falling into a state not unlike the waking coma I'd been in the first week we'd been on the ship on the way to Europe. To make sure he got as much rest as possible, I got up quickly and tiptoed to where Richards had halted once he'd seen me rise. He signaled me to follow him, and since he likely had a very good reason for this clandestine meeting at such an ungodly hour, I followed. Really, if he and some of the others had wanted to shiv me, they'd passed up so many chances that I'd long since forgotten to be afraid any longer.

We were halfway down the corridor to the front of the ship when he finally paused to explain. "I managed to get a call through to Emily Raynor," he offered. "I thought you'd like a moment to talk to her in private?" Which likely translated into "without Hamilton listening," not that I gave much of a crap about that anymore. How easily shifting perspectives could change things.

I nodded and we set off once more, heading for the secondary communications station deep down in the belly of the destroyer rather than the bridge. Sgt. Buehler was waiting next to the door and stepped in after us to close it. Besides her, there was only the technician who was making the magic happen.

And speaking of magic, as much as it was convenient to have Raynor on video conference up on a monitor in front of me rather than just hearing her voice, what made my heart beat faster was the man next to her, who was leaning against the frame of a hospital bed, but clearly standing on his own.

"Hey, chico," I said, hard-pressed to hide a smile. "Good to see you up and running again."

The fact that Martinez didn't even give me a grin in return sobered me up—and served as a good reminder of the bullshit they must have fed him about me—but didn't change anything about the sense of elation inside of me. Maybe I couldn't save the world, but I sure as hell had done what I could for one of my closest friends.

"Not running yet, and entirely his fault," Raynor informed me tartly, her accent crisp once more, telling of her exasperation. "He would be if he hadn't refused the serum. He insists that he prefers months of physical therapy and a good chance that he will only regain eighty percent of strength and range of motion in his legs."

"Well, that's his choice then," I quipped back in a tone not dissimilar from hers. "It's too bad that you can't force every single person on this earth to see things your way."

A hint of amusement crossed Martinez's face. If that was all I got, it was enough.

Raynor clucked her tongue but let her patient speak for himself as he straightened. "If I have the choice—which I do—I don't want that shit anywhere near me. No offense," he added, his eyes narrowing slightly. "I know you don't agree with me on that."

I was hard-pressed not to snidely ask what that was supposed to mean, but that was a conversation for a time when we didn't have anyone listening in, particularly those who I wanted to listen in the least.

"Glad you're doing okay," I said instead. "They treating you well?"

Raynor was ready to respond but Martinez, trained from hanging out with me and Burns for well over a year, talked right over her before he could get interrupted. "Surprisingly so. If I was a little more paranoid I'd say they're trying to either set a good example or want to recruit me."

"Probably both," I pointed out. He didn't seem very keen on hearing my opinion so I kept the rest to myself—which seemed to surprise him to the point where he looked a little guilty. Damnit, but I really wanted to have that talk right now. Sadly, that was impossible, and we both knew it.

Raynor, satisfied that we were done chatting, looked down at the notes she was holding. "Commander Parr earlier informed me that you will be reaching land within the next thirty hours or so, if the storm doesn't get any worse. So I expect you to be back here within the next three days. By then, Mr. Martinez will be ready for departure." I didn't miss that she refrained from using his rank, and considering the look on his face, it didn't go unnoticed by him as well. Ah, the games people play…

"That's good news," I enthused, careful to keep my tone neutral. "Thanks for that update, but if you're done now, I'd really like to get back to sleep. I know we're in different time zones at the moment but it's well past bedtime at your base, too."

As expected, Raynor didn't look pleased at my dismissal. "Richards here tells me that you've been quite busy. And ignoring normal day and night cycles for the most part."

Red got an amused glance from me for that. Of course he'd been tattling on me—and not unexpectedly so.

"I think we should have this conversation in private, Dr. Raynor," I said, stressing her title. "Or as private as we can make it under these circumstances."

Martinez looked annoyed that I actively cut him out of this, but looked somewhat mollified when I waved at him and promised to see him in a few.

It was somewhat vertigo-inducing as Raynor picked up the laptop she'd been using and carried it to another room—not her office but rather a maintenance closet, with packs of gloves and plastic lab material behind her. While she settled in, I glanced over my shoulder at the other occupants of my location. "If you'll give us a minute?"

The technician looked ready to protest, but at Buehler's nod he got up and left with her. Richards remained at my side, the stoic look he gave me letting me know that there was no way in hell he wasn't a part of this conversation. Fine, so be it.

"What have you found?" Raynor asked, impatient although she had been the one to cause the delay. "Lt. Richards has told me that you've compiled a lot of notes already."

I couldn't hold back a nasty smile. "Oh, what I've found and what I've written down are two very different things," I let her know, considering Red's presence for a second but then decided, oh hell. There was a chance he already knew, anyway.

"Notes first, if you will," I told her. "I found your solution."

"Solution for what?" She really didn't like the fact that I held all the cards right now.

"For the cure, if you still want to make it work," I offered. "Miller and Andrada were damn close to finding a way to reverse the terminal effects of the serum, both without them ever actually going into effect—which is pretty close to the weaker form of the serum that was mentioned in the letters." I paused, glancing at Richards. "You told her about the letters already, I presume?" He nodded. "Good. Hamilton has samples of that, and you should be able to extricate the compound from Munez's blood as well. I'd still treat him to the full version if I were you, unless you want to start full-scale production and distribution of said cure, and we all know that this was never your intention."

Raynor had the grace not to deny that accusation. "You know yourself that the powers that be wouldn't want to lose their most dangerous weapons," she stated, matter-of-fact. "And if presented with it, would you want to receive said cure yourself?"

A week ago, I would have said hell yeah. After gnawing my remaining fingernails down to the beds because Nate's recovery was going at a snail's pace... "Not really."

Raynor allowed herself a satisfied smile—one I intended to soon wipe off her face. "It's good that you haven't lost your grasp on reality yet," she surmised.

"Lack of realism has never been one of my weaknesses. Speaking of which, what are you going to do with my notes, besides checking that they make sense? I presume we're having this conversation now because you don't want it known what's in those notes? And in my head, by extension. We all know that there are some people who'd rather see all that gone."

She didn't seem very perturbed by that claim. I hated how much this underlined that Hamilton had been right with his assessment of that Decker guy. "Just because there won't be a direct application to some people doesn't mean it's not an important advantage to have," Raynor pointed out. "And I'm not even talking about threatening a prisoner with taking away his partial immortality." I hadn't even thought of that yet. My, I still had so much to learn. "There might come a day when we need that cure," she went on, oblivious to my thoughts. "Right now, our predictions are that the undead problem will eventually take care of itself or run its course. Should we prove to have been wrong, turning said cure into a vaccine for everyone not yet affected might be exactly what we need."

"Or just a choice few," I couldn't help but notice.

Raynor's smile was a little sardonic. "You mean, history repeating itself? If we hadn't been so cautious and only inoculated those we needed for fighting purposes but also most of the intellectual elite, we might not have had to send you across the ocean." What she didn't add was that she wouldn't have needed me at all, which she likely preferred. Too bad, really.

"What about those soldiers who got the faulty version of the serum? Taggard's boys, and a lot of others who were at that base in Colorado," I reminded her. "Your side promised to take care of them. Knowing what I know now, I'm sure that whatever bull you tried to sell us about the upgrade with the mind-control shit that you gave my husband, that isn't connected any way whatsoever." As I said that, I wondered if that was the reason why Nate's recovery was hampered, but I doubted it. Until the lab he'd been doing just fine. "The cure might very well be the cure for them, or at least a stepping stone."

Her utter lack of reaction told me more than I wanted to know. So much for holding to the finer points of our agreements. "They are being dealt with," was all she said. "And they are none of your concern, which you made obvious in your negotiation that day." Where she wasn't wrong. "Anything else? Because, if not, I'd appreciate it if you made sure that Lt. Richards gets all your notes, and—"

"I haven't told you what I've discovered yet," I said, making her shut up immediately.

Her eyes narrowed but not with the trepidation I'd expected. "Very well. What have you discovered, Dr. Lewis?"

One last time I considered whether I should just lie and keep this to myself—it sure didn't sound like a smart idea to burn the only bridge I had that was connected to this side. But like so often before, being right was imperative to being smart. Story of my life.

"I found some very interesting things on Dr. Andrada's laptop. On their own, they wouldn't have made me make the connection. Or the notes you sent with Hamilton to give to me once he figured I was mentally fit enough to evaluate them. Parts of it was in Raleigh Miller's documentation as well. So, so many clues, and no way to connect the dots," I mused. I wasn't sure if it was my words or my sing-song tone that tipped her off, but there it was, finally—dread for what I'd say next. Again I halted, but this time to wonder if I should call in the others, at the very least Nate and Hamilton, for this conversation.

"Are you intending to make any sense with this, or are you only wasting my time?" she quipped, but her voice was quaking. I glanced at Richards, finding him tense—but not ready to break my neck once I spilled the beans. He wanted to know just as much as Raynor, likely more as it was news to him, and only confirmation to her.

I was only too happy to oblige them.

"You're the one who caused all this," I told Raynor. "You, and Raleigh Miller, and Dr. Rosamie Andrada. You are responsible for the zombie apocalypse."

No dramatic sound effects appeared out of nowhere, and her neutral expression was rather anticlimactic.

"May I remind you that I was the one warning the world?" she stated, actually puffing out her chest a little. "And you and I both know that it was Dr. Alders and those idealist flunkies of his who—"

"Bullshit." There was only so much of her denial that I could take. "I have no clue how you convinced that idiot to take the fall for you. Mind control maybe? One too many LSD trips gone wrong that made him susceptible to believing he actually achieved something he had nothing to do with in the past decades? And I'm not claiming that you were the one who set the distribution of the virus and activator in motion. But you're the ones who created it." I stepped closer to the monitor, mostly to better read her face. "The virus was stable for generations. Alders had built it to be stable, with instant expiration of the subject as a loophole should anything happen. He created the perfect weapon, yes—as in a living, breathing, thinking soldier who was faster, stronger, and most of all more tenacious than his opponents. Turning into an uncontrollable monster was a consequence and drawback, but one everyone felt was acceptable considering the advantages. It was also a measure of control to make sure all your inoculated sheep remained in line. At best, you wouldn't have to pay pensions for retirees. But it was tantamount that the virus always remained stable. Nobody was fucking stupid enough to tinker with that—until you did."

Raynor listened to me without trying to interrupt, and even when I dropped that bomb, she didn't offer up anything. I was only too happy to continue with my tirade.

"I understand that Miller did it because he wanted to save his brother. I don't know what Andrada's motives were, but knowing what I know about you, I'd say you figured it was a challenge that you couldn't say no to. I'd think it wasn't a hard sell to the powers that be—give them a chance to disarm their perfect weapon. Who doesn't like a contingency plan? But you made two mistakes."

That sardonic smile from before resurfaced as she finally gave in. "You mean, besides allegedly kicking off the end of the world?"

I inclined my head, giving her that. "One, you never took the time to actually talk to the people affected by the serum. That's why you never really understood exactly how it works, and what it does to them." And, oh boy, had I gotten a good lesson of that down in that damn complex.

Confusion was her predominant reaction. "What has that got to do with anything?"

"The rage," I simply said, a glance at Richards showing that he understood. Raynor still didn't. "That's how the serum works," I elaborated. "It makes you so fucking angry that you push through all the natural barriers, those of the mind and those of the body, to accomplish superhuman feats. It's why you fight harder, and longer. It's what turns you into a single-minded, homicidal killing machine. And if you can't stop yourself, you're gone. You insta-convert from being so fucking angry that your mind shorts out and your body overrides everything that makes you hold back. All that's left is that rage. You know what separates us—and other primates—from so many other animals? We got those supercharged brains that turn us into the perfect killers although we lack the teeth and claws and whatnot. Because we can use tools, and strategy. But to balance that out, we became social creatures that operate with a very complicated setup of emotions and boundaries. We got smart because we learned not to act on impulse and kill that impertinent asshole beside us on a whim because we'd still need him later. And your damn serum eliminated exactly those boundaries. Those many layers of second-guessing and simple weighing of consequences. You took away the regulations. What was left was a superior killing machine without a conscience." I paused to let that sink in.

"And our second mistake?" Raynor asked without reacting to the first.

"You made it contagious."

She stiffened immediately, almost making me laugh. So that got under her skin? Which also gave me the understanding of what must have happened—a mistake. But it made sense. "You didn't plan it, did you? To make it work, you needed to make the virus unstable, and the consequence of it mutating was that it wasn't inert anymore. That it could jump hosts and didn't remain in the inoculated subject as it was." Thinking along those lines, something else occurred to me. "That happened after Miller's death, right? You and Andrada, you thought you could go on alone; that you didn't need him. But any virologist worth his salt would have told you that using a virus as a vehicle to introduce anything into a host always hinges on making sure that host never gets infectious. He also would have warned you to test for that, but you didn't. You just inoculated your test subjects, and because you weren't completely inhumane, you let them all sit together in a cell block, not their individual cells—because that would have been cruel. You let them kill each other in little contests and death matches, and it was all good. Until, one day, something happened, and you realized that not only were they all infected, no—they'd infected their keepers as well. And because once you take away our moral compass, we still remain team players and all they needed to do was to fight long enough to establish a hierarchy, but not to the death. That's why you shut down the lab and called for a state of emergency, right? Not because the lab went dark and you were alarmed; it was the other way around. You realized that it was a lost cause and the only way you could contain it was to slam the door shut and throw away the keys. Only that, somehow, the plan to end the world was already in motion, independent of the shit you are responsible for, and you inadvertently managed to still save thousands while watching helplessly as someone else killed billions."

If Nate's brother hadn't died, none of that would have happened—or if they'd pulled me into the fold the very next day, dumped all their research in my lap, let me sort it all out in my head, and tell them what to look out for. As much as presenting the facts to Raynor had made me want to gloat, that realization brought me right back down to earth.

Yeah, it's not every day that you realize you could have averted the zombie apocalypse.

And seeing that slight smirk on Raynor's face made it plain that she knew that I'd come to that conclusion—and would very likely die never breathing a word of any of that to anyone.

"That's a very interesting theory that you have there," Raynor said, toning down her mirth but not quite managing to get rid of it. "I'd love to talk about that in-depth with you at a later time. But I'm afraid that you were right—it is getting late, and science talk requires clear heads and rested minds. If that is everything, Dr. Lewis…?"

All I did was nod. Raynor smiled again and turned the camera off, the connection terminating a second later.

I probably would have spent an hour or two staring sightlessly at the dark screen if not for Richards clearing his throat.

"Exactly what did I just witness?"

A very odd way of phrasing it, but aptly done so. Turning to him, I crossed my arms over my chest, forcing myself to both relax and let my mind stop running itself into a rut. "Pretty much me trying to be a know-it-all but mostly schooling myself. It's a scientist thing. No need to worry your pretty head with such bluestocking matters."

He cracked a smile but I didn't miss the spark of interest that remained in his eyes. Good. If the world needed one thing, it was one more smart person who second-guessed the bullshit others tried to sell him.

"If you say so. Doctor."

That made me snort as I turned toward the door. "Oh, shut up, LT. Go be useful and tell that tech and Sgt. Buehler that we're done here. Or whatever else you still need to do with her, seeing as in a few hours from now, we'll be off this ship and it's anyone's guess if you'll ever see each other again. You should spend your time wisely. After all, Emily will be disappointed if you got rusty in the meantime."

Richards had the gall to snort at my insinuations but, ever the gentleman, pulled the door open for me. Considering how heavy these damn things were, I didn't mind not having to mangle my fingers just to leave a room.

"Does that ever work for you?" he asked just as I was about to step outside. "Throw people off track by pretending to be a lewd asshole?"

This time when I smiled at him, it was a real one. "More often than you'd think. People also tell me it's entertaining as hell to watch."

I left him to his devices, lewd or otherwise, and made my way back to the hangar, not quite sure whether I'd really burned a bridge or just tightened the noose around my neck. Hopefully, I'd never get a chance to find out.

Chapter 22

Our last meal together in the mess hall wasn't exactly a somber affair—actually, it was about as far from that as possible—but my heart was heavy throughout it, laughing and smiling as I might have been the entire time. I didn't even care that Hamilton called me Stumpy three times, but no one else did. The sailors now regarded the entire lot of us with pleasant weariness, about ready to be rid of us. We were just waiting for the snowstorm to die down enough that the boats could bring everyone who was leaving to the shore. Clearly, we hadn't returned to the same base where we'd come aboard for the first time but I was sure someone had given some thought to that. Nate and I still hadn't had time to plan what to do next, but that was likely a good thing—if we didn't talk, no one could listen in, and just maybe, an opportunity would arise. Even I would recognize it once it bit me in the ass. Burns was back to his usual joking and Gita seemed to be slowly reconnecting with the world at large. It was weird to admit it, but the last weeks had done a thing or ten to fuse all of us into a group. It annoyed the hell out of me that the idea that I'd likely—hopefully—never see a single one of them ever again made me weirdly melancholic.

I was sure that Hamilton knew we had no intentions whatsoever to come with him to that base. Richards, too, if he wasn't a complete imbecile, which he'd proven not to be. Gita pretended to be oblivious but Burns definitely knew, and that killed me. I didn't say anything when he brought me a steaming mug of coffee after lunch, and he didn't, either, but there was a silent world of understanding between us—and a lot of accusation as well. So what if he didn't like us tucking our tails in and running—he wasn't the one both sides might be gunning for.

As it was, I couldn't miss said opportunity as it grabbed me by the arm and pulled me into a room I had no idea what its purpose was, in the form of one perky marine sergeant. Nate was already standing next to Buehler, regarding her with a mix of annoyance and anticipation.

"You're probably asking yourselves what this is about," she whispered to us, casting one last look outside before she shut the door.

"Not really," I offered, making her blink furiously.

"We're special that way," Nate supplied, shifting his leg to take the weight off the one that wasn't quite up to par yet.

"You sure are," Buehler muttered. "I got a really weird message last night from one of my buddies at the Silo." She paused. "He said he's met you? Guy named Blake."

I had to rack my brain for a little but decided that must have been the grumpy guard who'd become my not-so-silent shadow when I'd last been at the Silo, trying to find out what was going on with me with Dom and Sunny's help. "Yup. What did he say?"

"It's not what he said," she offered. "Or rather, what he didn't say. He was contacting us on behalf of Commander Wilkes. Apparently, he's come to his senses that his Navy wusses won't save the day and has extended an invitation to the people who actually can." Her pause was a pointed one before she said to Nate, "No offense."

He gave her a toothy yet real grin. "None taken. If that chest pounding makes you feel validated, please, by all means, continue."

Great, another one of those "we are the bestest warriors in the world!" pissing contest—as if I hadn't had enough of that already on a daily basis.

"So Wilkes is rallying his best buddies," I surmised, cutting through whatever this was they had going on. "Good news for the Silo. They were concerned about staying independent last year, and I can't see how that's a bad thing."

"It's not," Buehler insisted, a little sore I'd interrupted her. "They're keeping some Army liaisons but trying to, ever so slowly, build up their own ranks. Apparently, a lot of the scavengers that bugged down there are quite happy to follow someone who provides them with training, gear, shelter, and food, and doesn't turn that into the next stage of a war of principles. The way Blake put it, they seem awfully tired of picking sides, so Wilkes is going for true neutral. But that's not the interesting part, besides what we'll be doing once we're done with doing duty here, I expect."

"And, pray tell, what is the interesting part?" I couldn't tell if Nate was actually curious or just yanking her chain. Buehler seemed equally undecided but went with dropping her posturing completely.

"Nothing concrete, but he said that about the time we took you on, people started talking. And then they did more talking. Nothing official, and nobody can pinpoint the origin, but then people started disappearing. Not in a creepy, kidnappy way, but, you know. People with a purpose following said purpose, just elsewhere."

"You mean like planted spies retreating to their home base?" I ventured a guess.

Her eyes narrowed at me. "So you do know what is going on."

I shook my head. "Nope. But let's say that some people here"—I glared at Nate—"have a past that's started to catch up with them. We'd greatly prefer not to be caught up with, to put it mildly."

"Right." Buehler scratched her head, looking from one of us to the other. "The thing is, also last night the captain mentioned that we have some extra space near the cargo compartments since we've used up so many of our provisions, and one of these days we should repurpose them." She let that hang for a second, barely waiting for Nate to nod that he'd gotten her meaning. Ideal for storing human cargo, at least for a while. "We start unloading in ten minutes. If you get into those crawl spaces right now, nobody will realize you're missing until everyone's off the ship and on the shore, maybe not even then. I've already sent one of my guys to make sure that whatever remains behind of your personal belongings mysteriously disappears to make it look like you packed everything up. Downside is, you can't say goodbye to your friends."

And, right there it was—the moment I knew I would one day point back at and say, yup, that started all the shit that came after, but no way I could have done anything different.

Nate seemed to agree, as he said, without checking in with me, "Where's that crawl space?"

Buehler looked a little disappointed but mostly because that ended our wonderful conversation as well. "Right behind you there's a loose panel. Twenty yards toward the stern you'll find a larger space where you can sit more easily. I'll fetch you once we've made sure we don't have any other stowaways and there's no chance anyone from the coast can still get to you." She paused. "Do you need a light? It's pretty dark in there, we only have a few vents high up near the ceilings."

"Not our first rodeo in tight, confined spaces," I snarked, pausing to offer her my hand. She shook it, as before not minding that it was lacking two fingers. Nate left it at a nod. Buehler waited until we'd crawled through the panel into the—comparatively wide—space behind before she turned off the lights and closed the door, the locks engaging giving me somewhat the creeps. Nothing I could do about that.

I followed Nate as he crawled the way Buehler had indicated, barely able to make out anything even after my eyes got accustomed to the darkness. We still found the larger compartment as it was hard to miss with one wall dropping away for several feet of distance, and while not roomy enough for either of us to get up, it wasn't so bad sitting side by side.

"So, this is it," I said, lightly tapping on my thigh to bleed off some nervous energy. "Think anyone will actually look for us?"

Nate shook his head. "I doubt it. Hamilton will be happy to be rid of us. Richards has the samples and your notes—"

"And I got to talk to Raynor," I supplied. He looked surprised but didn't question my statement further. "Burns will hate our guts, and I'm not sure Gita will get over two more people she cares about abandoning her."

Nate let out a low sigh. "Nothing we can do about that, either. It's just a few more hours and they'll be back at the base where they can put up with Jason hounding them for leaving him and Charlie behind."

"Martinez is doing okay," I supplied.

"You talked to him, too?"

"Briefly." My silence seemed to be answer enough but since we were stuck in here for a while… "I really wanted to tell him that I didn't do this for him. That I didn't betray all my principles just so he'd get another chance to walk. He should be smart enough to eventually get that where there's a carrot, there's also a stick."

Nate chuckled softly. "I'm sure he knows. But wouldn't seem like such a rift between us and the rest of the world if everyone we met was all, oh, sure, we understand! We forgive you! Just come back any time you want!"

That I hadn't considered—and I caught myself smiling in spite of myself. "Think the others will wonder where we are? You and me, we both survived that lab but we had chances aplenty to be killed off that Hamilton was directly responsible for. And I'm not even talking about your dumbass sacrificial stunt."

Nate's answering silence made me wonder what I'd missed.

"At least we know now that we can count on more help than we thought," he offered in what sounded like a non sequitur, but I didn't buy it.

"Like who? Zombified Aimes was only a thread more hostile toward me than human Aimes."

Nate snorted as if I'd recounted a fond memory. "Well, for instance, we now know that I still have some standing with the people who've been under my command in the past. I give Murdock a sixty percent chance that he will desert if he gets a good enough opportunity, and Davis would likely be sitting in here with us if he hadn't bitten it." He waited for me to protest and went on when I didn't. "Sure, there will always be lost causes, like Parker, but he's nobody's loss. People like Aimes, Wu, Russell—you can't win with them. They've been fed the same BS they still believe in since the very day they signed the dotted line in the recruitment office. You'll never change their minds. But it took you all of a single fight and some random campfire chatting and you got Cole and Hill firmly in your camp. They're both too married to the cause to turn their backs on what they've dedicated their lives to, but they don't follow orders blindly. They question, and they consider, and if one day down the line we all meet again and Hamilton tells them to pull the trigger on you, they might just say, hey, wait a minute—why don't you explain exactly why we should do that? And don't leave out the good details."

"And you think that's worth risking your life for?" I couldn't quite keep the incredulity out of my voice.

I got a smirk in return. "Maybe. Maybe not."

That was when I realized where I'd been wrong. "You fucking conniving, lying asshole!" I shouted, punching him in his arm, not caring how much that hurt. He sure deserved it. Of course he was laughing, although he also made shushing sounds to make me turn down the volume. "I thought you actually sacrificed yourself for me!"

"And whose fault is that, huh?" he teased, but caught my arm before I could aim for his face next. "I'm sorry. I really am. I didn't want to lie to you but, you know. You're a shitty actress on a good day. You would have ruined it all if you'd spent the last two weeks gloating at everyone, particularly Hamilton." I continued to glare at him, which made him laugh more softly now. "Oh, come on. Snap out of it. It wasn't just an opportunity served on a silver platter. It was a once in a lifetime opportunity. I would have kicked myself for the rest of my life if I hadn't taken it."

"Yeah, tell that to Tanner." I knew this was a low blow, but right then I was sore enough not to care.

Nate gave an appropriately chastised nod, which in and of itself was rather suspicious. "I will regret his death for the rest of my life, too. I tried to dissuade him but he insisted on helping me. And he was right. He would have been too focused on guarding Gita, which in turn would have made him an easy target and then they'd both have been dead. He knew what he was doing, and if you ask me, he died without many regrets. That's my burden now. As for doing it at all? We needed that diversion or we would have died for sure, one after the other. They might not have realized it at the time, but they were counting on me for getting them out of there. Shit, Bucky was counting on me to get them out, and if I wasn't certain that he would have loved to see me die for nothing, I'd say he set everything up like this."

That was awfully close to what I'd accused Hamilton of, only the other way round—yet as Nate seemed convinced of his view I felt my own conviction drain slowly.

"So you took the chance to turn from a traitor into a savior," I noted, not trying to take my acidic tone down a notch.

Nate didn't deny it. "You know how they all saw me when we joined up with them. How they looked at me, whatever I did. I'm the one who betrayed his own people's trust and got them killed for my own ulterior motives. I'm the one who ran when the shit hit the fan and my country needed me. I helped instigate a rebellion, and I'm still supporting the biggest pain in their collective ass there is right now. Which is you."

"Yeah, because I didn't get it right away," I grumbled, trying hard not to grin.

"Now?" he went on without dwelling on my childish glee. "I may not have changed everyone's mind, but you'd have to be one dumb fuck not to see that Hamilton was the one who stranded them down there, and I got them out. Sure, he had his orders—and while I know you will disagree with me on that, I'm certain that he did have them, and it was our mission to get the samples. No one would begrudge him acting in accordance with our primary target. But not getting torn to shreds and eaten by monsters does a thing or two for a man's psyche. No, I don't think that Wu or the likes will ever change their mind, but people talk. People listen. I didn't set out to clear my name, and there's still a lot of shit that's sticking to me, but one thing I hammered into their heads: I'm not a coward, and I won't waste their lives for no good reason whatsoever. That might make a difference if push comes to shove one day, far, far down the line. I'm sorry that I couldn't let you in on this. You would have tried to come with me, and I'd have had the exact same problem that Tanner tried to avoid. You wouldn't have been so convincing in rallying the troops to go hunt for my corpse. And you wouldn't have spent the past two weeks stalking around, hissing and spitting at everyone and everything because you felt like I made the ultimate sacrifice and nobody was grateful for that."

A lot came to mind to respond to that, but I left it at a simple, "Burns told you about that?"

"He sure did." I caught Nate's faint smile in the dark. "I'd like to claim that I'm deeply concerned about your priorities, but what can I say?"

"'Thank you' would be an appropriate choice," I harped.

"Too easy." He continued to laugh even when I smacked him good. Again he caught my hand on the second try, and this time I noticed.

"So, having some low-light vision of your own going on now, huh?" I summed up my razor-sharp conclusion.

"Not exactly," Nate admitted. "But I'd be lying if I said I didn't notice any changes."

"Like what?"

He shrugged. "Too early to tell. I'll let you know once I'm sure about it all."

"If you say 'monster penis,' I'm gonna slap you."

"You just did," he pointed out.

"Again."

"Still not that much of a threat."

I snorted, leaving it at that.

We ended up sitting there, listening to the ship groan and creak around us for what felt like a small eternity until the gentle vertigo of motion made my stomach queasy for a moment. "Guess this is it," I remarked. "Think we made a colossal mistake?"

"Wouldn't be the first," Nate enthused, grinning at my frown. "Oh, come on. It's not like this is for forever."

"And what if it is?"

He shrugged, unperturbed by our circumstances. "Then we'll die, old and alone, in the wilderness, knowing that we didn't drag any more innocents into drama that we didn't create."

"Not sure I'd call someone like Burns or Martinez innocent. They'd likely object."

"Vehemently," Nate agreed.

"Fuck, but I miss them. All of them." Nate held my gaze, not saying anything, a silent agreement if there ever was one. "You think it's worth that? Slinking away into hiding, on a whim? Bucky's the only one who ever really mentioned anything about Decker. He could be lying."

"He's not," he replied, sounding more convinced than I was about pretty much everything. "But I'm rather certain that, either way, we'll sooner or later find out. Let's hope it's later, and after someone else has taken care of the problem for once."

Somehow I had a feeling that wasn't going to happen—but hope was cheap, and something I realized I had in abundance after how the last months had gone down. It couldn't really get that much worse than both of us almost dying, right?

Buehler was back soon after the ship had started moving once more, ushering us into one of the abandoned crew quarters no one seemed to have inhabited for quite some time judging from the mildewy scent. She told us to stay put while she fetched what remained of our gear. Stuffed right into the top of my backpack I found a hastily scrawled note from Burns, reading, "You fucking assholes! Hope you have a wonderful life!" with a series of lewd smiley faces. I made sure to fold it properly and stow it away where it wouldn't get wet.

Most of our things were still there, plus Tanner's spare outer gear that would fit Nate in a pinch. Also some spare magazines and ammo—but only for our handguns. As it turned out, Hamilton had been very thorough in cleaning out the armory, leaving us with what contrabands we'd hidden in the packs. Nate didn't seem concerned so I swallowed my ire, and really, I'd get a new shotgun somewhere, I was sure. With just the two of us, going for stealth was the only option, and rifles would only slow us down.

There was also an entire pack of provisions left in Nate's pack, what Burns and Gita must have had left from the French. We'd need that soon enough as well, considering that winter might not be the best time to start a new pantry.

Speaking of which, Commander Parr dropped by our cabin a few hours later, looking rather conflicted, which made me guess that he hadn't expected us and Buehler to actually enact our plan.

"I presume you won't be sticking around with us forever?" he asked, still taxing the leader of the marines with questioning glares. Buehler ignored him.

"Wherever you want to drop us off is fine with us," Nate offered jovially. "If you have a map handy, my wife can give you a more concrete location if you will."

"She can?" I mouthed to Nate as we followed the captain to the bridge.

"Just pick a spot on the coast," Nate murmured back. "Carolinas or farther into the Gulf would be neat for winter." When I was still confused, he flashed me a grin. "You're the queen of randomness. Didn't you tell me once that was your strength, not following military code and strategy? Well, be as random as they get."

Viewed like that, not the worst idea. So it came that we were guests on the destroyer for another week before Buehler and a few of her marines piled into a boat with us and set off toward the Georgia shore. Since they'd already had to fuel up the RHIB, they used the opportunity to hit a few houses to see if anything worth raiding was to be found. By the time they returned to the beach, we were long gone, walking up the soft incline away from the ocean, side by side.

"Any idea where we should head next?" I asked as I studied a signpost, figuring that neither downtown Savannah nor the greater Atlanta area sounded like such a great idea. I'd always wanted to visit the CDC headquarters but that didn't sound quite that appealing anymore.

Nate shrugged, surprisingly relaxed considering that we didn't even have a map of the area. "It's all the same to me. You choose."

"So you get to blame me later? Fat chance." Shaking my head, I took a look around. "How about we head west?" The road leading in that direction was barely more than an access road, ideal for hiding in the ditches. Nate set out down that path without further comment, making me snort under my breath. "Really, no objections at all? You must have some place in mind. At least a general area. Doesn't have to be a fortified bunker but I'm not sure I want to spend the next years living in a cave."

"I thought more along the lines of a log cabin somewhere by a river. Good for fishing," he mused.

"Sounds good. Just, where?" He shrugged, still smiling. "Seriously? You're not fucking with me right now? You have no clue where we should go?"

"I have many clues," Nate replied, the smile disappearing. "And all those are places someone else knows about as well. But if I don't know where we'll end up, neither will they. I say, we wing it. We have provisions for a few weeks if we pace ourselves, and there's plenty of houses between here and the Rockies that are waiting to be looted. We find signs of any kind of habitation, we move on or backtrack into the wilderness. Sooner or later, we'll find something we like. We stay for the night, for a week, or for fucking forever. Who cares?" He let out a sudden laugh that was way more carefree than I'd ever heard from him. "Bree, we can do whatever the fuck we want! We have no obligations! Shit, I've never felt that free in my entire life!"

His enthusiasm was contagious, although I didn't much care for how his shout chased away a flock of birds. Of course he noticed, but he still didn't seem to mind. No mob of zombies came down on us as we continued down the road so it was probably okay. We were likely the only living bipeds in the county once the marines were back on the ship. "Hate to break it to you, buddy, but you still have obligations to me," I reminded him, sidling closer. "Don't forget about that."

"Never," he promised, leaning in for a quick kiss—before he retreated to the other side of the road, speeding up so he was walking a few paces in front of me, giving us both ample space to move should anything attack us. Ah, like good old times.

"We should probably stock up on gear," I observed. "The usual stuff, you know? Extra boots, sleeping bags, maybe a camping burner if we find one. And coffee. If I have to live rough for the next few months on the road, I need coffee. Else I'll be ready to kill you by the end of the week."

"Coffee, got it," Nate replied, his eyes still scanning the terrain ahead. "Anything else? Maybe a queen-size bed with an extra duvet?"

"You not being such an ass, maybe?" I suggested cheekily.

"You'd get bored in less than an hour," he shot back.

I snorted but didn't object. "Too bad we don't have any of that booster left. I could do with a little high just about now." And with it being just us, the other side effects weren't anything to be annoyed by, either.

Nate glanced back at me, a hint of worry quickly giving way to more unnatural levity. "You don't need the booster for that."

"Har, har, very funny. Like you ever complained."

He kept chortling under his breath. "I mean it. You won't need the booster to key up. It's a neat thing to have in sustained combat situations where you shouldn't let your guard down, but since we're not planning on getting into that, for any short-term stuff you won't need it. Trust me, you of all people won't. But maybe you should look into building a habit of meditating each day."

"What's that supposed to mean?" I complained, momentarily stopping to investigate a heap of rags by the side of the road. Months old, I decided, and of no interest whatsoever. "Both."

Nate sighed as if he was already sorry to have said anything. "You do realize that the serum works fueled by strong emotions, right?"

"Duh."

"And would I be so wrong if I said that you're a woman possessing a rather fiery disposition?"

That made me snort. "Did you just call me a raging bitch?"

His momentary silence was insulting enough but his words mollified me somewhat. "Do you hear me complaining? But you've felt the effects of it yourself now. The booster makes it easier to remove the shackles around your anger, but it's a tool, not a necessity. Remember how stir crazy you got last year on the road? And that was with many other people around to distract you. Now it's just you and me. Maybe learning to find a way to put a damper—or at least some shackles—on your temper might be worth a thought."

"Or we could just have sex until we're both exhausted and I've forgotten all about why I felt the need to beat you up in the first place?"

"Or we could do that," he agreed, laughing. "Or you could pick up something like Tai Chi. Or hunting with bow and arrow. Fishing."

"I still like my idea best."

"Of course you do."

"Like you're complaining."

"I'm not complaining, I'm pointing out that we have all the time in the world, and all options are open to us."

"Including sex."

He groaned but I could tell that he was still smiling—and so was I.

Sure, my heart was heavy with the knowledge that setting out on our own wasn't the ideal solution. It killed me to know that our friends and loved ones had no idea of where we were, or whether we were still alive—and the reverse was true as well. But it was a solution, and for right now, it was the solution. And when things changed, well—I'd learned to adapt to many things. I was sure that I'd take whatever may come in stride. Because giving up? Now that wasn't a solution at all.

To be continued in

Green Fields #10

Acknowledgements

You know the drill, right? Let's get this party started!

This book wouldn't be what it is today without my wonderful editor and amazing beta readers! You rock! And deserve some extra bacon! Also you, gentle reader, who you keep me happy and motivated, and all around doing this here writing thing! Last but not least, the guy who brings me my bulletproof coffee every morning, and has yet to complain about me ranting at my plot lines not behaving as they should.

Exodus was a blast to write—when it wasn't strangling me. Some books get written with consistency. This was not one of those. Either there were thousands of words of progress, or none. I wrote a huge chunk of it with my self-imposed deadline breathing down my neck, knowing I wouldn't finish it before my vacation. Not only did I finish it, but with enough time to spare to do the preliminary proofreading so I could send it to my editor and beta readers—with a day to spare. Took me half of my vacation to get off that super productive high, but so worth it in the end. I hope you agree. I sure had a lot of fun writing the second half of the book in one huge weeks-spanning session. I wish I could keep up that speed but let's be real—I'd go insane, and who knows what would happen then?

I also, finally, am ready to announce a new project: I'm now on Patreon! Patreon is a crowd-funding site for artists where fans can support their favorite creators. I'm doing a monthly subscription kind of thing. Depending on your level of support, you get updates, teasers, short stories, and behind-the-scenes info there. The first short story (well, really, novella. It ran a little long) is already available there—the prequel to the series, how Bree and Nate met, told from alternating points-of-view. Let's just say that Nate really didn't know what was going to hit him! If you want to, you can check it out there!
www.patreon.com/adriennelecter

What's up next? The remaining three books of the Green Fields series! 12 is such a lovely number for a series, and that's what I'm going for. I've actually already started on #10, rejoice!

Again, thank you so much for being the best audience any writer could wish for! If you have a moment, why not leave a review on amazon for the book? Reviews are an amazing way for readers to support Indie authors. Every single one counts, even if it's just to say you enjoyed the book and can't wait for the next one! THANK YOU!

NOTE ADDED TO THE SECOND PRINT EDITION:

While Patreon is no longer active, you can find alle the short stories from there in the two Beyond Green Fields omnibus editions.

About the Author

Adrienne Lecter has a background in Biochemistry and Molecular Biology, loves ranting at inaccuracies in movies, and spends increasingly more time on the shooting range. She lives with the man and two cats of her life in Vienna, and is working on the next post-apocalyptic books.

You can sign up for Adrienne's newsletter to never miss a release and be the first to know what other shenanigans she gets up to:

http://www.adriennelecter.com

Thank you

Hey, you! Yes, you, who just spent a helluva lot of time reading this book! You just made my day! Thanks!

Want to be notified of new releases, giveaways and updates? Sign up for my newsletter:
www.adriennelecter.com

If you enjoyed reading the book and have a moment to spare, I would really appreciate a short, honest review on the site you purchased it from and on goodreads. Reviews make a huge difference in helping new readers find the series.

Or if you'd like to drop me a note, or chat a but, feel free to email me or hit me up on social media. I'll try to respond as quickly as possible! If you'd like to report an error or wrong detail, I've set up a separate space on my website for that, too.

Email: adrienne@adriennelecter.com
Website: adriennelecter.com
Twitter: @adriennelecter
Facebook: facebook.com/adriennelecter

Books published

World of Anthrax
new series coming 2022

Printed in Great Britain
by Amazon

28668392R00187